THE BANNERS OF POWER is the
third novel in the sequence 'Destiny of
Eagles'; its predecessors were THE
BANNERS OF LOVE and THE
BANNERS OF WAR.

Before writing these novels the author,
Major Carnegie, spent a total of five years
planning and painstakingly researching into
historical details. The result is a splendid
saga of love revolving around Kasia
Radienska and Henryk Barinski set amidst
the turbulence of Europe in the mid-
eighteenth century.

In THE BANNERS OF POWER Kasia is
reunited with her beloved Henryk, but her
loyalty to her friend and mistress, Catherine
the Great, threatens to separate them once
again . . .

Also by Sacha Carnegie

DESTINY OF EAGLES: THE BANNERS OF LOVE
DESTINY OF EAGLES: THE BANNERS OF WAR

and published by Corgi Books

Sacha Carnegie

The Banners of Power

CORGI BOOKS
A DIVISION OF TRANSWORLD PUBLISHERS LTD

THE BANNERS OF POWER

A CORGI BOOK 0 552 09522 2

Originally published in Great Britain
by Peter Davies Ltd.

PRINTING HISTORY
Peter Davies edition published 1972
Corgi edition published 1974

This book is set in 10–11 point Plantin

Corgi Books are published by
Transworld Publishers Ltd.,
Cavendish House, 57–59 Uxbridge Road,
Ealing, London W.5.
Made and printed in Great Britain by
Cox & Wyman Ltd., London, Reading and Fakenham

For Alexandra and Jocelyn

My grateful thanks to Don Pottinger
my collaborator in planning and research

THE BANNERS OF POWER

Dramatis Personae

IN RUSSIA. *1763*

Captain Vlassiev and *Lieutenant Chekin*
> Officers guarding Ivan Romanov in the fortress of Schlusselburg.

Countess Kasia Radienska
> Polish lady-in-waiting to the Empress Catherine; also a childhood friend. Born and lived in the Polish Ukraine until, in her eighteenth year, Turkish marauders destroyed her home and family. After many adventures she reached St. Petersburg where she joined the Court of the Grand Duchess Catherine.

Catherine
> Empress of All the Russias.

Ivan Romanov
> The rightful heir to the throne as Ivan the Sixth.

Ensign Potemkin
> Officer of the Household Troops; later to become Catherine's favourite lover and adviser.

Grigori Orlov
> Catherine's lover. Eldest of the five Orlov brothers. Instrumental, with his brother, Alexei, in putting Catherine on the throne.

IN POLAND. *1763*

Henryk Barinski
> Son of a Polish noble family. Friend and lover of Kasia Radienska during their youth in the Ukraine. Separated

7

from her by the attack on her home by Turks he was drawn into political intrigue in Rome, Paris, and St. Petersburg and fought at the Battle of Rossbach.

Reunited for a few months of 1758 with Kasia in St. Petersburg, then arrested as a spy and sentenced to Siberia. Escaped in English ship only to be press-ganged into H.M.S. *Huntress*. Served during Seven Years War. Took part in Battle of Quiberon Bay. Left Navy and returned via Paris to his home, Lipno, in the Polish Ukraine, aged 34.

Count Branicki
> Grand General of Poland.

Josef Pulawski
> A lawyer who had met Henryk in Rome.

Jan Dombrowski
> Friend of Henryk's whom he had met *en route* from Paris.

Adam Barinski
> Henryk's elder brother. Trained as a soldier but now looking after the estates of Lipno.

Count Sigismund Barinski
> Henryk's father. A Polish nobleman of the old school. Proud and stubborn and filled with memories of Poland's past greatness.

Globnik
> Estate agent at Lipno.

Major Skurin
> Russian officer. Commander of a detachment of the Smolensk Regiment stationed in the Ukraine.

Ensign Potovski
> His second-in-command.

Father Krosinski
> The village priest of Lipno.

IN RUSSIA. The Coup d'Etat, 1762

Kasia Radienska

The Grand Duchess Catherine of Russia (Figgy)

Alexei Orlov
> The tallest, and the cleverest, of the five huge brothers.

Captain Bibikov
> Alexei's companion.

Father Alexei Mikhailov
> Regimental Padre to the Izmailovsky Regiment.

Colonel Razumovsky
> Regimental Commander.

Sergeant Levashov
> Of the Preobrazhensky Guards, *élite* regiment of Russia.
> Once in Imperial bodyguard of the Grand Duchess.

Major Voyeikov and *Captain Vorontzov*
> Officers who remained loyal to the Tsar Peter.

Peter the Third
> Uncrowned Tsar. Catherine's unpleasant and un-
> balanced husband whose behaviour and foreign policy
> since the death of his aunt, Empress Elizabeth, had
> alienated many of his subjects, especially the army.

Field Marshal Münnich

Count Vorontzov
> Chancellor of Russia.

Baron Goltz
> Prussian Ambassador.

Prince Trubetskoi
> Courtier and Statesman.

Field Marshal Count Shuvalov

All with Peter
at Peterhof

Countess Elizabeth Vorontzova
> Niece of the Chancellor, mistress of Peter who wanted to make her Empress in place of Catherine.

Admiral Nummers
> Commandant of the great naval base and fortress of Kronstadt.

General Devier
Colonel Neelov } Emissaries from Peter to
Prince Bariatinsky Admiral Nummers

Admiral Talyzin
> Emissary from Catherine to Admiral Nummers.

Grand Duke Paul
> Six year old son of Catherine and Peter.

Count Panin
> The child's tutor. Statesman and adviser.

Princess Dashkova
> The young sister of Elizabeth Vorontzova. Youthful, ardent and impetuous supporter of Catherine.

IN POLAND. The Carpathians. 1763

The Patriots

Henryk Barinski

Jan Dombrowski

Casimir Pulawski
> Son of Josef Pulawski. To become a famous cavalry leader and later to die at Savannah in the American War of Independence.

Father Gurowski
> Priest turned soldier.

Sergeant Nym
> Regular cavalry soldier.

Jacek Zalinski
Lazienski
Bludhorn
Ducek
Kolbe

PART ONE

THE great gates of Schlusselburg opened slowly with a squeaking and grinding of hinges as the small plain coach rattled into the courtyard of the fortress.

Two officers stood waiting by the steps to the main arched doorway.

'One thing,' muttered Captain Vlassiev from the corner of his mouth, 'at least she's punctual.' His companion, Lieutenant Chekin, had no time to answer, for the wheels rumbled to a halt and the postillion leapt down to open the door. The two men drew themselves up, rigid and motionless as the grey walls towering above them.

A small slim woman dressed in a sober travelling habit of dark blue damask stepped out and as he bowed low Captain Vlassiev was struck at once by her amazing grace and dignity.

'Gentlemen,' she said, inclining her small neat head under the large black straw hat, 'I trust I've not kept you standing for too long in this hot sun.' Her smile was warm and vivid. Her Russian was good thought Chekin but you could have cut the German accent with a knife. But the words and the smile had made an instant slave of the young man; he felt himself blushing. Getting a sharp nudge from Vlassiev he pulled himself together and clumsily kissed the hand held out for him.

It was a small hand, very white and cool, and so overcome was he by the moment that he almost forgot to let go.

'Please Lieutenant Chekin' – so she even knew the name of an unknown officer – 'May I have my hand back.' A suggestion of laughter trembled in her voice. 'And now,' she said, suddenly brisk, 'we must go into the business that brings me here.'

'Your Majesty,' suggested Vlassiev diffidently, 'if I may lead the way—?'

'Of course, Captain Vlassiev,' Chekin gazed at his Empress with goggling eyes; so she knew both their names, 'I should get utterly lost in here.'

For a moment she hesitated below the greatest fortress of Russia, built grim and massive on a little island near the source of the Neva at the southern tip of Lake Ladoga, standing guard over the old trade route to the Baltic; taken and retaken from the Swedes in the Great Northern War. Weathered and worn by the bitter blizzards of four centuries it was now used as a prison from which there could be no escape, not even across the ice of the frozen river.

Then as Catherine the Second, Empress and Autocrat of All the Russias, followed the tall figure of Captain Vlassiev up the worn steps and went from the sunlight, the feel of the place descended on her with a flutter of dark wings.

They walked along the endless labyrinth of stone passages, climbed up and down narrow winding stairs lit even on this bright afternoon by smoky rushlight torches held in iron brackets. Now and then they passed a window heavily barred or small dark doors. They met no one, heard nothing but the echo of their own footsteps and the swish of her wide skirt, yet Catherine had the feeling that unseen eyes were watching them, that ears were pressed to the doors listening with hope or fear to the steps as they approached then faded, leaving the occupants to the perpetual silence of cells that were no more than tombs.

At length Captain Vlassiev stopped at one of the dark doors, opened it and stood aside with a bow.

'In here, your Majesty.'

The room was surprisingly large, arched and well-lit by two large glazed windows; the sunlight which streamed across the floor and the plain pine table was cut into neat squares by the bars.

Two chairs were set at the table; a plain ewer and two pewter mugs stood on the scrubbed wood. Four books lay in a pile on a stool. It was cool in the room and smelt clean with the freshness of new laid rushes.

'Please, Your Majesty.' Vlassiev held the chair for her. 'I much regret the squalor and rudeness of this place.' He gestured round in disgust. 'But my instructions were—'

'Of course,' said Catherine smiling. 'I particularly wanted no pomp or ceremony. This is purely a private visit. And now, please will you fetch—' she hesitated slightly, 'the prisoner.'

Lieutenant Chekin withdrew. For a moment Catherine remained at the table; then, unable to sit still, she rose and went to the window. Two sparrows quarrelled on the sill, hopping about angrily and fluffing their feathers. So you've also got your problems, she thought, but surely not as great as mine. And yet, she admitted with her usual honesty, everyone thinks their own particular problem the thorniest. But this one – she looked up at the sky where clouds were moving towards the sun. Within a few minutes it would be covered, the warmth blotted out; within a few minutes the door would open – God, how she dreaded the opening of that door. Then why had she come, on her own, in secret like this, when she could have ordered the prisoner to be brought to Petersburg as the Empress Elizabeth had done before her? What on earth did she hope to learn or gain – from the forthcoming interview? Was it in fact merely a woman's insatiable curiosity to see what kind of a man life imprisonment had bred? But would a sight of him help her to decide his fate? Why had she come? *Why, why?* At that moment Catherine longed to be strolling in the gardens at Peterhof chatting with her friend Kasia, free for a while from affairs of state. She longed to be anywhere, anywhere at all except in this room, darkening now as the clouds reached across the sun, waiting for the sound of footsteps in the passage.

She could still leave; there was time; she didn't *have* to see him. If a mere woman is privileged to change her mind then surely an Empress can do the same. You needn't have come, it was your own fault – you could have left him a spectre in the back of your mind – bringing him to life won't do one bit of good. Turn back, urged the tiny voice of reason, before it is too late. Once you have met him face to face, spoken with him, it will make everything that much harder.

But it was not in Catherine's nature to turn back and, as the steps sounded outside, Captain Vlassiev saw the Empress straighten her shoulders and turn quickly towards the door.

Then, with her heart beating faster with apprehension, she

sat down again, her hands clenched out of sight beneath the table.

'Please,' she said with great composure, 'have him brought in.'

How regal she is, thought Vlassiev as he opened the door, every inch an Empress – and a woman.

'In here.' Catherine heard Lieutenant Chekin's quiet command. Forcing a small, calm smile, she looked straight at the figure which came in. Beside the two burly officers, the young man who stood before her, though tall, looked slight and frail. What struck her at once was the extraordinary luminous pallor of his skin, snow-white against the long fair hair and thick red beard. It was almost as if the darkness of his perpetual solitude had drained every drop of blood from his body.

No one spoke. He stood, twisting his long fingers together in front of him, staring at her with dull eyes that blinked continuously, unused to normal light.

He was dressed in a plain brown jacket and breeches, dingy white cravat and thick wrinkled stockings; his gaze, more puzzled than frightened, went slowly from the woman at the table to the expressionless faces of his two gaolers.

It was Catherine who broke the charged silence.

'Leave us,' she said.

'But, your Majesty—' Vlassiev looked horrified.

'Leave us!' she commanded, her words cutting the air like a blade.

Bowing, the officers withdrew, closing the door behind them. The young man glanced round with the look of a trapped animal.

'Sit down,' Catherine urged him gently. Very slowly, his weak, blinking eyes never leaving the face of the woman before him, the young man sat down on the edge of the chair.

'You know who I am?' she asked, quite in command of herself now the moment had come.

He did not seem to have heard. A strange, unpleasant smell came from his body, a sort of living decay, and she experienced a pang of fierce revulsion at his matted hair. She got the sudden feeling it might start to crawl and writhe on his scalp. Catherine repeated her question. This time he nodded and looked away;

16

when his eyes came back to hers she saw they were filled with tears. Again she wished she had not come. What in God's name was there to be said? That she knew who he was; that she knew he was the man who had the inalienable right to rule over Russia as Ivan the Sixth, the man with the true blood of the Romanovs somewhere beneath that ghostly skin? That he had been a prisoner, first in Siberia and now here, since the day, twenty-two years ago when his cousin Elizabeth had exerted her right as Peter the Great's daughter and taken the throne which had been left in trust for him?

Should she admit to this poor helpless creature that she knew all his history and that furthermore his presence here, his very existence on earth, disturbed her greatly?

None of these things could she speak of so she tried to win a few words from him with all her considerable charm and gentleness. But he could not answer except in dreadful spasms of stammering so bad as to be almost unintelligible; spasms that contorted his features and jerked his head. She had heard Kasia stammer under the stress of emotion or sickness but nothing like these incoherent explosions that left him panting and sweating and with his eyes filled with terrible tears of frustration.

So much was fighting to escape which had been penned up inside him, so much to explain to this poised and gracious woman who seemed so sympathetic.

Why was he here? Why was he kept in darkness all his life, never allowed to see the sun? He had got to his feet and stumbled to the window, blinking up at the open sky with the tears coursing down his thin cheeks. What harm had he ever done to anyone? He struggled on, arching his body, beating his clenched fists against the window frame until at length utterly exhausted he leant his head against the bars, sobbing quietly.

Alone with him, Catherine's heart was filled with pity. The only harm you've ever done in your life is being who you are – great-grandson of Ivan the Fifth, the only crime you've ever committed is that of having Russian royal blood in your veins. And for that you can never be pardoned, she thought, torn by her pity and her honesty. Never let him free, she thought, allow his mind and body to recover, educate him and this poor creature would pose a very real threat. She went to him and laid her hand on his heaving shoulder.

'I'm sorry,' she whispered, 'I'm truly sorry.' He reached blindly for her hand, nuzzling like a dog, the first comfort he had felt since his mother died in Siberia fifteen long years ago. Catherine's hand dropped to her side, wet with his tears.

After a moment to regain her composure she called sharply for Captain Vlassiev and did not look at Ivan as he was led away, walking with a curious shuffling step like a broken old man. But as he reached the door he suddenly stopped, ignoring Lieutenant Chekin's guiding hand. Turning he cried out in a strong, clear voice: 'I am a prince of this empire.' He clung desperately to the doorway as Chekin, embarrassed and fuming, tried to prise him away. 'Quiet! Keep silent!' Ivan shouted. 'I am your sovereign.' Catherine saw pride in the eyes now grown bright.

'Take him away,' she ordered imperiously.

'But,' she added in a lower tone, 'be gentle with him.'

As quickly as the pride had sparked in the young man's eyes, prompted by some half remembered stirring in his blood, so it died, leaving them dull again as he stumbled away mumbling unintelligible words. The door closed.

Captain Vlassiev stood silently, his hand resting on his sword-hilt, waiting as Catherine poured herself wine. He noticed the slight trembling of her hand as she raised the goblet to her lips and he glanced away. But when she spoke her voice was quite steady.

'You know your orders, Captain?'

'Yes, Your Majesty.'

Vlassiev knew them well. In the event of any attempt at rescue, then the 'nameless prisoner' whom not even General Savin, the fortress commandant, was allowed to visit, was on no account to leave Schlusselburg alive.

Peter, the late Tsar of unlamented memory had added a few refinements of his own. Should Ivan prove fractious or misbehave himself in any way then he was to be chained and beaten; in the event of illness no medical aid was to be given the poor wretch. And should Ivan succeed in getting away then a very terrible death awaited his two gaolers. Oh yes, Captain Vlassiev knew his orders all right.

'In this matter,' she said, getting up, 'you are in sole charge and must use your discretion should—' she paused, 'should any unforeseen occurrence arise.'

'I understand,' said Vlassiev impassively. A cruel mouth, she thought. A man without much mercy.

'You can consult no one.'

He nodded.

'Except myself or Count Panin. In the last resort,' she added slowly, 'you are the one to make whatever decision seems necessary. We understand each other, Captain?'

'Perfectly, Your Majesty.'

'I have the greatest faith in you and Lieutenant Chekin,' she said.

He bowed his head in acknowledgment.

'And in your judgment.'

'Both Lieutenant Chekin and myself are deeply honoured by Your Majesty's trust,' he said, not meeting her eye. Catherine nodded as if satisfied by a matter at least partially resolved.

'And now I wish to see the prisoner's quarters.'

Vlassiev's narrow Tartar eyes widened a fraction.

'As Your Majesty wishes,' he said without expression. She followed him along more cold passages passing no living soul though once she heard the tramp of feet, the heavy rattle of a bolt. The captain led her downwards deep into the very heart of the fortress and each passage grew colder and darker until they came to a small door thickly studded with rusty iron and heavily bolted. There was no sign of Lieutenant Chekin.

Vlassiev took a large key from his belt.

'There are only two keys,' he said slowly turning it in the lock. 'To get them they would have to kill us.' The door swung open and he stood aside. Unsuspecting, Catherine stepped forward, peering into the gloom.

Then, with a muffled exclamation she stopped abruptly, hit by the appalling stench of the place and put out a hand to steady herself against stone that was damp and slimy. Steeling herself she waited until her eyes grew used to the semi-darkness. Revolted, yet in some horrible way fascinated by what she saw,

Catherine forced herself to remain where she was though all her senses were crying out for her to turn and run for the air and sunlight.

Her unwilling eyes took in the macabre scene, flickering redly in the light of a single candle-lantern, rested with horror on the dull gleam of chains and fetters hanging from the wet green wall, the tiny hole high up in one corner which acted as window to the casemate cell.

There was a table, a stool and a low pallet bed, covered in what looked like bundles of rags. Water dripped somewhere, and with a shudder she saw the tiny ruby spark of rats' eyes in the shadows.

Ivan sat hunched on the bed, head bowed forward on his knees, racked by coughs or sobs and he did not look up or move. He was no longer dressed in the jacket and breeches but in tattered garments.

'My God,' Catherine whispered. 'Oh, my God.'

Vlassiev made as if to rouse him but she said in a strangled voice.

'Leave him.'

There was an awful chill in the stinking hole where a human creature eked out the dreadful hours, days, months, years, where he saw no sun, breathed no air but the stench of his own filth, spoke to no living soul and had for companions the hungry rats which shared his eternal solitude and his sickening food. She shivered, holding her clove pomander to her nose; she would have to leave, now, at once, for any moment she was going to retch and vomit.

With one more pitying glance at the young man who should sit not on a verminous bed but on a jewel-encrusted throne, the Empress of his country left him to the slam of the door and the silence and returned to the warm sweet air of the June afternoon.

Before she got into the waiting coach, Catherine gave Captain Vlassiev her last order.

'Have him moved to better quarters.'

'Yes, Your Majesty.'

So she was losing her nerve, he thought. One glimpse of that hole below and her woman's heart was softening.

'At once,' she said. 'And on his return, please inform General Savin with my compliments, that these are my personal orders. But always remember, Captain Vlassiev, that the other instructions still stand.'

They saluted as she drove away, remaining rigidly at attention until the coach had disappeared beyond the main gateway.

'Phew!' Lieutenant Chekin removed his hat and mopped his forehead.

'A remarkable woman,' said Vlassiev thoughtfully. 'Very remarkable.'

'But, by God,' said Chekin fervently, 'she's a damned attractive one. It's funny to think she's a German without a drop of Russian blood and yet she's Tsaritsa.'

And an Empress who travels alone without a massive retinue and a clattering escort of Household Cavalry, he thought wonderingly, remembering the visit of her late husband surrounded by a hundred of his precious Holsteiners.

'So we've got to improve conditions for "His Majesty",' said Vlassiev sourly. 'Why? He's half dead. But you don't disobey that one.'

'I wish to hell he'd die,' burst out Chekin bitterly, 'then we could get out of this damned place. Jesus Christ, we're just as much prisoners as he is. Three years we've been stuck here. How much longer, Sergei. In God's name, how much longer?'

'Patience,' Vlassiev replied. 'Have patience. I don't think we'll be needed here much longer.' He glanced up at the sky now overcast and blackening from the East.

The first fat raindrops plopped in the dust of the courtyard, thunder growled beyond the walls.

'No, I think we will leave Schlusselburg before the end of the year.'

The downpour drummed on the roof on the coach and slashed across the windows, driven by a sudden wind, drowning the uneven rumble of the wheels on the rutted road. Catherine sat back against the hard leather seat staring out at the storm. The road was taking a long curving turn to the north and she watched the rain squall running across the ruffled waters of Lake Ladoga, beyond which lay the lands of the Swedes, those dour, dangerous soldiers who had so often gripped Russia by the throat. The coach turned south again and she saw the endless birch trees, interspersed with stretches of swamp reeds, thrashing in the fierce wind; here and there a woodman's cabin squatted lonely and miserable in the desolate landscape.

The Russian wilderness, she thought, drawing her cloak more closely round her, shivering not only from the cold but at the vastness of her domains, which stretched far far beyond the limits even of her fertile imagination. A wilderness filled with peoples of a dozen races she would never get to know nor to understand, not even if she reigned for seventy years. The 'Dark People', Kasia called them: the bitter, poverty-stricken slaves of Russia. True they had run beside her as she drove up the Nevsky Prospekt to seize the crown; they had seemed to take her to their hearts but she knew they were as unpredictable and dangerous as children. Given a leader and one day – she switched off the unpleasant thought.

This is what she had wanted, had worked and schemed for. Very well then, she would be not only Empress but leader; she, Catherine of Russia, would lead her people from poverty and the stifling darkness of ignorance to greatness. Under her guidance Russia would become respected and feared.

'I *will* do it,' she said aloud. '*I will*.' She hit the seat with her clenched fist. She must succeed for she knew the penalty of failure. Her expression screwed up in disgust at the memory of the casemate cell where Ivan rotted like a decaying vegetable. She'd rather kill herself than end in a place like that.

Perhaps he could be persuaded to enter a monastery. For a moment her conscience lightened. Yes, that was it. There must be somewhere suitable, miles away from Petersburg where he could turn to God. But he'd still be alive. Her mind wrestled with the problem as it had so often. She knew what Panin advised in his subtle, oblique fashion but – again she put the insidious thought from her mind, and lowering the window, breathed slowly and deeply of the clean air.

The passing of the short storm had left the evening cool and fresh after the heat of the day. She leant out. They were entering the shabby outskirts of the city but the people moving among the little timber houses and dripping birches paid no heed to the plain coach splashing through the puddles. Ahead Catherine could see the golden needle of the Admiralty, the crooked spire of the St. Peter and Paul fortress, that other dreaded prison where her enemies languished, waiting on her pleasure. Beyond the wet shining roofs a double rainbow arched across the black thunder clouds and the watery sun struck gold from the cupolas and spires of her capital.

She settled back in the seat, resolutely putting aside the nagging question of the ragged prisoner in Schlusselburg and allowing her mind to cast ahead to other problems, no less pressing for being comparatively trivial. Often, she thought, these puny worries of everyday living were the straws to crush the unfortunate camel, for, like the tip of a tongue that is drawn again and again to a hole in a tooth, they kept on returning to clutter one's mind. And there were so many. So many personalities involved, so many people to be kept happy, to be soothed or scolded. Countess Bruce and her implacable jealousy of Kasia, the Polish woman, Catherine's childhood friend, who had come to her court after strange wild adventures. The hatred between the young impetuous Dashkova and Grigori Orlov.

Ah, Grigori. Her frown lifted for a moment, but not for long. What was she to do about her lover? Soon a decision would be required. Another decision. But not now, not yet. She shut her eyes and tried to smooth away the headache building up behind her temples. This secret journey, so nearly over, was the first time she had been really alone since the days, now no more than a dream, when, as Grand Duchess, she used to ride in the woods of Peterhof and Oranienbaum.

The coach rolled to a halt, the door was opened and, with a sigh Catherine the woman stepped out to become Empress and Autocrat of all the Russias as she entered her great palace on the Neva, smiling graciously up at the sentries of the Imperial Guard as they crashed into a thunderous salute.

*   *   *

The steady tramp of the heavy boots was loud in the still summer air, mingled with the monotonous thud and rattle of the drums, the raucous words of command as the soldiers came swinging into the great cobbled square below the Winter Palace.

A woman sat at one of the fifteen hundred windows watching as the men crashed to a halt below. Thin clouds of pipeclay rose through the early morning sunshine as they grounded their muskets and stood so utterly still that they might have been planted in the square.

There was no breeze to sway the lines and, even though the time was only just past half past six the sun was already well above the roofs of St. Petersburg, bright on the waters of the Neva and on the red-brown sails of a merchantman making down river for the open sea.

The woman turned her face towards the sound of a horse's hoofs, very sharp in the silence, feeling the warmth of the sun which played on her skin, drew coppery tints from the depths of her shining black hair, touched her long blue eyes every now and then with a hint of green the colour of the sunlit sea.

An officer of great stature rode on to the parade ground, very slim and dark against his white horse. She wondered with a little smile how Ensign Potemkin was feeling this morning. Yet his capacity for vodka, wine, even the newly popular Hungarian *tokay* equalled that of the five Orlov brothers whose insepar-able comrade he had become.

Alexei, Grigori and this young man riding slowly along the ranks, stopping here and there to speak to one of the ramrod figures, together they could outdrink, outsing, outfight a regiment.

And love? Well, she knew Alexei after all – had she not lived with him off and on for some years now? – and the Empress seemed well satisfied with his brother. But this one – Potemkin turned his horse just below and started along another rank and as she looked down she saw in her mind another figure in the long green uniform coat and gleaming top boots.

Henryk would look magnificent on that horse. Her eyes no longer took in the parade, her mind filled with warm thoughts

24

of his letter, locked safely away in her room. He was alive – *alive*. She was seized by a sudden urge to shout his name to the doll-like figures, see their wooden faces gaping up in surprise at her words.

Henryk Barinski lives. I know it. Soon I shall see him, be with him in Poland. She wanted to lean from the window and include them all, all those oafs with their great moustaches and huge boots in the intensity of her joy.

He had written in a code from Paris, the letter had reached her two days ago and had been opened by Shuvalov's minions of the Secret Chancellery, she knew that from certain tiny marks – she had not been dealing with the Empress's correspondence for all these months without being able to recognize the signs.

He would be in Poland now, waiting for her answer, waiting for her to come to him. Consumed by a sudden tearing impatience Kasia Radienska got up from her chair and began to pace the little study where Catherine, Empress of All Russia was wont to deal with a fraction of her work from half past six till nine in the mornings.

The swish of her wide blue dress moving across the inlaid parquet floor was soothing. In his letter Henryk called himself a horse breeder who had for sale an Arab mare named Rasulka and, knowing her love of horses wondered if she might be interested in seeing this beautiful little mare – if so he would keep the animal for her and if she cared to she could view it in Poland. As she would probably understand it was not possible for him to come to Russia. Rasulka. She remembered the first time he had called her that name, on the ridge separating their homes, a month before the Turks came and the nightmare years began. Today she would have to speak to Catherine, broach the subject of taking leave to visit Poland.

On the square, orders cut the air with all the sharp savagery of a knout. Two Negro drummers, ostrich feathers waving in their tall hats, stepped smartly from the ranks and began to tap lustily at their drums. Pigeons flew from the palace roof and wheeled high above the tall mitre caps, the green tunics faced with yellow, long twinkling bayonets and the drawn sword of Ensign Potemkin.

A door opened and Kasia heard Catherine's sharp voice calling her dogs. Two greyhounds came leaping into the room running to Kasia, standing on their hind-legs to greet her with splashing tongues.

'Get down you two! She doesn't want you all over her at this unearthly hour.' It didn't sound as if the Autocrat of All Russia had slept well last night Kasia thought as she went down in a deep curtsey. When she straightened up she stood half a head taller than Catherine.

'Shut the window, Kasia. Those damned drums. I've a good mind to make them drill on the Field of Mars in future. It's further away.' Kasia smiled, showing the little crooked top tooth which added so much to the attraction of her wide smile; she closed the window, muffling the military sounds and turned to Catherine.

On the Empress's head the usual crêpe mob-cap perched askew; two dark plaits of hair hung down to the shoulders of her dressing-gown, tied carelessly at the waist and in which she looked small, round and quite shapeless.

'You look happy,' Catherine said slowly. 'Quite radiant.'

She padded to the window in her small slippers looking down listlessly. Kasia saw she was carrying sheaves of papers in her hand. Catherine was rarely without her favourite gold-edged foolscap, usually thickly covered with her neat writing, for the sight of a blank sheet of paper set her mind and hand twitching as music will set another's feet tapping. She had to cover the empty whiteness with prose, notes, poetry and ideas, always ideas.

'A sheet of paper,' Catherine once told Kasia, 'is like a snow-field. Blank it's just a white wilderness, but people it with ink symbols and it becomes alive, like the steppes become alive when horsemen gallop over the snow.'

But this morning she looked jaded and tired, she was not her usual enthusiastic self, rubbing her little hands and bubbling with her incredible energy and vitality.

'I'm sorry,' she said, leaving the window and sitting down at her desk. 'I slept badly. It's the heat. Soon we'll leave this oven and go to Peterhof and feel the sea breezes,' Catherine spoke in French. Sometimes she used French to Kasia, sometimes Russian, never German which the latter could only speak very badly. The night had been sultry and oppressive with lightning flickering in the west but no rain to cool the stifling city.

Kasia watched her as she fiddled with things on the desk, picking up pens and putting them down again. She had seen her like this before; it would soon pass. Catherine was as resilient as a young branch that not the strongest wind can break. That was the secret of her amazing strength.

'I am thirty-five years old,' said Catherine heavily, 'and my God, this morning I feel every minute of them.'

Her chin, a little too full and fleshy, was sunk into her long neck; her very white fingers played absently with a plait. Her thick brown eyebrows were drawn together in a slight frown.

'How long have we known each other?' she asked suddenly.

'Since our first meeting at Volochisk, Ma'am?' There were times when Catherine, in private, liked her favourite lady-in-waiting to call her Figgy, the pet name of her youth. But this particular morning was clearly not one of those intimate moments.

Kasia's heart sank. She had to ask for leave to go to Poland for a month – at least a month – to visit her relations, yes that was it. Then, once reunited with Henryk they would see what was to be done. But how could she ask it this morning with the Empress out of temper and likely to refuse? She must though, before the day began and Catherine was caught up in countless problems of state.

'Well, you *are* dreaming this morning.'

'I'm sorry, Ma'am. It is a long time.'

'Seventeen forty three. Christmas. That was when we first met.' She worked out the years on her fingers. 'Good heavens, *this* Christmas will make it exactly twenty years. Twenty years,' she repeated in wonder.

Catherine's little Kalmuk servant girl brought in her mistress's favourite coffee and rusks and departed without a sound. Catherine poured out the coffee, blew on it for a moment and drank.

'Ah,' she sighed luxuriously, 'that's better.'

27

The two women sat in silence, Kasia remembering as if it were yesterday the visit of little Sophia von Anhalt-Zerbst and her errant, mischievous mother, Princess Joanna, to Volochisk, home of the Radienskis in the Polish Ukraine since the early fifteenth century. She remembered how the two small girls had instantly taken to each other; how impressed she had been by Figgy's air of sophistication, her grown-up talk of courts and castles and of how one day she would *be* someone.

Well, now she *was* someone; she ruled the largest country in the world and sipped her coffee, dipping a rusk into the hot black liquid, dropping pieces to her eager dogs.

How far we have come, thought Kasia, since the day Figgy drove away from Volochisk through the snow, waving from the furs of the sledge, tears on her small pointed face. What a long and bitter road we have travelled to reach this small room and still be friends.

'And how long is it since you first came to Petersburg?'

'Nine years.'

'Nine years. Is it really as long as that? How quickly the time has passed. How much has happened. How much we have seen together.' Catherine's eyes were clouded with memory. Kasia, looking at them, was struck as so often before at the extraordinary way they seemed to change colour from brown to hazel to blue. Poniatowski had called them blue and he should surely have known having been closer to them than most.

Catherine opened a little golden box and extracted a tiny pinch of snuff which she placed on the back of her left hand. 'I can't have all the kind people who kiss my hand going away sneezing,' she said but without her usual note of ironic humour. For a moment she stared at the little mound of brown dust then drew it up her nose with two sharp sniffs. This seemed to disperse the lethargy of her mood. With a shake of her head she pushed back her chair and walked quickly to the window, drawn by the gleam of the August sun.

'I feel like writing, writing, but this morning I think I'll get my ideas better in order if I talk,' She paused, her eyes on the square below.

'So Monsieur Potemkin is playing at soldiers this morning.' Something in her voice drew Kasia's attention. Catherine was smiling gently and her eyes softened as they gazed at the young officer.

'At the moment,' she said, 'he is a close friend of the Orlovs but—' she paused, 'too much wit and intelligence in a man does not always make him over-popular with his peers. Expecially if he has those looks,' she added softly.

Yes, thought Kasia, he was certainly witty, highly intelligent and possessed of all the cool bravado so admired by Catherine – who else, as an unknown young officer, would have ridden forward to offer his sword-knot when the Empress had dropped her own at the start of that fateful march to Peterhof at the head of her Guards? A young man of considerable boldness. Oh yes, they would hear and see more of Monsieur Potemkin.

Already many in the Court began to cultivate the tall young Ensign of the Horse Guards. For you never knew what the future might bring, how long Count Orlov might remain in the Empress's bed – and in her confidence. And of what use were sails if they were not trimmed to catch every new change of wind?

Kasia knew enough of the Court and of Catherine herself to realize, more clearly every day, that the position of Grigori Orlov was by no means so secure as he himself thought. For, in the matter of men Catherine was fickle in the extreme. Had Kasia not heard it from her lips? 'I cannot live without love. Love is a wonderful tonic – even for Queens. *Especially* for Queens.' Catherine had laughed. Saltykov, Stanislas, Poniatowski. Now Orlov and each one in his turn thought he was the one truly to win her heart. Of Henryk she tried not to think. Besides he had only been forced to Catherine's bed by the pressure of circumstances. Political love-making, that's what it had been, to further the ends of France – and Poland. Anyway what did it matter now when so soon she would be with him again?

'You remember I wrote a letter to Monsieur Voltaire,' Catherine's words broke into her thoughts, Kasia pulled herself back into the present, 'in which I said, my symbol is the bee, the motto is "Useful"?'

'Yes, Ma'am.'

Catherine had been delighted with her cleverness.

29

'Well, I've had an answer. D'you know what he wrote?' Monsieur Voltaire, she always declared, catered for her mind. Kasia shook her head.

'He wrote, if your symbol is a bee, you inhabit a terrible hive.' She returned to her desk and began rummaging among the papers. 'Now what d'you suppose he meant by that?'

For a moment Kasia did not answer. Outside a band struck up a march, the sound thumping against the windows and setting up a little rattle in the glass.

'I think he m-means we – you – are going through a d-difficult time,' said Kasia diplomatically. The stammer which had afflicted Kasia since the sack of Volochisk and the slaughter of her parents rarely troubled her except in moments of agitation or when she was tired or sick. 'That you are caught up in the reaction that was bound to follow you—' she hesitated 'your accession.'

'What you really mean is I'm a German without one drop of Romanov blood, reigning on sufferance. Isn't that it?'

'That's how some people see the situation, yes.'

'But, God in heaven, am I not ruling them to the best of my ability? Do I not slave at this business of ruling for fifteen hours a day? If they didn't want me why did they put me on the throne with guns firing and bells ringing and everyone swearing eternal allegiance? Why, Kasia, why?' Her colour had risen and in her sudden storm of agitation tears of resentment, of incomprehension, filled her eyes and she pushed the mob-cap further askew on her head with a fierce gesture. It was not often that Kasia heard self-pity in her voice.

'Why did they not send me back to Zerbst as Peter wanted?'

Because, Kasia thought with her uncompromising honesty, this is what you've always wanted, what you've worked for during eighteen long years.

'You're my closest friend. You tell me. What have I done wrong?' It was a cry from the heart.

'Nothing, Ma'am. You've done nothing wrong.' Kasia came round behind the desk and put her hand on Catherine's shoulder. A hand came up and pressed her fingers.

'This will pass, Figgy. They'll soon turn back to you. I know that.' Kasia wished she could sound more confident. But how could anyone except a blind fool be confident when all round one the tide of opposition was creeping closer, undermining what a year ago had seemed so completely solid and indestructible?

The carnival days were over, now came the reckoning. It was difficult in this growing atmosphere of suspicion and whispered hatred to remember the days, the weeks of rejoicing that followed the abdication of Catherine's husband, the Emperor, Peter the Third.

Weeks on end of unbridled gaiety when the whole of Petersburg went wild; when beer flowed in the gutters and even the most wretched beggars crawling in their rags felt themselves part of the human race. The great passed down the broad Nevsky Prospekt in their gilded coaches, and heartfelt *Te Deums* rose to the dingy, smoke-stained ceilings of the humble churches and the painted cupolas of the great cathedrals.

To the poor of the city it did not really matter all that much who sat on the throne, who rode through the streets smiling a false Royal smile, surrounded by the clatter of the escort, the bayonets of the Guards. But even to them Peter, with his obvious loathing for their country and his hero worship of the Prussian Frederick whose soldiers had killed so many of their husbands and brothers, had seemed something loathsome, something contemptible, not worthy to reign as Tsar.

At that moment when the vodka flowed and Russian pride was once more stirring with this woman, who as Grand Duchess had put up for so long with the insults from her miserable husband, as Empress; well, it seemed as if a new era was dawning for them all.

But now all this was forgotten, or in the process of being forgotten. The murmurings and the doubts were heard not only in Moscow and throughout the length and breadth of Russia but in Petersburg in the corridors and attics of the Winter Palace itself. Doubts were spreading like a dank autumn mist and dark rumours scurried like rats across the land. Rumour fed on such uncertainty and on the merest hint of trouble bloomed and waxed fat.

There were many, an increasing number it seemed, who remembered Peter's well-meaning reforms: how he had abolished the dreaded Secret Chancellery in whose dungeons confessions and half-truths were dragged from the shrieking victims with the rack and the knout and the glowing pincers; how he had stopped the salt tax, outlawed the use of the knout. All too quickly they chose to forget his imbecile behaviour and his unbalanced outbursts, his drunkenness and foul language. Now they only seemed to remember that he was a Romanov, grandson to the great Peter.

Already, not a month after her crowning, a conspiracy had been discovered among the officers of the Ingermanland and Izmailovsky Regiments, until that moment Catherine's most loyal supporters, to rescue Ivan the Sixth from his dungeon.

The two ringleaders, Semeon Guriev and Peter Khrushchev were sentenced to what the Senate, as supreme court, termed a lingering death, but Catherine, as Kasia well saw at the time, with a chance to regain popularity repealed this ghastly sentence to one of eternal exile to Kamchatka, on the very eastern fringes of Siberia.

Anonymous letter and tracts written by cunning literate hands were appearing in the streets of Moscow and St. Petersburg. What about Ivan, they accused. Is he not the rightful heir? The world knows he is kept in solitary darkness lying like an animal in his own ordure, but soon, very soon, he will be stripped of his rags and brought in triumph to occupy the throne of his ancestors in place of the German harlot.

Kasia knew that Catherine, though she had never once spoken of her visit to Ivan and though his name was a forbidden subject, was haunted in her dreams by the spectre of the 'nameless prisoner of Schlusselburg'. In the cold light of day the threat posed by the poor wretch seemed very real to an Empress as yet unsure of her hold on a foreign people.

'A ruler can brook no rival,' she had once said, 'nor even the shadow of one.'

Coming so soon after her moment of supreme triumph when the sable cap of Monomachus was held above her proud head, this attempted revolt shocked Catherine.

'It seems,' said Catherine dully, 'I must rule a people who can never be content.'

'Give them time. They won't desert you.'

Catherine sat staring with sightless eyes at the golden bowl of flowers on the desk. There was a defeated look to her hunched shoulders and a worried face that Kasia had never seen before, not even in the days when she was Grand Duchess and all the world seemingly against her.

'When I am dead how will people speak of me? Will it be with hatred and horror?' She leant back in the gilded chair, gazing at the painted cherubs on the ceiling on whose fat little legs half a dozen bluebottles crawled contentedly.

'I'm human enough to want them to think well of me when I'm dead. I want history to speak of me not as a monster wielding a blood-stained whip but a woman who made her dreams for Russia come true.'

'But surely,' Kasia suggested good humouredly, 'we're not thinking of history quite yet. You want them to think well of you now.'

Again Catherine got up and went to the window followed by the greyhounds. 'I have many dreams, Kasia. Since I first arrived in this city nineteen years ago I have dreamt them. And now at last – with their help—' she gestured at the soldiers marching and countermarching.

'Those men, those brave stolid men whose only trade is death, who die so stubbornly and uncomplainingly for Russia, they are the ones who put me where I am,' she said, 'and where I intend to stay. They put the first Catherine on the throne, they allowed Elizabeth to reign – and now me. Three women who owe them a lot, Kasia.'

Kasia heard the familiar vital energy returning to Catherine's tone as she spoke. Her shoulders lost their bowed look and her voice grew stronger as she continued.

'To join the Caspian to the Black Sea and both of them to the Baltic, to establish trade routes to China and the East Indies through Tartary.' Kasia saw the gleam in her eyes as Catherine glanced at her over her shoulder, a mingling of excitement, ambition and triumph. 'I want to take Constantinople from the Turks. I want my ships to pass freely into the Mediterranean – why should it remain a permanent preserve of the British and

French navies? Are they the only men in the world who can sail ships?'

Kasia remained silent. She knew nothing of the sea. Only her journey from Kerch, in the Crimea, to the mouth of the Don in the Cossack gallery with Pugachev as leader, but that was something never to be forgotten; part of another life, as far removed from gilded palaces as was a serf's ragged coat from a cloak of ermine and sable.

'Tell me this, Kasia,' Catherine's foot was beating time to the music of the band, 'who can resist the unlimited power of an absolute prince – or princess—' she added with a brief smile – 'governing a war-like people? And no one can persuade me they are not war-like; most of them have Mongol blood in their veins. Give them a leader and they will march to the four corners of the earth.'

Give them a leader. The words came to Kasia out of the past ... a hut in the village of Zimoveskaya and Emylyan Pugachev, Cossack of the Don, his eyes filled with strange, impossible visions of the future, staring at her from under black brows. 'Give them a leader to follow and they'll march to hell, let alone Moscow.' She had been that man's mistress, had borne him a son, had understood the fires which burned within him. 'Russia is not a country,' he had said, 'it is a world – a world – a world which I intend to see, and to conquer.' In his mind as he spoke those words were the tramp of feet and thud of hooves as thousand upon thousand gathered to his standard and flowed nothwards across the steppes, making for the rich soft cities of the north. He saw then, as he stood by the slow flowing sweep of the wide Don, the flames of burning towns; he saw the stricken land, the trampled crops, the nobles and Government officials who dared oppose him twirling slowly at the ropes' ends, blackening in the sun. He saw victory; he saw power, not for the people he professed to love and pity – but for himself.

Nine years ago after the death of her baby son she had left him and ridden westwards for Poland, but she had never forgotten the look in his dark smouldering eyes as he spoke of what one day he would achieve when he led the peasants on the crusade that would end in the Kremlin or in death.

34

'May I speak frankly?' Kasia asked.

'Since when have you not done so?' Catherine smiled and pushed the mob-cap to the back of her head.

'It seems to me that the worst mistake of the Tsars throughout the centuries – and not only the Tsars but kings and queens of other countries – has been their ignorance, innocent or deliberate, of the power lurking just beyond their noses, I mean the power of the people. Not the nobles, the merchants, the army officers, the priests, the officials but the serfs, the "Dark People" as we call them. They are the ones who—'

'My dear Kasia, don't you think I see that?' Catherine interrupted. 'That why I intend to improve the lot of the serfs: their present state is a stain on Russia's character. Why, my God, in the West they call this country a barbaric inferno as though at any moment they expect Batu's hordes to come galloping over their frontiers. Don't you think I see the weaknesses of this country – but, and this I think few people realize, I also see the strengths. But give me time. As you said yourself this is no moment for bringing in unpopular innovations – how d'you think the nobles would react if I were suddenly to deprive them of their serfs? And where would I be, what would I be without the support of the nobles? Perhaps you see me at the head of an army of ragged *mouzhiks*, the first sovereign to lead her "people" against her "nobles".' Catherine laughed.

'Cossack Countess,' she said in a bantering tone showing her small even teeth. 'Prascovia Bruce was right. Your years on the Don have tinged you with revolt. Besides, like all Poles you are an incurable romantic.' Since Kasia's first arrival at Peterhof in 1756, Countess Bruce, until then Catherine's closest confidante, had gone out of her way to belittle this Polish woman's challenge to her position.

'No, Ma'am. But they opened my eyes to a world I had never known before, a world you yourself don't know, a world which could—'

'Rise up and destroy me?' Catherine's question was on the surface lighthearted, a little malicious and yet tinged with concern.

'They are talking in the taverns, and at the street corners. There's ugly talk, and it's spreading.' Already in Moscow, the

35

people had been summoned by drum-beat to hear a manifesto read, banning idle gossip on affairs concerning the government.

'And you think I couldn't put an end to this – this nonsense – by turning out the Guards?' Kasia caught the uncertainty in Catherine's loud tone, almost imperceptible, but there nevertheless, a sudden loss of confidence.

'Oh yes, you could stamp out the w-whispering with musket butts and fill Siberia with—'

'That's enough!' Catherine's eyes were bleak, her voice hard, twin spots of colour appeared above her cheek bones.

How simple when you were autocrat, when millions of souls were yours, when the power of exile or torture, life or death, lay in your merest whim, how simple to snap, 'that's enough!' Kasia felt her temper rising, but controlled it; she had to for she had a favour to ask, a favour that meant more than life to her, and she lowered her eyes to hide their anger.

'You're surrounded by dangers, Ma'am,' she said after a pause, 'isn't it better to face the facts? The fence is lined with people waiting like a lot of crows to see what's going to happen. They'll cringe and smile today – but tomorrow? Nothing's more difficult to recognize than treachery – especially when it's smiling.'

'You've got a good head on your shoulders,' said Catherine with a smile, 'as well as a pretty one.'

'And I'd like to keep it there.' Kasia smiled in answer and Catherine was struck as so often before by the intense vivid life that animated Kasia's face, replacing the serious, almost sad expression which added a mature and haunting attraction to a face not strictly beautiful in that her mouth was too large, her nose a little too broad. In repose or lost in thought a shrewd observer might have noticed from the set of the mouth, the trace of lines on her tawny skin, the curiously withdrawn almost melancholy look in her eyes, what life had done to Kasia Radienska during her thirty-three years. But when she smiled or laughed she was a young girl again, without a care in the world, gaily challenging fate as if she knew nothing of its false and cruel ways.

Catherine took a deep breath, held it a moment, then expelled it explosively as if she'd come up from the depths, it was her way of clearing out one train of thought and replacing it with something entirely different.

'Your country worries me,' she said, picking a letter from among the pile on her desk. Kasia did not answer; her views on Poland were very different from Catherine's and when they discussed the Polish question it usually ended with Kasia's anger getting the better of her.

'Augustus is a sick man. It doesn't sound as if he has long to live. In fact very wisely he's taken himself off to end his days in Saxony with the comfort of his art treasures. To all intents and purposes Poland is governed by Bruhl. A vain, unscrupulous man whose insincerity is matched only by his enormous extravagance.' Kasia sat in silence, looking at a gay pastoral romp by Boucher on the silken walls.

'You're a Pole,' said Catherine tartly. 'Aren't you interested in what happens to your country?' Nothing annoyed her more than inattention to what she was saying.

'Count Bruhl is not a Pole, nor is the Saxon, Augustus. Why should I be interested in—?'

'Exactly.' Catherine struck the desk with her hand. 'Exactly. It's time Poland had a Polish king again, that is why I sent Count Keyserling to Warsaw with orders—' Orders, thought Kasia hotly. Orders? As if Poland was some province of Russia. 'With orders,' went on Catherine, her enthusiasm mounting, 'to make either Count Poniatowski or his cousin – *your* cousin incidentally – Prince Adam Czartoryski, King. And they surely *must* be Polish enough to please the most ardent patriot.'

Kasia had been away from her country for too long to be familiar with the intricate maze of Polish politics. All she remembered was the bitter feud between many of the Polish nobles, the Barinskis included, and the great family of Czartoryski whom they considered to be too liberal and too much on the side of Russia. Her own mother had been a Czartoryski. 'A crawling viper is no worse than a Barinski who consorts with a member of that accursed family,' that's what Henryk's father had told him in the days when his son, unknown to him, was riding to meet the eighteen-year-old Kasia every day.

'And now this is the answer I get from Stanislas.'

She began to read in her most theatrical tones:

37

'Do not make me King! Only call me back to you! That any other woman could have changed I could have believed, but you, never. What is left for me? Emptiness, and a frightful weariness of heart. Sophie, Sophie, you make me suffer terribly.'

With a petulant gesture Catherine flung down the letter. Poor Stanislas, Kasia thought pityingly, he had truly loved his Catherine, possibly always would.

'I offer him a throne and what do I get?' There was weariness and surprise in her voice.

'D'you want my opinion, Ma'am—'

'Not at the moment, but I'll get it all the same.'

'Count Poniatowski will no more make a king than I would make a queen. Oh, Ma'am, we both know he hasn't the—' she knew exactly what she felt but could not find the word.

'The ruthlessness?' asked Catherine gently.

'Well, yes, if you like. But more than that he hasn't the presence, personality or the dignity necessary to carry a crown.'

'You'll agree he was good-looking?'

'Oh, yes, he was that all right.'

'And that he had a kind heart, a cultivated mind and—'

'All that, yes. But that doesn't make a king.'

'Poor Stanislas, was I very cruel to him? I know how much he loved me – he thinks he loves me still, but I? Well he had begun to bore me. I couldn't help my feelings, sometimes they showed, then the whipped dog look came into his eyes and that disgusted me.'

'That's what I mean,' said Kasia, 'he's not a man to command respect.'

'My dear Kasia, the days of Sobieski are over. Kings are no longer required to go to war, or to lead their peoples personally in desperate ventures.'

'But you yourself, Ma'am—'

'Ah, but that was different. And somehow I do not see Stanislas at the head of his Guards marching to seize a throne.'

She said it in a pleased, complacent way and suddenly the truth of the matter struck Kasia with all the force and shock of a physical blow. Catherine wanted this man, once her lover,

38

to rule, not for any strength he might possess but for his very weakness. He was to be king in name but in fact no more than a puppet that would dance to Russian tunes, would jump obediently to every snap of his mistress's fingers.

'He can bring Poland other more lasting benefits,' said Catherine. 'Culture, the true meaning of the arts, a more liberal outlook, an appreciation of literature.' She was speaking rapidly now, caught up in her dream and her eyes shone with the excitement. 'I see a new golden age dawning for your unhappy country, not an age of conquest and battles but rather of enlightment and—' she broke off, glancing sharply at Kasia.

'You don't agree with me, do you? I see it by your face.'

'Do you, Ma'am?' Kasia felt her expression to be quite wooden. 'I was only wondering what the Poles will think of this idea.'

'Tell me,' asked Catherine, tipping back her chair in the way she had and regarding Kasia with her head on one side, 'do you want your quick-tempered country to become a battlefield yet again – or would you rather live and work in friendship with Russia?'

'Rather a battlefield than a slave market.' But Kasia bit back the words and her fresh spasm of anger.

'Well?'

'I think we should at least be allowed to elect our own King,' she said mildly.

'Ah you Poles—' Catherine smiled playfully. 'The thorns in so many sides.' She shook her head slowly as if in sad incomprehension over the fact that any people could be so troublesome as to want a say in their own affairs.

The squeal of the fifes of the square changed to slow time and the drums thudded with the measured pauses of a metronome.

'I feel better now.' Catherine poured herself her fifth cup of coffee. 'Much more refreshed. Now I shall work.' The Empress usually worked alone till nine when she returned to her red-lined bedroom to receive people with appointments.

Kasia rose to her feet. Now was the moment; she must make her request. Catherine's head was already bowed over the table her pen already scratching busily across the paper.

'Ma'am?'

39

'Yes.' Catherine did not look up.

'May I request a favour?'

'Later, Kasia, later.' The pen never stopped. But Kasia was determined.

'Will you grant me l-leave to go to Poland?'

This time the quill point squeaked to a halt. 'What in the world for?'

Kasia had planned this conversation for two days and an almost sleepless night.

'I've not been home for years, Ma'am. I feel I should like a change.' Since that night fourteen years ago when the darkness was rent by the flames roaring from the windows of Volochisk, consuming the great house and with it the bodies of her mother and father; that terrible night she rode away a prisoner of the Turks past the huddled shape of Henryk flung against the wall, his face a glistening mask of blood from the sabre slash. That was the first time they had been parted and thought each other dead – and now miraculously for the second time she knew him to be alive, and nothing, certainly not the risk of Catherine's displeasure, was going to stop her going to him.

'But my dear,' said Catherine gently, 'you have no home any more. This is your home here with me. Are you not happy?'

'You know I am,' exclaimed Kasia impulsively, 'and I think you know how grateful I am for all you've done for me.'

'It is I who owe everything to you, Kasia.' Absently she patted the sleek head of the greyhound which rested its muzzle on her thigh.

'For that reason of course you can go.' Kasia tried to hide the joy which lit up her face and the surprise. But with the Empress you never knew; sometimes she was like that, no questions asked, just a plain yes or no. At other times she put you through a regular inquisition. Why? Who? When and what for?

'But on one condition only.' Kasia felt the sudden empty stab of apprehension. 'That you return in – let's see, it's August now – in time for Christmas.'

'Thank you, Ma'am,' said Kasia simply. Christmas was an age away and within a fortnight she could be in Kiev and only a few days' ride from Henryk's home at Lipno. Catherine had not asked her why she was going. All she said, half laughingly, was,

'Should you visit your Czartoryski relations you can always tell them that I am not quite the ogre the world tries to make out – tell them that at least I mean well.' She glanced up at the bluebottles.

'I could of course make great use of you as a messenger and confidential agent. But I won't. Go and enjoy yourself and forget the arduous affairs of state. Though how I can spare you, I really don't know.'

'Countess Bruce will manage very well,' said Kasia stiffly. Kasia knew how delighted her rival would be to see her depart, how she would work on Catherine during her absence, dripping poison from her hard, beautiful mouth.

'When will you leave?'

'I hoped before the end of the week.'

'There'll be much to arrange for such a journey. You'll take a coach from the Imperial mews of course and then there's the matter of the escort – nonsense, Kasia, we can't have you travelling all that way on your own. I shall speak to Count Orlov; he will arrange it.' Catherine was entering into the project with all her infectious enthusiasm, and soon they were talking and laughing so loudly that neither of them heard the footsteps on the little staircase that led to the apartments below and only paused in their animated planning when the concealed door in the wall burst open and Grigori Orlov strode in.

Only her lover, disguised by the grandiloquent title of Adjutant General, would have dared to break in upon the Empress unannounced before the hour of nine and he seemed to fill the whole small room, towering above Catherine. He stopped to kiss her hand, nodded perfunctorily at Kasia and without a word, in two huge strides crossed the room, opened the glass window and leant out, drawing deep gulps of fresh air.

There was a dishevelled look to his magnificent coat of yellow velvet, the scarlet sash of the Order of Saint Alexander was stained and crumpled and a blob of candle grease was stuck to Catherine's portrait miniature set in diamonds and pinned to his coat, his white stockings were runkled and the blue ribbon at the tail of his tie-wig was half undone. When he turned to face them after staring at the troops below Kasia saw his eyes were bloodshot and his handsome face an unhealthy colour, puffy with dissipation. He looked as if he had either been up all night or had slept off a drinking bout in his clothes.

'By God, call themselves soldiers!' He scratched the back of his neck with nails that were none too clean. 'Half those brainless louts out there couldn't stand steady if a ball passed within a mile of them.' Orlov helped himself to a rusk and sprawled heavily on the gilded day-bed completely dwarfing it with his huge frame. No one spoke, there were only the sounds of his teeth destroying the rusk. A man's voice shouted an order, there was a crash of a thousand muskets struck as one.

'Potemkin! What the hell does he know about infantry drill. He's a cavalryman.' Orlov's tone was not only contemptuous but bordered on visciousness. That there was precious little love lost between the two men was very clear. Kasia glanced curiously from his heavy, sullen face – the face of an angel Catherine had once called it – to that of the Empress. Catherine sat expressionless, her pen poised above the paper and Kasia could see that she was very angry. Then, slowly, deliberately, she put down the pen and made a little pyramid of her fingers.

'To what do we owe the pleasure of this visit at so early an hour, Grigori?' she inquired coldly.

'I felt like it,' he said rudely.

From Siberia to Kiev there was not another man in the Empire who would dare to speak like that to the Autocrat of Russia.

'I see.'

The drums rolled, orders snapped out and the tramp of two thousand boots rang out as the men marched off parade. Orlov banged his shoe against a table leg in time to the drums so that the jewelled buckle flashed and sparkled. Kasia watched him closely.

Grigori Orlov, legendary hero of Zorndof where, three times wounded, he had fought on through those nine terrible hours at the end of which some twenty-five thousand Russians lay dead and wounded in the summer twilight. The eldest, but not the largest – Alexei was even more gigantic – of five brothers of humble origin, whose grandfather had been an archer in the palace guards of the Great Peter; the man who now rode at Catherine's side in her carriage and aspired to marry her, to

42

reign with her as Emperor Consort. A year ago she had borne his son and now he thought it no more than his right to be her husband.

It was amazing, thought Kasia, that he seemed entirely unaware, as did Alexei, of their growing unpopularity. Could they not see that Russia would not tolerate a man like Grigori who even as he planned to be Tsar had gone back to his old way of life: the drinking taverns, the cards, the nights with the gipsies – and with the women. All Petersburg knew of his behaviour, how could it fail to when he sat flushed with drink, boasting of his hold over the Empress in the lowest haunts of the city. Already there had been threats to his life – the lives of all five brothers.

An officer of the court, one Khitrov, acting in the sincere belief that disaster would strike at the Empress if she married her lover and came under the influence of the Orlov clan, had plotted to kill them. Impressed by his evident honesty and the fact that he was obviously expressing the opinion of not only the city and the court, but also other beloved Guards Regiments, Catherine merely banished him to his country estates.

But now she knew of the growing opposition of her subjects to any idea of marriage to Count Grigori Orlov. Perhaps Fate, like Catherine, admired boldness. Kasia remembered 'l'affaire Kurakina' when Orlov as a young adjutant had stolen the beautiful Princess from Count Peter Shuvalov, his commanding general, and had, from that moment become the talk of Petersburg.

Kasia could well understand why Catherine had fallen so desperately in love with him; she saw and sensed the strength, the huge virility of this man whose powerful masculinity was so different from the charm and gentleness of Poniatowski; the Grand Duchess, as she was then, had, like most other great ladies of Petersburg been intrigued and fascinated by the tales of his courage on the battlefield, his success at the card table and his irresistible attraction for women. Orlov was uneducated, boorish but, by heavens he was a man and at this moment in her life, as never before, she needed a man; she needed to face the hostile world with him behind her, to gather strength from him, but not as her husband.

43

Would he never understand this? He knew there was talk against him, even among the men of the Guards who had followed him so doggedly through the carnage of Zorndorf. He knew of the plot to kill him and Alexei. But in his supreme confidence and arrogance he shrugged away such things as the foolish nonsense of children, beneath his notice.

Catherine knew now what kind of man he was; how he had altered since her accession as Kasia also saw how Alexei had changed. She too, on her first arrival in Petersburg had needed someone to whom to lean and Alexei had been there, a young god in those days, filled with glowing strength and health – but now he too had become arrogant, insufferably pleased with himself, impervious to criticism or advice. In the early days the brothers had possessed their own fierce code of honour; devotion to their regiment, to Russia, but now even that seemed to have vanished.

Four years ago Grigori Orlov had become Catherine's lover and in those days she had such names as 'my slave unto death' and he, not to be outdone, had replied with 'my adorable goddess'. But now, such tender exchanges were becoming rarer, and could you wonder when he appeared like this, unshaven and rumpled after yet another wild debauch, having surely forgotten the fact that besides being his mistress Catherine was also his Empress. Take care, thought Kasia, eyeing him with distate, take care, or like Peter you will dig your own grave.

'Kasia is going on a holiday to Poland,' said Catherine brightly, breaking a silence that was fast growing intolerable.

'Is she,' he growled without interest. The antipathy between him and Kasia was mutual. She recognized his animal attraction and admired his bravery as a soldier but otherwise disliked him intensely. He for his part considered her influence on Catherine to be too great and inimical to himself; therefore, as he kept on urging Catherine, the 'Cossack Countess' should be dismissed. 'Send her back to the Don or the Ukraine or wherever it is she came from.'

He stared at her balefully with narrowed smarting eyes – my God, his head was like a rotting pumpkin. She was a beauty all right, with the look of a gipsy in her raven hair and a hint of the blazing Ukrainian sun still on her skin even after these last years in the hothouse atmosphere of the Court. He looked away from the steady glance of her dark blue eyes. She saw too much, damn her. Alexei had warned him of that; she sat there so often without speaking; just listening quietly, smiling to herself now and then, but always listening, always watching. Anyway, he loathed the Poles, treacherous swine. That poor fool, Poniatowski, all charm and sweet talk and nothing else.

'Tell 'em in Poland from me,' he said unexpectedly, 'there's only one man worthy to be King of Poland and that's Oginski. Understand? Oginski.'

'I hardly think we need discuss the matter now.' Catherine got to her feet as did Kasia but Orlov remained where he was, his lap full of rusk crumbs. The gilded white marble clock on the mantelpiece began to whirr, preparatory to striking.

'It is nine o'clock,' said Catherine, standing very straight behind her desk and Kasia was struck once again by the extraordinary dignity of her short body, the lively graceful manner in which she carried her head.

'At midday I shall see you again, Grigori.' There was no mistaking the command in her tone. 'That is should you not be feeling too unwell.' There was also no mistaking the fondness which had crept back into her eyes. He glowered but nevertheless heaved himself with bad grace to his feet, mumbling something that could have been meant as an apology. Kasia opened the door to the bedroom and, as she curtsied, she felt Catherine's hand on her shoulder.

'We'll talk of your plans this evening. Now go, for you'll have much to do, much to think of.' The door closed behind her. But, before Kasia could leave the room, Orlov began to speak.

'How long is it since you saw my brother?'

'What is that to you?' she answered stiffly, her hand on the door knob.

'Don't go yet. I have something I want to say.' Orlov summoned a cold smile. Unwillingly Kasia turned and faced him.

'Well?' He lay back on the creaking couch and repeated his question.

'Three weeks, a month – I don't know.'

45

He glanced at the door to Catherine's bedroom.

'Has it not struck you that you could marry Alexei?'

She did not answer.

'After all, he's asked you enough.'

'Apparently you and he have no secrets between you.'

'Very few.'

'Then you'll know my answer to him, won't you? And it'll be the same however many times he asks me.'

Kasia knew that Alexei had never really loved her. He wanted her body, that was all, but the matter of marriage had been a challenge to him. After all how could any woman resist the chance of being the wife of the man who, or so rumour whispered, had killed the late Tsar and put Catherine on the throne?

He regarded her reflectively, his manhood stirring. She was far more beautiful than Catherine and, when roused, every bit as spirited. He thought of the Russian folk legend that she who is to be the fairest of them all must have hair black and shining as a raven's wing. But she was not Empress.

'The four of us,' he said in a low voice. 'You as her friend and favourite lady-in-waiting. Soon perhaps, if you play your cards correctly she will make you her first lady-in-waiting.'

She knew he was watching her minutely.

'A word from the right quarter,' he went on slowly, 'and you would rank second only to the Imperial Family. I could do this,' he added with all his overbearing confidence. 'I could have Prascovia Bruce removed and—'

'Your concern for my future is most touching,' said Kasia with a ravishing smile.

'There would be one small condition,' Orlov said, also smiling.

She waited.

'Next time my fortunate brother asks your hand in marriage you will decide you love him most dearly and accept.'

Kasia stared at him in silence then burst out laughing.

'So then you and—' she nodded at the bedroom door, 'and Alexei and I would be the four most powerful people in Russia, is that it?'

His eyes had gone hard and dangerous, a tiny pulse was

beating above his left eye. In the silence the long drawn cry of a flower seller rose from the square: '*Tsvety Tsvetochki!*'

She went to the window. Below she saw the blooms piled in crimson glory on the tray borne on the man's head. 'Oh, no,' she said without turning her head, 'I've no great longing to oust Countess Bruce – even if I could, which I think's most unlikely. I'm very happy as I am, single—' the pause was almost imperceptible – 'and her Majesty's friend,' she added slowly.

'So you won't do as I ask?' he said with rising anger.

'No.'

Heaving himself to his feet, Orlov stood beside her in two huge strides.

'Remember it was the Orlovs who put the Empress where she is. Without me, without us,' he laughed harshly, contemptuously, 'she'd be back to Zerbst – or in Schlusselburg. And you—' he drew his finger across his throat in a crude gesture

Kasia felt the anger colouring her face. She faced him.

'I admire your w-wonderful loyalty, *Count* Orlov.' Serfs, roubles, decorations and jewels and ennoblement – all these rewards Catherine had showered on these brothers of lowly origin. 'But you remember this,' she added very deliberately, 'an Orlov can hang just as high as the next m-man.'

Her breathing was rapid, her breasts rising and falling in their curving bed of blue silk. His face was like thunder, his eyes red with anger. She thought he was going to strike her. But she faced him without flinching, her eyes steady.

'Why she surrounds herself with women like you and that silly little bitch Dashkova—'

He seized her shoulders in a grip that made her bite her lip to stop the cry of pain. Then one hand moved to her neck, caressed it roughly; the other went to her breasts.

'My God,' he said thickly, 'I could take you now if I had a mind to.'

She saw the sudden surge of lust glaze his eyes for a second.

'Don't worry your pretty head, brother Alexei has told me many juicy little titbits about your habits in bed.' He laughed coarsely at her obvious distress, his eyes cruel.

'The Turks and Cossacks are fine teachers of love it seems.'

Anger suited her, he thought with all the cold appreciation of a practised lecher; he had never seen eyes that really flashed and sparkled with rage.

'Your morals are not exactly stainless, my fine, arrogant Pole.'

'And you can't keep your dirty hands off any woman, can you?' Kasia turned on her heel without another word. In the doorway she paused. 'In the Ukraine we have a word, *chlopy*. It means lout.' She almost hissed the last three words.

In the passage she leant for a moment against the brocaded wall, calming her agitation. Her shoulders hurt cruelly where his fingers had bitten into the flesh, her mind was bruised by his vicious words; her anger such that if she had a knife she would have plunged it into his body, time and time again and with intense pleasure.

Many men wanted her. All her life they had wanted her; since she began to grow into a woman. Some had taken her; Diran Bey, the Turk in Kerch; Emylyn Pugachev, Cossack of the Don; Lev Bubin, that weak and worthless noble who had brought her to Petersburg and back into Catherine's life; and lastly Alexei Orlov.

But Henryk Barinski had been the first and to him she had given not only her body but her heart, mind, her whole being. And that was not something she could do more than once.

And now she treated all men as she considered they deserved. Some with a grave courtesy, others with smiling charm; the ones who pawed at her and tried to bed her she turned on with a sort of suppressed fury and scorn. She had built an invisible wall between her beauty and the men who craved to enjoy it, a wall she never broke down by flirting or encouraging or teasing. Rather, as a man became more and more importunate so she retired further within her armour of reserve.

But, she thought with a sudden surge of relief, soon none of this would matter for she would be with Henryk.

PART TWO

THE sun played among a few fat little clouds which sent short-lived shadows across the rolling Ukrainian hills thick with oak and birch. The mist still hung silvery in the small valleys and low above the river dividing the land of the Barinskis from that which had once belonged to the Radienskis, but which now since the sack of Volochisk was deserted, ghost-ridden, given over to woodcutters, charcoal-burners and wandering goat-herds.

The oak woods were full of roe-deer, foxes and wild-boar; lynxes moved swiftly and silently in the thickets and at nights the darkness trembled to the haunting cries of the hunting wolves.

To the west of Lipno the distant peaks of the Carpathians drew a dark, jagged line across the sky; to the east the great rolling plains stretched to the Dnieper, changing to the endless Don steppe, the land of the Cossacks, where the feather grass swayed and rippled in a wind heavy with the scents of sage and wild thyme, stretching in a bronze sea to the banks of the Volga and beyond, as far as a man could ride in twenty days, right to the very fringes of Mongolia; to the south lay the land of the Turks, and to the north, through the watery wilderness of the Pripet Marshes and the impenetrable northern forest, the way to Russia.

In one small valley, in a pleasant, secluded spot a house stood among orchards filled with the sound of bees and the soothing murmur of turtle doves: a squat house built of white stucco; four dormer windows broke the graceful fall of the green copper roof, steeply pitched to spill the snows of winter. At the front a wide gravel path swept round past a white-pillared porch. Green tinted windows in narrow blue frames reflected the sunshine as though the rooms within were full of green water. Smoke rose raggedly from one of the four tall chimneys, dipping this way, that way in an uncertain little breeze which rustled the leaves of the lime trees. A row of white pigeons sat along the line of the roof, nodding their little round heads and peering down warily at the three men seated in the shade of a spreading acacia on wooden benches in the garden below, ready to fly at an instant's notice if the sound of the voices should get too loud, or should there be any sudden movement.

'I've only known Henryk Barinski for about three months, since he got back from Paris in June, but I would trust him with my life. In fact I had to the first time we met when I tried to steal his horse, but that's another story.' Jan Dombrowski chuckled. He was a young man of perhaps twenty-six or twenty-seven, with red hair and a cheerful, freckled face inclined to split in a wide, infectious grin. One of his very blue eyes was slightly rounder than the other giving one half of his face an open-eyed look, the other a more sleepy expression, so that it was not very easy to guess what he was thinking. He had one quite black tooth in the middle of the top row so that it looked as if there was a gap. His clothes were brown and plain and slightly old-fashioned and he spoke in quick, breathless snatches, caught up by his own sudden enthusiasms. A likeable fellow, but as quick to anger as to laughter.

His two companions were older than he; in fact, one Count Branicki, Grand General of Poland, was in his early seventies, with a worn, lined face and tired voice. The other man, Josef Pulawski, lawyer by training, soldier by inclination, was in his early fifties, a man of distinguished, scholarly appearance and untidy dress.

'He can be trusted all right. I'd stake everything on that,' he said. 'I knew him once in Rome about seven years ago. He was drifting then, another of the many Polish exiles wandering about Europe – like the Scots, we make good soldiers and good exiles.' Pulawski smiled briefly but without much humour in his small eyes.

'But even at that time, so soon after the tragedy of Volochisk and the loss of the girl he loved, when he was full of drink and self-pity, even then I was impressed by something in him, a hint of strength and purpose hidden somewhere if only it could be dug out.'

'And now I think it can,' said Dombrowski.

'We stood on a balcony one night in Rome and he told me he'd never go back to Poland. What is there to go back to, he said, and I've never heard such a depth of desolation in any man's voice before or since.'

In the silence that followed Pulawski's words they heard children's laughter from the village lying beyond the far corner of the garden, and a sudden frenzied outburst of cackling geese among the blue-washed cottages.

'Well,' said Count Branicki, 'now he's back and we must hear what he has to say, what views he has on the—' he hesitated – 'the matter in hand.' He pulled a watch from the fob pocket of his heavy travelling breeches and frowned. 'How much longer is he going to keep us waiting? I must be back in Loov by tonight. It's damnably inconsiderate—' He did not actually say, the Grand General of Poland has more to do than sit about in the garden of an obscure country house, however pleasant the surroundings, but the words hovered over them nevertheless. Dombrowski grinned to himself and fell to whistling tunelessly between his teeth.

Count Branicki regarded him with his hooded, lizard eyes wondering what they were doing here, what they hoped to achieve. And yet the biggest oak often started from the smallest acorn; the most powerful armies grew round the first few men to don its uniform. He himself had travelled from Krakow, Pulawski from Warsaw, and Dombrowski – God only knows where he had come from. An oddly assorted trio he thought drily, and a fine start to what they hoped would be Poland's new future – waiting on a hard bench in a sun already uncomfortably hot listening to a young fool whistling. He was too old to start new adventures, to talk of a war that might bring nothing but disaster and ruin to the country he loved more than anything in the whole dark and uncertain world. Too old, and too tired. He leant his head back, closing his eyes, the corners of his mouth pulled down by disillusionment and despair. Ostensibly, he thought, the three of them were at Lipno simply on a social visit to their good friends the

Barinskis. It would be many months, possibly years, before the true purpose of this first meeting together would burst upon Europe.

'His father is not well today,' said Pulawski. 'Henryk is with him. He'll join us as soon as he can.'

'Let's hope the son is even half the man his father was.' Branicki did not open his eyes. 'For Poland needs men like this, my God, how she needs them.'

'He's been a soldier,' Dombrowski wiped away the sweat gathering on his forehead. 'And he's been a sailor,' he paused a moment for effect, 'in the English Navy.'

The Grand General opened his eyes. 'What in heavens name was he doing in the English Navy?'

'Fighting the French,' answered the young man. He laughed, enjoying the surprise his words had caused. 'Think of it. A Pole who'd never even *seen* the sea having to spend five years in a stinking ship. He told me it stank. Among other things.'

'And how will this doubtless interesting experience help us?' asked Pulawski acidly. 'After all, there are not many opportunities of fighting a war at sea on the Polish plains.' Again the humourless, strangely inhuman smile.

'Ah, but I said he'd been a soldier. He fought against the Prussians at Rossbach, and that time in the uniform of France.'

'He appears to have led an active life,' remarked Count Branicki, drily.

'He can speak good Russian. He was in St Petersburg on the staff of the French Legation – that was before Catherine's time of course.'

'So he's a diplomat as well as a soldier and, for all we know, an admiral.'

'Oh no, sir, he was only a common seaman,' said Dombrowski ingenuously.

'Ah, I see.'

They looked towards the house and the sound of footsteps. The pigeons flew up with a loud clatter of wings as Henryk Barinski walked with a slight limp down the path towards the waiting men.

'I must apologize, gentlemen, for having kept you like this –
and without refreshment.' He turned his head and shouted,
'Stepan! Bring wine and cakes!' Then he gave his attention to
the others.

'Count Branicki. I am honoured to meet you sir.' He
inclined his head in a little bow.

'Jan.' He nodded with a quick smile at Dombrowski, then
held out his hand to Pulawski.

'It's been a long time, Josef. How long since Rome ?'

'Seven years. And your grip hasn't weakened.' Pulawski
glanced down at his fingers ruefully. 'Later we must talk of old
days.'

'Yes.' Henryk smiled again and Branicki thought how a
sudden movement of the lips, a sudden expression in the eyes
can change a man's personality – anyway on the surface. In his
long life the Grand General had seen many smiles, some true,
some false, but this one, he decided, this had a real spontaneous
warmth – and that could mean a lot.

'My father begs to be excused but—'

'I can't see your father begging for anything,' interrupted
Count Branicki drily. Again the quick smile as Henryk
answered.

'You know him well.' He watched the pigeons as they
swooped back to their accustomed perches. 'But his gout is
troubling him even worse than usual today. Next time you all
visit Lipno he hopes to be able to entertain you himself.' His
voice was deep and surprisingly slow somehow, when taken
with his looks. You'd expect, thought Branicki, a quick,
impetuous rush of words.

Henryk sat down on the warm grass. Count Branicki
fumbled in a capacious travelling pocket and finally discovered
his favourite pipe; as he filled it the old man regarded Henryk
with interest. The same long grey eyes and dark almost
swarthy skin as his father, black curly hair – his own – touched
here and there with grey. His mouth was wide and generous,
and made for smiling.

Yet in repose the face was intensely serious and older than
that of a man of thirty-six. But it was the scar that fascinated
Branicki; never in his long and eventful life had he seen a man's

53

face so marked. And yet it did not altogether mar his face; somehow it went with his looks, added the final touch of authenticity to a man with his turbulent history. The dull red line ran from the broad brow diagonally between the eyes across the bridge of the short straight nose and down the left side of his cheek, God had been kind: the steel had cut between his eyes.

The tinder rasped, smoke billowed from the stained bowl of the pipe; Count Branicki tamped the glowing tobacco with a brown square finger, wondering briefly what it must have been like to receive such a wound.

'Well,' he said without preamble, 'you know why we are here.' It was not a question.

'Yes,' said Henryk.

'And you agree with what we must do?'

'Yes,' Henryk plucked a stalk of grass and put it between his teeth. His hand was thin and brown, the fingers long. 'With all my heart.'

'So we are all agreed then, in company with many thousands of other Poles,' said Pulawski, 'on what we should do?'

'But not on *how* we do it,' remarked Branicki. 'And, as we all know to our cost, it has never been easy, in most cases not even possible, to get more than two Poles to agree over anything. If it had we would not be in our present unhappy state.'

In the silence that followed his words, Stepan the old butler shuffled from the house with a tray. He placed it with great deliberation on the rough table and stood quietly waiting.

'Thank you, Stepan,' said Henryk. 'That will be all.' A man of great natural courtesy, thought Branicki. That was good; arrogance alone would not serve them well; brains, intelligence and courage, yes. Above all, courage.

Henryk poured out the wine, raised his glass. 'To the future of our country,' he said quietly. They touched glasses and drank.

'Russian troops are on Polish soil and we sit drinking and talking about some vague future which no one seems to know how to achieve,' burst out Dombrowski in a sudden quick flare of anger.

Behind his pipe smoke Branicki shook his head. It was not easy for the old and exhausted to hold back the fiery young, but for Poland's sake it must be done, at least until the crucial moment.

'So far the Russians have committed no offence,' said Pulawski in a flat voice. Ah, thought Henryk, the cautious lawyer speaking.

'Only that of being on Polish soil at all. By what rights has the German whore sitting there on her damned throne in St Petersburg sent her troops into Poland? We're not at war, are we?' Dombrowski looked from one to another, a mixture of rage and puzzled incomprehension on his young face.

'They have not pillaged or burnt,' went on Pulawski in his strangely expressionless voice.

'Catherine, as far as we can gather, merely asked that her soldiers should march through Lithuania from Courland en route for the Ukraine.'

'A strange route surely for a Russian army to take to reach the Ukraine,' remarked Henryk. He had a sudden vision of Catherine sitting at her desk, straight as a small drill sergeant, signing with her own particular flourish, the order that was to send her soldiers into Poland – and that was to put in train a chain of events the outcome of which no one could possibly foretell. And had Kasia been standing at her shoulder? What had she said to such an order? Had she tried to argue, to remonstrate with her royal mistress and friend? He shook himself free of memories that threatened to engulf him.

'Technically they are not here in aid of any particular faction,' said Pulawski.

'Then why in hell's name are they here at all?' Dombrowski banged the table so that the glasses and the silver wine jug leapt and rang. 'I've seen them, marching about as if they owned the whole damned Ukraine. And if they start to kill and rape what are we going to do? What *can* we do?' The desperation trembled in his voice.

'That surely is what we are here to discuss,' said Henryk soothingly. He looked at his friend with understanding and liking. It was men like Jan who had led the Winged Hussars

55

to the gates of Kiev, who had shattered the Turks outside Vienna.

'Keep your anger for the battlefield,' he said. 'For, by God, that is the right place for it.' He spoke with a great intensity of feeling.

'You know about war, I believe?' said Branicki. Henryk did not answer at once. The sudden crying of a child in the village drowned the deep drone of the bees in the lime trees.

'Yes, too much. But don't worry,' he added with a short laugh, 'I'll fight again. But never for foreigners.'

'Where privilege is concerned Poles have always strained at a gnat,' said Branicki after a short pause. 'Who is to lead? Which way are they to go? Why should one take orders from another?'

'Petty bickering,' muttered Dombrowski.

'It's ironic, isn't it, that there's no word in the Polish language nor phrase for "follow a leader". We can imitate one, we can even love one, but we cannot follow.' Henryk grinned and looked, for all the shocking scar, like a mischievous little boy. He got to his feet and refilled their glasses. Branicki shook his head.

'The sun is too hot. At my age—' he broke off, fell into a sudden reverie, then stirred himself and said, 'How very peaceful it is.'

He let his eyes roam slowly, and for a moment contentedly, over the garden. At the far end, visible between the apple trees, the cherry trees, the clumps of Tatar honeysuckle and wild jasmine, a pond shone in the sunlight. Little earthen paths wound among gooseberry bushes, buckthorn and lilac. He sighed. This was the place for a tired old man to end his days, watching the dragonflies, the sparrows soothed by the soft music of the turtle doves. Here he could doze and dream of his long life, his faraway youth, of how once he had thought himself someone on his own little bit of stage. 'Are men not mad always to be talking of war and conquest when they could be sitting in a beautiful garden listening to the birds and the sound of childrens' happiness?' He sighed again more deeply. Henryk, looking at him curiously, wondered, and had an idea of what it must be like to feel you had to begin all over again in your seventies. To give up the well-earned rest and tranquillity of old age and force your tired body and mind back into the turmoil and hatred.

He could understand, for his years on the lower deck of the *Huntress*, though in many ways toughening his spirit and body, had left him with some unpleasant legacies. Damp weather would bring on a persistent cough; the wounds received at Rossbach and the effects of the actions at Quiberon and against the *Richelieu* had left their mark. Often he suffered vivid nightmares, often he suffered much pain, often he felt exhausted, utterly drained mentally and physically. But at the moment, with the sun warm through the branches and the wine pleasant on his palate, he felt he could take on the world. He sat up, clasping his knees, glancing up at the others with a sidelong look from smiling eyes.

'During the late war with France I had the misfortune – or perhaps in some ways, the good fortune, to spend some years in a British man-of-war. Among experiences I learnt the value of leadership. To my mind a good leader is worth ten thousand men on the battlefield.'

'If – if – what we hope takes place,' asked Dombrowski, 'who will lead us?' His question tailed off as he saw the expression on the three faces.

'At this stage we cannot be concerned over such a vital matter,' said Pulawski.

'But surely—'

'Let us make certain first that horses are harnessed to the cart and that they are all pulling in the same direction before we appoint a coachman.'

Count Branicki spoke with a new voice, the voice that had made him Grand General of Poland. 'At this moment Poland has no national army. Ah, to be sure, Prince Radziwill commands a private force in the north, but to achieve what I believe we all have in mind we need before anything a new Polish army. Are we agreed on this at least, gentlemen?'

They nodded.

'In the past,' said Henryk, 'our cavalry was supreme in Europe. No troops could stand against the Winged Hussars. The Polish knights saved Europe for the first time at Lignica when they halted the Mongols.' He smiled. 'Tatars! The

Creatures from Hell. And that's what we'll face again, for Hell lies to the East.'

'We beat the Turks outside Vienna,' said Dombrowski, 'and the Teutonic Knights at Grünwald. Can we not do the same again? In the name of God, what have we become? A nation of spineless old women?'

'With the improvement in artillery,' said Henryk, 'as you know as well as I do, the entire concept of great set-piece battles has altered. Or, if it hasn't yet, it'll have to. Otherwise the cavalry – and the horses of every civilized,' he laughed, 'country are heading for massacre.'

'We will not talk of strategy and tactics now,' put in Branicki, 'these details will come later.'

'Augustus is not expected to live much longer,' said Pulawski, firmly changing the subject. 'And after our Saxon King has gone to his art treasures in Dresden, who is to step on to the throne in his place? For surely on that unknown quantity many of our future plans must hinge.'

'They all say it's to be Poniatowski. Put there on the orders of his mistress, Catherine, Empress of All the Russias,' Dombrowski cried scornfully.

'A weakling who'll do nothing for Poland except on instructions from that German. Why, it's well known she's already sending expensive presents to anyone she thinks can influence the election.'

'We should go back to a hereditary monarchy,' said Henryk, 'then perhaps we'd get a little more stability.'

'Like Augustus, I'm afraid that Stanislas Poniatowski may turn out to be a stupidly good prince.' Count Branicki relit his smouldering pipe. 'And such men often do more harm to their countries than the worst of tyrants. His moments of greatest success will perhaps serve only to mark the final destruction of his country.' As if exhausted by his words, the Grand General without an army closed his eyes and leant back.

'Therefore he must not be allowed to reach the throne.' Dombrowski's fists were tightly clenched on the table. 'He *must* not!'

'Unfortunately he hasn't the moral strength to go with his intellectual abilities,' Pulawski said.

Henryk watched a small beetle negotiating a strenuous path among the jungle of grass stalks, remembering a slim, good-looking boy poring short-sightedly over his books at Volochisk while his cousin Kasia Radienska and little Figgy von Anhalt-Zerbst and he, Henryk Barinski, had gone riding in the snow; remembering a charming, amusing young man, the passionate, ardent lover of Figgy, Grand Duchess and wife of Peter, one day to be uncrowned Tsar for a few short months. And once again the question rose in his mind, was it the gay, witty Stanislas who had betrayed him into the bloodstained hands of the Secret Chancellery? The haunting question that would probably never be answered.

'Who is to wear the crown of the Piasts, the Jagiellos, of Sobieski? Who's worthy of it?' No one answered Dombrowski's indignant cry.

'Oginski? Radziwill? Even Czartoryski? Surely any of these are preferable to a poor player like Poniatowski. You yourself, sir, will you not stand for election?'

Count Branicki slowly shook his head without looking up.

'I agree,' said Pulawski. 'But there are some in Poland who would welcome a man like Poniatowski, liberal minded men like the Abbé Konarski whose greatest ambition is to revive Polish literature and Bishop Zaluski who has just given some two hundred thousand books to the nation.'

'Better to have given two hundred thousand muskets,' said Dombrowski.

'Exactly,' agreed Henryk. 'As a boy I studied under the excellent Abbé.' He paused, then went on. 'Not so very long ago, though it's difficult to imagine now, Poland was great. Yet, among the things he taught me – or tried to teach me – was that national glory was of no importance compared to peace. Peace at all costs. That was his sincere belief. One day perhaps men will no longer think it worth while to fight for their freedom – but not yet—' He was speaking more rapidly now, roused by his own words.

'Besides,' he added fiercely, 'this is a time for the sword, not the pen. What use are books to slaves?' The fire within him glowed in his eyes.

At that moment Pulawski knew that this was the man they needed, that Poland needed. As romantic as all Poles but with romanticism tempered, supplemented perhaps, by the experiences of the last years. A romantic realist. A man who could be kind and understanding and yet, or so Pulawski thought, Henryk Barinski would be hard and, if circumstances demanded, ruthless, and men would certainly follow him.

Henryk was speaking again. 'One of the French *philosophes* – Rousseau, I think – has said of us, "Poles, if you cannot prevent your neighbours from swallowing you, you can at least stop them digesting you." Or something like that.' He raised his foot to allow the beetle to pass.

'In our present state of weakness it looks as if that's about all we can do. But some day very soon, I hope – perhaps when winter comes – we'll stop them getting us anywhere near their mouths.' They all smiled with him except Dombrowski.

'It would be more use if the French sent us men and arms instead of highflown phrases,' he said. 'But they can't fight any more. They're effete. Useless. This last war has drained them.'

'I think you're wrong,' said Henryk gently. 'The French can fight.' The sweet scents of the garden were replaced by the stink of gun smoke; he saw the burning hulk, smashed and splintered, of the *Richelieu* drifting on a bright sea, her colours clinging stubbornly at the mizzen peak, her last few guns firing, still manned by blackened, bloody scarecrows. He remembered with a sudden tightening of his throat, even after all these years, the sight of the little drummer boy, Cornu, beating out the *pas de charge*; the memory of how the men of the Régiment de Mailly turned to face the Prussian cavalry as they charged with Seydlitz along the red stream to finish the battle by the village of Rossbach.

'Oh, yes, the French can fight all right, you needn't worry about that. But there's only one way we'll keep our freedom and that's through our own efforts. It's no use depending on the French or the Tatars, or the Cossacks.' Henryk gazed towards the village and the golden hills lying beyond the lazy haze of smoke.

'Those devils are just waiting for the chance to throw us out of the Ukraine,' put in Pulawski.

'How does your brother feel about these affairs?' asked Count Branicki.

'Adam?' Henryk considered for a moment. 'He thinks as we all do but – well, he's got a cautious head on his shoulders and, being the eldest, he'll be responsible for Lipno one day, and—'

'Is he here?' Pulawski broke in.

'No. He's not back from Uman. He's gone to buy a new stallion.'

'From the Potocki stud?'

'Yes.'

Count Branicki knocked out his pipe on the corner of the table. 'There's to be a meeting of the Diet within the month. Privately I'll sound out opinion and in public try to make some sense from all the endless speeches and argument. Perhaps your father will be there.

'If his leg allows him to travel,' said Henryk. 'Otherwise nothing would stop him from attending the Diet. He enjoys losing his temper too much.'

Stepan appeared from the house and spoke to Henryk.

'Excuse me, Your Honour, but there's a man in the yard who says he must speak to you.'

'Can't it wait?'

'He says the matter is very urgent. The man has ridden a long way by the looks of him.'

'Oh, very well.' Henryk jumped to his feet.

'I must go,' said Count Branicki, consulting a huge watch. 'I have to be in Lvov by nightfall. But before I go, I should like to visit your father. That is, if he feels like meeting anyone.'

'If you go without seeing him he'll be in a filthy temper for days – and I have to live here,' Henryk chuckled. 'But are you sure you won't stay for a meal, sir?'

'Thank you, but no. Our talk has been most agreeable and I hope it will not be too long before we meet again. I will send word of when and where.' He held out his hand.

Henryk took it, saying, 'I shall be here, sir. And I'll work on various ideas which may be of use in the future.'

Count Branicki nodded without speaking.

'Stepan, take His Honour to my father.' They watched the two old men vanish into the house.

'A great man,' said Pulawski. 'If anyone can achieve unity among us it's him.'

'We haven't achieved anything else so far,' Dombrowski muttered. 'And don't tell me Rome wasn't built in a day,' he added seeing Pulawski's expression. Henryk laughed and clapped the young man on the back.

'Don't worry, Jan, one day you'll get all the action you want – and more.'

Against his will Dombrowski grinned. 'The sooner the better,' he said. 'I've almost forgotten how to draw a sabre.'

They went into the house and through to the yard. On the way Henryk heard his father's great bellow of laughter.

'Something has made him forget his gout,' said Pulawski. 'I wouldn't have thought the Grand General possessed that amount of humour.'

A man stood, thickly coated in dust, beside his lathered horse.

'I'll see you in a moment,' Henryk called out. 'Have they given you something to eat and drink?'

'Yes, Your Honour. A pot of beer and some cheese.'

Count Branicki's coach waited in the shade of the house.

'It won't be long, Henryk,' Pulawski said. 'What we need more than anything at the moment, even more than soldiers or arms, is patience.'

Dombrowski mounted his chestnut mare and raised his arm in farewell. 'I'll be back next week,' and rode out of the gates with a great clatter of hooves.

'Where does he go? What does he do?' Pulawski shook his head slightly as he spoke.

'Half the time, God knows. The other half he spends playing at looking after a small estate about thirty miles away. But his heart's not really in the land or in checking tallies of grain and fruit. He'll make a good soldier.'

They talked for a while until Count Branicki came out to join them. The two men got into the coach.

'You have a beautiful place here, Barinski,' said the Grand General as he settled back against the stiff leather. 'I hope to visit it again quite soon.'

'You will always be very welcome, sir.'

'Goodbye Henryk.' called Pulawski.

'*Au revoir*, Josef. Only *au revoir*.'

Henryk crossed the yard to the messenger.

*   *   *

It was only when the rumble of the coach wheels had faded down the road which led to Lvov that Henryk, pacing slowly in the garden, could allow his mind to concentrate on the news the horseman had brought him. Kasia at Kiev. No more than a hundred and fifty miles. So she *had* got his letter. Six hours on a good horse; ten in a coach, call it twelve with two changes of horses. Twelve hours and she could be at the birch tree.

'Countess Radienska said, the usual place Thursday or Friday and that she would not fail.'

'Was that all, man? Did she say nothing else?' Henryk had longed to shake some expression into the man's impassive peasant face.

'Nothing else, Your Honour. Those were her very words.'

He stopped by the pond. Fat ducks swam towards him among the water lilies, hoping for food.

'Good morning you stupid-looking birds,' he said, squatting on his heels, holding out empty fingers. The ducks inspected them beadily then swam away chuckling in disgust. Henryk laughed aloud. The joy of the news from Kiev was so intense it hurt and almost choked him.

Two round-eyed village children peered at him from the branches of a lime tree beyond the high wattle fence. He smiled and waved and called out, 'Mind you don't fall, little idiots!' and did not notice the sound of the long riding boots on the path until his brother stood right beside him.

'My God, it's hot,' said Adam.

Henryk turned. 'Hello, Adam. Good trip? Did you get the stallion?'

'Yes,' Adam Barinski was burnt darkly by the Ukrainian sun, his face, longer and thinner than Henryk's, showed traces of his fatigue. His clothes were travel-stained, his blue eyes bloodshot from the glare and dust of the six-hour ride. He removed his cravat, stroking his neck with the same long fingers as his brother's.

'They may be our cousins,' he said wearily, 'but by heaven, they drive a hard bargain. The lord only knows what Father's going to say.'

'Have you seen him yet?'

'I just looked in to say I was back. He's giving old Globnik hell about the wheat. I wouldn't be Father's agent for all the furs in Siberia.' Henryk laughed.

Though the two brothers had never been really very close they shared one thing in common and that was a very healthy respect for their father.

'I gather from Stepan that the Grand General's been here. And that crazy young fool, Dombrowski.'

'Oh, I don't know, Jan's not such a fool as all that.' Henryk wanted either to be alone with his whirling thoughts or to blurt out that wonderful, unbelievable news to someone, anyone.

'Who was the other fellow?' asked Adam.

'Pulawski. Josef Pulawski, a lawyer from Warsaw. I hadn't seen him since we met in Rome.'

Adam looked down at his brother from his greater height, his eyes troubled.

'Look here,' he said, 'are you sure you know what you're doing?'

'Yes.' So he's going to play the heavy elder brother again.

'But, good God, Henryk, you've only been home for three months and already' – he lowered his voice – 'you're busy planning a war. A war that Poland cannot hope to win—'

'At least she can try,' retorted Henryk hotly.

They stood in silence broken by the sharp tap of a riding whip against leather. Henryk put his hand on Adam's dusty sleeve.

'Adam.'

'Yes?'

'If I fight will you come with me?' For a moment Adam did not answer.

'I'm the one trained as a soldier and yet I've never heard a shot fired in anger. And you. You get yourself educated at a most liberal-minded establishment and know as much about war as any man.' He smiled sadly, a smile showing stained uneven teeth yet of peculiar charm. Adam smiled rarely and seemed to find it hard to laugh.

'I think someone will have to stay and look after Lipno,' he said quietly. 'And there's more chance of keeping this place safe and intact if we try to save the country by peaceful means. Can't we do it politically and not by turning our country into a battlefield? Surely the black earth of the Ukraine is sufficiently soaked in blood; do we want to start it pouring again?'

So this is the trained soldier speaking, Henryk thought, but without surprise.

'When the time comes you may change your mind.'

'I hope so,' murmured Adam very softly. 'My God, I hope so.'

'Surely all this is worth fighting for?' Henryk made a gesture with his hand, embracing the house, the garden, village and surrounding hills.

'Keep that persuasive tongue of yours to yourself,' answered Adam, but his smile was understanding.

'Now I'm going to get something to eat and then a few hours' sleep. We'll talk about this later.' As he turned to walk away, Henryk said:

'I've heard from Kasia, Adam.'

His brother stopped dead as if struck by a sharp blow.

'*Who* did you say?'

'Kasia.'

'But – we – I thought—' Adam faltered.

'That she was dead. No, she's alive. Alive and coming here.'

'*Here*?' Adam's voice rose in pitch. 'But no Radienska has been to Lipno since – since before God was born.' His eyes were wide with surprise.

'Don't look like a frightened owl.' Henryk laughed. 'One day I'll tell you her story. Or perhaps she will.' He became serious. 'Should I bring her here, Adam? Does Father still feel the same about the Radienskis?'

They both fell silent thinking back to the bitter feud which had split the two neighbouring families; which had kept the children apart and which had meant that when Henryk and

Kasia had fallen in love thirteen years ago they could only meet in secret by the little birch tree on the ridge where the Turks had ridden from the trees that terrible August day.

They were both remembering the evening at Volochisk when their father, shouting at his young sons to mount and get away from the 'blasted place', had galloped furiously through the snow followed by the bellowing voice of Kasia's father telling them never to return. And none of them except the two fathers had ever discovered the true cause of the quarrel.

'You'll have to tell Father,' said Adam at last.

'I know. How will he take it?'

'Like everything else, it'll depend on the state of his leg. But I don't think you'll find him unsympathetic.' Adam paused. 'I'll tell you something I've never mentioned to anyone. The night that Volochisk was sacked, after you had been brought home unconscious with your face like a sliced melon, he just sat hunched in his saddle staring at the smoking ruins, the tears rolling down his face. And he didn't care who saw it. He sat for an hour, never moving and during that time he only spoke – murmured rather – one sentence. I remember his words as if it was yesterday.

'He said, "Marie, Jan, the children. All gone. Oh, God, why should such a thing have happened?" Then it took four of us to hold him back from riding after the Turks on his own.'

'Thank you,' said Henryk gravely. 'I'm glad you told me that.'

So she's coming back from wherever it was she had been for all these years, Adam thought with a little flicker of envy for a love which could withstand so long a separation. But who knew if she still loved Henryk? He did not want to see his brother hurt. In the old days Adam had found her gay, amusing and immensely attractive, and, in his own slow way, he could have loved her, but it was to the younger, more vital brother that she had entrusted her heart.

'Now, I'm going to see Father, before my courage fails me.' Henryk grinned. 'One thing, he can't take his riding whip to me as he used to. Wish me luck, Adam.'

Adam watched the slim figure limp quickly up the path and vanish into the house.

'God help him,' he muttered. 'God help us all.' But whether his heartfelt plea was because of their father's unknown reaction or the return of Kasia Radienska into their lives he could not have said.

* * *

'Come in!'

Henryk paused with his hand on the latch. He had never fully conquered the nervousness his father inspired in him. Taking a deep breath he went in.

His father sat in his worn armchair, his right leg heavily bandaged and stuck out on a stool. Beside him stood Globnik, the elderly agent, clutching a sheaf of papers. A look of relief spread over his grey, worried face as he saw Henryk and a chance to escape, back to the musty little den where he sat for hours on end totting up figures when he wasn't out riding round the estate on his thin, moth-eaten nag.

'Right, Globnik, you can clear out now.'

Count Barinski glared at him from beneath bushy, untidy eyebrows. Henryk had never heard his father address a civil word to the unfortunate man, yet Adam always insisted that the two old men were really devoted to each other.

Globnik hurried out, blinking at Henryk through his wire spectacles. The door closed respectfully behind him.

'Stupid old goat! Well, don't stand there, sit down, sit down. My leg's like a damned furnace and he has to come pestering me with some long-winded rigmarole about the horses. Why the devil doesn't he go to Adam with his whining old problems? Why not, eh?' Because, thought Henryk with an inner smile, you'd be like a bear with a broken head if anything went on at Lipno without you knowing every last detail. He sat on an uncomfortable chair, heavily carved in dark oak. A bar of sunlight lay across the room full of bright, dancing dust, lighting up the portrait of Henryk's mother, the mother he had hardly known though he could just remember the hushed grief in the house when, on his third birthday, she had died of the smallpox. Except for the painting it was entirely a man's room; a room of animal skins and furs on walls and floor, of oiled sabres, riding whips, saddle pistols and precious trophies of

Sobieski's war against the Turks. In one corner stood the great feathered wings worn by Henryk's grandfather when he charged with the Hussars outside Vienna; in another, a green standard of Mahomet gathered dust. Crossed scimitars hung on one wall between the skins of lynx and wolf and part of a silken Turkish tent.

And still that same smell Henryk remembered so well, a mixture of leather, oil, stale tobacco and *kvass*.

'Have a glass of mead.'

Henryk poured himself a tankard. 'And you, Father?'

'Can't touch the stuff today. It pours straight into this infernal leg.' And he the man famed for miles around for his ability to down enormous quantities of vodka, mead and dark Polish beer. Henryk sipped slowly, not really enjoying the honey-sweet taste. A bluebottle droned round the smoke-stained ceiling.

'Branicki told me why he was here.' Count Barinski winced and swore savagely as a fresh stab of pain shot up his leg.

'I'll tell you one thing, Henryk. The only way to deal with a Russian is the same way you'd deal with a Turk or a Cossack – with a sabre or a lance.' His very blue eyes lit up at the thought.

'I've sent a good few of the brutes to their Maker – if they've got one, the heathen devils.' He chuckled under his heavy, drooping Tatar moustache.

'Never waste talk on a Russian. Don't waste powder either, make every shot count, there are too damned many of them.

His father was a Polish nobleman of the old school who scorned the newfangled clothes and notions creeping in from the West. He wore the costumes of the past, barbaric, magnificent. Caftans of rich crimsons or blues, fur-trimmed pelisses flung back over his broad shoulders. Jewels pinned plumes to his hats of lynx or leopard fur. When he rode to the hunt, which he still did whenever his gout allowed, sometimes being heaved into the saddle amid volleys of oaths by three sweating grooms, he dressed in the fashion and style of the old Polish Kings, hating the cravats and breeches of contemporary Europe.

He lay back in his red silken dressing-gown closing his eyes. Henryk studied him with a sudden stirring of affection and a sort of awe. When he and his like finally vanished from the earth it would be the end of an era for Poland. Her Golden Age had long ago been dissipated by internal squabbling and the Winged Hussars were already no more than a romantic dream.

He remembered Kasia and why he was here. But as he opened his mouth to speak his father said, 'Some seven hundred and fifty years ago the first Barinski rode with Boleslav the Brave to the gates of Kiev.'

Henryk waited.

'Last century Poland stretched from the Baltic to the Black Sea, from the Dnieper almost to Moscow. And now—?' His face twisted in disgust. 'Now we're nothing. D'you understand that, Henryk? *Nothing.*' His voice was bewildered, desolate. 'What are you going to do about it? You and Branicki and that lawyer fellow? Are you going to fight?'

'Yes,' said Henryk.

'Thank God,' his father whispered. 'Why in Heaven's name does a man have to grow old so soon?' He blew his nose angrily.

'How will you fight?'

'I've got various ideas,' answered Henryk. 'I hope the others will agree.'

'Agree, yes, that's it. If we Poles could only agree then no one can stand against us.' He fell into a reverie.

'Father?'

'Mm.'

'You remember Kasia. Kasia Radienska?'

Henryk, gazing into the tankard, felt his father's eyes fixed on him.

'Yes.'

Henryk took a deep breath. 'She's coming back.'

For a long moment there was silence broken by his father, surprisingly quietly. 'Coming back? But I thought—'

'She escaped from the Turks and got to Paris. That's where I met her again after leaving the Navy.'

'But – Paris? It's fourteen years since Volochisk was destroyed. What in Heaven's name has she been doing since then?' He paused, utterly confused. 'Paris. How could she have got there?'

'The Turks took her from Volochisk. The rest I'll leave her to tell you herself.'

'And the brother, what was his name? Yes, Jacek – that was it.'

'They took him too. She's never seen him again.'

'I suppose the swine dragged him to one of their filthy slave markets in Constantinople or made him into a Janissary. Nice-looking lad,' he added inconsequentially.

Kasia rarely spoke of Jacek. Once she had told Henryk she hoped he was dead. 'The thought of him alive in the hands of people who—' She had fallen silent remembering the horror of what the young Turkish boys had done to her brother the last night she had seen him.

'Did you ask her to come back to Poland?'

'Yes.'

'Why?'

'Because I love her, and want to marry her.'

Sparrows chirped happily on the window sill: the sound of horses' hooves was loud as Globnik rode from the courtyard on some ploy to do with the estate.

'And does she still feel the same?'

'Would she come back if not?'

'Perhaps, yes. Curiosity, Henryk, curiosity. Most women would travel to Hell, crawl if they had to, simply to see what it was like there. They're damnably inquisitive creatures.' Count Barinski fell silent, his eyes far away, then he slapped the arm of his chair.

'Well, by God, who'd have thought it, eh? It seems only yesterday that I'd have taken a whip to you for seeing her and now—'

If these two loved as he and Wanda had loved then they were a very lucky pair. He looked at Henryk through half-closed lids. This is the one who should have Lipno, he thought. Adam was the eldest, but secretly his father found him altogether too precise and prosy; too meticulous, always tidying something. What did it matter if a sabre hung crooked on a wall, provided it was sharp. The blood of the Barinskis flowed more strongly in Henryk's veins. If anything were to happen to Adam would this one ever in fact settle down to running an estate? Would he not always be riding to war? Perhaps behind that dark, serious face, in that slim, hard body lay the brain, the strength of purpose, the selfless courage that would carry the white eagle of Poland once more across Prussia and deep into the empire of the Muscovites.

He remembered Kasia, her spirit and her beauty even as a girl of seventeen. Very like Marie, her mother, he remembered. The same eyes and smile. She would make a fit mate for this son of his. There would be sons. The deserted lands of Volochisk would be joined with those of Lipno; a new house could be built in place of the sad ruins.

Count Barinski shifted in the chair, grunting with pain. 'Never get old,' he said with great feeling. 'Shoot yourself or jump into the Dnieper but don't get old. All you've got is a lot of damned pain and memories.' He shook his head.

Henryk had never heard his father speak like this before, revealing his inner thoughts. Suddenly it was brought home to him how dreadfully lonely life must be for this proud old man, chained to his chair by a failing body.

'Kasia will help to cheer you up,' he said softly.

'Yes,' agreed Count Barinski, his eyes lightening. 'It'll be fine to have a pretty face about the place for a change.'

Time may have played havoc with his body, Henryk thought, but it has certainly mellowed his spirit.

After a pause his father said, 'I'm happy for you, Henryk.' Then, as if ashamed of his sudden moment of tenderness he cleared his throat loudly. 'There's a Latin saying I used to think very apt. "*Carpe diem, quam minimun credula postero.*" I think that was it but like everything else my Latin's as rusty as a dagger in a swamp.' He chuckled. '"Make the most of today – tomorrow's not to be trusted." Now go. I'm tired.'

Count Barinski lay back. So the wheel had turned full circle and the families had come together again. How happy Wanda would be, and Marie too, that their children were to marry. He had so little time left. It would be pleasant to spend it within the sound of a woman's laughter. Closing his eyes he slept contentedly.

* * *

71

September in the Ukraine is often a golden month. That afternoon was a perfect example with the sunlight turning the birchwoods to pale fire and the autumn oak leaves to a rusty brilliance in which a multitude of birds flickered as they moved swiftly among the light and shadows. A few clouds, luminous as gauze, moved across the sky, very high, coming from the south, from the Black Sea.

Henryk stood in the shade of the birch tree on the ridge looking down at the gleaming river, running slow and shallow between sun-bleached rocks; he saw the beautiful flash of a kingfisher, heard the hollow booming of a bittern from the marshes in the valley, felt the brief tickle of a fly on his nose but hardly noticed any of these things.

Kasia had not appeared. He had waited by the tree – their tree, taller now, matured and strengthened by the winds and snows and sunshine of fourteen years – for nearly three hours, his mind a turmoil of anxiety.

Had something happened to her? These were unsettled dangerous times. Henryk began to pace round the little hollow, *their* hollow, until he had beaten a flat path in the dry grass. Often he stopped to listen but heard nothing except the birds and the chuckle of the water below. His eyes prickled with weariness for he had hardly slept, lying staring into the darkness, thinking of today: how would she look, how would she be, what would she say? And the question that teased and tormented him beyond all others. Why was she coming? Was it on some secret errand of Catherine's, or to tell him she had married Orlov? It would be in her nature to tell him face to face, and five years was a long time to wait, especially if she thought him dead in Siberia. Or was she coming to him as he hoped and prayed, because she still loved as he did?

Then, on the path that led down to the ghost-ridden valley of Volochisk, he saw a quick glint of blue between the trees bright as a kingfisher, and his heart began to choke him, his hands trembled.

She came out of the trees, very straight and proud in her blue riding-habit, the colour that suited her, just as he remembered her; he went to meet her, not speaking as he helped her down. He felt her trembling too.

'We're shaking like leaves,' he laughed unsteadily. The white feather in her little velvet hat waved softly as she nodded in answer, unable to speak.

'You look well,' he said lamely, suddenly as shy as she was. He was shy of her, the woman with whom he had always been so close that his thoughts were often hers at the very same instant, so that he used to say, 'I don't know why we bother to talk at all.' For five years he had dreamt of this moment, the only bright gleam that had kept him going in the mindless hell of the gundeck, and now that she was here before him he was as tongue-tied as some love-sick youth.

'S - so do you. But tired.'

'I didn't sleep very well. D'you wonder?'

'No. Nor d-did I. I spent the night at Kazatin. A lot of bugs.' She smiled and he held out his hands to her; she took them and for a moment they stood like that utterly still, staring into each other's eyes.

Then she began to cry, quite silently.

'Oh, Rasulka. Oh, my darling.' He drew her to him, and gently took off her hat, holding her head to his shoulder, stroking her hair soft and dusty against his cheek. She drew back her face and gazed at him with radiant eyes; he wiped the tears from her cheeks with the tip of his finger. Then he kissed her, his hand reaching for the tight curve of her breasts. Laughing and crying they clung to each other then, wordlessly, they went down into the hollow where they had loved each other for the first time.

Her horse threw up his head with a loud rattle of the bit, startled by Kasia's cries of ecstasy, then resumed his patient grazing unheeding of the frantic movement in the grass below.

Above, the birch tree rustled its golden leaves in the breeze, the little clouds went slowly across the sky touching their bodies, one brown and scarred, the other white as milk, with alternate light and shade.

'Oh, my darling, these scars!' Her fingers traced the rough ridges of hard flesh.

'The knout,' he said shortly. 'Don't talk, darling.'

They knew nothing except that it was as complete and perfect as always.

Panting, Henryk rolled away from her.

'It was worth waiting for five years – for that,' he gasped.

'Thank you, my love,' she said.

'Thank *you*, darling,' he said.

There was always mutual gratitude after such an experience. They lay quietly, her hand in his, the sun hot on their flushed faces.

All that had happened to them in the years since they had last been together in this hallowed spot melted into nothing like the snow that lies between the summer and the new spring.

'It was better than the first time,' Kasia said.

'You were only a gawky girl then.' Henryk plucked a piece of grass and put it in his mouth. 'Remember?' He remembered her in her scarlet Ukrainian skirt, a very lovely girl but without the mature beauty of this woman, without her depth of feeling – or her experience, he thought with a tiny sneaking twinge of jealousy.

'And you were only a young man insufferably pleased with his amorous prowess all over Poland.'

'Now you're an old thing of thirty-five,' he said.

'At least get your facts right,' she countered. 'Thirty-three.'

'And I'm thirty-six, and with you I feel twenty.' Leaning on one elbow he tickled her nose with the grass; he brushed the damp hair from her forehead.

'The years don't make much difference to us, do they?' he asked. 'To how we feel, I mean.'

'A hundred years wouldn't alter how we feel. You know that.'

'Yes, I know.'

He drew the feathery tip of the grass between her breasts down the length of her body and tickled the sole of one small foot so that she squirmed and laughed.

'Brute,' she said fondly.

He lay back with his eyes closed.

'Henryk?'

'Yes.'

'D'you remember the game we used to play when we said we'd ride to Kiev—'

'Then we'd sail down the Dnieper till we reached the land of the Cossacks, Zaporozhia, the land that lies beyond the rapids,' he cut in. 'Where we'd reign as king and queen.'

Well, she thought, she had been beyond the rapids; for six long, hard years she had lived in Zaporozhia, that fairy land of their youthful dreams, and had found life hard, cruel and not so magical.

'What made you remember that particularly?' he asked drowsily.

'I don't quite know.' After a pause she said, 'There's so much to tell each other, so much to talk about.'

'It can't be done in the first half-hour.' He opened his eyes and looked at her. 'But we've got our whole lives. It's rather a wonderful thought.'

Kasia thought of her promise to return to Catherine and wondered with a sudden sharp twist to her heart how she could ever tell him.

'Do you remember I said, lying here as we are now, that I wanted more than this, that I wanted a home and children – and I wanted them with you?'

'Yes.' It was a whisper.

'In Petersburg you said when we reached Paris. Well, we're not in Paris, we're in Poland, our home. I'll ask you again, Kasia. Will you marry me?'

And her answer came at once.

'Yes, my dearest heart, I will.'

Henryk uttered a sound, half sigh, half gasp, but did not speak; instead he buried his face in her hair and she could feel him shaking. With an immense tenderness she stroked the back of his neck.

'Fourteen years ago you tied my red hair-ribbon round our necks, and said – what?' she asked.

'Now we're truly one,' he murmured in a choked voice.

'Forever,' she added.

'Forever.'

'And now after all that's happened to us both—' she paused in wonder. 'Now our dream's coming true. Can you really take it in, Henryk?' She held his face between her hands, gazing deep into his eyes.

'Can you?' she repeated.

He nodded and wiped his eyes with the back of his hand, quickly, like a child.

'I never knew,' he said with a grin, 'that one could really cry with happiness. I always thought it was a privilege reserved for young maidens.'

They laughed together; they kissed and made love again and then slept for a while, waking when the sun left their faces as it dropped towards the trees from which the Turkish horsemen had ridden.

'Now we'll go home,' he said, impatient to take her to Lipno. 'Come along, make yourself decent, woman.'

As they dressed and she tried to rearrange her hair without brush or mirror Kasia told him about the trooper who waited for her near the blackened ruin of her old home.

'Catherine sent an escort with me,' she explained buttoning the front of her blue jacket. 'Men of the Imperial Guard. But not in uniform. She thought it better.'

'That was thoughtful of her,' he said drily. There were so many questions about Catherine he wanted to ask, about Poniatowski and Orlov and Karzel, that unpleasant little dwarf who had established himself as her self-appointed major-domo; Lev Bubin, tool of Shuvalov.

'The others are still at Kazatin with the coach and baggage. I'll ride down and tell him to have it brought to Lipno.'

'I'll wait here. Catherine knew me as the Frenchman, De Bonville, not as your childhood friend Henryk Barinski. We don't want her to know they're one and the same. And this—' he touched the scar across his face. 'Yet,' he added, 'does it matter any more? You're here now.' Safe from the long arm of the Secret Chancellery. Home and safe. Yet he had a moment of dread at the thought of her in one of Shuvalov's terrible dungeons: the glowing iron against her shrinking skin, the flaying knife.

'Perhaps it might be wiser, darling.'

'All right. I'll wait and dream of our wedding night.'

While she was away, Henryk lay in the fading evening sun and sang softly to himself.

Then they rode to Lipno. On the way they saw geese flying south.

'They're early this year,' she said, remembering her youth. 'It'll be a hard winter.'

'Yes,' Henryk agreed thinking of what might lie ahead when the snows came, 'it will.'

As the green roof came in sight ahead among the trees Kasia grew silent.

'Don't be nervous,' Henryk smiled his encouragement. 'Father's quite resigned to the fact that a Radienski's coming to his house. He's looking forward to a pretty face, he said if it wasn't for his gout he'd soon be chasing you round the dining table.'

The little lines at the corners of his eyes etched deep by wind and sea crinkled as he smiled. 'But I'll be there to protect you.'

'Yes, my love, I know that. Forever.' Her voice was serious, her eyes dark with love. She put out her hand to touch him as they rode up to the house.

*   *   *

PART THREE

COUNT Barinski sat staring intently at Kasia and she, sitting opposite him, returned his gaze very steadily. Since their arrival not much had been said. A little about her journey. From Paris, they had explained diplomatically. Count Barinski, as if suddenly bereft of speech, kept muttering, 'Well, I don't know,' in tones of amazement. Henryk, leaning against the window-sill, watched them apprehensively.

'So you're to be my daughter-in-law,' his father said at last.

'God willing,' she answered with a smile.

Yes, he thought, she's like her mother, the same long eyes, the same way of holding herself; the same look of serenity, but tempered by God knows what experiences. When they came to know each other better perhaps she'd tell him of her life since the Turks took her from Volochisk. She had her father's wide expressive mouth and his chin. He allowed himself to dream.

'It's what w - w - we both w-want more than anything else in the whole w - w—' She gave up with an angry little shake of her head.

Kasia's stammer was bad; part shyness, part fatigue, part the emotion of the day.

Count Barinski had never heard a woman stutter, only that waffling old fool – he couldn't remember the fellow's name – who used to splutter away in Diet, until he had either emptied the place or sent them all to sleep; and her painful hesitations caused within him both pity and a powerful longing to help.

'We had our squabbles, your father and I.' Kasia gave Henryk a quick glance and they smiled with their eyes. Squabbles, she thought wryly, when the very name of Radienski was forbidden at Lipno as that of Barinski had been anathema in her home, except as a target for furious abuse or cold contempt.

'What the devil are you grinning at, Henryk?' he demanded.

'Nothing,' said Henryk, smiling even more broadly.

'We may have argued now and then, but only in the manner of gentlemen. We were not peasants or Jews bickering by the village pump. No, there are times, I have to admit, when I miss him.' His eyes were sad. After a pause he said, 'Never let your damned pride keep a quarrel going long after it should have died.' He added gruffly, 'You're very welcome to Lipno, Kasia.'

Then he buried his face in his mug of mead. Drops of dark gold clung to his drooping moustache; little tufts of grey hair sprouted from his ears and a livid network of red veins covered his prominent nose. But his eyes of piercing blue were still bright, his hands steady.

Kasia thought, I'm going to like this old man who is trying to repair the damage of years in a few short minutes.

'Drink up,' he urged. Obediently she took a sip of the red wine finding it raw and sour. 'Perhaps you prefer this new-fangled tokay from Hungary?'

She had drunk it once in Petersburg with Alexei and been near sickened by its sweetness.

'Or d'you have a taste for vodka, eh?'

The squeak and rattle of wheels and horses came faintly from the yard.

'That'll be your baggage,' said Henryk. With relief Kasia heard the sounds. Now she could escape and rest; after sleep her body and brain would cope with this infuriating, exhausting challenge of speaking.

'She's tired, Father. I'll take her to her room.'

Wanda's room, thought Count Barinski. If anyone had to occupy that room of memories then it was fitting that it should be Henryk's wife. Once again it would be filled with life.

'Yes, yes, of course. Off you go, the two of you.' He shooed them from the room like a couple of children.

'Send Katushka to see me,' he shouted after them. He lay back in his long chair, his mind full of thoughts and memories which had lain dormant for many years but now, stirred by the sight of Kasia Radienska, came surging back from out of the past.

'Yes, what is it now?' The old housekeeper, bent as one of the hairpins that kept her sparse grey hair under some semblance of control, came shuffling in, keys clinking at her fat waist. As if she hadn't enough to do preparing the old Countess's room and getting the house fit for a lady to live in. Her small brown eyes shone angrily.

'She's to have the best,' said Count Barinski. 'Understand, Katushka? The very best.'

'Don't I always do my best?' demanded the old woman aggressively, adding, 'Will she be with us long?'

'How do I know?'

'I've got the maids to organize – and an idler lot of sluts I've never seen – the meals to order, and Heaven only knows what else—'

'For God's sake stop grumbling, you old devil! And just remember what I said. The best.' His voice softened. 'She's beautiful.'

'Oh, she's beautiful all right. But a sad face, until she smiles, then the sun comes out. And a real Court lady, the way she dresses. And her baggage, you should see her baggage. Brought by a couple of Russians.'

'Russians?'

'By the sound of 'em, yes. Great hulking brutes but civil enough. From Kazatin they said, and before that Kiev – well, if you're not listening I've got plenty to do without wasting my breath.' She departed, snorting and grumbling.

Russians? Kiev? But she had come from Paris – he shook his head frowning. Well, later they'd straighten it out. He was too tired and the pain of his swollen foot was stabbing up his leg. What did it matter where she had come from? She was here and that was all that mattered.

He heard her laughter from along the passage and despite his pain he smiled.

*   *   *

For the first few days they were rarely out of each other's sight for more than a few moments at a time. In the day-time they walked in the garden or the golden, autumn woods; they rode in the light September rain and they never stopped talking.

At nights they made love, talked, made love again, then, often not until dawn was creeping above the steppes, they slept.

Henryk told her of his escape from the chains of the *prut* as the procession of the damned dragged itself to Siberia; of the kindness shown to him by Pavel the fur trapper and Uliana, his wife. He told her of the Navy and she, who knew nothing of the sea except the glassy summer waters off Peterhof and the voyage in the Cossack galley from Kerch to the middle reaches of the Don, listened wide-eyed to his stories of his years in *Huntress*.

He described things well and through his words Kasia could see Captain Primrose as plainly as though he walked beside them; she heard the shrill whistle of Jem Pike's bos'n's pipe calling them on deck in the middle of a howling black night; she heard only too clearly the screech of the shot, the vicious hum of the musket balls, the shrieks of men pierced by jagged splinters of wood.

'I learnt a lot in that ship. Those officers and men taught me the real meaning of courage and discipline. They had a discipline we Poles have never been able to tolerate. That's why we're in the mess we're in now.'

She remembered the savage discipline of the Cossacks. 'But that was the discipline of fear,' she said.

'Not entirely, not with a captain like Primrose. Fear was at the back of it, but there was also respect.'

He told her of the months in Paris after his discharge from the Navy: of his meetings with the Chevalier D'Eon and his evenings at the *salon* of Madame Geoffrin. He did not feel it either necessary or politic to mention his brief, tempestuous reunion with Amande de Valfons.

Kasia never asked about other women, but sometimes she made some teasing little comment which showed that though she very well knew she was the woman he really loved, she equally knew that even if his heart had remained faithful his body had undoubtedly strayed. As indeed her own had, she thought with a shame she had not felt before.

Next day, as they rose in a soft drizzle, Henryk asked, 'What happened to Karzel?'

He had always hated the dwarf who had left the service of Alexei Orlov to become her servant; he had disliked and mistrusted the stunted little devil, but at least he had been loyal to her.

'He's gone back to Alexei.'

Henryk did not answer as he bent his head to avoid an overhanging branch. Alexei Orlov. So far they had left his name unspoken, but now was the time to exorcize a devil by bringing it into the open.

'How is he? Alexei, I mean.'

'When I last saw him he was in good health,' she said gravely, but smiling with a swift sidelong glance at Henryk's wooden expression.

'Have you seen much of him lately?'

'Yes, darling. But not in the way you think.'

'How d'you know what I'm thinking?'

'It's staring out of your eyes.' They left the shelter of the trees and she spurred ahead; he followed more slowly, swallowing the sharp pang of jealousy, the hot, tight rage he always experienced at the mere thought of her body beneath that of another man. She reined in and waited for him.

'He and Grigori are always close to Catherine so I could hardly fail to see him.'

'D'you still like him?'

'Not as much as I did, no.' She put up a gloved hand to wipe the cool rain from her face. 'He asked me to marry him.'

'Marry him? What did you say?'

'Well, no, of course.'

'Why? As far as you knew I was dead.'

'I knew you had been taken to Siberia. That didn't mean you were dead. But even if you had been I wouldn't have married him, or anyone else. I happen to love you. I could never have lived with any other man for the rest of my life.'

'I've said it before, my sweet, and I'll no doubt say it again: you're a very remarkable woman.' He leant down to adjust a stirrup leather. 'How did you know I had been sent to Siberia?'

'Lev Bubin.'

'That slimy brute. Is he still working for Shuvalov?'

'Yes. At least when he's not busy chasing the younger ladies of the Court all round the Palace. At the moment he's tied up with the wife of an elderly courtier who can't run so fast.'

'I always found him a singularly unattractive fellow,' said Henryk.

'Yes, but if it hadn't been for him I would never had got to Petersburg – and we would not be here now.'

'Well, God bless Bubin then.' Henryk raised his whip in a mock salute, thinking perhaps if it had not been for Lev he would not have been condemned to the lower deck of a British man of war via the torture chambers of the Secret Chancellery.

He had still not talked to her about who it was had betrayed him. Bubin? Orlov? Poniatowski? Countess Bruce? What did it matter now anyhow? It was over, in the past. He and Kasia were together; she had promised to be his wife. Nothing else mattered.

He looked at her hardly believing that this woman was going to marry him, that by her he would, if God smiled on them, have a son.

She looked back at him thinking of the agonizing weeks she had lain in bed after his disappearance, in a state of nervous collapse, not knowing whether or not he had died on the rack or by choking in the hangman's noose. And then, with a shock at the thought of what she had to tell him she prayed for the courage to find the words. Taking a deep breath she opened her mouth to speak, but he spoke first.

'What about Catherine? Didn't she show any curiosity as to why her tame Frenchman, de Bonville, that supremely handsome fellow with the intriguing scar across his face, had so suddenly vanished?'

Kasia stroked the wet mane of her horse before answering.

'She only mentioned you once. She said, "He was a spy in the pay of either France or Poland. He had to go."'

Kasia remembered very clearly the tight-lipped anger with which Catherine had uttered that short sentence.

'It's getting too wet,' said Henryk. 'Let's go home.' They turned their horses' heads away from the rain so that it drove heavily against their backs.

'The awful part,' Kasia said, 'was that I couldn't ask Catherine for your release. What was some vague Frenchman to me? – especially one who had been in her bed.' But her tone was without bitterness. 'Anyway, at that time she had little or no influence. But I'd made up my mind that once she was Empress I'd throw myself on her mercy, tell her who you were, that De Bonville was Henryk Barinski, the man I loved.'

'And you think that out of gratitude for what you did to get her to the throne she'd have forgiven all and ordered my release?' His question and smile were quizzical.

'Yes,' she answered without hesitation. 'Yes, I think she would. But, thank God, you released yourself.'

'So we'll never know,' he said.

'We'll never know.'

They rode the rest of the way home in silence, under the dripping trees, and Kasia's heart was heavy with the thought of what she must tell him tomorrow.

*   *   *

Count Barinski watched his son and future daughter-in-law as they walked slowly down the path towards the pond at the bottom of the garden. Thank God, he thought once again, the ridiculous, bitter quarrel between their two families had been resolved. Never go to bed on a quarrel, he had once been told. More important, never die on one. It warmed his heart to see them so happy: and the morning was on their side; the last hot sun of the autumn and the birds behaving as though it were spring. The two of them reached the pond and he watched Kasia throwing crumbs to the ducks. What grace she has, he thought, seeing her arms shine in the sun, the black gleam of her hair as she turned her head towards Henryk.

And Kasia, as she fed the eager birds, thought, dear Lord, how can I tell him?

'What's the matter?' Henryk asked quietly.

'Nothing.'

'Oh, come on, I do know you. There's something wrong, isn't there?' It was not until she had thrown the very last crumb into the water that Kasia answered.

'There's something I've got to tell you, my darling.'

'Yes?' His heart was suddenly heavy as lead though he had no idea why. She went straight on without hesitation, 'I m-must go back.'

84

As she said the words he knew exactly what she meant but he said nothing. Instead he bent down and very carefully picked up a small piece of bread from the grass and threw it to one of the ducks.

'Go back?' he asked bleakly. 'Go back where?'

'To Catherine.'

In the silence the cries of the village children came to them very clearly.

'Say something, Henryk. Please say something.'

'What is there to say?' Then, after another dreadful pause, he burst out, 'In God's name, why?'

'I promised her.'

His face was hard and a tiny pulse throbbed in his temple.

'You know I'll come back to you. I'm going to be your wife.'

'She won't let you.'

She could see how desperately every word she spoke stabbed his heart, as it stabbed her own.

'D'you think I *want* to go?'

'I've no idea.' His voice was dead.

He had withdrawn into a wall of icy anger and misery. To prevent any further pain he was closing up and she knew there was no point in saying anything further at this moment.

'All right then,' he said unexpectedly. 'We won't discuss it further. If you've given your word—' He shrugged, turned and walked towards the house.

With clouded eyes she watched him go but made no attempt to call him back.

Count Barinski, still watching from his window, thought, Now the young fools have had some stupid quarrel. He saw the frozen anger on his son's face as he came up the path. Ah well, thought the old man, many's the time that Wanda and I wouldn't drown our pride and make it up.

Kasia slowly approached the house, her shoulders lowered dejectedly. Her father-in-law longed to call her in and console her but was old and wise enough to know he would probably only make things worse. He shifted his sore leg, reflecting that by the evening everything would probably be fine between them and there they'd be, billing and cooing like a couple of doves.

The first thin snow of the winter whirled round the house on a bitter north-east wind straight from Siberia that rattled the windows and, now and then, gently billowed the heavy red curtains of the long low dining room and bent the candle flames.

'It's early this year. We'll have a hard winter eh, Globnick?' Count Barinski rubbed his hands happily; he loved the clean frozen world of snow. 'There'll be some good hunting.' His eyes twinkled at Kasia seated on his right.

'"Prepare a bed before going to hunt wild boar but prepare a bier before hunting a bear." Isn't that so my dear?' He threw back his head in a great shout of laughter that filled the whole room. She smiled in answer, looking through the smoky candle-light at Henryk who sat in gloomy silence, twirling his goblet sullenly, not meeting her eye. Kasia felt a quick flare of anger. Damn him and his black moods – did he think she *wanted* to go back to Russia? Couldn't he understand what the decision meant to her?'

She turned with another bright smile to her future father-in-law.

'My father used to say that,' she said.

They were very alike, the two men, always coming out with their well-worn aphorisms like 'The nobles *are* Poland' and 'All one can hope for is a quick, clean death.' Already she had become very fond of Count Barinski and he, for his part, was, as Adam kept saying, eating out of her hand.

'On time,' said Adam, glancing at the big bracket clock in the wall. A particularly ugly clock, Kasia thought fondly, but then it was not a very lovely room. Long, low and dark, the walls badly hung with indifferent portraits of earlier Barinskis, some with Henryk's swarthy good looks, some podgy looking, most of them flat and wooden with dead blue eyes. The satiny sheen of highly polished brass candelabra, pewter goblets, silver spoons and forks bright against the dark oak table all glowed warmly in the soft light of the tall tallow candles. It was warm and cosy, her feet were buried deep in the bearskin rug, the heat of the great tiled stove played pleasantly on her shoulders through the *fichu* of dark blue chiffon. The tokay was golden sweet on her tongue.

'I don't know how you can drink that sickly stuff,' said

Count Barinski, grimacing in mock disgust. He took a swig of his corn brandy. 'Good, foaming stuff,' he always called it.

Kasia dipped her fingers in the little crystal bowl of warm water and dried them on her napkin.

'Is it as sweet as m-mead?' she asked.

'We don't need anything from the Hungarians – except perhaps arms.' Count Barinski was scarlet in the face from drink and food. It wouldn't take much more brandy to turn him belligerent, she decided.

'Yes,' put in Globnik unexpectedly. 'That's what we need, arms, plenty of arms.' They all stared at him, disbelieving what they had heard, for old Globnik rarely ventured an opinion beyond the narrow confines of his own profession. Twin spots of colour glowed in his thin cheeks, his rheumy little eyes darted fiercely behind his flashing spectacles.

'My God,' said Henryk, stirring himself from his gloom, 'Globnik's going to war.'

'Yes, Master Henryk. Globnik would go to war if he had to.' His dingy wig was slightly askew, his speech was thick but he spoke with surprising conviction and dignity. 'And if he were not so old,' he added sadly.

'Well,' said Adam breaking the amazed silence, 'well, who'd have believed it.'

Kasia felt she might easily cry.

'Don Quixote,' murmured Henryk. 'On his horse. The Russians are beaten already.' He softened his words with a smile and added, 'Sorry, I was only joking. I'll find you a post in my army, don't worry. We'll need a good quartermaster.'

Kasia looked at Henryk doubtfully; even after all the years she had known him there were times when she could not tell if he was joking or serious. One thing she knew for certain: he hated to be unkind with his tongue except when he lost his temper when he would burst out with bitter, thoughtless words he did not really mean and which, when he had calmed down, he very much regretted. She winced at the memory of his cold rage and scorn of the previous night.

'We'll ride together, Globnik,' said Count Barinski with surprising gentleness. 'You and I, side by side, and we'll show these young firebrands how their fathers can fight. They think we're

87

senile, Globnik, old friend. But we'll show them, by God, we'll show them.'

Henryk caught Adam's eyes. Never in all their experience had their father called his agent anything but the most uncomplimentary names.

'I'm sure you will,' put in Kasia. 'And will there be a place for me? I know a little about war.' She remembered the Turk at Volochisk, the first man she had killed, clutching the spouting wound in his throat; her musket ball taking the Tatar full in the gaping mouth in the gully beside the shore of the Black Sea – the savage war-cry of the charging Cossacks – *Netchai! Netchai!* Cut! Cut. She'd never forget to her dying day the soft jarring thud of the sabre as she brought it down on the neck of the Tatar as he raised his long dagger above Pugachev's twisted, sweating face.

The eyes of all the men turned on her. Yes, thought Henryk, looking at the colour in her cheeks, her sparkling eyes with great love and pride, she knew more of war than anyone in the room except perhaps himself. With such a woman beside him and an army of Dombrowskis behind them he could ride to St. Petersburg – he could conquer the world. She sat there, regal as any Empress, as feminine as any woman born, and yet in her memory she carried the hissing of the sabres, the ugly hum of musket balls, the screams and groans of dying men. Blood had stained those beautiful shoulders; those small hands he loved so much had dealt out death. He emptied his goblet and as he reached for the chased silver wine flagon, a sudden commotion broke out in the passage, then the door burst open and Dombrowski rushed in throwing his cloak to the startled Stepan panting along behind him.

'He's dead,' he cried dramatically. 'At last he's dead.'

'Another place, Stepan, beside Countess Radienska. Wine for Jan Dombrowski,' ordered Count Barinski calmly. Dombrowski's face was wet with melted snow, his eyes shone as if with fever. He seized the goblet and raised it high.

'The King is dead! Long live Poland!'

He drank deeply, standing by the stove, his red hair like flame in the light, wine gleaming on his chin.

'How d'you know this, Jan?' asked Henryk.

'I heard this morning in Lvov. A courier from Dresden. The whole city's mad with the news. We have no king.'

'We hadn't got one when he was alive,' said Henryk.

'No, by God, you're right there. But now—' His voice faded and Henryk saw Dombrowski's eyes come to rest on Kasia in sudden surprise. For an instant he watched in silent amusement then stood up, very polite, very correct.

'I don't think you know Countess Radienska – Jan Dombrowski.' Henryk resumed his seat, adding lightly:

'Kasia. Jan.'

Utterly clumsy and taken aback Dombrowski stepped forward with a stiff little bow holding out his hand in which, unfortunately, he still held the goblet. Blushing furiously, he put it down hard on the table, slopping wine. Her hand was cool and her grip firm. Mumbling something inaudible he took his seat beside her and applied himself in noisy haste to the dish of roasted goose before him.

'They say our late, lamented King somehow managed to find the time from his regal duties to collect enough porcelain in the Green Vault at Dresden to equip and arm any number of huge armies,' said Adam with heavy irony.

'Well, we know he gave a regiment of damned dragoons to Frederick of Prussia in exchange for twelve vases.'

'Obviously a man with the true interests of Poland at heart.'

'A vase to roughly eight dragoons,' remarked Henryk. 'I wonder if they thought themselves sold too cheaply?'

Kasia listened to their words, tossed lightly across the table but nevertheless loaded with a deep and terrible bitterness.

'Now Catherine will move,' said Henryk.

'This is the moment she's been waiting for since Keyserling first arrived in Poland.'

'Now all her carefully laid plans for getting Stanislas Poniatowski to the throne will be put into action,' Kasia added. 'But one thing's certain: he'll rule as her puppet and dance to her tune. And Poland will dance to the same tune.'

Adam and his father glanced at her in surprise.

'You seem to know a lot about her intentions,' remarked the latter, looking at her suddenly shrewdly and inquiringly. 'Not only a pretty head, my dear, but also a clever one.'

Kasia acknowledged the clumsy compliment with a smiling inclination of her head so that the diamonds in her upswept hair shone and twinkled.

'It seems clear enough,' she added quickly, seeing Henryk's warning glance. 'Good heavens, all Paris was talking of Count Poniatowski and his royal future.' To change the subject she turned to Dombrowski who was busy with the *kluski* – the small fat dumplings – before him.

'You must have had a very unpleasant ride in this w-weather,' she said.

'Not too bad,' he mumbled into his food. Faced by her beauty and poise he felt tongue-tied, all fingers and thumbs, for he knew nothing of women beyond the whore houses of Lvov and Krakow, and this woman in her shimmering flowered brocade and with her round white arms and slender hands and delicate ruffles hiding the shadowy cleft of her breasts both frightened and excited him. He felt the sweat start on his forehead and plunged the fork angrily into his food, like a gauche, red-faced schoolboy.

Henryk smiled to himself. Poor old Jan, he wasn't doing very well. But once he got over his shyness they would get on, for, given time, there were few people, men or women, Kasia could not make into friends or, at least, admirers.

'No more spineless neutrality,' Globnik almost shouted into the silence. 'At least we shall have a king with a Polish name.'

'You really think *King Poniatowski* will lead us on a crusade against the Muscovite?' Dombrowski flared, very conscious of Kasia's eyes upon him.

'Ah – well – perhaps—' Globnik relapsed into his usual depressed silence, morosely sprinkling pepper into his vodka.

'I thought it was only the Cossacks who did that,' said Kasia.

'You're remarkably well informed on – on everything,' remarked Adam in his most pompous tone.

'I'm a walking encyclopaedia of almost w-worthless knowledge,' she flashed him a brilliant smile. 'Whilst we're on the subject of the Cossacks—'

'Lazy, shiftless blackguards,' growled Count Barinski.

'Stick a knife into you with one hand while the other one patted you on the back. I know what I'd do with the whole damned brood, I'd—'

She waited patiently until he had exhausted his various blood-thirsty ideas then went on quietly, 'They have a saying, "Buy with silver, save gold, don't scorn copper, defend yourself with iron."'

'What's that got to do with it?' demanded the old man belligerently. He was getting drunk and soon he would talk of mounting up and riding through the storm, across the steppes on and on, hell for leather till with naked sabres they encountered the first Cossacks.

'I merely thought they might make good allies,' she said mildly – and bravely.

'*Allies*? Cossacks? Great God, I'd rather fight beside the Tatars. They may be the Creatures from Hell but those – those devils' spawn from the steppes, why I—' words failed him, as he sat back, panting slightly.

'Poland shall have no arbiter but God,' said Globnik for no very good reason.

'. . . God has forgotten this country.'

The voices beat against Kasia's brain; she hardly listened; they were all repeating themselves, shouting each other down, no one really listening to anything but his own very loud voice. A typical Polish argument, she thought sadly, yet with a warm, fond surge of feeling. She was home.

Her head had begun to ache from the smoke of Count Barinski's pipe, the stink of the candle grease, the food and drink and the din of voices. She wanted only to go to bed.

'That imitation Empress . . .'

They were back on Catherine again, swapping insulting remarks.

'German bitch!' shouted Dombrowski thickly.

'Murderess!' That was Globnik's final contribution before he subsided slowly into snoring insensibility.

She felt anger rising. What did they really know of the woman who was her friend, these drunken men who ripped her character apart so savagely? And yet, and this was partly what caused her anger to mount, yet she knew deep in her heart that

91

she herself was part of these men. She belonged here, in the world that held nothing but hatred for Catherine.

Henryk was very silent leaning back in his chair staring at the smoke gathering below the ceiling, now and then reaching for his drink. His eyes, when they rested on any of the others, were dark and thoughtful. Once when they met hers, he smiled faintly and went back to his study of the smoke.

'If you'll excuse me,' she said to Count Barinski, 'I think I'll go to bed.' But noisily involved in a spirited, one-sided argument with the unconscious Globnik, he did not hear.

Dombrowski made desperate efforts to get to his feet as she left the room but his legs failed him and he sank back lazily to follow Adam's long rambling assertion on the true function of heavy guns in modern warfare.

Upstairs Kasia got ready for bed. The dull mutter of talk rose through the floor, then Dombrowski's voice raised in song.

'. . . Poland is not yet dead while we are alive. . . .'

She found herself humming the tune of Poland's anthem. What would that shy, fiery young patriot say when he discovered that she, soon to be the wife of his friend, was so close to the Empress of Russia, had helped to place her on the throne?

Let her worry about that in the morning. She got into bed, pulled the bed clothes to her chin and lay with the candle still alight luxuriating in the warmth, watching the shadows flickering about the small room, listening to the slight hiss of the squat stove, drowsily waiting for the moment when Henryk would come to join her.

*　　*　　*

'What in hell's name *are* you going back for then?' Henryk stood by the stove his face dark in the shadow.

'Because I promised her,' said Kasia wearily.

'You promised her.' He mimicked her savagely.

'I thought we weren't going to discuss it any more.' She held out an arm to him. 'Come to bed, darling.'

He did not answer for a moment then all the pent-up misery and fury burst out in one short vicious phrase.

'I suppose it's Orlov.'

Kasia drew in her breath sharply as if she had been struck across the face.

'Oh, Henryk!'

'Well?' His voice grated harshly. But she had turned her head away and the thick black hair hid her tears from him.

He railed and stormed at her and she, understanding the misery eating at his heart, bore with his cruel words in silence. He in his turn said things he knew to be untrue, things he did not want to say but which were forced from him by the drink in his brain and by the black demon working on his mind.

She let him finish and then, as he slumped on to the chair, said very gently, striving to control the stammer that threatened to render her speechless:

'If I th-thought you m-meant one w-word of those horrible things I'd g-go away now, I'd leave you, Henryk – I w-would and never come back. I mean that.'

In the silence a dog began barking in the yard; a voice shouted angrily and the animal shut up. Henryk shook his head as if in disbelief.

'I'm sorry,' he whispered so low that she only just caught the words. 'Oh, God, I'm sorry.' He kept his gaze on the floor.

'My darling, I understand.' She strove for calmness, utterly shaken by his bitter fury. 'You can't think I exactly enjoy the thought of leaving the only man in this sad silly world that I really l-love.'

He looked up, staring at her in a sort of wonder. 'You still love me – after those – after what I said?'

'Unfortunately for you, darling, I'm not the sort of w-woman who stops loving in five minutes.' She gave a shaky little laugh. 'Even though they were a very unpleasant five minutes.' Again she laughed, trying to coax him from his bitter mood. 'It was the little black monkey again. He's—'

She broke off as she saw the tears rolling slowly and silently down his cheeks.

'Oh, my darling, don't,' she cried in sudden anguish at what she was doing to him. 'Please don't.'

She went to him, sitting on the floor, laying her head in his lap. At first he did not move and she felt the tiny splash of a tear on her skin. Her hand tightened on his thigh; she pressed herself closer, murmuring little words of love.

'Marry me, Kasia,' he said. 'Marry me now this moment. I'll go for the priest.' He was stroking her hair.

'We're being married in three days, dearest. And I do want the church, you know how much I want it.'

'Yes, I know.'

He bent and kissed her ear and she moved against him.

'We're married already,' he said. 'We've been married for the last fourteen years.' Her heart lightened to hear his tone. Gone was the moment of misery, the cloud had lifted, the black monkey had been sent scurrying back to the shadows whence it came.

'Don't say it, my sweet,' he went on. 'Not in God's eyes. But is God blind? Hasn't he watched over us for too long, not to have noticed what we do?'

'So He won't really mind if you come to bed now, will He'?

Henryk raised her to her feet. He gazed at her in silence, taking in with the wonder that never faded, the shining beauty of her hair, her great long eyes, grown very black now, the wide mouth slightly parted. He stroked her shoulders, feeling far more than the simple stirring of lust.

'I'm sorry, my dearest,' he said in a low voice. 'I'm truly and deeply sorry.'

In answer she leant towards him and kissed him on the lips. He opened his mouth to hers, feeling the sharpness of the little crooked tooth against his tongue. His hand went to her breasts. She jerked back her head laughing in her pleasure and desire.

'Take all those ridiculous things off.' She teased him with her hands; the hands he called 'her little white animals'. She went to the window, drew back the curtains. The snow had stopped and the half moon shone brilliantly among tattered scraps of cloud.

Henryk laughed softly as she turned towards him, looking up at the moon over the smooth curve of her left shoulder.

'You've always been superstitious, haven't you?'

Her eyes were dark and serious as she answered. 'When we have a love like this – it's w-wiser to be just a little superstitious.'

'It's a gift of God,' he said, half teasing. 'Your water-spirits and frog fairies have nothing to do with it. Only God can take this love away.'

To him his words sounded a little fanciful but she did not smile and suddenly he felt strangely elated, almost exalted. Nothing could touch them, not at that moment, no power on earth could tarnish the love he felt for this woman.

She held out her arms to him.

Henryk watched her as the nightgown fell to her feet and she stood naked in the moonlight. With his arm round her waist they stood looking out. The snow had stopped but the clouds still drove in silvered flocks across the moon and among the chimneys.

They stood and watched, savouring the wait; now and then they teased each other, gently at first and then with more urgency, until with a short gasping cry, Henryk picked her up and carried her to the bed.

*   *   *

Though the sun was warm, traces of the night's frost lay in the shadows of the apple trees and there was a sharp bite in the morning air.

Count Barinski lay on a backed bench wrapped in furs, a wolf-skin cap crammed low over his forehead, a long-stemmed Cossack pipe gripped firmly between his teeth, listening with an expression of frowning incredulity on his face to what Kasia was saying. When she had finished he sat puffing furiously at the pipe, watching her as she leant forward from her seat beside him and plucked some stalks of grass. He removed the pipe from his mouth and asked very slowly.

'You mean you were a *friend* of Catherine's?'

'I *am* still a f-friend,' said Kasia busily plaiting the grass. It had taken all her courage to tell the old man the truth. She knew full well how he felt about the Empress of Russia, yet if he was to be her father-in-law there could not be this secret hanging over them. Pretending an overwhelming interest in her grass-work she waited nervously for his reaction.

Would there be a wild explosion of rage that would leave him purple and shaking and their friendship impaired: that might even kill him through apoplexy? She took a quick sidelong glance and was surprised by what she saw; she had expected anger, contempt even, but not this look of utter stupefaction. Then the rage came.

'A friend and lady-in-waiting to – to—' Words failed him. He uttered a sort of furious groan. His moustache quivered.

'My son's not only going to marry a Radienska but a – a—'

Again he gave up. His face was dangerously suffused, his eyes red. It did not seem to the worried Kasia that he would survive the next few minutes. She put a hand on his arm.

'Please,' she begged, 'c-calm yourself.'

'Calm myself, she says. *Calm* myself! Stepan!' Involuntarily she winced at his roar, drawing her red cloak closer round her. 'Bring mead!'

There was silence until Stepan had gone hobbling away and Count Barinski had emptied half a mug down his throat. The liquor seemed to restore his composure, for after a while, he asked more quietly, 'How long have you been with her?'

'For six years.'

'Six years,' he mused. 'You must know her well then.'

She nodded. 'Yes, I think I do.'

Count Barinski refilled his mug from the big silver ewer.

'You know you're crazy to make a friend of such a woman.'

Kasia did not answer.

'But by God, at least you're loyal. That I understand – and admire. What's she like, this – this Empress of yours? As a woman, I mean. Not a ruler.' Although he spoke casually, he could not keep the curiosity from his voice.

'That's not a very easy question to answer.' Kasia sat in silence, her eyes far away. Then for the first time she tried to put into words her honest opinion of Catherine.

'I think,' she began slowly, 'she's finding it harder and harder to separate the two rules – ruler and woman. She's kind, understanding and highly intelligent, hard working and, to her friends, intensely loyal.'

'Has this paragon of a woman got no vices then?' he asked sourly.

Kasia regarded him thoughtfully. In many ways this old man with his fierce loyalties, his burning patriotism and pride, would get on very well with the capricious, courageous and utterly dedicated woman who sat on the throne of the Romanovs.

'Oh no,' she said with a smile. 'Little Figgy has never been an angel. She's enormously ambitious, she's wilful and scheming – and she's a superb actress.'

And quite ruthless, she thought with a sudden little cold feeling.

'For practically all the time her heart is ruled – and very strictly too – by her head. Very little she does or says is thoughtless or pointless. She calculates the effects of her every action, however small. For instance, she has the gift of winning the love and respect of those who serve her; the ordinary soldiers, grooms, servants and so on. You see, she has always remembered to say "please" and "thank you" – and, my God, it has paid her.'

Count Barinski snorted.

'Women on the whole bore her. She prefers the company of men, and not only for the more obvious reasons, she really enjoys talking to them. Catherine rather fancies herself as an intellectual. She longs to enlighten people.'

'And how d'you suppose she proposes to enlighten us ignorant Poles?'

'You think of her as an enemy, don't you?'

'What else could she be?'

'It's not that she hates Poland. It's more that—' Kasia paused, 'that she loves Russia.' He snorted again. 'From all I've heard she loves nothing in the world as much as herself.'

'No, that's s-simply not true.' Kasia's colour had risen.

His angry blue eyes snapped under his shaggy brows. 'Hell's name,' he burst out, 'above everything I admire courage – and you've certainly got your fair share.'

'Well, you asked about Catherine and I've told you a little – or tried to – there's plenty more.'

He sat silent, his head sunk in his shoulders.

'She'll be a formidable enemy,' he said. His voice was sad. Then he suddenly brightened. 'Tell me,' he asked, 'these lovers of hers, these Poniatowskis and Orlovs and God knows who else, what part do they play in her life, except as players in bed?'

'Not as much as they'd like to think,' she said simply. 'Though I think she has loved both Stanislas and Grigori, each in a different way. But Catherine keeps her – her love l-life in a little compartment of its own, separate from her political and intellectual lives. Perhaps one day she'll find a man who dominates her mind and body. He'll be very remarkable.'

'They say she's a hot-blooded woman.'

'She is.'

Kasia tried vainly to avoid the sudden twisting memory of those awful months four years ago when Henryk had been forced, through political intrigue, into Catherine's arms. If Henryk's father ever discovered that his favourite son had been the Empress's lover—! Kasia shut her eyes. Blackbirds were chinking in the garden and somewhere in the pale blue sky geese were calling on their way to feed.

'Does Adam know?' he asked.

'No, only Henryk – and now you.'

'It's better that way. Keep it in the family. Dombrowski, Branicki, the rest of them wouldn't be so kind. My God,' he added, 'how in hell's name *can* we tell them?'

'You mean, they wouldn't trust me?'

'Why should they?' he said, but not unkindly. 'Even though you are going to be Henryk's wife. Wives have been known to—' He broke off, his eyes twinkling. 'But not the woman who marries my son.' He patted her hand. 'You know my feeling towards Russia and Catherine. You know my feelings for you. Let us leave it at that.'

She leant forward and kissed him on the cheek.

'Thank you,' she said. 'You've no idea how I've b-been dreading this m-moment.' She felt light-headed with relief and so filled with confidence that, there and then, before she lost her nerve, she told him she would have to go back, and he seemed to understand her reasons.

'But you must marry Henryk before you go,' he insisted firmly. 'Yes, of course you must,' he reiterated, warming to the idea. 'We'll get hold of that lazy old dog Father Krasinski and for once in a while he'll have to stir his idle carcass.'

'Please,' she urged with a smile, 'please not so fast.'

'You want to marry him don't you?'

'You know very well I do.'

'Well then, what are you fussing about?' She shook her head silently and he saw the glint of tears as she turned away her head.

'You think I m-might not come back otherwise. Is that it?'

'Of course you mean to come back but—' He spread out his hands and shrugged. 'Who knows what's in a woman's mind? Least of all Catherine's. Supposing she orders you to stay or claps you into one of her stinking dungeons, what then, eh?'

'She won't keep me,' said Kasia with a quiet conviction that impressed him and he nodded without speaking, then said:

'I'd like to see my grandson playing in this garden before I go. This house has been empty of children's voices for too long.'

'I'll do my best,' Kasia promised him and he laughed.

Unbidden, the memory of her baby son by Emylyan Pugachev, Cossack of the Don, dead in his third month of the choking sickness, came to her. As she sat talking lightly of new sons she remembered the day they had buried little Mikhail beneath the cold winter earth, his requiem the moaning dirge of the *chorny vetier*, the black wind of the steppes. The tears were long since dry but the ache still came secretly to her heart.

'Will you do something for me, my dear—' he asked very gently. 'At your marriage will you wear the dress my wife wore on our wedding day?' His eyes were dark with a never forgotten grief. Kasia nodded, unable to speak.

'I know it will be old-fashioned and probably won't fit – though she was very like you in build – but we could have it altered, couldn't we?'

'Of course we could.'

'Thank you, Kasia. It will make her very happy. Though she never knew Henryk he would love you as a daughter, as I do,' he added gruffly, burying his face in the mug. She put out her hand and touched his.

At that moment she felt close to the lonely old man. Since her arrival they had got to know each other well, had come to like and respect each other.

He loved her for her gay courage, her honesty with him as much as for her beauty which entranced him and drove away the leaden feel of age from his aching old limbs.

PART FOUR

As Kasia and Adam Barinski rode slowly through the village the horses' breath was steamy in the bright, frosted air and the clop of the hooves on the hard earth road had a hollow sound. The gay cries of the children rang out cheerfully as they scampered alongside the riders, gazing up with adoration at the beautiful lady who always talked and laughed with them and often gave them poppy-seed cakes or sugar-coated buns. To the children of Lipno, to their parents also she was a companion, a friend. And was she not to become Count Henryk's wife – or so rumour had it? A fit mate for the man who made the women's hearts beat faster; who weakened the legs of the young girls as they watched him gallop by, dark and scarred, always in a hurry; quite unlike Count Adam, his serious methodical brother.

'They love you,' said Adam.

Kasia smiled at him. 'Laugh with them, talk to them as human beings and they'll love you – why shouldn't they?'

Scrawny hens scuttled out of the way and geese, hissing angrily, moving more slowly and with a sort of waddling dignity; thin curly-coated pigs rooted along the edges of the wattle fences or lay suckling their litters in the cold sunshine. A long, rangy boar faced Adam's two greyhounds as if he were one of their true wild cousins but the dogs could not be bothered with something so far beneath their notice and loped proudly at the heels of Adam's grey mare.

Outside his grimy little house stood the local village Jew who held most of the village's meagre wealth in his thin, hairless hands. Looking at his long greasy side curls below the little black hat, the long black coat, also greasy – everything about him was greasy like an unwashed cooking pot, she thought with an unwilling aversion. His gestures servile, the expression in his black eyes shifty and ingratiating as he watched the great ride by. And yet, as she remembered from the Jews in the Cossack villages, he was a man of considerable power in Lipno and the surrounding countryside; there were few men not in his debt to greater or lesser degree.

But the day was fine, she felt utterly happy; wanting to share this happiness with others so she smiled and he smiled back a little secret, furtive smile as he turned away from Adam's hard look.

'Bloodsucker!' Adam spoke angrily after they were past. 'If there's ever trouble in the Ukraine it's us who suffer for the greed of these damned Jews. Father hates them. So do I.' Kasia had never heard him speak with such bitter anger. 'They descend on a country like a pack of black lice and bleed it white. How can you think otherwise? Look what Poland has suffered from them.'

'If you're brought up from childhood to think that a wolf is nothing but vermin with every man's hand against it then it's not easy to change your opinion,' said Kasia in answer.

'Henryk used to talk as you do,' she went on. 'But now, since his time in the British ships, he feels differently. He served with a Jew and became his friend.'

'Henryk has changed a lot since he left Poland,' Adam interrupted shortly.

'Are you surprised?' she asked with a smile. 'He's not exactly led the luxurious life of a nobleman for the last few years.'

They rode in silence, leaving the village behind and climbing one of the long rolling hills that lay along the fringes of the southern steppes. Kasia's horse was high-spirited; with ears pricked and sharp little snorts he fought for his head as they followed the rough track leading into a wood of birch and scrubby oak. A brown dove flew ahead weaving low below the branches as though guiding them into the silent forest.

'But he has come back with the most extraordinary ideas,' Adam persisted. 'All about what he calls the freedom of the individual. Something he seems to have picked up from those mad English. Why, he's sometimes almost a revolutionary,' he concluded indignantly.

'Perhaps,' she suggested gently, 'he's just a little before his time.' Her experiences with the Cossacks had taught her that the common people were no better nor worse than the nobles and that they also were human beings. In Petersburg these views were received with either tolerant amusement or open scorn. Only Catherine seemed interested enough even to discuss such a crazy idea.

Kasia did not really want to talk, not even about Henryk. The morning was too glorious; but once Adam got his teeth into a subject he would not let go until it was sucked completely dry.

'Not that he talks much about the past,' he said, 'only the future.'

'Isn't that more interesting?'

'But it's the past that makes a man.'

'And what he becomes must surely lie in the future?'

Kasia smelt wood-smoke and heard the distant thud of axes, and remembered with startling vividness the charcoal burners of Volochisk, the old man and his son, whom the Turks had cut down so savagely in a wood very like this one. And because of that terrible day she had become what she was. Adam was right: in a person's life the past was all important. You did not discard the past as though it had never happened, not if you were wise. Adam broke into her sudden moment of reflection.

'What do you know of his future?' he asked abruptly.

'Only that we're going to be married,' she said and gave a little laugh that cut his heart like a dagger. He looked away from his future sister-in-law so as not to see the happiness in her eyes.

Ever since he had first seen her as a young girl, long-legged in her bright Ukrainian skirts and wrinkled red boots he had been attracted to her, not only to her slender budding body but admiring her dignity and air of serene tranquillity tinged with a kind of youthful, beautiful arrogance; envying her wild spirits, courage and occasional reckless defiance of grown-up authority though she had loved her parents most deeply. He remembered her flaring anger, her hot contempt – none of her emotions could ever have been cold – her moments of grief and tenderness over the death of some bird or animal she had tried

vainly to save. More than anything he remembered sadly –
bitterly now as he suddenly realized how very much he loved
and wanted this woman who was to be his brother's wife –
how it had always been Henryk to whom she had turned even
at the age of thirteen. Henryk with his curly black hair and
brooding good looks, his air of self-sufficient confidence, his
proud 'it-really-doesn't-matter-what-you-think-of-me' look.

Adam glanced at her eyes shining, skin aglow from the cold,
her body erect on the side saddle, the high rounded curve of her
breasts, the shape of a long thigh moulding the blue skirt. Her
beauty made him tremble, so that to hide the burning desire in
his eyes he leant down pretending to adjust a stirrup.

Kasia hoped Henryk would catch them up very soon for she
liked Adam and did not want him to say anything they all
might have cause to regret. But all he muttered was, 'He's a very
fortunate fellow,' and did not speak again until they reached the
top of the hill.

'Oh, Adam, what a view!'

Below them, stretching away to the east the steppes shone
golden bronze; here and there in the little hollows and ravines
mist still hung in white patches.

'On a clear day you can see right to the Dnieper,' he said,
calm again. And over the Dnieper, many hundreds of miles
away, she thought, lay the Don, finding it almost impossible to
realize that she had once lived there, far beyond, over the rolling
horizon, had lived and borne a son beside the mighty river.

Two steppe eagles circled slowly across the cold blue sky; a
fox barked in the wood behind them and then from a copse
about half a mile below and to their right came the long-drawn
howl of a wolf. The greyhounds whined in their eagerness,
looking up at their master, imploring him with liquid eyes to
let them go. But he did not appear to notice.

'You're a very exceptional woman, Kasia,' he said, staring
into the distance.

'No, not exceptional. Only very, very lucky.'

'If,' he began hesitantly – 'should anything ever happen to
Henryk—'

'Why should anything happen to him?' she asked slowly.

'He talks always of war,' said Adam uncertainly.

'What Pole doesn't? For five hundred years we've known war.'

He turned to face her, suddenly impulsive.

'For God's sake, Kasia, don't you see what I'm trying to say? If – well, I'll always be here.'

Softened by the anguish in his voice and understanding the reason for it Kasia said with great sympathy:

'Dear Adam, I know and I thank you. With all my heart I thank you.'

And with that gentle touch on his arm Adam had to be satisfied for they heard Henryk's voice shouting for them and the sound of his horse cantering up the slope.

'I had the devil's own job to get away,' he called before he reached them. 'You know what Father's like once he starts on politics.'

He was bareheaded, and his eyes lit up as he rode to Kasia's side.

'Has this solemn brother of mine been entertaining you well?'

She nodded, her eyes smiling in answer to his own.

Very sadly Adam wondered if any woman would ever look at him in that way.

'There's a wolf down there,' he said pointing with his whip to the copse.

'Well then, why are we sitting here? Come on!'

With a shout he was away down the slope at full gallop, the greyhounds leaping ahead. Kasia touched her horse with the whip and set off in pursuit, the rush of the morning air scouring her face, her eyes on Henryk's faded green hunting coat; smoky vapour fresh from the melted frost rose under the racing hooves. Her horse was moving so smoothly and with such power that she gave him his head, exulting in the feel of the superb body beneath her. She saw the hounds vanish into the oak thicket and heard Henryk's cry as a wolf broke cover and made across the open valley towards the woods, the greyhounds racing ahead to cut it off. She was laughing aloud with the wild excitement of the chase, the cold burning in her throat, and then, with no warning, her horse was going down and she was hurtling into the air in a great arc that seemed to go on forever until she hit the hard earth in whirling, smashing darkness.

Just behind her Adam managed to swerve violently and rein in. He leapt from his horse and ran to where Kasia lay, horribly crumpled, on her face. Very gently he turned her over. Beneath the blood oozing from the wound somewhere in her hair her face was ghastly grey; her breathing was quick and shallow.

'Oh, my God!' He felt quite helpless and began shouting for Henryk, waving his hat to attract attention.

By the time Henryk reached them, the blood covered her face and was dribbling very slowly from the corner of her slack mouth. Henryk's eyes widened and the fear sickened him as he knelt beside her.

'Ride for home and bring a cart, blankets, brandy. Hurry, for Christ's sake!' He removed his coat and covered her still body. By now her breath was coming in little snoring gasps; he wiped away the blood from her face, not daring to touch her head.

Her horse stood trembling, one foreleg, broken in the marmot burrow, hanging useless. Adam rode close to the poor beast, pulling the long pistol from his belt and the horse, as if realizing what was coming, rolled its eyes piteously but did not move as the muzzle was pressed close behind its ear. The report echoed in the hills as if ten men had fired. The animal sank to its knees and rolled slowly over, dark blood bubbling over the quivering satin neck.

Then, putting spurs to his horse. Adam rode hell-for-leather for Lipno, using the whip unmercifully, urging the animal to its utmost limits with his voice and his knees.

For an hour Henryk waited with her. The old bayonet wound in his thigh grew unbearably painful from his cramped position but he never moved. Now and then he wiped her face with his soaked handkerchief listening to the awful little sound of her breathing; once he whispered:

'Kasia, Kasia.'

In the distance the hounds were barking as they bayed the wolf, waiting expectantly for the hunters who never came.

With incredible relief Henryk heard Adam's voice urging on the driver of the long peasant cart.

'How is she?' Adam hurried to his side.

'The same. Help me get her into the cart. Gently, you fools!'
Henryk snapped at the two men who had come with the cart.
With infinite care they placed her on the straw and covered her
with blankets.

Very slowly they took her home.

*   *   *

It was night and still Henryk sat at her bedside, his eyes
never leaving her face. Since they had laid her on the bed
twelve hours before he had not moved. The doctor had come;
he had cut away the hair from around the deep scalp wound
and bathed the long scratches on her forehead. He had wanted
to bleed her but Henryk pushed him out of the room.

As dusk darkened the room old Stepan brought candles and
quietly drew the curtains then he came with food which remained on the table cold and untouched. He put logs into the
stove then departed, muttering mournfully to himself and
shaking his head.

Adam came in with their father; for a while they stood in
silence at the foot of the bed, then with a few words of comfort
which Henryk hardly heard they went and Henryk was alone
with her.

Mice moved in the shadows; the chill of the small hours
crept into the room as a wind moaned round the house. His head
nodded and for an instant his eyelids closed. With a sick spasm
of fear he jerked himself awake, feeling death's icy presence in
the room, heard the curtains rustle, but it was only the wind,
the candle flames dimmed but did not go out. For a terrible
moment he thought she had died, slipped away in the second
his eyes were closed. He put his lips to hers and felt the uneven
flutter of her breath.

At some time before dawn his father hobbled in again.

'Any change?' he asked in a low voice.

Henryk shook his head and felt the comfort of his father's
hand on his shoulder. Count Barinski stayed, huddled in a
chair beside the stove.

The last hours before dawn were very slow in passing. Twice
Henryk thought she had gone. Already in her bandaged drained

face there was the look of a skull. He had seen many men die but none like this, slowly and quietly, slipping away in a candlelit room with an old man snoring by the stove.

Her hand was limp in his; she lay motionless as a corpse.

It was daylight now and Henryk heard his brother urging him to get some sleep.

'I'll watch for you.'

But Henryk shook his head.

'At least eat something.'

He forced down a little soup, tasting nothing.

Throughout the day people came and went, speaking in whispers as if already in the presence of the dead; throughout the day Henryk sat, his face a mask of stone, only his eyes showing the anguish of the endless vigil. Now and then his lips moved in silent prayer. He had never found it easy to pray and he used simple words to beg God for the life of this woman he loved so completely. Often he held the hand-mirror to her lips, hardly daring to look at the glass so faintly clouded. Food was brought and taken away; he drank a glass of wine.

At some time in the evening he felt her hand growing cold in his, the glass was barely misted. He called for Adam.

'Fetch Father Krasinski.'

There was an awful note of resignation in his voice, hoarse and thin from exhaustion and strain. At that moment he had begun to give her up to God.

Father Krasinski entered very quietly. He came to the head of the bed and stood looking down at the beautiful face already touched by the awesome serenity of death.

'My poor son,' he said with deep compassion. In a few weeks he was to have joined these two in marriage and now he was called to make easier their last and final separation.

With a heavy heart he prepared for the last rites, placing a crucifix on a table within sight of the unconscious woman, beside it a single wax candle, a pewter plate with six small squares of cloth and a little vessel of holy oil. His preparations completed he turned to face the bed.

'Peace to this house,' he said.

Count Barinski had come in with Adam; Stepan stood in one

corner and the rest of the servants spaced themselves solemnly along the walls.

Father Krasinski sprinkled a few drops of the holy water on Kasia's face, murmuring, 'Our help is in the name of the Lord.' He then anointed her closed eyes.

'By this holy unction and His own most gracious mercy, may the Lord pardon thee whatever sin thou has committed by sight.' His voice was slightly harsh and pitched in one key. Slowly, deliberately, he touched her on the mouth, ears, nostrils and hands, wiping away the shiny stain of the oil with the little squares of cloth.

'. . . whatever sin thou hast committed by touch.'

Henryk heard the words from far, far away. This macabre ceremony by candlelight could surely have nothing to do with Kasia. Kasia, so intensely, so vividly alive, being treated as a lump of grey clay. He hated what the priest was doing but knew the man believed sincerely he was helping her.

'*Salvam fac ancillam tuam.*' Save thy handmaiden. It was too late for that now: why had not God prevented the horse from going down?

'Lord have mercy on her.'

Henryk remained sitting beside her, holding her hand as the others knelt, Count Barinski grunting from the pain in his swollen leg.

The old priest bent over her and began to speak into her very ear.

In the extraordinary unpredictable way of memory Henryk had a quick vision of Captain Primrose saying the burial service over the bodies of the men smashed by *Richelieu*'s guns.

'Oh Lord Jesus Christ, receive my spirit——' Someone in the room was sobbing quietly.

'. . . and receive me at the hour of death.' Father Krasinski traced the Sign of the Cross on her bandaged forehead and then, with tears in his eyes did the same to Henryk. For an instant he let his hand rest on Henryk's bowed head.

'May God help you, my son, and grant you strength,' he said with a deep and terrible compassion. 'For you will surely need it.'

Gathering up his holy things the old man in his stained vestments and his cracked boots went from the room.

No one moved until, at a nod from Count Barinski, the servants filed slowly past the bed, paying their last respects to the woman whom they had so quickly come to love and respect. All were in tears. When it came to Stepan's turn he spoke in a strained whisper.

'Bless you, my lady, and thank you for bringing light and joy to this house.' He shuffled out like a drunken man, blinded by his grief.

And now only the Barinskis remained, and the faint smell of the oil.

'Go,' said Henryk into his hands. 'Please go.' He would save her, or lose her, on his own; he wanted no one else to see her die. Suddenly something broke and he began to weep, silently with bowed back, the tears squeezing between his fingers.

His father and brother stood, one on each side of him: their eyes, full of suffering, met above his shaking shoulders. Count Barinski mouthed the word, 'Go.' Adam bent and kissed Kasia on the cheek.

'God's will be done,' said Count Barinski quietly after Adam had gone. It had been the same when his Wanda had died; she too had just slipped away and he, like his son, had been condemned to watch, unable to do anything. God was often horribly cruel, he thought not for the first time.

'If you need me,' he said, 'I'll be outside.' He had never felt closer to Henryk than at that awful moment. Henryk's answer was muffled.

The door closed; the candle flames settled to a steady light; the stove purred contentedly then, when the man could weep no more, he sat up, eyes burning in his unshaven, tear-stained face, and whispered with a desperate intensity,

'Don't die, Rasulka. You must not die.'

He was leaning close now, speaking more loudly so that his father, seated in his chair beyond the door, heard the words which tore at his heart.

'You cannot leave me. Do you hear, my dearest love, you cannot leave me.'

He pressed her hand with a grip of steel, willing her to live.

'Please. Please. *Please.*' He was begging her to stay with him. There was so much to say, so many years to spend with her. Was she going without so much as another whisper? Would he never again see her smile, see the love and laughter in her eyes? Never. This little word was the executioner's axe poised above his shrinking neck.

She lay as if in her coffin, calm and very peaceful, leaving, as always, the agony to the living.

But as Henryk waited for her to die, fighting with every last scrap of his will to call her back, he felt, disbelieving, a tiny miraculous pressure of her fingers, slight as the merest breath of wind that barely stirs a leaf. Trembling, he held the mirror to her lips and a great sigh escaped him as he saw the thick clouding of the glass. Her colour had deepened, her breathing though still quick and shallow had lost the nasty little snoring sound. For the first time since she had hit the ground Kasia moved her head and her eyelids stirred but did not open.

Henryk put his hand to her brow and found the skin hot and dry to touch. All the gods in the world be praised, there might be a chance. He knew these fevers of hers. Ever since her ride from the Don she had been prone to periodic bouts of boiling fever that set her whole body aflame.

Now her head was tossing from side to side and for the first time in nearly forty hours he heard her voice, weak at first but slowly gaining strength.

'. . . don't you see, they loathe the new Tsar, they despise him . . .' Her words slurred and, through his dazed senses he could not make out what she was saying. Then her voice was clear again.

'The people did not laugh at his childish antics . . . not when he betrayed Russia and made peace with Frederick . . . and called you an idiot at that ghastly dinner. . . .'

Through his fatigue and indescribable relief Henryk realized that in the twilight world of her fever she was talking to Catherine.

'Then how he gives the late Empress's jewels to his mistress – a fat, black pig in pearls – and talks openly of marrying her and sending you back to Zerbst or shutting you up in Schlusselburg . . . he's a brute, Figgy, no one knows it better than you. A brute must be got rid of . . . must . . . somehow . . . don't you see, it's *you* they want. You, Catherine of Russia.'

Fascinated, Henryk listened, stroking her face with gentle fingers now and then, murmuring little words of love. . . .

'Now is the time. He has insulted the Guards . . . they'll carry you to the throne . . let the Orlovs lead them, already they're giving them beer and vodka . . . that's the way to lead the Dark People.' Her voice trailed off; she moved uneasily on the bed and he put his hand on her shoulder to restrain her.

'If Henryk was here, he would lead them,' she said. 'They would follow him.'

'I'm here, my darling. I'm here with you.' But she did not hear him.

'Don't let Dashkova spoil everything, I beg of you, Ma'am, don't trust her too far . . . too young and indiscreet . . . if we fail . . .' Kasia jerked violently in agitation, trying to sit up but Henryk held her down.

'Oh, my God, the penalty if we fail.' Then in a loud clear voice she cried out. 'Is God on our side?' And as she fell silent the sweat broke, pouring from her body in torrents.

Henryk wiped her dry and sponged her face.

'The Guards are warned to march for Denmark at the end of June. They won't obey and this is our chance. Next week . . .' Suddenly her strange dream world faded and she opened her eyes.

'Henryk.' She smiled weakly, reaching up to the bandage on her head.

'What happened? Why am I—'

He put his fingers to her lips. 'Not now. Later. You must sleep.' She put up her hand to his stubbled chin, saw the deep black shadows beneath his bloodshot eyes.

'How long?'

But he shook his head with a smile and bent to kiss her. 'Sleep, dearest. I'll be here if you need me.'

With a small contented sigh she closed her eyes; when her slow even breathing showed him she slept, Henryk tiptoed to the door. His father was asleep in the chair and woke guiltily with the unspoken question in his eyes as Henryk gently shook him.

'You can go to bed, Father. She's all right.'

Wordlessy Count Barinski stared at Henryk, his eyes brimming, then rising slowly and stiffly to his feet he embraced his son.

'The Lord has worked a miracle,' was all he said, and hobbled away to his bed.

Henryk stretched himself beside Kasia.

'Thank you, God,' he murmured. 'Thank you for letting her live.'

With her hand in his Henryk slept.

*   *   *

Major Skurin of the Smolensk Regiment bent forward in his saddle, cursing the icy wind and the sleety snow which stung his face, cursing the fate which had chosen him to command the column of infantry plodding sullenly along behind him.

Here they were, marching and countermarching about the Ukraine for God knows what reason when he should have been snug in Petersburg, warm and satisfied in the arms of his plump little mistress. Damn these miserable peasants and their flea-ridden cottages, damn the mud of their cart-track roads, damn more especially the Poles who treated him and his men with such lofty contempt. But just you wait, you arrogant swine, you'll soon get what's coming to you. His hands tightened on the reins. You'll find we've become something to be reckoned with.

'Hold up, can't you!' He swore as his horse stumbled in another pot-hole. For the moment sleet lifted and screwing up his eyes against the wind, Skurin saw in the far distance the usual thatched cottages of a village, and beyond, the green roof of a big house. He turned in his saddle and shouted for his second-in-command, a wet-nosed boy with six months' service.

'Halt the men. Let them fall out and light fires – if they can find anything to burn in this God-forsaken place. But if any man so much as touches a single stick from a peasant fence I'll have his head – and yours.' If I had my way, he thought savagely, I'd let 'em tear every village apart.

Sourly he watched his men fall out and begin their search for firewood. God knows what keeps them going he asked himself, not for the first time, the patient dogged infantry of Russia whom he had seen die on half a dozen battlefields. Mute and long-suffering as cattle but when roused the most ferocious and ruthless of fighters.

For twenty years of his life Major Skurin had been a soldier. His fellow officers claimed he had been weaned on gunpowder. Among them he had few friends, being very much a lone wolf and, besides, of too cold a character for the easy warmth of friendship. The only man to whom he had ever felt remotely attracted was a withdrawn embittered officer named Mirovich, whose family had forfeited their estates in the Ukraine for some misdemeanour committed in the Great Peter's reign. After surviving Gross-Jägersdorf, Kunersdorf and the carnage of Zorndorf, he had come to respect war but yet still to enjoy it. A professional to the tips of his bayonet-scarred fingers, he regarded war as a game to be played entirely without rules. Once the fighting had begun there was no room in Major Skurin's mind for chivalry or mercy. In his heart there was one aim – to destroy his enemy as swiftly and efficiently as possible and by any means available.

'We're not at war,' he said sourly to the young officer. 'Unfortunately.'

'No.' His subordinate was huddled miserably in the saddle, the blue grey tinge of fatigue frozen on his sharp features.

No, my little cock sparrow, thought Skurin contemptuously, this isn't what you expected when you first put on your smart new uniform in Petersburg and went strutting down the Nevsky Prospekt, proud as a stuffed peacock.

'What we're doing now, whatever it may be, is three-quarters of soldiering. The sooner you learn that simple fact the better for your immortal soul.' With a grim chuckle Major Skurin spurred his horse and vanished into the murk, calling over his shoulder, 'Wait here till I'm back.'

'But sir – will you be all right alone?'

His only answer was the fading thud of hooves.

The young officer felt the apprehension tighten his stomach. He peered uneasily into the sleet, prey to every sort of wild fancy, expecting the terrible thunder of Polish cavalry, the sudden roar of cannon, the tramp of enemy boots, God knows what else.

'We're at peace. There's no war,' he reassured himself. Only cold and hunger and homesickness, and this feeling of vague dread which weighed him down.

It was the first time he had found himself in command on his own.

*　　*　　*

Kasia lay on the day-bed by the window of her room looking out listlessly into the thinning sleet. She was still very weak and at that stage of her convalescence when most of the world seems drab and pointless. Without much enjoyment she sipped the wine prescribed as a tonic by bumbling old Doctor Kossak. A final flurry of sleet smacked against the glass then the afternoon brightened, letting a few cold rays of sunshine through the heavy dark clouds.

Above the bare branches of the orchard she could see the road stretching to the whitened village and beyond, and, as the lone horseman appeared, riding slowly towards the house, so the sun disappeared again. But, before the light had faded back to greyness she had seen the vivid green and yellow of his uniform, the whiteness of the breeches against the big black horse.

With the sight of that solitary figure riding slowly towards Lipno her lassitude fell away like an unwanted cloak.

This Russian officer had ridden a long way from the Palace Square, she thought, remembering the motionless ranks of infantrymen, identical in their tunics of green with yellow facings. And was it by order of his Empress that he came to the Ukraine? Once long ago in another life, she had watched a lone Cossack ride slowly across the frozen Don and had experienced this same feeling of uneasiness, of inexplicable dread. Her heart was now filled with foreboding but she knew not why. This man rode up the road to Lipno on his own. He did not send an underling, he came himself, riding with a great air of purpose on his big black horse.

Someone else had seen the rider or a messenger and run ahead from the village for she heard voices shouting below; Count Barinski bellowing for his riding clothes, footsteps pounded along the passages. Henryk stuck his head round her door,

'There's a Russian officer coming. Father's beside himself – I think he'll have a stroke—'

'Henryk!' The old man's voice shook the house. 'Adam! Where the devil are you?' Henryk hurried across the room, kissed the top of her head, whispered, 'I love you,' and ran out.

Kasia lay back smiling. On the road, half-hidden by the poplars, the Russian had reined in and sat staring at the house. For at least fifteen minutes he remained thus, never moving, while the pandemonium in the house gradually subsided. She heard the clatter of hooves on the cobbles of the yard and a moment later saw Count Barinski as he rode out with his two sons to meet the Russian.

He had found time to dress in all his finery: hat of lynx fur, plumed and set proudly on his grey head, long caftan, braided and frogged with tarnished gold, sable-trimmed pelisse flung back over one shoulder, long soft riding-boots, silver hunting-dagger at his belt. Beside him his sons looked plain and dowdy. As Kasia watched the officer urged his horse into a slow walk, going forward to meet the three Poles.

Within a few yards they all halted and Skurin raised his tricorne hat politely in greeting.

They saw a tall clean-shaven man with prominent cheek bones, a thin mouth and cold blue eyes set a fraction too close above a beaky nose.

'What's he saying?' growled Count Barinski.

'He wishes us good day,' Henryk translated.

'Oh – ah, yes. Wish him the same.'

'You speak excellent Russian, sir,' said Skurin, looking curiously at Henryk's dark, scarred face.

'I know Petersburg well.'

'May I ask when—?'

'Come on, Henryk,' broke in his father irritably, 'get on with it. What does the fellow want? It's too damned cold to sit here all night.' In reply to Henryk's question, Skurin spoke rapidly for a moment.

'He asks whether we can provide shelter for the night for a hundred and forty-six men, two officers and twelve horses.'

Henryk was struck by the punctilious manner in which the Russian phrased his request.

One day, thought Skurin, and God grant it may be soon, we shall not have to ask these arrogant Poles. We shall simply take, as is the right of conquering soldiers.

Count Barinski's face became dangerously suffused.

'By God—' he began then remembering his manners and the laws of hospitality he pulled himself taller and said, with all the politeness he could muster:

'Of course. Arrange it Adam. Put 'em in the barn. The officers will naturally stay with us. Tell him, Henryk . . . Less likelihood of trouble if we have the officers under our eyes,' he added in an undertone.

But Skurin shook his head at the last invitation, no emotion showing on his hard pale face. Henryk listened, also quite impassive save for a small dangerous light in his eyes, to the transparent excuse.

'Major Skurin regrets,' he translated curtly word for word, 'but he feels that he and Ensign Potovski must remain with their men.'

Count Barinski stared hard at the Russian who returned the angry look coldly and calmly.

'Very well,' he said flatly. 'I shall not ask him again.' Wheeling his horse the old man cantered towards the house. Seeing Kasia at the window he raised his whip in salute, shouting to her:

'The place is going to be overrun with bloody Russians!' Moustaches bristling, he vanished from view, roaring for Stepan.

'But you'll perhaps take a glass of wine with us,' suggested Adam through Henryk. Major Skurin gave a short nod.

'Thank you. When I have seen to the quartering of my men.' His smile matched the sleet which had begun to increase in the rising wind.

The brothers watched until he had disappeared over the ridge beyond the village.

'Well,' said Henryk in a tight voice, 'that's the first Russian to appear at Lipno.'

'But not the last.'

'I didn't like the look of him. Unpleasant mouth.' Henryk's eyebrows met darkly above his nose as he gazed with an angry frown at the distant ridge.

'Why on earth did you have to go and ask him to drink with us?'

'Common hospitality,' answered Adam pompously. 'Besides we may get some information out of him.'

'Father's going to be delighted,' said Henryk with a quick grin. 'Still, that's your funeral.'

       *   *   *

But they discovered nothing from Major Skurin, except the fact he could speak bad German. The visit was no great success. Count Barinski remained in his room, leaving his sons to make whatever excuses they thought fit. Through the floor of her room Kasia could hear the brief bursts of conversation, the even louder pauses.

Major Skurin stood, stiff as a ramrod, refusing the offers of a chair. 'I've been in the saddle all day.' Young Potovski was obviously far too frightened to sit when his superior was on his feet. So the four men remained standing.

Henryk tossed down two vodkas in quick succession and felt better.

'And how was Petersburg when you were last there?' he asked affably.

'It was very well,' said Skurin in his slow, stilted German. His eyes were never still, Henryk noticed; darting about the room, taking in every detail – curiosity to see the interior of a Polish manor house had been the only reason for this visit – but always returning to Henryk. Each time the cold eyes rested on his face Henryk saw in them a faint look of puzzlement, as if some vague memory was stirring.

At last during another silence Skurin asked, 'Have we not met before?'

'Quite possibly,' Henryk said, 'if you were in Petersburg during 'fifty-eight.'

'I thought so. Were you not attached to the French Embassy!'

Henryk nodded. 'You have a good memory. Of course,' he added with a smile, touching the great scar, 'this is fairly easy to remember.'

'How—' began Ensign Potovski, then, catching Skurin's look, buried his burning face in the glass.

'The Turks can use their scimitars with considerable skill—' Henryk glanced at Skurin, 'as you may know.'

Skurin shook his head and for the first time Henryk saw a trace of a smile on the thin lips.

'I have not yet had occasion to meet Turkish steel.'

'Then,' said Henryk cheerfully, 'let's hope for your sake that you never do. It's very sharp.'

Silence fell on the room. Ensign Potovski shifted uneasily in his huge riding-boots. The sleeping wolfhound twitched and growled by the stove.

'Do you expect to be in these parts long?' Adam asked.

'My orders have specified no exact date for our return to Russia.' Skurin's eyes were wary.

'It's difficult for a professional soldier to plan far ahead,' remarked Henryk blandly.

'Yes,' agreed Skurin from behind the pale mask of his face. 'And now if you'll excuse me I must return to my men. May we thank you for your hospitality?'

'Indeed you may,' said Henryk heartily. With a muffled sort of grunt which they took to be an expression of thanks, Ensign Potovski stamped heavily from the room in the wake of his superior.

'Well,' Henryk said, flinging himself into a chair and unbuttoning his waistcoat with a loud sigh of relief, 'what did you think of friend Skurin of the Smolensk Regiment?'

'A hard man,' Adam said seriously.

'One thing,' said Henryk in a mocking tone, 'he must love his men very much to spend the night with them in the barn.'

'He doesn't want to let himself become too friendly in case—'

'Friendly! It was like talking to a snake. Good lord, the oak of a gun-deck was warmer than that man. You mean, in case the next time we meet it's looking down the wrong end of a musket?'

'Yes.'

They heard shouted Russian orders, the rumble of waggon wheels in the yard.

'I'd like to see Father's face at this moment.' Henryk chuckled then grew serious.

'There's one thing I'm certain of. I'd rather have Major Skurin on my side than against me.'

*　　　*　　　*

That night Kasia lay beside Henryk and listened to the songs of the Russian soldiers. They were singing of sad love. 'Do not shine, bright moon, begs the girl, for anyone but my beloved. Should he fall in love with another girl, then dear moon hide yourself behind the clouds. The moon hides herself and, heart-broken, the girl weeps.'

Kasia's eyes prickled with tears; she put out her hand and softly touched his arm.

'I love you so much, Henryk.'

He turned and kissed her. 'Thank you,' he whispered. 'Thank you for your love.' They lay listening, her hand in his.

'Men who sing like that surely can't be all bad,' she murmured.

'I've heard British sailors sing gay little sea shanties,' said Henryk. 'Then seen them fight like devils, without any sort of mercy in their hearts. You've heard the Cossacks sing, haven't you? And they're not exactly the world's most kindly fighters.'

'I know.'

A man accompanied by the plucking notes of a *bandura* began to sing in a voice of magnificent power and tone.

'Listen to that, darling. What a voice!'

In the song that flooded the broken stillness of the night was all the haunting melancholy of Russia, all the desperate peasant yearning for release from serfdom. The singer held a high note steady for an unbelievable time, the instrument throbbed and trembled, then others joined in and the sad swelling chorus rolled across the silent village.

'They're no worse nor better than any other soldiers,' Henryk said. 'It's not their fault they're here, poor brutes.' He did not share the violent hatred felt for all things Russian by so many of his countrymen. His experiences had taught him a real understanding and a great admiration for the patient long-suffering men in the ranks who bore the brunt of war, whether they wore the uniform of Poland, Russia, France or England.

Shouts of applause greeted the ending of the song, hand clapping, loud laughter.

'Catherine's making them a nation that'll leave its mark on history,' Henryk said. 'She's carrying on where the first Peter left off.'

Then a hundred voices burst into a rousing, marching song.

Wide awake, Kasia lay remembering the Cossack songs; in her head the words of one, Pugachev's favourite:

> ... as this camp-fire burns out slowly
> so our love must have an end. ...

She could not dispel from her mind the vague feeling of dread and pulled the blankets over her head to drown the splendid sound of Russian voices, clutching tight to the comfort of Henryk's hand.

Beside her he lay thinking not of the past but the future, staring open-eyed into the darkness, thinking fiercely yet sadly of how he was going to have to fight and kill, perhaps these very men who sprawled so full of song and life on the fragrant hay of a Polish barn.

*　　*　　*

To the raucous shouts of the non-commissioned officers the men fell in on the road outside the courtyard. Henryk leant against one of the great gates watching with a length of hay between his teeth. Stepan came out wearing his greasy apron, one of Count Barinski's long boots in his hand.

'I'll be glad to see the back of that lot. Rowdy devils.' He spat on the hard earth. 'But they're smart enough. I'll grant 'em that. For foot-soldiers,' he added with all the scorn of one who, in the long distant days of his youth, had served in the heavy cavalry.

Muskets gleamed, sidearms were bright, belts and pouches

dazzling white. No naval captain, not even Primrose, could have improved on the turn-out of these men, Henryk thought, in his mind a sudden vision of white sails and twinkling brass-work as *Huntress* sailed close-hauled across a bright sunlit sea.

A word of command rang out and the green lines stood rigid as Major Skurin and Ensign Potovski appeared. They mounted and rode to the front of the ranks, Skurin looked slowly along the motionless figures, then, hardly raising his voice, gave a sharp order.

With a crash of boots the company executed a smart right turn. Another cold, sharp command and they set off down the road stepping out smartly to the brisk tap of a drum. If they fight as well as they drill, Henryk thought, the future will certainly not be all roses.

The waggons rumbled along in the rear, each driver sitting bolt upright; the coats of the big draught horses shone with a splendid lustre in the sunshine, even the iron wheel rims looked as if they'd been polished.

'Bah,' said old Stepan. 'It's too cold to stand about here all day.' With a muttered, 'Good riddance, that's what I say,' he shuffled off back to his lair which stank of wax and smoke, where he cleaned and polished and argued endlessly with Mika the toothless old head groom.

But Henryk did not move. Watching the tall mitre caps bobbing as one above the thin dust he thought grimly that courage alone would not be enough to beat such men as these. As well as bravery and the legendary dash of the Polish horse-men they would need one vital thing – discipline.

His grandfather had always contemptuously dismissed the Russian troops as a ragged, ill-fed rabble. But now – with officers like Skurin, armed with good weapons which they'd been taught to use, no, now the story would be very different. He frowned, then smiled at the thought of trying to discipline Dombrowski. It could not be the iron discipline of the British Navy, but rather of a kind that would hold together irregular troops who would have to fight, not in serried, stubborn ranks wheeling and manoeuvring like soulless automatons, but as will-o'-the-wisps, striking swiftly and hard before vanishing back into the forests, swamps and mountains.

His vision of the future was shattered by the brisk thud of hooves as Major Skurin cantered back from the column. The man rode well, erect and motionless in the saddle, a part of his big black horse. Henryk screwed up his eyes, shading them against the sun as he squinted up at the dark figure above him.

'On behalf of myself and my men I thank you at Lipno for your hospitality,' he said. If next time we meet I have to burn this place round your ears, he thought dispassionately, I shall do so without a qualm.

'I'm delighted we were able to help,' Henryk replied with equally cold courtesy. Next time we meet, he thought, it'll be your head or mine.

Raising his whip to his hat in salute, Skurin wheeled the horse, touched the satin flanks and trotted after the fading tap of the drum.

Henryk pulled the chewed stalk from his mouth, threw it on the ground and with a long sigh went slowly into the house.

*　　*　　*

When Henryk had arranged the chessmen on the ivory board he sat back with a smile. Kasia sat opposite, a white lace shawl round her shoulders, very attentive, very serious. In the candle-light her face was warm and serene. At last she's looking better, he thought with the first real relief for many weeks; more colour in her cheeks and she was losing the drawn, exhausted look, the black smudges of illness under her eyes were fading.

Except for occasional headaches she had recovered but Henryk still insisted on treating her firmly as an invalid, hardly allowing her to lift a spoon to her mouth unaided.

'Warm enough?'

She nodded, smiling. 'You coddle me too much,' she said fondly. There was no wind and outside, beyond the soft folds of the wine-red curtains, the night was still and very cold. Count Barinski was safely in bed; Adam away in Lvov on estate business. They had the house to themselves.

'Now, let's see how much you've learnt so far,' he said. 'Tell me the names of all the pieces.'

The chessmen glowed in the soft golden light, stolid ranks of red and white. In front the pawns carved as Roman legionaries, behind them the figures of power: the bishops in Chinese robes, the castle on the back of elephants, Persian knights with delicate lances, the Kings and Queens dressed as Mogul rulers.

'He's beautiful.' Kasia held the red king close to a candle flame, running her finger over the minute carving of the little face.

'Beautiful, yes,' he agreed, 'but in this game not so powerful in the end as these' – he pointed to the pawns – 'if they're used properly. They're the peasants of the game. For instance if you get one of them to your opponent's back line it becomes a queen.'

'Serf to Emperor,' said Kasia, thinking of Pugachev and his dreams of glory.

'Play your ivory peasants with skill and – the great ones are helpless.' Henryk removed the white king with a flourish. 'He's gone – he can be trapped and harried by these little men until he has no way to turn. Very frustrating it is too.' He replaced the king.

'The French are great players,' he said. 'I've seen people take two days over one game.'

'I don't think I'd have the patience.' Kasia laughed. 'Imagine just staring at these little things for two days. But on the other hand Catherine would enjoy this game, I think. It's got an intellectual ruthlessness to it that would appeal to her.' They sat in silence. A sudden whisper of wind sighed round the house falling away to utter stillness again.

'Just before the *coup* the weather in Petersburg was like this,' she said the chess lesson forgotten. 'Except it was hot and sultry. As if the whole world was held in a strange sort of breathless hush.'

'Like the eye of a storm.'

'I expect so. I've never been in one.' More like the day of the eclipse, she thought, the day the sun went out, the day the Turks came.

'The whole thing must have been superbly planned,' said Henryk absently, twiddling a castle on its base. 'By all accounts it all went like clockwork.'

So far they had hardly talked about the weeks in the previous year when Catherine took the throne from her weak and hated husband. Kasia laughed again.

'You've no idea how disorganized everything was. That was the whole trouble. There was no real leader, no proper overall plan. The Orlovs said this, Panin something else, Razumovsky argued it should be done this way, someone else put forward quite a different idea and Dashkova twittered about getting over-excited and talking too much.'

'How on earth didn't Peter find out what was going on?'

'God knows. Or, if he did know then he must have been on our side. Luck certainly was,' she paused, 'and a sort of spontaneous explosion of anger and hatred against Peter which swept her to the throne. But if he had been a stronger character and had taken immediate counter-measures Catherine would either be back in Zerbst, in Schlusselburg – or dead, and I certainly wouldn't be sitting here with you.'

Henryk raised his glass of wine. 'A toast then. To you my love, and in company with Bubin to the late Tsar Peter for letting you come home.' They touched glasses and smiled; he saw that her eyes were troubled.

'Tell me how it all started.' Getting up he fetched the jug of wine. When the glasses were filled she said,

'Where do I start?'

'At the point when it was decided to *do* something.'

Kasia leant back with her eyes raised to the ceiling.

'I suppose the moment was when we went to Peterhof. That was, let's see – yes, the seventeenth of June. We stayed quietly at Monplaisir – and waited, trying to pretend it was just another summer holiday. At least I was trying. And then on the twenty-eighth in the early morning Alexei arrived with Vasili Bibikov in a little carriage to take Catherine to the throne.'

'Just like that?'

'Just like that.'

Logs spluttered in the silence and small fat puffs of smoke were forced from the stove by the wind.

'And that was the beginning of those incredible days.'

PART FIVE

JUST after midnight on Friday the twenty-eighth of June, 1762, a light carriage clattered at speed through the outskirts of St. Petersburg taking the road that led to Peterhof. Alexei Orlov held the reins, stinging the two powerful horses with the long curling lash; beside him his friend Bibikov sat in silence as the two young officers rattled and swayed along at the start of the greatest adventure of their lives.

The last of the houses fell away and on each side the deserted countryside lay silent in the eerie, luminous light of the 'white night'. Now and then sheet-lightning flared to the west but the rumble of the wheels drowned the thunder. Within an hour the sun would rise again beyond the Gulf of Finland.

'God help us,' said Bibikov suddenly.

'Losing your nerve?' Orlov flicked at the horses. He laughed harshly.

'No. But – my God, d'you really realize what we're doing? That the destiny of Russia's in our hands?' Awe trembled in Bibikov's voice.

'Yes,' Orlov answered grimly. 'I realize.'

They did not speak again until the sun was well above the horizon and shining on the golden domes of Peterhof. By the steps leading down to the gardens they stopped and Alexei sprang out.

'Wait here,' he ordered. 'There are never any sentries round this place but should one of the Holsteiners appear and question you, say we have driven out to arrange an entertainment for Peter's name-day.'

He hurried between the lime trees towards the miniature palace of Monplaisir.

Kasia heard his boots on the gravel as she lay awake. She had slept only fitfully, tossing in the hot night, listening to the grumble of thunder, hoping for rain, filled with an excited apprehension, feeling that something would happen before the night was through, that something must happen; the tension *must* break.

Catherine had gone to bed in a calm, reflective state of mind which completely hid the turmoil Kasia knew was raging in her heart, and she would have slept like a child as though totally unaware that her fate was already balanced on the sword blades of her Guards.

The wheels ground to a halt and as Kasia jumped out of bed she heard Alexei's voice calling her name. She went through to the little hall, noticing that the time was exactly six. His huge frame filled the doorway, the light strong behind him and even as he spoke Kasia realized once again that she felt nothing for this magnificent young giant who had been her lover, that he had died like a withered leaf from her life.

'We've come to fetch her,' he said abruptly without preamble.

'Come in,' she answered equally abruptly. 'I'll wake her.'

Catherine woke instantly to Kasia's touch.

'They're here, Madam. Alexei and Bibikov.'

'What's the time?'

'Just after six.'

'And the day? Is it fine?'

'Lovely.' Kasia drew back the curtains and the room was radiant with sunlight. Catherine's dark hair fell across the pillow; her face looked very small.

'Within six hours – perhaps sooner – we shall know,' she said in a low voice. 'Whatever the outcome this day will go down in history.' She seemed reluctant to move, to leave the safety of her bed.

'For eighteen years I had to suffer indignities, insults, contempt – and now today?' She closed her eyes. 'Will it all have been worth while? Will it, Kasia, *will* it?'

'Only God can answer that. And,' she added with a smile of encouragement, 'some regiments of Russian soldiers.' It seemed as if Catherine had dropped back to sleep. What an amazing woman, Kasia thought, to be able to lie in bed as though there was nothing more to plan than another picnic in the gardens or a sailing trip to Kronstadt.

'Tell Shargorodskaya. And come back yourself.' Catherine sat up in bed rubbing the sleep from her eyes with the gestures of a child; for a moment she remained motionless and in her eyes was something close to fear. But the moment passed and she swung her legs briskly to the floor.

'When the time comes, wear black,' Kasia had advised. 'It suits you and besides is a most effective colour.'

On this day it should be Kasia who would dress colourfully in blue, flowered brocade, with a large scarlet breast knot and a wide-brimmed hat bright with feathers.

'On the day you shall steal the show, my dear.' They had laughed gaily, for at that time the day lay still in the distant future.

No rouge but powder to accentuate the natural whiteness of her skin. They had discussed such seemingly unimportant trivialities backwards and forwards for, as Kasia insisted, 'not only a throne may depend on a dress but your life – our lives.'

'Well,' asked Catherine, getting up from her dressing-table half an hour later, 'will this please my soldiers?'

Kasia looked at the small figure clad in the simple black dress unrelieved by jewellery or flowers, no colour except the crimson sash of the Order of Saint Catherine across one rounded shoulder and bosom.

'A little more powder.' Kasia stood back, her head on one side.

'Yes, that will do very well.'

Catherine's personal maid, Shargorodskaya, nodded. 'Perfect, Madame.'

In the heightened pallor of her face Catherine's eyes were huge. Suddenly they filled with tears and she held out her hands to Kasia. For an instant the two women clung together.

'Oh my God, Kasia, I'm frightened,' she whispered.

'Don't, Figgy, don't. They'll take you to their hearts, I'm sure of it.'

Catherine composed herself, dabbed carefully at her eyes; the maid put finishing touches to the lightly powdered hair and laid a soft scarf over her head to shield it from the dust. A knock sounded on the door.

'Madame, we must leave. All is ready for you to be proclaimed.' Orlov spoke urgently. Catherine sighed.

'Very well then.' Kasia opened the door.

'I am ready, Captain Orlov.' He bowed and stood aside, looking down from his great height with undisguised admiration in his handsome eyes.

The three of them went swiftly through the gardens already filled with the peaceful hum of bees, the cheerful song of birds. Kasia wondered if they would ever return, if she would ever hear such sounds again and turned her head for one last glimpse of Monplaisir, 'my little red and white summer house', as Catherine called it, where they had spent so many peaceful and happy days.

Catherine arranged herself with Kasia beside her. Bibikov sat opposite very stiff and nervous and Orlov got up on to the coachman's seat. He took up the reins and, holding the whip poised, turned towards the women, a strange, twisted smile on his scarred face.

'To Petersburg and a crown – Your Majesty.'

'No, Alexei, not Your Majesty, not yet, don't tempt the gods,' Kasia burst out.

As the wheels of the carriage began to turn Catherine spoke.

'Now there will be no going back.' She sat straight, her hands folded in her lap, staring intently ahead beyond Orlov's broad back as if trying to pierce the hazy mist and see what awaited her in the city.

They went fast, bumping and swaying in the dust so that Kasia had to cling to the side to avoid being flung against Catherine. She saw the lather, white and shining on the straining rumps and heard Orlov's loud exhortations. He sounded gay and carefree as a boy riding to an assignation and for an instant Kasia felt a resurgence of her old admiration for him. Then, in place of the broad uniformed shoulders she saw in a flash of amazing clarity Henryk's slim figure, the curly back of his neat head. Her hand gripped the door as if to splinter the woodwork. They *must* succeed; Catherine *must* be Empress for then she would have the power to pardon Henryk and bring him back from the awful loneliness of Siberia – if indeed he still lived. *If* they failed – Kasia smiled grimly to herself – at least she might be permitted to join her love in perpetual exile. She tried not to think of the immediate future, to control the breathless pounding of her heart and fight the painful emptiness of her stomach, striving to emulate the icy calmness of the woman beside her.

But at least she wasn't the only one, she thought wrily: Bibikov looked as if he was going to be sick at any moment and the hand gripping his sword-hilt showed white-boned. There was dusty sweat on his face which he kept mopping with a grimy handkerchief. His smile at her was more like the grimace of a skull and she felt hers to be even worse. She took a quick glance at Catherine; her mouth was set too tight, her fingers were plucking at the lap of her dress, but except for these small signs she showed nothing of the almost intolerable anxiety she must be feeling. Kasia tried to lose herself in the heavy thud of the hooves and the iron rumble of the wheels.

The mist was melting in the mounting heat and on their left strips of dark blue sea glinted between the little wooded rises where the country mansions of the great lay pink and white, smug among the oak trees. A few miserable peasant huts huddled among the reeds and their owners paused at their work, leaning thankfully on shovel or hay-fork to gaze without much interest at the speeding carriage. After all, at most hours of the day or night, the nobles or their sevants passed to and fro along the poplar road between the city and summer palaces. That this particular carriage was going at such a rate caused little comment. Why should they care? What did it matter to them? As the clatter of the wheels faded and the dust settled they turned once again to their toil.

Some miles farther on a man sat his horse in the middle of the road, his hand upraised. Catherine shaded her eyes against the glare.

'It's Grigori,' she cried in surprise and alarm. Kasia's heart dropped. Had he come to warn them, to turn them back? Was this the end of the attempt before it had even begun?

Grigori swept off his uniform hat with a smile and a flourish, bowing with an unaccustomed courtesy to his mistress, addressing his brother:

'You've made excellent time.'

'What news d'you bring?' Catherine asked.

'So far all is well,' said Grigori. 'The city's quiet, the troops still in their quarters. Now,' he went on briskly to Alexei, 'I'll ride on to Kalinkina to warn the officers of the Izmailovsky.' He leant down from the saddle.

'If you can win the Izmailovsky, Ma'am, then you are half way to the throne, for the other Guards regiments will certainly follow.'

'God willing,' said Catherine simply.

'Give me ten minutes, then follow slowly to the parade ground of the barracks. Stop for no one except myself.'

'If there's resistance, what then?' Kasia asked. 'We have two pistols and three swords between us.'

'Crowns have been won with less,' Alexei said.

'We know how to use them,' put in Bibikov speaking for the first time. His eyes shone with a sudden new resolve.

'No,' said Catherine, 'there must be no bloodshed. I would rather surrender myself than that my reign should be launched in Russian blood. If there are any signs of dissent among the soldiers then you will return and tell us at once – is that clear?' And even Grigori Orlov did not argue with Catherine when she spoke in that tone. With a grim smile and a nod of agreement he wheeled his horse and galloped towards the village of Kalinkina, visible in the far distance.

The ten minutes that followed were the longest in Kasia's life.

A peasant cart driven by a woman approached and went creaking past very slowly with a young foal prancing and kicking up his heels behind. The woman had a lined, leathery face and small blue eyes which lit up momentarily as they took in the magnificence of Kasia's dress. Catherine smiled at her but the woman did not smile back, merely muttered something as she urged her horse into a quicker pace.

The road to Kalinkina stretched before them white and empty as they approached what, at that moment, was the most important village in Russia, possibly in the world.

Glancing at Catherine, Kasia saw that she was rigid and trembling, her face taut with the strain. Under the powder her skin was deathly white; now and then she bit her underlip and wiped the palms of her hands on the leather of the seat.

They were close now and could see movements; figures ran here and there; and they could hear distant shouts.

'God,' whispered Catherine. 'Oh, God—' Kasia put her hand on Catherine's wrist and felt the quivering, like an overwound spring.

'Courage, Figgy, courage.'

A drum was beating out the alarm and more men came tumbling from the barracks; some were dragging on their tunics, some carried muskets. A few were properly dressed and accoutred as if for parade. Grigori Orlov towered above the seething mass of soldiers, his drawn sword glittering in the sunlight, he was shouting something. A great blur of faces confronted the slowly moving carriage.

'Now is the moment. I will rule,' said Catherine, 'or perish,' she added in a low voice. Kasia just caught the words above the loud rattle of the drum, the pounding of running feet, then the carriage stopped – and there was silence.

It was a silence which could go on and on or it could suddenly explode into violence, terror and death.

For the most part the soldiers' expressions were impassive, curious as they stared at the two women; many, seeing the richness of Kasia's dress and her regal mien, took her for the Tsar's wife whom Captain Orlov had told them was coming to ask their support.

'You can change the history of this great country of ours,' he had cried. 'The future of Russia lies in your hands!'

They had come pouring into the sunshine chattering like magpies among themselves, gathering with their officers round the big bay horse, gazing up at the hero of Zorndorf, the lover of the little Tsarina.

'What are we to do?' shouted a tall, grizzled soldier. 'Tell us now.'

'Yes,' they echoed eagerly. 'Tell us!'

Orlov held up his sword for silence and his great voice rang out.

'Make her your Empress. March with her to the Winter Palace—'

And then the little carriage came slowly on to the parade ground and the silence gripped them all. No one spoke, no one moved; the drum was silent. Grigori Orlov sat his horse like a statue. A few men moved their muskets nervously, glancing at their fellows doubtfully as if for guidance. Kasia caught the sudden swift gleam of a bayonet above the mitre caps. Faces peered out, framed in the barrack windows. Waiting to see which way the cat would jump before venturing out, Kasia thought with a quick contempt. There'll be plenty of them.

The first person to move was Catherine. At her slight nod Bibikov got out of the carriage and held the door open. Slowly and with an immense dignity she climbed down and, taking a step forward, stood quite still.

As she stood there, her bearing, a mixture of courage and defiance tinged with a certain pathos, seemed to imply – Look, my soldiers, I am but a helpless woman who casts herself on your mercy and kindness; do as you will but in God's name be quick. There was also the suggestion – Accept me and I will lead you to greatness. I can do it. Just give me a chance.

Looking at the small pointed face, so effectively pale against the black dress, held high on the slender neck, Kasia thought, not for the first time, what a superb actress she would have made. At this, the supreme test of her life, Catherine showed nothing of her true feelings to these men who faced her and who could, if they wished, destroy in a few wild minutes her dream of eighteen years.

The moment grew almost unbearable. Kasia found she was praying more desperately than ever before in her life, yet she smiled at the nearest soldier who regarded her gravely, impassively from his slightly slanting eyes but without animosity, more as he would have looked at some gorgeous bird of paradise who had suddenly wandered into his little Volga village. He had a mole on the side of his chin, she noticed. Whatever the outcome of the next few minutes she would never forget the face of this peasant turned soldier.

Sweat ran down Bibikov's face. His eyes were watchful and his hand shifted restlessly on his sword-hilt. On the seat of the little carriage Alexei sat with a pistol on his knees. Grigori

Orlov was tense in the saddle, his sword ready. But still no one moved, no one made a sound; the men seemed mesmerized by the sight of the small, slight woman standing so steadily before them.

Then, somewhere behind the barracks a cockerel crowed brokenly, and the normal, homely sound released what had been building up within them.

'It's her! It's Matushka.' The grizzled soldier pushed his way to the front and turned to face the men.

'Our Little Mother's here with us. Are we to betray her?'

And in a roar that echoed round the barrack square came the answer.

'No!'

'Well spoken, lads.' Alexei Orlov threw back his head with a great shout of laughter.

'Hurrah for our Matushka!' The cheers and cries were taken up. 'Long live the Empress! To Petersburg . . . To the city! Yes, we'll take her to be crowned . . . she shall sit on the throne of the Tsars . . . and wear the cap of Monomachus. . . .' They pushed forward, jostling and shoving to get a closer view of this woman who stood alone with the tears trickling slowly down her cheeks as she held out her hand to a soldier who had darted forward to throw himself at her feet, crying out in a strong young voice.

'Matushka, Matushka!'

'Please get up. Please.' She bent to touch his bare head.

Kasia choked with emotion as she heard Catherine speak softly. 'It's marvellous,' she whispered to herself. 'It's so marvellous.' Her feeling was one of unutterable joy and relief.

And Bibikov blinked rapidly and kept clearing his throat. But Alexei was unaffected by anything but a sense of personal triumph.

'They're with us, Grigori,' he shouted to his brother. 'By God, they're with us!' Again he laughed and this time he was joined by his brother who waved his hat above his head, half crazed with the excitement of the moment.

'Make way. Make way for Father Alexei!' the crowd parted respectfully as the regimental priest walked slowly towards

Catherine with a crucifix high in his hands. The young soldier was on his feet and standing near her with shining eyes ready to give his life for this woman who had spoken kindly to him.

'Your Majesty,' Father Alexei Mikhailov gave a bow. Then, without a word he held out the crucifix. Catherine very gently kissed the ivory Christ as a murmur of approval and respect swept through the throng like the sigh of a warm, fresh wind in a forest of young trees. Kasia crossed herself.

Assisted by the young soldier the elderly priest climbed up on to the seat and stood beside Alexei Orlov raising his arms in their wide sleeves so that to Kasia he resembled a black bat with wings spread against the blue of the sky. The jewels on the cross twinkled and flashed as he began to speak in a high, firm voice.

'Kneel, my children.' They went on their knees, their eyes fixed raptly on the figure of their beloved priest.

'In the name of God and on this cross let us all swear our eternal allegiance to Her Imperial Majesty, Catherine Alexeevna, Empress and Autocrat of All the Russias.'

But she looks far too small to bear such a title on her small sloping shoulders, Kasia thought, knowing as the thought flashed through her mind, that in fact the woman standing there was strong enough to carry the whole world.

'In the name of God and on this cross we swear—' Kasia found herself uttering the oath of allegiance drowned by the deep throated thunder of male voices.

And then, as all the heads were bowed in prayer, Catherine herself kneeling on the hard-baked earth, her face hidden in her hands and Father Alexei passionately begging God to show His favour to the new Empress and to all who assisted her, the Colonel of the Regiment arrived in a flurry of hooves.

Taking in the scene at once, Colonel Razumovsky flung himself from his horse and to his knees.

The priest's voice ceased. Slowly he got down and going to Catherine, he raised her to her feet saying quietly, 'And may God bless you, Catherine Alexeevna.'

Silently she acknowledged his blessing with a look of deep humility then she smiled with brimming eyes. 'Thank you, Father Alexei.'

With a clink of spurs Colonel Razumovsky approached, a tall, ramrod figure, his long boots white with dust.

'Forgive me, Your Majesty, for not having been here in person to welcome you to Kalinkina.' He knelt and kissed her hands. 'But I see my regiment has already done its duty.'

This time her smile was dazzling.

'Every man, Colonel.' The men were on their feet now and the cheering was breaking out anew.

'I would like to speak to them, please.' She took her place in the carriage, on her feet, where she could be seen. Gradually the noise subsided.

'Men of the Izmailovsky Regiment,' she cried in a clear voice that carried to all corners of the parade ground. 'I say at this wonderful moment, this unbelievable moment in my life that I am doing what I am, with your help, for the sake of our orthodox religion – and for the sake of my infant son – and, my soldiers, most of all, for Holy Russia.' She paused, tears shining in her eyes.

'And now, what more can I say but thank you, with all my heart. I thank each one of you for what you have done today, I—' Her voice broke and she could not continue, for she was weeping, openly and unashamedly.

And down the rough, weather-beaten cheeks of men who had lain horribly wounded without a whimper the tears ran freely.

When she had recovered her composure Catherine turned to Razumovsky and asked so that all could hear, 'Colonel Razumovsky, will you and your men come with me to Petersburg?'

His answer was swept aside by that of his men.

'Aye, we will!'

'To the Winter Palace then,' shouted Grigori Orlov, pointing with his sword towards the golden spire of the Admiralty.

'And God help anyone who gets in our way,' added his brother whipping up the horses.

So with Razumovsky and Father Alexei seated opposite Catherine and Kasia, and Grigori Orlov and Bibikov riding one on each side of the carriage, they set off, in the midst of the Izmailovsky Guardsmen, on the next stage of the venture.

The shouting and acclamations were deafening and all the two women could do was to smile at each other; now and then Kasia reached out to touch Catherine's hand. But Kasia sensed that she no longer needed encouragement, there was colour in her cheeks, a defiant sparkle in her eyes. She sat very straight and proud, flashing smiling glances to right and left, nodding her head graciously in response to her soldiers' wild enthusiasm. With some eight hundred men surrounding her Catherine set out to conquer Russia.

One regiment marches, thought Kasia with a sudden cold stab of reality, and she thinks it already over and the crown on her head.

As they approached the outskirts of the city the people gathered at the doors of their little cottages staring in amazement at the strange cavalcade. Children ran out on bare feet, adding their own shrill cries to the din, pointing at Kasia's hat, laughing all over their dirty little faces at the grand lady who smiled at them so happily; Catherine they hardly noticed

'Come with us, friends,' urged the soldiers gaily, 'we're taking our Empress to the Palace.'

After doubtful glances many of the peasants ran out to join the procession, sensing that there might be silver at the end of this day – or at least free beer and vodka.

And so, as they went along they collected more and more people and children and dogs who, catching the mood of infectious excitement, barked and leapt in the sunshine.

'Who is it? What's happening?'

As the news spread and ran ahead, carried on the swift legs of children – 'Catherine's coming! The Empress is on her way!' – large numbers of townsfolk were waiting, waving, crying, many on their knees. Pigeons flew overhead as if escorting the carriage, high above the dust clouds rising from countless feet. Grigori leant from his saddle.

'Should we not send warning to the Semenovsky and Preobrazhensky, Colonel?'

'They'll surely have heard us coming a mile off,' laughed Catherine.

'They're overrun by children already,' said Kasia.

'Nevertheless Captain Orlov is right,' said Colonel Razum-ovsky. He waved and called up a young officer who forced his horse through the press. Saluting, the lieutenant rode ahead to warn the other two regiments.

*　　*　　*

A young officer of the Izmailovsky Regiment galloped into the barracks of the Preobrazhensky Guards, calling urgently for the officers.

The guardsmen stood on parade in stolid ranks of red and green, never blinking an eye as they watched their officers hurry to the middle of the square, gathering round the excited young officer. There were few among the ranks of big, stolid men who did not know that something was afoot this fine June morning and as the voices of their officers, some raised in anger, came to them muttering broke out, travelling quickly from man to man.

'She's coming to . . . Little Catherine's on the way. . . .'

'Silence in the ranks!' The sergeants and the corporals bellowed and yelled but the spark of excitement would not be quenched.

'The time's come! This is what we've been waiting for since Elizabeth died.' Soldiers who would have stood utterly steady in a howling storm of cannon fire now began to turn their heads, to fidget and stir; even the older sergeants were all staring at the group of officers, not knowing what to do.

'Voyeikov doesn't like it,' growled Sergeant Levashov in a deep, rumbling voice. Six foot four inches in his long black gaiters and scarlet tunic, his moustache waxed to twin ramrod points set fiercely on a broad, battered face, the sergeant was a veteran of the Seven Years War. Twice wounded, he had fought in all the bloodiest engagements. When the pike wound in his side was healed he had gone to join the Imperial body-guard to the Grand Ducal household of Peter and Catherine. Now he was back with his own regiment.

'No,' he repeated in a louder voice to no one in particular. 'He doesn't like it. He's going to make trouble.'

'And Captain Vorontzov's with him,' put in another voice.

Slowly Levashov drew his long bayonet from its scabbard and with a sharp, experienced twist fixed it to his musket. All along the ranks other followed his example and no one said a word in protest. They stood silent, watchful, their eyes going from Levashov to the little group of officers; though they still stood properly at ease, the bayonets began to thrust further forward; muscles were tensed and hands gripped the muskets more tightly. Like a crouching beast poised to spring the soldiers waited.

The noise of argument among the officers grew louder and more acrimonious.

'Are we then to break our oath to the rightful Tsar?' demanded Major Voyeikov angrily. His face was red, his eyes red with rage.

'He's right,' said Captain Vorontzov. 'We are officers in the service of Tsar Peter, and no one else.' The Captain was brother to Elizabeth, Peter's misshapen mistress, and to Princess Dashkova, Catherine's friend; his uncle was Grand Chancellor. His divided loyalties were tearing him apart. So he took refuge in his first duty as a soldier: loyalty to his rightful sovereign.

'Our regiment is the oldest, the greatest in all Russia. And who founded it?' He glanced round his brother officers, many them close friends.

'Who first formed the Preobrazhensky Guards?' His tone was impassioned.

'The Great Peter,' answered half a dozen voices.

'Yes, and was he not a Romanov?' he shouted above the mounting hub-bub of discord.

'So how can we – the Little Father's personal troops – turn against him?'

There was silence at this. The officers looked at each other in some dismay until a burly lieutenant answered Vorontzov's question.

'This precious Tsar of yours is no more than a lackey to Frederick of Prussia.' He spat between his boots, glaring at Vorontzov and Voyeikov as though daring them to argue with him. But neither said anything in answer.

'Our brothers of the Izmailovsky want no more of him, why should we fight for a man who cares so little for Russia?'

'He and his damned Holsteiners,' snarled a scarred captain. 'What does he think of us who've risked our damned necks killing his Prussian friends? Nothing, I tell you – nothing. We're just Russian dirt.'

'Puts us into Prussian uniforms and won't even speak our language.'

The tone grew ugly, the words more bitter. And meanwhile the men waited, restrained by Sergeant Levashov.

'Wait, boys. Steady. We want no blood spilt today.'

Major Voyeikov had courage. Stepping from the group of officers he addressed the silent ranks.

'Men of the Preobrazhensky, listen to me. You – we – are soldiers of the Tsar and as such cannot—' He was not allowed to continue. In his best parade-ground voice Sergeant Levashov interrupted:

'Listen to *me*, boys. He's no Tsar of ours.' Some of the men looked startled at this near blasphemy but a dull rumble of approval told Levashov and Voyeikov that there was precious little sympathy for Peter the Third among his own personal troops.

'I say we march to join Catherine – our new Empress – and to Hell with anyone who stands in our way.'

'He's right. Levashov's right.'

'To the palace with Catherine.' Men began to move eagerly from the ranks.

'Stand firm!' the sergeant's voice thundered. 'You're soldiers, not a crowd of bloody moujiks!' Sheepishly they resumed their positions. He turned to Major Voyeikov and said, almost apologetically, for he liked the officer, 'You see how it is, sir. We won't follow Prussian Peter any more, whatever you or anyone else says.'

Voyeikov flushed with anger. 'You'll lose your head for this day's work, Levashov.' His voice trembled.

Captain Vorontzov came forward to stand by his side.

'They'll protect Peter on their own, with their little swords,' called out an anonymous voice from the rear ranks. A man laughed and the laughter spread, derisive, mocking, but lacking anger.

The other officers did not laugh but with glances of mute

sympathy towards their two comrades they moved to take up their positions in front of the men, drawing their swords. A loud cheer went up, followed by an interested silence as the regiment watched to see what would happen now.

With tears of rage and humiliation in their eyes the two officers snatched at their swords and the rap of the steel was loud and vicious. At the sound bayonets jerked threateningly.

'Steady,' came Levashov's voice. 'No man's to move!'

'Men, I implore you—' But once again Voyeikov's final appeal was drowned in a spate of cat-calls and whistles.

With a gesture of helpless fury he took the sword in both hands and snapped it across his knee, flinging down the pieces; Vorontzov did the same. The snap of his breaking blade cut the silence like a whip-crack. With head held high the two officers, defeated but not disgraced, turned and strode from the parade ground.

'Why are we waiting? Lead us to join Catherine!'

Sergeant Levashov hesitated, looking to the scarred captain who nodded.

Orders rang out, a fine white dust rose from the pipe-clayed equipment and then, with drums beating, the sunlight twinkling from the bright metal gorgets hanging at their necks, the men of the Preobrazhensky Guards marched out to meet their Empress.

*　　*　　*

At the Semenovsky barracks the officers and men, watched by hundreds of expectant eyes and with dogs running among the kneeling soldiers, swore allegiance to their Empress on Father Alexei's crucifix.

Then amid scenes of mounting excitement the procession, even more disorderly, moved on and came eventually to the broad Nevsky Prospekt. Every window was filled with craning heads; from every doorway people ran to see the woman who, like the Empress Elizabeth before her, was rising with her Guards to claim the throne of the Tsars.

'It's forty-one all over again,' was heard on every side.

'She's beautiful,' said those who mistook Kasia for the Empress.

'That's not Catherine, dolt. She's the small one, the one in black.'

'What, going to her funeral, is she?' But few laughed at that kind of remark and the man, a cynical young clerk with ink on his fingers and fire in his diseased lungs, was fortunate to get away with no more than a shower of oaths.

'What does it matter to us who sits on the throne?' He was a brave young man and his hatred of Emperors and nobles twisted his heart so that he did not care what he said.

'Would you rather have Peter then?' snarled a man with one leg. 'I lost this,' he tapped his clumsy wooden leg, 'at Kunersdorf. A bloody Prussian ball took it – phft! – just like that. And now Peter makes the bastards into allies. What d'you want me to do, dance a jig? He spat angrily. 'No, my friend, let little Catherine take the crown and then perhaps we'll be treated as Russians again.'

'Oh yes,' said the clerk with a bitter smile, 'oh yes, we'll be treated as Russians all right – that I can promise you.' Coughing violently he turned and pushed his way into the crowd, away from the procession.

'Bah, that sort of whiner should be put down.' The ex-soldier turned his attention to the excitement, cocking his head in the direction of a new sound insistent and regular above the din.

'Drums,' he said, sniffing the air like an old war-horse.

'What can it mean?' Fear showed on the faces of those round him. 'Is the Tsar coming?' They stood on tiptoe striving to see over the seething, bobbing heads.

'Can you see? Can no one see?'

'Is it Peter himself?'

'God help us if they fight here.'

The crowd pressed along the fronts of the houses swaying this way and that in their agitation. The carriage had stopped in front of them and they could see Catherine gazing anxiously ahead along the Prospekt towards the Kazan Cathedral as the rattle and thunder of the drums grew louder. Gradually the shouting faded and the drums echoed and crashed among the buildings; people began to move towards the safety of their own doorways; the street was no place to be with musket balls flying.

Then the ex-soldier, who was a big man, called out, 'Don't worry, friends! It's the Preobrazhensky!'

'The Preobrazhensky!' The cry was taken up.

Until they drew close to the mass of people blocking the Prospekt the men marched as a machine, arms swinging rhythmically, every pace exactly equal, every bayonet at the very same angle. Big men, proud men, they marched as if they owned the whole city – which indeed at that moment they did. But as soon as they recognized Catherine waiting for them even their magnificent discipline cracked and with a swelling shout of enthusiasm the leading files broke ranks and, shoving the drummers aside, rushed forward calling her name and uttering noisy apologies and excuses as to why they were so tardy in joining her.

Catherine thanked them and held out her hand for their joyful but respectful kisses. A face she knew well appeared, half a head above the others.

'Well Levashov, this is a great day for us all.'

'Your Majesty – Your Majesty—' was all he could say.

'Stay beside the carriage,' she ordered kindly. With moustaches quivering with pride the huge sergeant walked beside the coach, his large hand gripping the door possessively as the cortège made its slow, triumphal way towards the Kazan Cathedral.

*   *   *

The heat in the great cathedral was overpowering and many women in the close-packed body of the church fainted or dizzily leant against those round them for support.

Twice Kasia felt her senses reeling from the hot stench of candle grease, incense and the rank smell of dirty, overheated bodies. She knelt a few feet from Catherine and wondered again at the amazing reserves of strength hidden in that small frame. For they had been on the road for some three hours without food and drink and under a strain which for Catherine must have been well-nigh unendurable. And yet she knelt there dead still, back straight, head bowed, listening to the golden-garbed priests as they intoned the blessing on her as 'the Autocrat, Catherine the Second'.

'. . . and on the heir to the throne, Tsarevitch Paul Petrovich.'

Kasia caught Grigori's eye and saw mirrored the same relief that filled her own heart. Thank Heaven, so far no one had mentioned Catherine's son as anything but the heir to the throne. The Church had made no attempt to interfere with the *coup*. And what the Church agreed to, so would the people – anyway until Catherine was safely on the throne. But Peter? What would Peter do? Kasia's thoughts flew beyond the stifling cathedral, hardly taking in the high chanting of the priests and patriarchs, the swelling triumph of the *Te Deum* rising into the vast painted dome. The flames of the candles in the massive gilded candelabrum high above the bowed heads shivered and swayed to the mighty sound of the singing.

As they knelt on the hard marble and sang their thanks to God, what were Peter's plans? Did he already know his days as Tsar were numbered? Had someone slipped from the city to ride hell-bent for Oranienbaum where Peter had gone with his mistress and his Holsteiner and Prussian cronies?

Kasia's knees were sore; she wanted to get out and to the Winter Palace. There were plans to be made, measures to be taken in case the Tsar marched on the city with the troops assembled for the coming war with Denmark. It was too soon for this sort of celebration, she thought with a swift flash of anger. Never celebrate, not until the bird was safely cooking in the pot, until the wild pig was hanging head down ready for the knife; life with the Cossacks had taught her that.

These crazy Russians crying and cheering and dancing round like clowns at a fair when the whole desperate business wasn't even half begun. She felt a wave of contemptuous pity for these people who could lose Catherine the crown before it was even on her head. Henryk would feel exactly as she did. With the familiar pain, a dry, empty ache, she longed to turn her head and see him kneeling beside her, to see the fond love in his grey eyes and feel the comfort of his hand on hers. Perhaps with Figgy on the throne – Kasia prayed then: for Henryk to be alive.

People round her were getting to their feet, making way for

Catherine as she went out into the sunshine, into the storm of cheering.

Household cavalry were now drawn up on each side of the carriage; the Guards Regiments had formed up in front and behind. All was orderly and disciplined again.

For a moment Catherine stood on the steps regarding the brilliant scene, waving to the people, then re-entered the carriage. At a walking pace, preceded by priests sweating within their heavy embroidered vestments, among them Father Alexei, like his Empress plain and simple in black, the procession, by now a true Imperial cortège, came to the vast square before the green and white palace on the banks of the Neva.

At the arched entrance Catherine got down for the last time from the faithful little carriage, dusty and travel-stained, aching in every limb, but not feeling the pain. All stood aside; priests, Guards, officers, the bear-like Levashov and after one last wave to the crowds surging across the square, Catherine, followed by Countess Radienska, the two brothers Orlov and Colonel Razumovsky, entered her palace as Empress.

*   *   *

Peter the Third, uncrowned Tsar of All the Russias was in a happy carefree mood on the morning of the twenty-eighth as he prepared to set out for Peterhof where he was to join his wife to celebrate with her his name-day.

The morning was very warm but cooled just sufficiently by a slight breeze from the sea; the sun shone brilliantly on the blue coats of the Holsteiners drawn up for inspection and Peter hurried along the ranks, walking so fast that the string of equerries, ADCs and the like had to trot briskly to keep up with their royal master. Pronouncing himself delighted with the men's turnout Peter rubbed his hands, grinning broadly.

'With such soldiers we should have no trouble in giving the Danes a good drubbing, eh, Münnich?' He poked the field marshal hard in his uniform waistcoat.

'The Danes should not be under-rated, Your Majesty,' answered the old soldier stiffly. In company with most of the

Russian army Count Münnich viewed this coming expedition against Denmark with the deepest suspicion and disfavour. Why, was asked on every side, should Russians be killed simply to regain Schleswig – and who had ever heard of the damned place anyway – for his ridiculous little duchy of Holstein?

'Stuff and nonsense.' The Emperor snorted. 'You talk like an old woman.' Laughter rose from Peter's toadies.

'And speaking of women, we should be off. We must not keep my sweet wife waiting, must we gentlemen?' Peter winked at his favourite of the moment, Baron Goltz, the Prussian ambassador. More laughter. In great good humour and calling for 'my Romanovna' as he named Countess Vorontzova, his extremely ugly mistress, he went off towards the waiting horses and carriages, whistling loudly.

Within two hours the cavalcade swept past the gates of Peterhof and down to the little palace of Monplaisir. Peter dismounted, stretched and yawned and called in his high voice:

'Catherine. We're here.' No one answered; only the white fantails rose in a cloud from the roof and vanished among the trees. Nothing else moved except the leaves and flowers in the little breeze. The sound of the countless cascades and fountains was very clear as Peter strode into the house, his long face darkened with anger.

'Catherine! Where are you?' He hurried from room to room gripped by a growing anxiety. Damnation, where the hell was she? Where was everyone? No ladies-in-waiting, no servants. He even reached the kitchen, a place he had never seen before. The big table showed signs of hasty departure; a large bowl lay in pieces on the floor; a carving knife was stuck in the wood, under the big ovens the fire smouldered half dead. With a loud oath the Tsar went back to the little hall where some of his suite were gathered, others jammed in the doorway, craning to see what was going on.

'Don't just stand there like a pack of stuffed dummies,' he snapped irritably, his pale blue eyes popping, which they did at moments of stress. 'Search. Search the house, the grounds, they must be *somewhere* – some of you go up there,' he jabbed a long forefinger at the palace.

'They must be somewhere,' he repeated, then his face

brightened. 'I know,' he chortled. 'She's hiding with them all. It's a joke for my name-day. Oh, this is fun.' He rubbed his hands together. 'Spread out all of you and the first to find her shall have a bottle of burgundy all to himself.'

So Vorontzov, Chancellor of Russia, field marshals and Princes were soon creeping about among the trees and shrubs playing at hide-and-seek, some of them hoping to surprise Her Majesty with her ladies and stifling her giggles.

Meanwhile Peter and Baron Goltz searched every corner of Monplaisir, the Tsar poking his long nose into cupboards, dressers, under the beds, even opening drawers as though, Goltz thought sourly, he imagined that Catherine and her entourage had been turned into midgets. Goltz was not only very hot but frightened as well for he had a good idea of what had happened. My God, the signs had been there for all to see for the last few months.

He sat in the small, panelled dining-room.

'Have you looked in the cellar, Goltz?' He heard Peter's high-pitched voice. Could it really be that he had no inkling? He had refused to listen to advice. 'Rumours,' he had said, 'nothing but silly rumours. Catherine would never dare to raise a finger against me. I know that.' Well now the rumours were proved and God knows what was to happen in the next few days, hours even. At that moment Goltz began to think of two things: the first was his own future and, more immediate, how to tell Peter that almost certainly his wife had gone to Petersburg to usurp his throne and seize power as the Empress Catherine the Second. And she was no friend of Prussia. This he knew as surely as night follows day while he listened to Peter, by now in all probability no more than a minor princeling of Holstein, hallooing through the rooms.

Prince Trubetskoi came in, removed his wig.

'I'm too old for such capers,' he grumbled, sinking into a chair.

'By heavens, but he's a child sometimes.' Goltz stood at the open window staring out across the blue Gulf towards the island of Kronstadt, hazy in the afternoon heat.

'How to tell him,' he said without turning round. 'That's the question.'

'Tell him what?' Trubetskoi mopped his shaven head.

'You know as well as I do,' said Goltz in a tight voice. 'We both know where she's gone *and* what she's doing. Vorontzov knows, Münnich knows. They all know. The whole damned country knows – all except him.'

'Yes,' Trubetskoi agreed equably, replacing his wig, slightly crooked. 'Even at this moment she is taking over Petersburg – probably sentencing us all to Siberia, or death.' The old Prince did not seem particularly worried. After all, had he not gone through all this before, with the late Empress Elizabeth?

'But what do we do?' Goltz whirled round.

'It's not what we do. It's what *he* does.' Trubetskoi rose to his feet as Peter came bouncing in.

'Well, any luck?' His expression changed as he saw their faces. 'What's the matter with you two? You look as if you'd just met your own ghosts.' The two men glanced quickly at each other then, with a little shrug, Prince Trubetskoi began to speak, slowly and clearly as if to a child.

'Your Majesty, it grieves me deeply to be the one chosen by Fate to speak to his Tsar in this manner but—'

'Get on with it.' Peter's flat sloping forehead creased in a frown. Trubetskoi's mouth tightened but he continued calmly enough.

'Very well, Sire. Her Majesty, your wife has gone to Petersburg.' There was silence, disturbed by the gentle hiss of the tide on the pebbles of the beach.

'To Petersburg? But this is my name-day; she was supposed to meet me here, we were going to celebrate.' His mouth had fallen open, the heavy lower lip quivering. 'Why should she go to Petersburg?'

'Oh, Your Majesty, can you not see?' Goltz burst out.

And at that moment Peter understood. His face went ashen, his eyes bulged alarmingly, sweat broke on his skin. His lips moved but no sound came. He doesn't look like an Emperor, thought Trubetskoi, he looks more like a pockmarked cod. But he felt a pang of compassionate pity and pushed forward a chair. Peter slumped into it and began to chew his nails still saying nothing but shaking his head so that Goltz thought the shock had finally unhinged his already unstable mind.

'Get Vorontzov, Shuvalov and Münnich,' whispered Trubetskoi. 'Bring them here quickly. No one else.'

'Romanovna,' said Peter in a strangled voice. 'I want Romanovna.'

Trubetskoi nodded. Goltz went out.

'What am I to do?' Peter moaned. 'Oh my God, what am I to do?'

Prince Trubetskoi poured wine, put the glass into Peter's shaking hand, and said nothing for, when you really thought about it, what was there *to* say?

*   *   *

But Münnich had other ideas. With all the vehemence at his command he urged that Peter ride to Petersburg and regain the loyalty of his Guards.

'Now, Your Majesty, now this very moment. Every second you delay will make the task more difficult.' Impossible, thought Trubetskoi, not difficult. Yet he could see that Peter's courage was stirring under the soldier's words; the field marshal was putting backbone into the Tsar. He had stopped biting his nails and colour had returned to his cheeks, brought there perhaps by the wine he had drunk.

'Remind them of their oath to you as their lawful and rightful sovereign,' said Münnich. 'Remind them that you are great-nephew to the first Peter, that you are a Romanov.'

Peter's dull eyes brightened as hope was kindled in his heart.

'You're right, Münnich. We'll ride at once. Don't you agree, my dear?' His gaze rested on his mistress.

'You shouldn't go alone,' she said speaking thickly through a heavy summer cold. 'If you go to Petersburg then it should be with soldiers at your back.' At her words the look of irresolution returned to Peter's eyes. Trubetskoi, watching them, wondered for the hundredth time how two such unattractive creatures could love each other; how they could bear to touch each other, he thought with a fastidious little shudder.

Her eyes were like wet brown marbles set in her dark olive skin also badly marked by the pox, daubed with twin patches of bright rouge. There was a rounded, hunch-backed look to her squat body. An attraction of similarities, he supposed drily. And yet, was there not something a little sad, a little touching about such a relationship?

'Cards,' suddenly cried Peter. 'A pack of cards.'

Oh, God, thought the Prince, he's going to decide his fate, our fates, on the turn of a card. No one spoke until Vorontzova placed the cards in front of the Emperor.

Slowly and with infinite care he began to build a house. Goltz cleared his throat. 'Countess Vorontzova speaks wisely, Sire. We should march with the troops assembled at Narva.'

Peter placed another card, an expression of intense concentration on his long, horse face.

'And you, Chancellor, what are your views?'

Chancellor Vorontzov drummed lightly with his fingers on the oaken table. His was a tricky position. In his own mind there was little doubt that Catherine was firmly in control of the capital. She would be difficult to dislodge. He did not like Peter but he was his Tsar and should Peter's head fall it would not be the only one.

'Well?' said Peter impatiently, pouring himself more wine.

Vorontzov gazed round at the pictures brought here by the first Peter from England and Holland, glowing softly in the dark panels, as if seeking inspiration. His eyes settled on a small painting of warships becalmed and he made up his mind.

'Kronstadt, Your Majesty. That is the key.'

The Fleet lay at Kronstadt as well as a considerable military garrison.

'Win the navy and you have won the day,' went on the Chancellor. Trubetskoi could see the distant island framed in the open windows. What was happening in the fortress? Had Catherine's couriers already reached the sailors? Were they even at this moment weighing anchor and loading the guns?

'With the city under the guns of the fleet the people will turn to you, Sire,' said Goltz, throwing in his lot with Vorontzov.

'We've got the troops,' argued Münnich. 'What do we want with ships?'

'There's another alternative,' said Field Marshal Count

Alexander Shuvalov, speaking for the first-time. They all stared at him except for Peter who seemed utterly engrossed in his growing card-house.

'Your Majesty could accept the inevitable and return to Holstein.' There was a moment of stunned silence followed by a general outcry.

'You'd have the Emperor creep away like a whipped cur,' shouted Goltz, now on his feet.

'Shame,' cried Vorontzova. 'What a terrible suggestion.' She flapped her large red hands in agitation.

The Chancellor regarded his niece with distaste. A fine kettle of fish: on top of everything else, one niece here with Peter, the other steeped in treason.

But Shuvalov, he thought with admiration, a cunning fellow, running with the wolf, hunting with the hounds. Get rid of Peter without bloodshed, go to Catherine with clean hands –
'Look, Your Majesty, it was I who solved the problem.'

'Great heavens, man,' Münnich was purple in the face. 'You call yourself a soldier and yet – and—' Words failed him.

'It could be a solution,' Shuvalov answered calmly.

'Not one I'll have any part in,' snarled Goltz. 'I'd rather die, sword in hand than—'

'Does anyone have to die?' Shuvalov asked quietly.

'No, no, this must not be.' Vorontzova blew her blocked nose, trembling with indignation. 'Your Majesty, you cannot, you *must* not. You must stay and fight.'

Everyone else seemed to have forgotten Peter. His house was now five storeys high. Ideas and counter-ideas flew about the little room. Trubetskoi stood by the window breathing in the summer air, the scent of the limes and the fresh smell of the sea. He wished, how very much he wished, to be walking alone on the beach, far from all this human turmoil. Behind him the room echoed to the various arguments.

Suddenly there came a blow as Münnich struck the table, a stricken silence and then a shrill cry:

'Oh, you clumsy fool, it's fallen down!' Peter sat staring at the wreck of his house. The cards lay scattered on the table, flat and useless. And Prince Trubetskoi, turning from the window, and seeing Peter's hands wandering blindly among the cards, thought with a nasty little twinge, this surely is an omen. They all looked at the destruction of his building and saw disaster in the scattered cards. All of them, expecting an uncontrolled outburst were surprised at Peter's next reaction.

'Very well then, we will go to Kronstadt. I've decided. I shall call upon the sailors to take the Fleet to Petersburg. If necessary I shall order them to fire on the Winter Palace.' It amazed them to hear him speak in so firm a voice; at that moment there was no doubt who was in command.

Peter rose from the table and joined Trubetskoi by the window. The others, stunned to silence, watched his narrow back. A dove called in the garden and another answered from further away; a bee zoomed past the window.

'You, Münnich, will arrange for vessels. See to it at once!'

'But—' began the field marshal doubtfully.

'At once, I said.'

Trubetskoi listened wonderingly. He had never heard Peter speak like this, with such authority. Perhaps, he thought a shade uneasily, perhaps the Tsar would succeed in rising to the occasion.

'Sire?' said Vorontzov.

The Chancellor, like the Prince, was puzzled by this unexpected show of decision and courage. He must love this fat, ugly woman, he must really love her.

'I have an idea for Your Majesty's approval,' he went on. 'It is that Prince Trubetskoi, Count Shuvalov and myself should go immediately to Petersburg.'

'What on earth for?' Peter demanded.

'So that we may speak to Her Majesty and—'

'She's not Her Majesty,' said Peter very loudly. 'She's a woman who has committed treason, that's all she is. How *dare* she? How dare she?' He thumped the window-sill. 'And yet, didn't I once say she was capable of anything?'

'Exactly, Sire,' put in Vorontzov suavely. 'If you will allow me to use my undoubted – ah – influence to persuade her – ah – your royal wife to give up her present unlawful course of action I feel that perhaps I – ah – we, may have a chance of improving this tragic situation before it has gone too far for—'

'Do whatever you like,' said Peter indifferently.

So he's losing interest again, Trubetskoi thought. His brief seizing of the reins was no more than a flash in the pan.

'Kill her if you want to.' There was a horrified gasp from Countess Vorontzova.

'No, oh no, not that.'

'If you have to,' said Peter coldly. 'I'll never forgive her, never.'

Vorontzov watched him from narrowed eyes. Kill her, he says, and let us be torn apart by the Guards. That remark would reach Catherine somehow. God in Heaven, what a cretin. And were they all to be tarred with the same ugly brush?

'I hardly think that such a – ah – such an extreme measure will be necessary,' he said. Peter did not answer but simply shrugged his shoulders and turned to his mistress.

'I'm hungry. See that dinner is served.' Obediently she went from the room, wondering hopelessly how to manage without cooks or servants.

The Chancellor signalled to his two companions, nodding towards the door.

'You have no message for your wife?' asked Prince Trubetskoi, making one more effort.

Peter again did not answer. The three men bowed and withdrew leaving the Tsar alone with Baron Goltz.

'They go on a difficult mission,' said Goltz when the silence had become too tense.

'My dear Goltz, you're a bigger fool than I took you for if you expect to see any of those three again. My sweet, dutiful wife will twist them round her little finger. Besides,' he added with a sudden terrible bitter sadness, 'they already know where their new duty lies.' He gazed at the sea, watching a small coasting vessel struggling up-river slowly against the breeze.

'And you, Goltz,' he inquired softly. 'Where does your duty lie?'

'All is not yet lost,' said the ambassador diplomatically.

'God help your poor country if *she* gains power.' With that Peter slumped on to a chair and began drumming on the table.

'Shall I call the others?' Goltz asked. 'We should be ready I think, for when the boats arrive.'

'Boats?'

'Kronstadt, Your Majesty,' reminded the Prussian patiently.

'Oh. Yes, of course,' said Peter vaguely.

'I should warn them.' Goltz moved towards the door.

'If you like. On the way see what's happened to my dinner. I'm damned hungry. And tell someone to bring some wine.'

Baron Goltz left his Emperor staring morosely at the panelled walls of this little room built by his great uncle, the giant Peter who had been a real man, a real Tsar.

Outside, the ambassador found the rest of the entourage gathered in a silent, sombre group. They had ceased their merry game of hide-and-seek among the summer flowers and Goltz could see from their faces that they knew why Catherine was not hiding with her ladies in the lovely, shaded garden of Monplaisir.

*　　*　　*

As they made their way along the coast to where the boats awaited them there were some among Peter's retinue who thought secretly, well, if the worst occurs then we can at least use these boats for escape. Whether Peter himself had any such idea no one could tell. He had, with the assistance of much wine, regained his good spirits and with them his courage, for he joked and laughed with 'Romanovna' and her attendant ladies, almost as though, Field Marshal Münnich thought sourly, they were off to a merry rustic picnic.

'Cheer up, Münnich. It's a lovely day for sailing.' Peter's loud, neighing laugh was echoed by the others, but their gaiety was forced and hollow. For all they knew every pace taken by their horses, every turn of the wheels took them closer to Siberia – or the scaffold.

'There are the boats! I see them!' a voice called excitedly.

A galley lay alongside the little wooden jetty; beyond her, further off shore a small sloop rode at anchor. On the other side of the jetty men were at work unloading what looked like stores under the command of a young lieutenant of the Preobrazhensky. Shading his eyes against the afternoon glare he peered at the approaching cavalcade. Beside him a soldier with keener sight suddenly exclaimed,

'Jesus be praised, it's the Tsar himself!'

Replacing his wig and hat and straightening his tunic the officer hurried forward.

'You,' shouted Münnich in a hectoring tone. 'What are you doing with that barge?'

'Fireworks,' said the flustered young man sweeping off his hat to Peter, who repeated,

'Fireworks?'

'Yes, Your Majesty. For delivery to the Palace of Peterhof.'

'Someone, it appears, is proposing to celebrate something,' muttered Goltz.

'On whose orders?' snapped Münnich.

'I – I don't know,' stammered the officer. 'I was simply told to bring them to Peterhof.' He knew perfectly well for had he not seen with his own eyes, heard with his own ears, the delirious proclamation of Empress Catherine? But as he very much wanted to live to enjoy the glorious new reign, he strove desperately to keep cool.

'What time did you leave the city?' asked Peter not unkindly. The sweat stood out on his flushed face, making tiny pools in the pock marked skin.

'Nine this morning, Your Majesty.'

'And did you notice anything unusual happening?' The officer hesitated.

'Well, did you?' Münnich thundered. 'His Majesty's waiting.'

Upon his answer the young man's life depended, or so he felt, looking round the faces above him, hard, curious or simply blank. His brain worked frantically. Honesty, it said, honesty is your best hope.

'Forgive me, Your Majesty, but –I—'

For no apparent reason Peter burst into uncontrolled laughter. When the paroxysm was exhausted and the Tsar, with an airy wave of his hand, had encouraged the young man to continue, he went on hesitantly:

'Your Majesty, at nine o'clock, the Guards – my own regiment – were acclaiming the Grand Duchess Catherine—' Seeing Peter's livid face, he stopped, aghast at what he had said.

'So it's true,' whispered the Emperor in a stricken voice. At last here was the proof his mind had been trying desperately to reject. Now he really knew. He heard Münnich's low voice beside him, felt the field marshal's hand on his bridle.

'Sire, I must speak privately.'

They rode a short distance away.

'We must block the road to Petersburg. That is imperative. Your Majesty's Holsteiners—'

'How dare she?' asked Peter listlessly.

Münnich brushed aside the remark.

'Someone should be sent at once to Kronstadt with orders to Nummers, the commandant, to dispatch at least three thousand men to Peterhof. I suggest Colonel Neelov.'

For a moment Peter visualized himself riding in triumph at the head of three thousand men and Catherine prostrate at his feet pleading for mercy. His eyes gleamed.

'Yes, yes, Münnich, you're right. He shall go at once.'

So Colonel Neelov set off for Kronstadt in the sloop while the rest sought what shade they could find where, hot and dusty, they bickered or dozed as the sun rode high and merciless in the cloudless sky.

Peter fell asleep in a coach, his head on Elizabeth Vorontzova's ample shoulder, snoring with his mouth open, an empty bottle across his lap, dead to the cruel world.

His Holstein guards barred the way from Petersburg gazing down the white, empty road, cursing the heat and the flies; it was too bloody hot for fighting and besides, they knew only too well what manner of men they would have to face if the Guards appeared through the haze.

The young lieutenant, forgotten by all, continued his task of unloading the fireworks, wondering in a daze in whose honour they would blaze and burst, pretending not to notice the whispering and muttering among his men.

Slowly the afternoon dragged past and turned to evening as the sun hung low above the fortress of Kronstadt.

*　　*　　*

A courier from the Emperor, sir. A Colonel Neelov. He says he must see you on a matter of the utmost urgency.'

Admiral Nummers groaned. It was close on eight at night; he had spent a hot and exhausting day of inspections and was looking forward to a peaceful evening, followed by an early bed.

'Oh, very well, show him in.'

The Admiral sighed and prepared to greet the Tsar's emissary.

'Great God,' was all he could say when Neelov had finished. 'Great God in heaven.'

'You mean you had no idea, Admiral?'

'Not an inkling.'

The day that was coming to an end had been like a hundred others at the great naval and military base; until this staggering moment not a word, not a whisper of what was afoot had reached the fortress.

'Three thousand men you say, and at once. How in hell's name do you arrange for three thousand soldiers *and* their equipment to get to Peterhof at once – just like that?'

Nummers paced the room, frowning deeply. Inwardly he wasn't certain he wanted to save Peter. Russia needed a leader like Catherine, and yet, his oath bound him. He wrestled with the problem while Neelov, guessing what was going through his mind, watched him with interest tinged with anxiety.

'The answer lies here,' he murmured respectfully. 'Kronstadt holds the key.'

'You mean, the man who commands at Kronstadt holds the key,' growled Nummers. He halted and swung round, his face a picture of racking indecision.

'I'd rather be facing the whole damned British Navy than be where I am at this moment.'

'I'm sure you would, Admiral,' said Neelov with real sincerity, adding: 'You have my deepest sympathy.'

'Sympathy,' exploded Nummers. 'It's not sympathy I want, man, it's advice.'

But, before the Colonel could open his mouth the door opened and the officer on duty announced two new arrivals.

'General Devier, sir, and Prince Baryatinsky.'

Without wasting any time on formal greeting the Prince hurried forward.

'You know everything, Admiral?'

'Everything,' Nummers said.

'Have the men been dispatched yet?'

'I may be in command here but I'm not God. I cannot perform miracles. Three thousand men you must understand—'

'Yes, yes,' interrupted Devier with obvious relief.

'I appreciate that, so you'll be delighted to know that Colonel Neelov's orders are countermanded.'

'Countermanded?' demanded Neelov. 'By whom, may I ask?'

'Field Marshal Münnich, acting on behalf of His Majesty, the Emperor.'

'May I inquire whether either of you gentlemen carry anything in writing countermanding my orders?' Neelov asked. At such a time it did not seem wise to take anyone simply at their word, even Emperors.

In reply General Devier handed him a scrawled note. He read the order slowly then gave it to Nummers.

'The troops are now to remain at Kronstadt. You will be prepared to hold the fortress under your command loyal in the name of his Imperial Majesty, the Autocrat, Peter the Third. Signed this twenty-eighth day of June, 1762. Münnich, Field Marshal.'

'Well,' said Nummers, looking round at the others. 'This puts a different complexion on the whole affair.' He was beginning to see things more clearly: three thousand men under his hand put him in a stronger position to face the future, very much stronger. From being a relatively undistinguished admiral destined to drag out the remainder of his career on an island he had suddenly become at that moment the man with the destiny of Russia in his hands. He smiled.

'My ships can be ready for sea within six hours,' he said quietly, conscious of his own power. 'And the troops of the fortress,' he paused, 'I give you my word they can be relied upon to withstand an attack – from whatever quarter it may come,' he added blandly. No one spoke. Through the narrow window they heard the sounds of sentries being changed; when the tramp of feet had faded below, Baryatinsky said,

'As there's no time to be lost, I suggest that either General Devier or myself return at once to Peterhof and inform His Majesty that Kronstadt, through the influence of its commander, will remain loyal to the Romanovs.'

'Yes,' replied Nummers, 'I agree with the suggestion that you return to His Majesty.'

'And I can assure him that he has your loyalty?'

The Admiral nodded. When he answered it was very deliberately. 'At this moment, yes. The Tsar has my loyalty.'

Baryatinsky took his leave. From a window the sailor and the two soldiers watched the boat conveying the courtier back to their Emperor as it danced over the water, the shadow of the sail running ahead of it, darkly across the little silver ripples.

'And now gentlemen, all we can do is wait for news or instructions from Petersburg,' said Nummers calmly.

They did not have long to wait. Within half an hour after Baryatinsky's departure the arrival was announced of Admiral Talyzin.

'In the name of Her Imperial Majesty, Empress Catherine the Second, I have come to assume command of the fortress of Kronstadt.'

That was what he said as he came in. He held out a piece of paper. Nummers read aloud: ' "Admiral Talyzin has been vested by us with full power in Kronstadt, and what he orders must be carried out. Catherine, June 28th day of the year 1762." '

There was silence disturbed only by the sound of banging and hammering from the shipyard.

'And this is written in her own hand?' General Devier asked slowly.

'Yes.'

Another silence was broken by Nummers who remarked drily, 'I am being bombarded by paper today. And it's all very much more dangerous than cannon-balls.'

'Are you alone?' General Devier asked.

'If you mean, have I come with half a dozen ships of the line or with an army at my back—' He smiled. 'No, I am alone.'

'You're a brave man, Talyzin,' said Nummers.

'Hell's teeth, what a position to be in,' exclaimed Colonel

Neelov, drawing his sword a short way from the scabbard and slamming it back.

'What in the name of God are we going to do?' General Devier demanded.

'That, gentlemen, is what we have to decide very quickly indeed.' Admiral Nummers indicated the table and chairs. 'Please be seated and I'll tell you what I think.'

* * *

It was just after midnight when the galley carrying Peter and his immediate companions approached the outer harbour of Kronstadt. Standing in the bows he could see the fortifications dark against the pale golden glow of the northern summer night; the masts and rigging of the ships – *his* ships – rose black and menacing, and seeing them, his spirits lifted slightly. Catherine could never stand against these ships.

His head ached cruelly and there was a foul taste in his mouth, left by the effects of the wine; rubbing a hand along his chin he scraped the bristles. For a brief instant he felt a real soldier, a true campaigner engaged in a desperate venture; he straightened his shoulders and cried in a ringing voice,

'We are here! Now let us see who is the rightful ruler!' He was lightheaded from the strain of the last ten hours. The wind blew cool on his cheek and little wavelets slapped against the side of the vessel as she rose and fell to the small, choppy seas.

From somewhere came the disgusting sound of someone being sick. Poor Romanovna, he thought dispassionately, she'd be seasick on a lily pond.

With a squeak of block and harsh flapping of canvas the mainsail came down, the long oars remained clear of the water and the way of the boat fell off rapidly.

'Let go the anchor!'

There was a heavy splash. Peter whirled round.

'Why are we stopping?'

'The boom, Your Majesty. The boom is closed,' explained the captain apologetically.

Peering ahead Peter made out the black shapes of the caissons low in the water, joined by heavy chains.

'Well, tell them to remove it.'

'Ahoy there!' called the captain. No answer came, only the slap-slap of the sea.

Field Marshal Münnich joined Peter in the bows and cupping his hands round his mouth he shouted, 'Open the boom for His Majesty the Tsar!'

Again no answer, but a boat moved slowly out from the shore, creeping like a black beetle along the inside of the boom.

'Lower a boat,' Peter commanded. 'I'll make these idle louts open up for me.'

'Are we going ashore? Oh, please God, take me off this terrible boat.' Countess Vorontzova's plaintive plea was weak and shaky. No one paid any attention to her.

The long-boat dropped with a rush into the water.

'No, Münnich. I shall go myself.'

His courtiers lined the rail, chattering and wondering, as the boat, with Peter in the stern-sheets, pulled away and headed for the boom.

*   *   *

In command of the other boat Midshipman Skavronsky gripped his drawn dirk and kept up his ebbing courage by remembering his orders. Heavy guns, he knew, were trained over him, covering the boom; that knowledge should have encouraged him but he had the nasty feeling that one midshipman and his boat's crew were probably expendable, for cannon balls were notoriously impartial.

He heard the shouts from the vessel at anchor beyond the boom.

'Rest on your oars,' he ordered in a loud whisper. 'No man's to make a sound.' He felt the sweat trickling down his flanks and hoped the sailors did not notice his shaking knees. They waited, leaning on their oars, pistols and cutlasses on the thwarts beside them, and watched without expression as the other boat drew closer. He could see the solitary figure in the stern and wondered who it might be, with whom he would have to deal. Well, whoever it was he had his orders.

The strange boat reached the boom and a sailor grappled the chains with a boat-hook.

'Who is there?' Skavronsky's voice was barely broken for he was only fifteen. 'From what ship?'

'The Tsar,' came the answer.

The boy's heart gave a huge leap; his men stirred uneasily; the coxswain swore under his breath.

'Open the boom!' It was light enough for Midshipman Skavronsky to see that it was indeed the Emperor who gave the order. He swallowed violently.

'I cannot.' His answer came out as a sort of strangled squeak.

'It is your Tsar who orders you. Open, I say!'

Again the boy said, 'I cannot.'

His men took hold of their weapons. Only the Lord could know how such a situation would end. None of them were thinking of Russia's future; they were thinking of the guns of the fortress and praying the gunners would not be such crazy fools as to open fire before they could get out of the way.

'For the last time, I command you. Open!'

And then came the words that so shocked Peter that he nearly fainted and had to hang on to the gunwhale for support.

'There is no longer a Tsar.' The boy's voice grew firmer and louder as he continued. 'There is only the Empress Catherine the Second.' He was on his feet, the point of the little dirk directed at Peter.

'If you don't go away, we'll open fire!'

The words were curiously childish but the meaning very clear.

Peter's face went grey and he sat down heavily, his mouth slack with disbelief and fear.

'What orders, Your Majesty?' There was a trace of contempt in the coxswain's tone; the rest of the crew glanced nervously from Peter to the other boat to the menacing embrasures where the gun muzzles showed as small black dots.

'Let's get out of here,' muttered a man. Without further orders he dug his oar deep into the water; one by one his companions followed his example and the boat turned and made off amid noisy ragged splashing. A bright flash from the fortress, followed by the deep boom of the gun. The straining men flinched at the vicious howl of the shot as it passed directly above them. Peter cried out in terror, ducking his head as the boat drove through the falling spray.

'Pull,' Peter screamed, his features twisted with fear. 'Pull, you fools!'

The gun did not fire again and all he heard, from far astern, was the sound of cheering as his sailors and soldiers sent him on his way with derision and scorn.

So, his cheeks wet with tears, his expression utterly fallen apart, the Emperor returned to the Imperial galley, a broken man.

And Midshipman Skavronsky, standing proudly in the stern sheets, was rowed back into the harbour to the mighty gale of cheers that proclaimed him, for the most wonderful moment of his life, the hero of Russia.

* * *

A shoving, heaving crowd packed the square below the Winter Palace roaring their pleasure at the sight of Catherine and her son on the balcony. The little boy leant his head against her not understanding the frightening noise, or why all these people should be shouting and cheering and calling for his mother, yelling his name.

His tutor, Count Panin, had woken him and carried him, still in his night-dress, to Catherine.

'The people will want to see the Grand Duke, Madam.'

'Wave to them, dear,' said Catherine, smiling and nodding to the sea of upturned faces. Obediently and sleepily, Paul waved and the people cheered themselves hoarse.

Behind her within the room, Kasia stood beside Panin listening to the rapturous thunder of sound, marvelling at the ease with which Catherine had achieved her ambition, but still apprehensive about the immediate future. As if sensing her thoughts Panin said in his clipped, precise way,

'We must ensure that they continue to cheer like this.' He was a small, neat man, fastidious in appearance and manner. As Kasia knew, he was in favour of a Regency until Paul came of age; for, though he admired Catherine he did not think that as a German, she should occupy the throne of the Romanovs.

'A mob is more unpredictable and deadly than any wild animal,' he added wrinkling his pointed nose in faint disgust. 'Today they're acclaiming her, tomorrow they could be screaming for her head.'

With a final graceful wave of her hand Catherine left the balcony hand in hand with her son. She was flushed and excited, her eyes shone with triumph; she kissed Paul and hugged him, much to his astonishment for she was rarely demonstrative to him in public.

'Go with Count Panin and get dressed,' she said fondly. Looking solemn and slightly dazed the little Grand Duke trotted off with his tutor.

'The greatest day in his life,' she cried. 'In all our lives.'

She held out her arms to all in the room: Kasia, the Orlovs, Razumovsky, members of the Senate and of the Holy Synod, generals, courtiers.

'My friends, from the bottom of my heart I thank you.' The tears in her eyes were genuine, she was not acting.

'And now,' she said returning to her brisk purposeful manner, 'there is much to be done, many people to see.'

For two hours the room swarmed with officials of the Court, more generals, more statesmen and humble folk – for Catherine ordered that none should be turned away. All Petersburg seemed to Kasia to be in that stifling room and Catherine never once ceased to talk, to smile, to hold out her hand to all who came to swear allegiance and eternal loyalty.

'You should rest, Ma'am. Just for an hour,' Kasia whispered in Catherine's ear.

'Not yet. Not yet.' The excitement kept her buoyed up, acted as fuel for her body.

'At least eat something.'

'Later, Kasia.' She smiled radiantly at an old man who stood twiddling his dirty felt cap, struck dumb by the surroundings, the satins and velvet and jewels.

'Thank you for coming to see me.' She could have been addressing a great noble. He was bearded and ugly and a huge boil disfigured his neck; his little eyes were bewildered.

Mumbling some sort of a blessing the old peasant backed from the room.

'Pah,' exclaimed a voice, 'how he stank.'

'He is the Russian people,' said Catherine sharply and Kasia detected the underlying note of fatigue and strain. There were others like him, many, many others, old and young, men and women most of whom prostrated themselves on the parquet floor at her feet.

Still the people came and went as outside the day grew hotter and hotter and inside the sweat streamed down the faces of the great dignitaries of State and Church, and the courtiers and officers wilted inside their heavy braided clothing.

Throughout the city the crowd were noisy and boisterous but despite the free beer and vodka they were surprisingly well-behaved; only those too old to walk, the sick and the dead remained in their homes.

But under orders of the Orlovs, mounted troopers guarded the gates to prevent anyone leaving and taking news to the Emperor; patrols of guardsmen pushed slowly through the crowded streets. But they saw no sign of trouble, heard no voice raised against Catherine for all were too busy taking advantage of the free alcohol. After all, these days one never knew when and how things could change from one hour to the next and when, instead of great carts laden with beer barrels, it would not be cavalry beating at their heads with the flats of sabres.

Heralds read out her first Manifesto to people brought to comparative silence by the harsh beat of the drums.

'By the Grace of God, we, Catherine the Second, Empress and Autocrat of all Russia etc. etc. . . . To all true sons of the Russian Fatherland . . .' Cheers and waving of hats and beer mugs . . . 'It has been clear what danger has indeed begun to threaten the Russian nation . . . Russian prestige, raised so high by our victorious army at the price of shedding so much blood . . .' Here the cheering was wilder, many openly wept and loud voices were heard calling for vengeance against the Tsar.

'Did I lose my Mikhail so that the Tsar should make friends with those lousy Prussians?' shrieked an elderly woman.

On the balcony where Kasia stood, for a moment escaping the heat and press of the room, she heard the screaming anger of the woman's cry. If Peter was to appear in the square she knew with a little shiver that he would be torn apart as wolves would rip a piece of carrion. She wondered if Catherine fully realized what she might have released; she looked down at the ragged, unkempt throng and, remembering Pugachev's words . . . 'The *golytba*, the naked ones . . . only give them a leader . . .'

As she watched she saw a coach enter the far side of the square; for a short while the horses managed to force a passage through the crowd but closer to the palace the press became too thick and the vehicle slowed to a halt. A woman's head popped out of the window and Kasia saw it belonged to Princess Dashkova; an arm appeared and waved.

'Quite the Royal Progress,' Kasia thought a little sourly. She held no great opinion of the nineteen-year-old Princess, ever since their first meeting when Catherine had so obviously wanted them to be friends; she had distrusted her passionate, almost hysterical declarations of loyalty and love and suspected her ability to hold her tongue.

'Good people,' Dashkova cried with a youthful disarming smile. 'Help me. I must reach the Empress. Please help me.'

'Come,' called out Sergeant Levashov who stood near the coach. 'I'll carry you to the palace.' He forced his way to the door and took her in his massive arms like a child, then, with a party of his men clearing a path the gallant sergeant brought the madly excited, giggling Princess to the doors of the palace, encouraged by laughter and well-wishes.

Kasia turned from the balcony to witness Dashkova's fluttering, dishevelled entrance, the grabbing for Catherine's hand and the lingering holding to her lips.

'Oh, Your Majesty, how can you ever forgive me? At a time like this and I was not at your side. I could not get through . . . Oh, Ma'am, you should see the streets and hear the people – they're quite mad with joy.'

Catherine smiled down at the radiant, tear-stained young face and, gently raising Dashkova to her feet, she embraced her.

'As you see, my dear Princess, I am here. No harm has been done and the good God has allowed you to come to me in the end.' Dashkova's large brown eyes glowed with delight and her small bosom heaved with the supreme emotion of the moment.

Kasia smiled to herself at the gentle irony in Catherine's voice, smiled openly at Dashkova – this was no moment to allow one's private feelings to intrude. On every side there were warm words of welcome for the Princess, praise for her determination; only Grigori Orlov turned his back on the gushing girl with studied rudeness. But what did the bad manners of one man matter on a day like this? Had she not been publicly embraced by the Empress – and before all the great in the land? Could she ever be so happy again in her life?

Catherine seemed indefatigable, her smile was the same for everyone, warm, gracious, sincere; her voice remained clear and charming; she never sat down except to dash off written orders in her own hand to commanding officers: to administer the oath of allegiance and to accept only orders with her signature: to Count Cherneyshev, Commander-in-Chief of the Army and others,

'. . . you will ensure that the popular will is carried out,' she wrote '. . . and you will crush all opposition, however *legal*.'

Having done this she returned to receive more people, more and more, so that the hours of that long hot day passed for Kasia in swirling waves of sound, movement, colour, of acute thirst and nagging hunger. Food was brought but Catherine seemed oblivious to physical wants and naturally no one could be seen eating before the Empress had taken the first bite, so with watering mouths and dry throats the ever-changing mob of generals and statesmen eyed the golden dishes piled high with tempting food, and the tall jugs of wine.

Kasia saw a high dignitary surreptitiously secreting a cold chicken leg and envied him his wide pockets, watched another dip his fingers into a wine flagon, and lick them dry. People came up to her, said things she could barely hear above the parakeet screech of the voices echoing from the gilded ceiling, thrown back by the tall wall-mirrors, misted with heat from a seething mass of bodies and breath. She smiled automatically, wondering if they had all completely forgotten that Peter was still to be reckoned with.

Almost as the uneasy thought passed through her mind they were reminded sharply of the fact.

A voice bawled above the chattering din:

'His Excellency, Count Mikhail Vorontzov, Grand Chancellor of Russia.'

Silence fell on the gathering. A few guilty glances darted from face to face as Vorontzov strode towards Catherine, followed by Prince Trubetskoi, hobbling slightly, and Count Shuvalov, very pale and set. Other eyes went to the door to see if the Chancellor had soldiers at his back.

Kasia saw Catherine draw herself up very erect; her hands clenched for an instant at her side then relaxed. The only sound was the heavy tramp of the three men; the room held its breath, every eye fixed on the small figure in black; in the background was the dull, beehive roar of the crowd in the square below.

'Well, Count Vorontzov,' she asked in a voice extraordinarily clear and calm, 'have you come on the orders of the Tsar to arrest me?'

Without reply or hesitation the Chancellor gave his answer. He went down on one knee and pressed her hand to his cold lips. Silently he rose to his feet and Prince Trubetskoi took his place, a grimace of pain flickering across his face as he strove to get down.

'Please,' Catherine insisted, graciously. He bowed low. When Count Shuvalov had affirmed his loyalty a great sigh swept the room and a woman's high laugh touched with hysteria rang out, abruptly cut off.

'Your Majesty,' Vorontzov said, 'there is much we must tell you.' He glanced significantly at the gaping faces round them.

'You have already told me the most important thing, Count Vorontzov.' Her smile included all three of Peter's emissaries.

It had taken the three of them little time or argument en route from Monplaisir to realize where their duty lay, or where, as Prince Trubetskoi put it to himself, the butter was spread thickest.

'But if you wish to talk privately we will retire – and leave the ladies and gentlemen to enjoy themselves,' she added with a gay little laugh.

As Kasia followed Catherine from the room she saw with envy the rest of the room hurl itself in a jumble of velvet, satin and brocade at the tables where the food and drink was spread. Being a friend and confidante had its disadvantages, she thought wistfully.

Beside her old Prince Trubetskoi muttered, 'By God, I need a drink.'

'Amen to that,' Kasia breathed fervently.

*　　　*　　　*

'But will he fight?' Catherine asked when the Chancellor had finished his account of the events at Monplaisir.

'That, Ma'am, depends on two men.'

'Goltz, you mean?'

'Yes, and Field Marshal Münnich.'

'So Münnich will resist.' Catherine paced the room like a small, restless animal, now and again striking her fist into her open palm.

'His loyalty is misplaced,' put in Panin. 'But in his own eyes he is at least loyal.'

'Then I say damn those eyes of his,' Grigori Orlov snapped. 'I say march now, at once, before he has time to rally support.'

'Who will support him now that Her Majesty is so firmly in control?' Shuvalov asked.

'The Fleet for one.' Orlov towered arrogantly above them. 'How do we know what those rascally sailors will do? And what about the troops at Narva, and his own Holsteiners?' He glowered down at them, demanding action, demanding a soldier's only answer to the problem.

'We have, as you know, Captain Orlov, already sent Admiral Talyzin to Kronstadt to ensure the assistance of the Fleet and the garrison.' Catherine spoke sharply.

'But he hasn't come back yet. For all we know he may be dead and the Fleet on its way up-river, at this very moment.'

Orlov was angry and when angry he did not mind to whom he was rude.

Catherine gave her lover a withering look, which he returned with furious eyes.

'We are well aware that the Admiral may have been detained – or have changed his mind when face to face with the – the Tsar. It is a time for the changing of minds.' The shadow of a small smile. No one spoke; some feet shuffled uneasily.

'A lot depends on my sister,' cried Princess Dashkova impetuously. Catherine stopped pacing and sat down.

'Countess Radienska, your fan, please. The heat's dreadful.' It's fatigue, excitement, strain, hunger, Kasia thought as she handed Catherine her fan.

For a moment of silence the figures of Diana, stags and hounds painted on the chicken-skin fan fluttered to and fro before Catherine's flushed face, then she said quietly:

'For a long time much has depended on your sister. I could have been on my way back to Zerbst and you, my dear Dashkova, would have been the sister-in-law to a Tsar.'

'Oh, Your Majesty, I never meant – I—'

Silly little fool, thought Kasia. And yet, perhaps she was right. If Vorontzova put some backbone into Peter. . .

'While the Tsar is still at large Your Majesty cannot regard her p-position as secure.' With all eyes on her Kasia found herself speaking out with unaccustomed authority.

'Yes? Go on.' Catherine was listening intently. The Chancellor was nodding in grave agreement.

'So, I agree with Captain Orlov that instead of waiting for news from Kronstadt that we – that Your Majesty – takes the initiative and—'

'What you are saying in fact is that the Emperor should be arrested? Is that it?'

'Yes, Ma'am, it is.'

If the coup failed Kasia knew there would be no lack of tongues to tell Peter how it was the Cossack Countess who had first used the word 'arrest'. And when the time came it would take her a long, long time to die. Orlov unwillingly grunted his approval. The others looked variously startled, amazed or disbelieving, as if the idea had never so much as entered their heads. Catherine stopped fanning and stared fixedly at the gilded mother of pearl mounts. Then in the way she had when she reached a decision she sat up very straight.

'So be it then,' she said. 'Captain Orlov, you will see that orders – strictly confidential orders – reach General Savin at Schlüsselburg to arrange for quarters to be prepared for the reception of a—' She paused, uncertain of how to continue.

'A high-ranking personage,' suggested Count Panin tactfully.

'Excellent.' Catherine's fan swished briskly. Now that she had gone well and truly beyond the brink and left all doubts and indecisions behind her she was once again bursting with enthusiasm and courage.

She got up.

'See that this is done without delay.' She gave the order as if to an obscure, unknown officer, a stranger. Grigori Orlov left the room at once. And that was the man in whose arms Catherine surrendered her body to the most passionate excesses. Kasia wondered once again at this amazing ability to separate her love-life entirely from affairs of state.

'I have decided something else. Tonight we shall march to Peterhof. I shall ride at the head of my Guards. See that all is ready for ten o'clock precisely.' Alexei Orlov bowed and hurried after his brother.

'You will be tired, gentlemen,' said Catherine, smiling at the Chancellor and his two companions. 'It has been an active day.'

They kissed her hand, this time with a very real reverence and withdrew, followed by Count Panin. As the door closed she slumped into the chair, kicking off her shoes.

'And now, my dears, you may do something for me. You, Katharine, may fetch me a plate of food and – yes, I think for a change, a glass of wine.' Dashkova, brimming over with love and loyalty, hurried away.

'And you, Kasia, will please see that I am not disturbed. By anyone. In four hours' time we leave for Peterhof and until I have to dress I want to be left in peace.'

'I understand.' Impulsively Kasia came forward and kissed Catherine on the cheek.

'You were wonderful, Figgy.'

'I must go on being wonderful until this business is successfully completed.' She gripped Kasia's hand. 'It will be successful, won't it? It *must* be.'

'Of course it will.'

'If it is it'll be because I have friends like you.' Her voice broke and for a second her mouth quivered then she regained her control.

'Heavens, how my feet hurt.'

They laughed together, as in more carefree times.

* * *

The Guards Regiments stood at ease waiting for their Empress. Though they knew they faced a gruelling march the men were cheerful and even the sergeants and young officers had difficulty in controlling their own ebullient spirits as they strolled among the ranks, smiling and chatting in low voices.

A loud command rang out and the regiments crashed to attention as Catherine rode from the palace. She was dressed in the uniform of a Preobrazhensky officer and sat proudly, on a magnificent saddle-cloth of gold and crimson, astride a white Arab mare holding a drawn sabre in her hand. Behind her came Kasia, very striking in her favourite blue riding-habit, the one that showed her magnificent eyes to such advantage, Princess Dashkova, also in a Guards officer's uniform, the Orlovs and other assorted officers.

As she rode out into the luminous sunshine of the white night Kasia heard Catherine exclaim:

'Oh, they're in Russian uniforms!'

On their own initiative the regimental quartermasters had re-issued the old uniforms of the Great Peter's day worn on so many a bloody field. With oaths and laughter the men had flung away the hated Prussian tunics forced on them by the present Tsar.

Colonel Razumovsky, in command of the parade, rode forward and saluted with his sword.

'Your Imperial Majesty, the Guards are ready for your inspection.'

Not a muscle moved as she passed alone slowly along the

ranks, not an eye looked anywhere but straight ahead; the men did not appear to be breathing, only the Colours stirred very gently in a fitful little breeze, and the palace pigeons wheeled and dipped as if in graceful salute.

'My deepest congratulations Colonel,' she said when the inspection was completed. 'They wear the uniform of Russia well.'

'They will thank you for those words, Madam.'

'Soon, I hope very soon, they'll be rewarded with more than words.' As she spoke the sword-knot fell from the hilt of her sabre and almost before it struck the ground an officer trotted from the contingent of Household Cavalry; a tall, slim young man, of dark good looks.

'Will Your Majesty do me the great honour of accepting this?'

Ensign Potemkin held out his own sword-knot, looking straight into her eyes.

With a smiling nod of acknowledgement Catherine accepted.

'Let me, Ma'am.'

He tied the knot and handed back the sabre, his dark eyes never leaving her face as he saluted and returned to his position in front of his troop.

Catherine's glance followed him; for a second she seemed to be dreaming, to have forgotten where she was, then with a tiny shake of her head she sheathed the sword and raising her gold-braided tricorne high in the air she cried in a ringing voice:

'And now, gentlemen of the Guards, to Peterhof!'

With the thunder of drums and the stirring squeal of the fifes echoing from the palace walls; with colours flying out bravely and bayonets flashing in the sun the Empress's Guards marched from the square.

And at their head, raising her hat again and again to her people, by now delirious with joy and drink, Catherine held back the white mare so that the beautiful animal pranced and cavorted, fighting for her head. Beside her rode, on one side Princess Dashkova, quite beyond herself with the excitement and drama of this historic march, on the other, Countess Radienska, her childhood friend, and Count Grigori Orlov, her lover.

Razumovsky, two field marshals, Princes and Counts and senior officers of the Guards: a glittering cavalcade just ahead of the bands whose little drummer boys thumped at their drums with a new and unaccustomed vigour. Troopers of the Life Guards rattled and jingled on each flank forcing back the crowds that ran beside the Imperial procession calling again and again for—

'Catherine! Catherine!'

And behind, the guardsmen marched with an extra swagger as they took the road to Peterhof.

*   *   *

They stopped at the inn of Krasny Kabachok for five hours.

For five hours, Catherine, almost exhausted, rested. In the little room with her, Kasia and Dashkova lay on the rough beds teeming with bugs which did not care whether the blood they drank belonged to Empress or peasant.

The innkeeper and his wife, like Princess Dashkova beside themselves with the drama of the occasion, bustled about serving the grand folk with the very best they had, fearful of the soldiers who shouted for beer outside. The nobles were few but were all powerful; the soldiers were many and also all powerful. It was a difficult position for humble people.

'How are the soldiers?' asked Catherine as she drifted into sleep.

'Very happy,' Kasia said, listening to the songs which rose on the short summer dusk.

'Thank God.' On that Catherine slept.

Kasia lay awake thinking of the first time she had come to this inn. With Alexei Orlov when first they became lovers and the innkeeper and his blowsy wife had scuttled about like frightened hens tending to the wants of these two grand nobles so obviously wanting a meal, plenty of wine and more than anything else a bed.

'We've seen her before,' said the innkeeper to his plain, slow wife.

'Have we? When?' She was too flustered to care.

'I don't know. Four, five years ago. I don't know, but we've seen 'em. They came here for a night. You remember, it was early snow that year and the cow had twins.'

'Oh, them. They all look alike to me.'

The man polished industriously at a dirty mug. 'But look who we've got this time,' he said. 'They say its the new Empress.'

'What? The one who came here last time?'

'No, you fool, the other one. The one dressed as some sort of an officer.'

'Her? You mean she's Empress?'

'That's what they say.'

'*They*!' she said with an oath.

He continued with his slow, methodical polishing.

'Who are *they*?' she asked.

'I don't know – everyone,' he said lamely.

'But what's happened to him then?' she suddenly asked.

'Who?'

'The Tsar, of course.'

'Why ask me, you old fool. I'm not God, am I?'

In the frowsty little bedroom Dashkova sat up on the edge of her bed, too excited for sleep, and whispered:

'It's a dream. It's a dream come true.'

'Mm,' murmured Kasia. Why couldn't she stop talking? They'd need all the sleep they could get before tomorrow was out. No, she thought as she drifted away, it's already today.

'Get some rest,' she said.

But the Princess just sat there gazing raptly at her new Empress who lay with her mouth open, snoring a little.

*   *   *

At six in the morning, just before they set off again, a courier arrived from Oranienbaum with a letter from Peter. Catherine's face was hard and contemptuous as she read his agitated, scrawly writing. Round her, mounted up, her entourage waited in silence and the long column of troops stood leaning patiently on the muskets. The sun was already uncomfortably warm.

When she had finished Catherine slowly and carefully folded the letter and put it in the pocket of her tunic.

'There is no answer,' she said shortly.

The courier saluted and rode away.

'He admits he has treated me badly,' she said to no one in particular. 'He promises to be good in future.' She laughed, but without much humour. 'And suggests we rule together—'

'Oh, but—' Dashkova burst out.

'Don't alarm yourself, Princess. Such a thing is highly unlikely to take place.' Someone chuckled nervously.

'Well,' Catherine said, 'we had better go on.' For the first time she sounded weary, just a little uncertain.

'Ma'am,' suggested Kasia cautiously, 'should we not send cavalry in advance, to f-find out the position at Peterhof? There may be troops still loyal to – to him.'

The Cossacks had taught her the use of scouts, how to avoid riding into a Tatar ambush. Only this time the ambushers would be men in the light blue uniform of Holstein, armed not with arrows but with cannon and muskets which could just as easily kill an Empress as a common private. Catherine nodded. She called to Alexei Orlov.

'Captain Orlov, will you ride to Peterhof, and see what we may expect there.'

With a squadron of Hussars at his heels Alexei galloped out of sight beyond the cloud of dust; the crisp thunder of the hooves faded, the dust settled and Catherine sat her horse very still, gazing intently down the empty white road that led to her future.

*   *   *

But the Holsteiners blocking the road to Peterhof, knowing little of what was happening, had no great wish to fight. As Alexei approached with his Hussars and halted with upraised hand an officer walked slowly forward, watched by his men from their positions behind the poplars.

'Remove that gun!' Orlov ordered peremptorily. The six-pounder squatted in the middle of the road; by the touchhole a gunner swung the burning linstock so that the end glowed dull red in the bright morning glare. The rest of the crew stood, careless but at the same time expectant. If any fool gives the order to fire, Alexei thought grimly, and that thing's loaded with grape, we'll be blown apart. The officer shrugged; he could not speak a word of Russian.

'Get it out of the way!' Alexei shouted, sweeping his sword in a flat decisive gesture. The meaning was unmistakable but the officer did not move.

'Draw sabres!'

Steel rasped and glittered. Alexei saw fear in the man's eyes, but he still did not shift his ground, looking up at this giant on the big bay horse.

'At a walk – advance!' Alexei was an infantry officer but imagined that a simple order would do for such a moment. He pricked his horse and began to move forward towards the round black muzzle of the gun which grew larger, and larger until it seemed to fill the whole road, the whole world.

Behind him the horsemen came on slowly, irresistibly, like the tide. The officer moved out of the way but gave no command and among the trees a few soldiers fingered their muskets longingly: at this range they could topple the Hussars from their saddles just like that and then run for it through the trees.

The gunner blew on the linstock so that tiny sparks hung on the still air, glancing up savagely at the huge Russian officer who rode by so contemptuously.

Then a sword swished and cut the linstock and three fingers from the gunner's hand. With a howl of pain and shock the man staggered against the gun, staring stupidly at the gush of blood spurting over the black metal.

The tide parted and flowed by on each side of the silent gun.

Hearing their comrade's scream several men levelled their muskets at the Hussars' backs. One went off. But the ball had gone wide, humming away among the branches towards the golden domes of Peterhof, and the Hussars rode on their way unharmed.

'No man to fire! Hold your fire!' the officer yelled. For in the distance he had heard the roll of drums and seen dust billowing above the trees. It was as he had thought: Catherine was coming.

* * *

'I will not sign. I *will* not. Nothing can make me!' Peter screamed the words. He's like a spoilt little boy forced into something he does not like, thought General Izmailov.

'But—' The General hesitated. It was difficult to know exactly how to address a man who was neither legally deposed nor still in most eyes a sovereign.

'But Sire, what else can you do? Her Majesty's sentries are at the gates. You are at her mercy.'

Peter stared at him uncomprehendingly.

'All I want,' he got out at last, 'is to go back to Holstein. I don't want to rule any more. Can't she see that?'

'Well then, Sire, all you have to do is to sign this statement of abdication.' Poor devil: General Izmailov watched covertly as Peter sat gazing as if hypnotized at the sheet of paper spread before him.

'Who's with her?' Peter asked.

'There are many.'

'Yes, yes, but who – at her side?'

'The Orlovs, Sire.'

'One of them is here.' When Peter looked out of the window he saw one of the sentries posted round Oranienbaum by Alexei Orlov pacing slowly and steadily beneath the lime trees: now and then the tip of his bayonet tore down a leaf which floated softly to the ground.

'Yes. The other—'

'Grigori?' Izmailov was surprised at the venom in Peter's tone.

'The other,' he continued calmly, 'is with her. Princess Dashkova—'

'Ah!'

'Countess Radienska.'

Peter turned the paper round and round on the table with a chewed finger-nail.

'I always rather liked her,' he said. 'A brave woman. An understanding woman.' Izmailov agreed.

'Count Vorontzov,' he went on, 'Prince Trubetskoi, Vice Chancellor, Prince Golitsyn—'

Peter cut him short. 'They'd all be there, naturally.' He stabbed his finger at the paper. 'There's one thing rats can do very well, General. D'you know what that is?'

'Sire?'

'Swim, General, swim. If the ship sinks then they damn well swim.'

With that he took up the pen and signed and to Izmailov the scratching of the pen was the loudest sound he had ever heard – until he heard the sigh that Peter emitted as he sat back in the chair.

'And now it's over,' he said in a dead voice.

Izmailov looked away and cleared his throat. 'The coach is waiting,' he said gruffly.

No answer came.

'The coach, Sire. To take you and Countess Vorontzova to Peterhof.'

'Yes, I see,' said the ex-Tsar slowly. 'To Peterhof.' He stood up and Izmailov could see he was shaking.

'Very well, I am ready.' He looked as if he was going to cry.

An hour later the coach containing the ex-Emperor and his ugly, faithful mistress rolled slowly out of the great court of Oranienbaum and, surrounded by a strong guard, headed along the coast road towards his wife.

*　　*　　*

Kasia looked out of the windows while two senior officers stripped the Tsar of his decorations.

The fountains in the gardens below rose in white columns and burst in rainbows of sunlit spray. At the end of the long straight canal the sea was very blue. Marble statues cast shadows on the grass and a man was scything, slowly with wide sweeps. It could have been any ordinary day.

A voice commanded, 'Your sword, please.'

They had been at the palace since eleven that morning when

they arrived from the inn of Krasny Kabachok, but Catherine had not rested. At once she was at work again, planning, discussing, sending out orders in every direction.

In the afternoon Peter's arrival had been announced.

'Have His Majesty taken to his old quarters,' Catherine ordered and then seemed to forget about him as she turned back to the preparation of another manifesto. But later she refused to see him.

'Go to him, Countess, and say that I do not wish to see him.'

When Kasia entered the room she had found the two officers at their distasteful task.

'Is that all, gentlemen?' Peter's voice was trembling.

They did not answer but stumped heavily from the room leaving her alone with him.

'They touched me,' he mumbled. 'They dared to lay hands on me, their rightful Tsar.' His voice rose. 'They'll pay, oh my Christ, they'll pay. I'll have them branded with hot irons. I'll have them broken and quartered alive. I'll have their right hands burnt off in sulphur.' He glared at her with mad red eyes, panting, thin foam at the corners of his mouth.

'And you too, my fine lady. You'll die screaming with the rest of the traitors, who are trying to take my throne for that – that whore!' He spat out the word and flecks of foam stained the shining surface of the table. Then he collapsed into a chair and letting his head fall forward on to his arms he abandoned himself to a wild paroxysm of weeping.

One of the officers returned with a dressing-gown and slippers.

'All I want is to be with my Romanovna,' Peter sobbed. 'Please tell my wife that's all I want. Don't let her separate us. Please. I must see her. I must talk to my wife. She will understand; she's not a cruel woman. Ask her to let me see her.' He was wheedling now and despite her contempt Kasia could not help a pang of something approaching pity.

She had to steel herself to remember his behaviour to Catherine, the insults he had heaped on his wife, his behaviour towards Russia. She thought of his drunken orgies with grooms and servants, his unbalanced outbursts of rage, his complete and utter lack of dignity, his callousness and childish selfishness.

'I am sorry b-but Her Majesty will not see you.'

'You've never been able to speak properly, have you?' he said maliciously between the sobs. Even in his moment of extremity he knew how to wound. Kasia flushed; her mouth tightened but she did not answer. He continued to weep and she left him, a snuffling broken creature. Without his orders and ribbons he was nothing any more, not even a man.

'Please, I beg of you, persuade her to see me, just for five minutes.'

And you, she thought in the doorway, not so long ago you were talking openly of divorcing Catherine and making Vorontzova your Empress.

'Oh God, what's to become of me,' he cried as she left the room and she wondered what was going on in the minds of the two sentries at the door who must have heard his heart-stricken cry.

On her way back to the Empress she met Count Panin hurrying towards her with his quick, precise little steps.

'How is he?' he asked.

'Finished,' said Kasia. 'Completely finished. He'll do anything Her Majesty says – anything anyone says.'

'A sad business.' Panin shook his head, pursing his lips. After all, in his eyes, a Tsar was still a Tsar whatever his circumstances, and yet he must definitely go.

'But it has to be,' he added. 'He could not be permitted to rule.'

'Are you going to see him?'

'Yes. To tell him he is to be taken to his country estate at Ropsha and there kept under guard until quarters are ready in Schlusselburg. Alexei Orlov is to command the guard of officers and they are to leave tomorrow.'

'He wants Romanovna with him,' Kasia said.

'I don't know about that.' Panin clicked his tongue and shook his head doubtfully.

'What harm can it do? If it makes them happy.'

'You're not only a very attractive woman,' he said giving

her elbow a squeeze, 'but you have a kind heart, as well.' He smiled his prim little smile, his eyes lingering for an instant on the proud swell of her breasts. 'Not always the most common of combinations.'

She drew back a step. She did not really like Count Panin; he seemed so totally without warmth or feelings. His next words surprised her.

'I wish to Heaven it were anyone but myself who had to break this news to him. I don't count myself fortunate to have to see him at this moment.'

Kasia watched him disappear into Peter's room and stood lost in thought. She sighed and went slowly down the long corridor, the rustle of her wide silken skirt a soft accompaniment to her confused thoughts.

*   *   *

'No, no, no,' said Catherine decisively. 'He can have everything else he asks for. Let him take his violin, his Negro, Narcissus can go and his Holstein servants and even Mopsy, that horrid little dog if he wants her – but I will not permit Countess Vorontzova to be with him.'

'But—' Kasia tried.

'My mind is made up. She will not go to Ropsha. He can have his favourite bed from Oranienbaum if he likes but not that woman to share it.' Spots of colour burnt in her cheeks. Kasia had seldom heard her so angry.

Kasia glanced at Alexei Orlov who was studying the painted ceiling with sudden intense interest.

Catherine calmed her moment of agitation. 'Are you ready, Captain Orlov?'

'Yes, Ma'am. We are ready.'

'Guard him well but treat him well.'

'You have my word that no harm will come to him.' Beside his great bulk Catherine looked minute.

He was still magnificently handsome, Kasia thought, though slightly more gross looking, yet I feel nothing for him, nothing at all. And he, for his part, was simply going from woman to woman: prostitutes, Princesses, young ladies-in-waiting – it did not matter for, like his brothers, his virility was not only immense but, as she remembered without the faintest stirring of lust, almost insatiable.

His face was in profile and the sword scar down his cheek, like Henryk's, enhanced his looks and did not disfigure.

Strange to think we were lovers. I enjoyed his body, she thought as she listened with half an ear to his deep voice explaining the arrangements for Peter's reception at Ropsha, but never once did I love him, not real love.

'. . . the house will be closely guarded and a sentry on his door day and night. No one will be allowed to see him unless by my express permission. All food and wine will be tasted before it is put before him. . . .'

At this very moment, Kasia suddenly realized, Peter and Romanovna would be undergoing the slow torture of parting, almost certainly for the last time. Those two unattractive, unlovable creatures clinging to each other in the last minutes, seconds, of their strange, pathetic love. It hardly bore thinking about.

The door closed behind Alexei. Kasia waited for Catherine to speak.

'If he goes to Schlusselburg, then there will be two of them.' Catherine was musing aloud. 'Can we afford that?' She had begun her pacing again.

'Could you not send him back to Holstein?'

Catherine paused by the window and watched a group of her ladies laughing and chattering among the gilded fountains, bright and gay as tropical birds in their rich dresses.

'I don't know. I must think. Only I can decide. I must think. Leave me, my dear. And get some rest, for this evening we return to Petersburg.' She smiled absently but her eyes were clouded with worry.

*   *   *

Kasia's room overlooked the wide gravelled space between the main palace and the stables. Two coaches stood ready with a troop of Life Guards drawn up beyond: the doors were open, a postillion in Imperial uniform at attention beside each. All eyes were turned towards the big arched doorway directly below Kasia's window.

As she watched she heard the muted sounds of a woman's screams, racking, hysterical. The horses tossed their heads nervously as the awful screaming came closer and louder. And now they could hear the voice of a man, cracking in high-pitched entreaty, blending horribly with the shrieks.

With her skin crawling Kasia saw Peter, being half-supported, half-dragged by two officers towards the nearest coach. Tears were streaming down his face and the sounds issuing from his mouth were barely human.

Then the scream came from the archway.

'Oh, my God,' Kasia whispered. Countess Vorontsova was led, still screaming, to the other coach. As her ladies somehow got her to the coach she looked back over her hunch-backed shoulder for her last view of the man whom she loved and Kasia saw her contorted face. Then Countess Vorontzova lost consciousness.

For a few ghastly seconds Peter fought with his guards, shouting obscenities, clinging desperately to the sides of the coach door, crying out for Romanovna.

Appalled, fascinated, Kasia watched the dreadful scene. At last, prying free his fingers, the dishevelled officers bundled the ex-Tsar, now the Duke of Holstein, into the carriage and slammed the door.

First Vorontzova's coach drove away from Peterhof, then a few minutes later the carriage bearing Peter to Ropsha moved off, and the last view Kasia had of the Autocrat of all the Russias was of a broken figure huddled in the corner of the coach.

*   *   *

The morning of the thirtieth was overclouded but that did not mar Catherine's triumphal return to her capital. And this time she rode through the streets as Empress in more than just name. The main threat had been removed and her smiling responses to the wild acclaim that greeted her were genuinely happy and carefree.

Deafened by the swelling roar of cheers, the heavy rumble

of the guns following behind the marching Guards, and the clangour of the bells, Kasia rode in a daze of wonder.

So they had done it. She rode beside an Empress who was also her friend. The people had taken to their hearts a woman without a drop of Russian blood in her small body, one of the hated Germans, and were sweeping her to the throne on a great tide of joy. Above the crash of the bands and the happy tumult raging round them could be heard the booming of the guns, adding their tribute to little Sophia of Anhalt-Zerbst, riding her white horse to the Palace.

*   *   *

Catherine sat at her desk, frowning and fiddling with some letters. Kasia, as was her habit, sat by the open window working slowly and methodically at a piece of embroidery. She had little aptitude or liking for sewing; she had not the patience. Over large issues she had learned to harness her impatience but it was a great test of self-discipline to concentrate on small, finicky tasks.

'What am I to do?' Catherine picked up the letters and slapped them down with a gesture of frustrated annoyance. Then she seized one at random and read extracts in quick bursts:

'". . . have the goodness to order that the sentries be removed, from the second room," mm, mm ". . . because as you know, I always run up and down in my room and if I can't, my legs swell . . ." mm ". . . order that the officers do not remain in the same room when I have necessities; it is impossible for me."' Catherine made a note.

'I agree, there are times when one wants to be alone,' she said. Her frown returned as she read on:

'". . . I entreat you to let me go to Germany with such persons as I have named."' She scratched her head as she did when worried or upset.

'Always this request. Always, always, *always*!'

Kasia said nothing; they had discussed this question so many times, she had given her views and had nothing more to say.

'He knows I cannot do this.'

Does he? Kasia wondered. To him it must seem the obvious solution.

'He adds a postscript, "Your Majesty may rest assured that I will do nothing to imperil the security either of yourself or your reign".' She glanced across at Kasia.

'Why don't you say something?' she demanded sharply, in a sudden flare of unfair irritation.

'What can I say that I haven't said before?' replied Kasia calmly, not looking up from her embroidery.

Catherine made a noise sounding like *Tchah*! 'Sometimes, you're quite impossible, Kasia.'

'I'm sorry, Ma'am.' Her lips quivered on the edge of a smile. This happened frequently and she knew exactly how it would end. And it did.

'No, no, I'm the one to be sorry. Forgive me, my dear. I was hasty, but – ' she slapped at the letters again, 'it's all this.' She took up another letter.

'"If you do not wish to murder outright a human being who is already sufficiently wretched—"' Catherine stopped and stared into space, her thoughts miles away; perhaps somewhere far in the past when she had first met her husband-to-be.

He may have been in many ways half mad, unkind and boorish but he knew how to stir pity with written words, Kasia thought.

'". . . have pity on me and grant me my only comfort, Elizaveta. Romanovna. . . ."' Here there was a longer pause '". . . For the rest, if Your Majesty would but visit me for a few moments my highest aspirations would be fulfilled".' Catherine shook her head.

'No,' she said flatly. 'Never.'

Is that because you fear you might weaken if face to face with him? Kasia wondered, pushing the needle with slow persistence through the canvas.

There was a discreet knock at the door and on opening it Kasia saw a young officer of the Guard, dusty and crumpled, straight from the saddle.

'A letter for Her Imperial Majesty.'

Kasia caught Catherine's muttered: 'Oh, not another one!'

'From Captain Orlov,' said the officer, handing the sealed paper to Kasia.

Catherine slit the letter with a jewelled paper-knife. Kasia watched her face as she read it but saw no change of expression. Without a word she handed it to Kasia.

Little Mother, Gracious Sovereign,

Our monster has become very sick from an attack of colic which has unexpectedly seized him. And I fear he might happen to die tonight and fear still more that he might recover—' Kasia hoped her expression was a blank as Catherine's had been – 'I fear the first, for he babbles pure nonsense and that is no joke and the other because he is really dangerous because he often talks as if he had his former power. Following your Imperial orders I have paid the soldiers with the exception of Captain of the Guard, Potemkin, who is serving without pay. One thousand roubles were lacking, Little Mother.

                    Till death, your faithful servant,
                              Alexei Orlov.

Ropsha, 2 July.

An old beggar was hobbling across the square below helped by a small boy in tattered breeches. Kasia watched until they were out of sight.

Neither woman spoke nor did they allow their eyes to meet, but their thoughts shrieked aloud.

At last Catherine said, 'May I have the letter please.'

She held it in her hands and they were posed to tear it across but they did not; instead she unlocked her private bureau with the key at her waist and put it away, shutting the drawer with a sharp slam.

'Will you make the necessary arrangements for this extra money to be sent to Ropsha at once.'

'Yes, Ma'am.'

'We cannot have our soldiers going short, can we?'

Kasia shook her head.

Next day the second letter came. In it Alexei wrote that Peter was very much worse.

'. . . but now the valet, Maslov, has also fallen ill, and he *himself* is so sick that I do not believe that he will live till evening. He is almost unconscious, of which the whole command is aware and praying to God to be rid of him as soon as may be. . . .'

'But can we rely on God?' Dashkova stood behind Catherine's chair trying without success to read Alexei's words over her shoulder. Catherine did not answer but drummed her fingers on the table.

Kasia sat in her accustomed place. The afternoon was heavy and sultry with the threat of thunder and it was an effort even by the open window to breathe. Hot, sticky and dusty. How she hated the city during the summer months, full as it was of smells and overpowering, trapped heat.

She was overcome by a great longing for the open hills of the Ukraine, to be riding through the tall grass with the shrill whistle of the marmots on every side, the whirr of wings as partridges rose from the steppes; to be far away from this dreadful time of hints and half-spoken thoughts; she felt somehow unclean, and wanted to creep away until, one way or another, it was over. They all knew the only solution but no one, least of all Catherine, could voice their real thoughts.

'Can we?' Dashkova repeated the question. As usual she was in a state of high fidgeting excitement, dancing about in her small embroidered shoes. Kasia's demeanour annoyed her to bursting point: sitting there so calmly, hands folded in the lap of her flowered skirt of crimson satin. Could she not see what was at stake, that this was *life* or *death*? Really, sometimes one wondered if the woman was human. These Poles, she thought with a sniff of disdain, cared for nothing but themselves.

'But, Ma'am, surely Providence—' she began in another quick gush of words.

'My dear Dashkova, the ways of Providence are far beyond the understanding of a humble being such as myself.' She saw Kasia smile.

Catherine looked at the letter again.

'He called for his Lutheran pastor. I hope they let him come to him.' She spoke with quiet sincerity.

'We must send for Alexei,' she continued. 'Where is Grigori?'

'He has not been seen since he left the Palace late last evening.' Kasia could almost see Dashkova licking her rosy lips as she gave Catherine this news. Catherine ignored her smug tones, but her mouth set in a thin hard line and her eyes were stony.

'I want Count Alexei here by tomorrow. See that this is done, Countess. He is to ride at his best speed.' As Kasia made for the door Catherine called out, 'We shall meet him in the Summer Gardens.'

'I don't like her,' Dashkova blurted as the door closed. She spoke with all the unthinking honesty of youth.

'That I had realized,' said Catherine coldly. 'And I am sorry, for I *do* like her.'

'Your Majesty – I – you know I would do anything for you. I would willingly give my life—'

'I know,' answered Catherine more gently. 'But at the moment you are not required to die for me. You can however do one thing for me.'

'Yes, Ma'am,' cried the Princess with brimming eyes. 'Anything! Anything in this world!'

'You may go, Princess.'

*   *   *

Though the thunderheads were building up low above the western horizon the great blister of heat holding the city in its airless grip had still not burst by the next afternoon; people moved through the streets, mopping their faces and puffing from the exertion of putting one foot before the other.

Guardsmen posted by Sergeant Levashov barred the entrance to the Summer Gardens for the Empress was walking beneath the chestnut trees in company with Count Alexei Orlov and her lady-in-waiting, Countess Radienska, and no one else on any pretext whatsoever was to be allowed in.

Usually the gardens were alive with bees and the shimmer of wings as birds darted among the yew trees, clipped to the fanciful shapes of cockerels, owls and demure seated cats, but nothing moved except the three humans deep in earnest conversation. The weight of the black clouds piling from the west pressed down heavily on the trees; not a leaf moved. It began to grow dark and a purplish light came creeping among the tall trunks of the motionless trees, bringing an eerie look to the statues bordering the neatly kept paths.

'He has been pronounced completely recovered by the two doctors sent to Ropsha on your orders.' Alexei was speaking very formally, bending down from his great height to Catherine who walked with slow, deliberate steps, watching the path in front of her as though it might explode at any moment.

'He is no longer in danger,' he said flatly.

Kasia tried to put herself inside Catherine's mind at this moment but found it difficult.

'The Little Father—' the contempt in his voice cut through the breathless silence of their surroundings '—has recovered so well that he's already asking for his fiddle and—'

'And his tobacco and an unlimited supply of Burgundy. I think I've a fairly good idea what he'll be asking for,' said Catherine coldly.

They walked in silence, their feet crunching on the small gravel.

'If the icon remains,' said Alexei slowly, 'then there will always be the people who will worship it.' They continued for a few more yards, hearing the first distant mutter of the thunder.

'More than anything the idea of treason is abhorrent,' Catherine said, so low they could hardly make out her words. But treason has already been committed, Kasia thought. How much further can it be taken? What more can be done? And in her heart, cold against the oppressive blanket of heat, the answer was clear. The Lord knew, she had experienced her share of fire and death; she also knew how to kill. But, if you kill, then kill cleanly and quickly so that the victim has no knowledge of what awaits him.

'Kasia, would you be so good as to go to the house and see that all is ready for us.' It was Catherine's tone of dismissal.

As she walked away she heard Alexei say, 'There is such a thing as divine intervention.'

For an hour Kasia waited in the little palace while the thunderstorm gathered above and it became so dark that candles had to be lit. She organized food for the Empress; she arranged everything for her comfort, yet the hour was very long in passing.

The thunder rolled across the sky, torn by the savage bolts of lightning. Then the rain burst from the bloated clouds and roared on the roof so that Kasia could hardly hear herself speak. It rushed in the gutters and gurgled in the pipes and the thunder crashed immediately overhead so that she was stunned, dazed and a little frightened.

With a breathless cry Catherine ran in from the downpour, rain glistening on her face which was flushed and rosy.

'What rain!' She laughed and shook the water from her hair, brushing it from her wide, brocaded skirt.

Servants came to light the fire, and Catherine crouched over the heat. In the glow of the flames Kasia saw she was smiling as though a weight had been lifted from her mind. The lightning flared, filling the little room with blinding white light and Kasia, glancing up at Alexei who stood with his back to the fire, saw his face frozen in a look of – was it worry, apprehension, fear?

They ate cold chicken and cucumber in sour cream and even Catherine had a glass of wine. She chattered away gaily, enjoying the picnic atmosphere and the sound of the rain outside; the thunder exhilarated her. After all, for an Empress to be caught in a summer drenching is quite a little adventure.

Slowly the rain slackened, the intervals between the lightning grew longer, the thunder faded into a distant mutter.

'It's clearing.' Those were the first words Alexei had uttered since he came in. He was deeply preoccupied and filled and refilled his glass too often.

'But there's still a lot more to come. We'll have a wet ride.' He stood up. 'With your permission, Ma'am. I will join Prince Bariatinsky and we will start back at once.'

The two women came to the door. He bowed low and took his leave, his face grim and unsmiling.

'God go with you to Ropsha, Count Orlov,' Catherine said and this time she did not smile.

He strode away beneath the dripping trees. Catherine gave a little sigh, then drew a deep breath.

'How lovely it is after the rain.' The air was cool and fresh, cleansed of the oppressive oven-heat so that Kasia's skin felt clean again, no longer sticky. Blue sky had reappeared through the wet green leaves but all round the horizons the city was ringed by black banks of cloud.

'Shall I send for the carriage?' asked Kasia.

'No, Kasia. Not yet.' Catherine watched a butterfly.

*   *   *

It was after midnight when the two riders dismounted in the courtyard of Ropsha, water dripping from their hats. They were drenched and sore after their journey from Petersburg; all they wanted was food, drink and warmth.

Count Alexei Orlov and Prince Bariatinsky had returned from the capital. Ropsha was a small estate, given to the Grand Duke Peter by his aunt, the Empress Elizabeth, in happier days when she had still thought him worthy of the throne of Russia. There was a house, stables, a certain number of serfs to make sure he endured no discomfort; there were horses, carriages and servants by the score. Ropsha was very well furnished.

'What news?' It was Count Alexei who asked. The guard expected that. Bariatinsky might be a damned Prince but he would never open his mouth unless forced to.

'The same,' said the officer of the guard. 'Still crying for Countess Romanovna.'

'But his health?'

'By the sound of it, much better.'

Christ, thought the officer, I wouldn't like to cross that one. But he thought nothing of Bariatinsky who gave him a warm smile. That was not the kind of man you needed at a time like this: it was not smiles you needed now, but orders.

All that night the thunder rolled across the skies above Ropsha; all that night the lightning flashed and crackled among the swollen clouds and the rain cascaded without a pause on the roof of the room where Peter, once the Tsar of Russia, lay awake, his mind filled with demons. Through the roar and crash of the storm he heard faintly, now and then, the raucous laughter of his gaolers and his whole body froze for he was not a brave man.

And in another room, also unable to sleep, Alexei Orlov paced the floor, his mind entirely attuned to the storm.

In St Petersburg the humble folk of the city crouched in terror and some were heard to say that it was the judgement of God for their wickedness.

'What wickedness, woman?'

'The Tsar has been deposed.' Her words were whispered lest the Lord of the storm were to hear her and reduce her house to ashes. And the man, however brave he was, did not reply.

The morning was beautiful. A faint mist smoked in the sunshine, drawn from the sodden earth, and the birds, free from the terrors of the night, rejoiced loudly and joyfully. But Peter, who had never thought about birds or what sounds they made, woke with dread in his heart.

The morning went on; all was as usual; he began to feel better. At noon he called for a bottle of Burgundy. It was brought. He drank it and felt better, bolder.

'I wish to see Captain Orlov,' he demanded.

'Count Orlov cannot be found,' he was told.

'*Count.*'

That he could not understand. These adventurers, these common descendants of some minion of his ancestor. Count! The world was going mad around him.

'Very well then, send me Prince Bariatinsky.'

But they had another excuse.

'Am I not the Tsar?' he again demanded. And this time no one answered. So throughout that long day he smoked his pipe, he drank his Burgundy, he played with his little dog, Mopsy, until the evening when Count Alexei Orlov came to ask him to dine with him and his friends and Peter, longing for human companionship, accepted thankfully.

There were seven of them at the table. They placed Peter at the head, beaming and smiling as he took his place. Although it was light outside the curtains were drawn, the candles lit so that in the room there was a sort of false dusk or dawn.

At the start the meal was heavy, the conversation laboured. Peter was morose. Why should he make an effort with these boors? But then the wine circulated and tongues, frozen by shyness, embarrassment, fear, began to loosen. With the wine running through his veins and the laughter of the others at the table to encourage him, Peter emerged from the shell into which the last week had thrust him.

'A toast, gentlemen,' he cried. Six faces turned towards him. He thought they looked like owls. 'To Russia.' There was no answer. The faces stared into their glasses.

'To my wife then – who has been badly advised.' The silence was louder. Peter took a long drink then he belched and giggled.

'To you—' He hiccoughed and fell back into his chair. 'All of you. Great gentlemen, very loyal. I thank you.'

The silence was awful.

They all stared fixedly into their glasses. A distant mutter of thunder vibrated through the heavy curtains.

'Don't you think I am still Tsar of Russia?'

The question was a whiplash across the face of every man at that table. One last fading thunder-roll underlined the silence.

'Well?' He giggled again. 'Am I or am I not your Emperor?'

No thunder came to break this silence, only the splash of Peter filling his glass.

'As you have not answered – obviously I am.'

Oh, you fool, thought Prince Bariatinsky. You poor, poor fool. He had drunk a certain amount and was a friend to all the world. But this time he was cast in the wrong role: this was no time to be a friend to anyone.

'Do you still think yourself Tsar?' Alexei Orlov's voice was very hard. Peter jerked his head out of his glass.

'Of course. I am a Romanov.'

'And would the Russian people accept you as a Romanov?'

'What do the Russian people matter to us? Can't we understand each other? We're different. Can't you see that?'

The light between the curtains faded, the candles threw a stronger beam, the shadows grew blacker.

For an hour, two hours, Peter raved, growing more confident as the time passed and no one argued with him. They sat in silence, stony silence, and he did not notice. Soon he had become Emperor again and Catherine might never have existed. 'I shall do this,' he said. 'I shall do that.'

And the six men sat and listened.

The candles were burning down. He was still talking. They were still listening, but in silence. If he had looked he would have seen their hands clenching, he would have heard the harsh splintering as Prince Bariatinsky's glass cracked in his clenched hand. But he neither looked nor listened. For that moment he saw himself as Tsar again with the world hanging on his every word.

Alexei Orlov stood up. He had drunk a lot but he was not drunk. It did not seem to make sense but he knew it to be true. He saw it all, shaking his head. But more clearly than anything he saw Peter's face at the head of the table, grinning, fawning, striving for power he had lost, begging for it, crawling for it. He looked at the faces of the others at the table. All he could see were the tops of their heads. But he knew the moment had come, someone had to act or for the rest of their days they would lead a half-life, not knowing from day to day what was going to happen next.

His fingers were beginning to curl but he did not want to kill. This creature – this thing was too pathetic to kill. Send it away; throw it away, but don't kill it. But if it lives, what then? He heard Peter's crazy laughter at some mad joke; he thought of Kasia. He didn't have to be drunk to think of her as a woman.

'Well, for God's sake, come on!' A voice shouted the words but he had no idea who it was.

He saw Peter's face and he hated it. He is small, you are big. You can kill him; with your hands you can kill him. It was all so simple, and looking round the table he saw the same thought mirrored on every face.

But Peter did not notice. He was shouting by now and giving orders as if he were still Emperor and not a helpless prisoner.

'Gentlemen, get to your feet and drink another toast.' He raised his glass unsteadily. 'To His Majesty, the King of Prussia.' The wine ran down his chin. 'And may he—' He stopped abruptly with his mouth hanging open as he saw the expression on Orlov's face. Peter tried to back away and knocked over his chair; the glass fell to the floor and the smash of glass seemed to release any hesitation they might have felt.

They came at him slowly, moving along both sides of the table, their faces masks of drunken hatred. At that moment they were animals, not men; animals out for the kill.

It was Orlov who first laid hands on him. Peter ducked away, blood running from the tear of Orlov's nails.

Just for a second Alexei was dumbfounded by what he had done and called out, 'What have I done to you?' But Englehart pushed past and swung his fist, knocking Peter to the floor, then standing over him he kicked him viciously in the side; Teplov joined in, then Volkov.

The kicks thudded home on the squirming body. Peter gasped and moaned, struggling to get to his feet, but Englehart, cursing horribly, flung him down. Two of them knelt to hold him, someone smashing their fist into his livid face.

'Stop that,' Orlov shouted. 'Don't mark him!'

Other hands groped for his thin throat.

And Peter realizing they were going to kill him began to scream. The screaming now and then changed to a strangled gurgle as hands found his windpipe. But he fought for his life with incredible strength and fury, sinking his teeth into the clawing hands.

'Come on, finish him!' They were panting, falling over each other to get at him, lusting for blood.

His screams were shrill, despairing. 'No! No! Please, no!' He shuddered with the agony of another savage kick deep in his kidneys.

'Get cushions! Put cushions on his face!'

They drew back, panting and sweating, a ring of murderous faces looking down at him as he writhed and sobbed. Volkov staggered back with cushions.

'Oh, no, not that, please not that! Don't kill me. Send me away. Put me in prison, do any—' His wild pleas for mercy were cut off as they jammed the cushions on his face but his struggles were desperate and every now and then he got his gasping mouth free, gulping air; his eyes stared from his head his heels beat at the floor. In a frenzy of murderous rage they jumped on his stomach so that wine and blood gushed from his mouth.

But he still did not die. His limbs threshed among the litter of food and broken glass scattered over the room; his fine velvet coat was ripped half off his body and one leg, stripped of its stocking, was already purple with bruises and his shoes lay beneath the table.

In the kitchens, far from the dining-room the servants huddled, white-faced, listening to the distant screams.

'Holy Mother of God,' said one of the cooks, 'what are they doing?'

'It's just another of their drunken brawls,' a footman said, but his words were uncertain.

'That's no brawl,' exclaimed one of the coachmen. 'That's a man screaming for his life.'

They looked at each other with frightened eyes, knowing full well who it was who uttered those terrible sounds.

Alexei Orlov felt his hair rising at the appalling scene; his stomach turning at the bungling horror of men trying in a drunken haze to kill one helpless human being.

'For God's sake,' he shouted, 'there are five of you. Can't you kill him?' The screams were muted now, half choked with blood as once again they tried to kick him to death.

Swaying slightly, Prince Bariatinsky gathered the napkins from the debris of the table and with intense concentration knotted them together to make a rough white rope.

'Stand back.' They shambled out of the way, stumbling and clutching each other for support. He kicked the cushion from Peter's face, and the latter seeing his death in the knotted linen, lay rigid not uttering a sound. The time had come, and he knew it.

But as the knots tightened and the air was cut off, his hands began to beat the floor and his legs to kick frantically as if his very feet were striving for breath.

Alexei Orlov had seen death on the battlefield but he had never stood by and watched anything like this.

Supposing the eyes squeezed out, he thought; supposing they fall on the floor and roll: roll under the table. Christ, he muttered through the dreadful sounds of a dying man, oh, Jesus, why have I got mixed up in this? I've killed; I'm a soldier so I've killed. But at least I've killed cleanly, with steel. Not this awful botched horror.

The thudding on the floor had ceased. There was silence in the room, except for the heavy breathing, the voice of someone saying, over and over again, 'Oh, God, oh my God!'

Prince Bariatinsky moved slowly to the table like a man in a dream.

The others stood in utter silence looking down on the blackened face, streaked with blood; the body, the limbs somehow disconnected, the eyes staring as they would stare until they dissolved into empty hollows.

Another candle flickered and went out; the room grew darker. They moved away from the body, furtively, not daring to say a word. In fact, what was there to say?

And on the floor Peter, once Autocrat of Russia, whose very frown could send people to the torture chambers, to Siberia, lay sprawled in an ugly death, no different from any of his soldiers torn apart by grape. At least they had died for something, but this – with it's blackened face and swollen tongue, this—?

'It is done.' No one knew who spoke.

'For God's sake, cover it.'

Again, no one knew who had spoken.

They threw a carpet over the remains of Peter the Third.

'What now?' This time the voice was Bariatinsky's.

'What the hell do we do now?'

All round the room were the deep breaths of those who try to be sober. As one they turned to Alexei Orlov. Why should they all hang if one neck would do for them all?

Orlov looked at them. He saw in their eyes what was in their hearts.

'Who killed him?' he cried again. He had his hand on his sword and no one argued.

'But what do we do?'

'Yes, for God's sake, what do we do?'

Two candles still burned and threw a little light on the livid faces.

In the silence was the slow drip, drip of wine into one of Peter's empty shoes.

'Leave him.' Alexei pointed to the corpse. 'I will deal with this.'

With the responsibility lifted from their shoulders they reached for the wine again.

'Get out!' They gaped at him. 'Get out! Leave me!'

They left him, stumbling over themselves in their eagerness to leave that room.

For perhaps half an hour he sat beside Peter's dead body. He did not drink. He hardly moved. The others had gone – where they had gone he had no idea. Silently, furtively, they had slunk away, appalled and yet not appalled at what they had done.

He went out into the garden. The air revived him; he breathed deeply and slowly he felt better. He saw the dawn of the summer night and he knew that his future, his life, depended on his actions now.

Beyond that garden wall, shining in the light of a full moon, lay something which could send him to the scaffold. Because, asked one small part of his brain, how far could he trust Catherine?

And yet, beyond the moon, lay the summer dawn. Play your cards right, he told himself; just play them right and your future is made.

For an hour, two hours, he walked in the garden. And by now he was entirely sober. Then he went indoors. He took a sheet of paper, a pen and he wrote. He wrote, he tore up; he wrote again, and again he tore up. Sometimes he listened and heard nothing. He went on writing until, at last, he was satisfied.

He went from the room and called quietly for the officer of the guard.

'This is to go to Her Majesty. At once. Is that understood?'

'Yes, sir.'

'If you kill one horse, two horses, it doesn't matter.'

'I understand,' said the officer, quickly. He had heard the screams and knew exactly what was at stake.

'Get this to the Empress and you will be well rewarded.'

Alexei Orlov listened to the sound of the horse disappearing into the dawn and thought, 'We've done this for Russia. In God's name, surely we have done this for Russia?'

* * *

That morning, after Catherine's greyhounds had been fed and she had drunk her cups of coffee a courier arrived from Ropsha.

'Well, what is it this time. Colic? A fever?'

'I don't know, Ma'am.' The officer stared down at the square toes of his mud-stained riding boots, not able to meet her gaze.

'All right then, you should rest,' she added kindly. 'You look exhausted.' She was standing up when she took the letter but when she had read the first few lines she sat down letting it fall on the table. Her face was very white. Absently her hand went out to stroke the head of the dog that came nuzzling at her skirt.

The little golden clock on the mantelpiece whirred softly and began to strike eight o'clock. Outside the sun was bright; she heard the voices of the people moving in the square. From next door came the sounds of her bed being made, her room being cleaned. It was a morning just like any other. But – against her will her eyes were drawn back to the letter. No, today was not the same; today was very different. She rang the small handbell on the desk. Her little Kalmuk maid came in.

'My compliments to Countess Radienska and would she please come at once.'

Catherine sat without moving until Kasia's arrival; her heart was beating uncomfortably fast; frequently she had to wipe the sweat from her brow and at one moment she thought she was going to faint.

'What is it, Ma'am?' Kasia cried in alarm as she entered the room. 'Are you ill? Shall I send for the doctor?'

Catherine shook her head then indicated the letter.

'Read it.' Her voice was no more than a whisper. Her colour was ghastly and Kasia could see she was trembling.

The writing sprawled unevenly, shakily across the paper; the ink was blotched and smudged. But the meaning was very clear.

'Little Mother, merciful Empress! How shall I tell or describe what has happened? You will not believe your faithful servant, but, before God I speak the truth. Little Mother, he tarries no longer on this earth. But no one would have believed it, and how could we have thought of laying hands upon the Emperor? But, Sovereign, the mischief has happened. He fell into a quarrel at table with Prince Bariatinsky; we could not separate them and already he was no more. We ourselves could not remember what we have done, but we are all guilty to the very last one and deserving of death. Have mercy on us, if only for my brother's sake. I have made my confession and there is nothing left hidden. Pardon, or else command quickly that an end be made. I do not wish to see the light; we have angered you and consigned our souls to eternal perdition.'

There was no signature, just a mess of letters scratched out.

'This was written in a drunken panic,' said Catherine, controlling her voice with an effort. 'It may not be true. He may only be injured.'

'No, Ma'am. It is true. It has happened.'

'An accident. It must have been an accident.' Catherine's brain was racing. What to do? All had been achieved without the shedding of blood, and now this. Kasia, watching her wondered: Will she betray Alexei, make an example of him? Will she put them all to death in as public and horrible a way as possible? She found to her surprise that her thoughts were quite calm and dispassionate. If I were in her position I would at once suppress any hints of murder, which would run like fire through the city and across the land to the very furthest corners of Russia.

She remembered Catherine's mood of lighthearted relief in the Summer Gardens. What had she said to Alexei as they walked alone? That, no one would ever know.

'You will need the Orlovs, Ma'am,' she said and Catherine nodded.

'Sometimes you read my thoughts, Kasia.' Catherine sounded a little uneasy. She took the letter and with one final glance at the damning words she locked it away in a small casket.

'One day that may become part of history.'

'First there must be an autopsy to establish the cause of death.' Catherine might have been talking of a dog or horse. Kasia was neither shocked by Catherine's reaction, nor surprised by her own.

'Then I shall issue a *ukaz* announcing that he died from natural causes, I think, a colic. He will lie in state in the Nevsky Monastery and those who want to pay their last respects—' Then a new thought struck her, puckering her forehead with worry.

'Soon I shall have to face the Senate and see Vorontzov. What face shall I show them? They all know how I felt about him. Am I to weep or fall flat in a dead faint?' Her voice held a note of bitter irony. God, how she had hated him. Kasia realized this fully for the first time at that moment.

'Your Majesty should not see anyone for at least a few hours,' she advised formally. 'As you say, they will not be expecting a show of wild grief or a state of shock.' She had seen that when she first came in. 'You will need some hours to yourself, Ma'am. Then you can face them with,' she paused, 'with sad c-composure.'

Though Catherine gave an outward impression of complete control there might be a sharp reaction of shock; in fact, as Kasia watched, Catherine's face changed abruptly. The look of careless unconcern vanished and, in its place, an expression of bewilderment crept into her eyes.

'I can't believe it. I can't take it in.'

'Why not lie down for a while?'

'Yes,' she answered uncertainly. 'Yes. Yes. I think I will. But the Chancellor, Count Panin, they should be told. There's much to do—'

'Later, Ma'am, later.'

'I suppose so,' said Catherine dully, and moved towards the door of the bedroom.

And as all the tension and strain of the last weeks, all the relief, the horror perhaps, as her brain began to take in what could have happened at Ropsha, was released in her mind, it showed clearly in the slow, dazed drag of her steps, the lifeless way in which she fell on the bed.

'Keep them away,' she murmured with closed eyes. 'Please keep them all away.'

'I will, Ma'am. I promise.'

With a long look at the pale, pinched face on the silken pillow Kasia went from the room, closing the door softly behind her.

PART SIX

HENRYK picked up the white queen then substituted the red one; he studied the little figure reflectively in the light of the dying candles. The stove gave out a small, red heat just sufficient to keep out the creeping cold. The house creaked and contracted with the frozen stillness of the night.

'Quite a story for the history books, isn't it?' Henryk leant back with his hands behind his head; he yawned. 'It's late, darling. You should be in bed. Besides, it's getting damned cold in here.'

But Kasia did not move and he saw her thoughts were far away, her eyes dark with memories. He felt the tiny spark of jealousy which he always felt over those parts of her life he had not been able to share. He knew it was childish and stupid; in time perhaps he would overcome it.

'What is it, my love?' He stretched across for her hand.

After a pause she said:

'It's – it's just – well, did he have to d-die in such a terrible way?'

'One of the things I've always loved about you is your wonderful imagination.' Henryk smiled. 'How do you know he died like that? You weren't there, were you?'

Kasia did not smile back. 'He died violently. That I do know. I saw him lying in the Nevsky Monastery.' Dressed in the light blue of the Holstein Dragoons, his hands concealed by heavy gauntlets and his face, half hidden in bandages, had been almost black. She remembered peremptory commands of the officers on guard at the catafalque. 'Come along! Move along there!'

The long procession of shuffling people had been hustled past the open coffin, allowed not more than a brief frightened glimpse at the remains of their Tsar.

'He died horribly,' she said. She shivered slightly as the dark horror of Ropsha cast its shadow across the room.

'But you were not exactly heartbroken when he died. Nor was Catherine. For her, for everyone, it was, as Orlov so aptly put it, surely divine intervention.'

There had been a long time to think since those bright summer days and the picture of Peter's death had grown and blossomed in her mind.

'I'm sure it wasn't Bariatinsky by himself,' she said. 'They all killed him.'

'Orlov?'

For an instant she hesitated, then replied. 'Yes, I think so.'

'So do I,' he agreed with heavy emphasis.

Killing a miserable thing like Peter would have meant no more to Orlov than squashing a wasp. Henryk knew that.

'Do you think,' he asked very deliberately, 'that she arranged it?'

Kasia sat silent for so long that he thought she was not going to answer. But at last she said, 'I don't know. Honestly, Henryk, I don't know. Nor do I want to know. It's over and done with and—'

'But she wanted it, surely?' He persisted.

Kasia nodded.

'All Europe openly accuses her of murder,' he went on.

'I know.' Her voice was flat.

'It wouldn't be the first time in history. Remember there was that Scottish queen. No one really knows what part she played in her husband's death.'

'Don't let's talk about it any more. Please, darling, not at the moment.' One day, she thought, I'll tell him what I think.

'Let's go to bed.' She stood up, holding out her hands to him.

As she snuffed out the melted heaps of wax spilling over the brass candle-sticks Henryk looked at her in the fading glow.

'Do you realize that this time next week you'll be my wife?

In answer she put her finger to his lips, shaking her head with a smile.

'Never tempt Fate, my dearest.'

Taking her in his arms Henryk kissed her.

*   *   *

The village church was crammed, people packing the pews like fish in a barrel. A thin haze of steam rose from their thawing clothes and mingled with the smoke from the heavy brass candelabra – Father Krasinski's great pride – for many of the wedding guests had travelled far through the snow-storm to attend the marriage of Count Barinski to Countess Radienska.

In the front pews were the friends and relations of the Barinskis. To Kasia's secret relief none of her Czartoryski relations had come from Pulawy. One reason was that she did not really like any of them and the other was that her father-in-law might have disgraced himself and the laws of hospitality by drinking too much and telling them what he thought of them.

For a small country church it was very grandly carved and decorated inside; painted in dark blue with golden stars on the roof. Banners hung from the walls, placed there by generations of Barinskis. And today the village women had helped their priest to hang garlands of evergreens, entwined with the red and white ribbon of Poland.

Kasia and Henryk stood before Father Krasinski.

'By Heaven,' Count Barinski kept whispering loudly, 'by Heaven, she's beautiful!'

That brought murmurs of agreement from those within earshot and a general nodding of kerchiefed heads. It also brought a glance of benign disapproval from the old priest over the top of his rickety wire spectacles.

'Wilt thou, Henryk, take Kasia, here present, for thy lawful wife, according to the rite of our Holy Mother the Church?'

'I will.' Henryk's firm answer rang round the church.

He glanced sidelong at her, smiling his encouragement.

Kasia's responses were also firm and steady. Only once did she hesitate.

'. . . till d-d-death do us part, and thereto I plight thee my troth.'

'Well done,' said Count Barinski even more loudly. Well! Good God, if a man couldn't even say what he thought in his own church!

On the priest's instructions Henryk took her right hand in his own. For a moment he regarded them with his wise, kind little eyes. Heads craned and peered round other heads to see better what was going on.

'I join you in Holy Matrimony in the name of the Father, and of the Son, and of the Holy Ghost.' He placed his own hand gently on theirs. 'Amen,' he finished, and smiled, showing his few remaining teeth.

Henryk, returning the pressure of her hand, felt the cold drops of the holy water. After these long years; after endless deserts of separation she, like him, had clung to her dream, her love, against Fate itself. Her faith had carried her through the darkness and brought her to stand here beside him, to become his wife in this little country church.

Not really conscious of what he was doing, Henryk placed the gold and silver coins and the ring on the salver presented to him by unseen hands.

'Bless, O Lord, this ring . . . that she who shall wear it, keeping true faith unto her husband . . .'

Henryk took the coins and gave them to his wife. His wife! He had never thought much about God but someone had brought this miracle to pass.

'. . . and with all my worldly goods I thee endow,' he repeated after the priest.

Father Krasinski, with his hands raised and held above their heads, intoned, 'May the Lord God Almighty bless you with the fullness of His Benediction; may you see your children's children even to the third generation and may you attain to a happy old age. Through Christ, Our Lord. Amen.'

He let his gaze wander slowly over the intent faces before him; it returned to Count Barinski. Today Henryk's father was dressed in all his old-fashioned finery, a fur-trimmed pelisse flung back from one shoulder, long caftan of heavy red velvet frogged in gilt; the jewelled hilt of his long dagger twinkled. His mane of grey hair was as thick as that of a man half his age, his moustache trimmed and combed, his face scarlet from the heat of the church. 'Get on with it, man,' said his haughty blue eyes. 'Get it over with and let's get back to the house: to the music and the drink.'

'And now,' said the priest, much to the surprise of everyone, 'all I can say to you, Henryk and Kasia Barinska' – Kasia felt a flood of warmth flow through her body as she heard the name – 'is that you are now well and truly married in the sight of God and before all these good people.'

They smiled at each other in a kind of wonder; their hands crept out and joined together.

'Be faithful to each other both in body and in thought. I hardly need to tell you to love each other,' he said with dry humour. 'That would be presumptuous. But this I do say to you: live in humility—' he thought he heard a slight snort from Count Barinski – 'and in awe, not fear, of the God who has spared you both for this day. And now,' he turned towards the altar, 'in the name of the Father—'

With a great rustling of best skirts and creaking of old knees the congregation knelt for Father Krasinski's blessing.

Henryk took his wife down the short aisle. At the door Adam stood waiting with her hooded cloak; smiling, he handed it to her without a word.

It was still snowing, the small flakes drifting slowly on an icy little breeze. But if she had been wearing nothing but her shift Kasia would not have felt the cold.

They waited while Count Barinski, with Count Branicki, Grand General of Poland, at his side, got into the sleigh and drove off to the house, for custom dictated that the master of the house must be at his door to greet the newly married couple.

The wedding sleigh drew up, garlanded and strung with ribbons.

There were cheers and cries of 'Good Luck,' 'Long happiness,' as the whip cracked and they drew away feeling the the snow sharp against their faces.

When they were hidden in their own small white world Henryk turned to her and drew her close beneath the bearskin rug. But they did not speak. Kasia nodded at the rough leather coat of the coachman in front of them. She brushed Henryk's lips with her fingers, laid the softness of his head against her cheek, murmured something in his ear.

A little mound of hard snow perched on top of the coachman's rabbit-skin hat and this struck Henryk as being enormously funny. He was seized by a sudden wild urge to laugh, to sing, to shout at the broad, stolid back. 'Heh, don't you realize what you're carrying in this sleigh of yours? We're not ordinary people, this is no ordinary day. Nothing like this has ever happened before, never in the whole huge world. She's my wife. *My wife*!' He wanted to prod the man – Peter, the blacksmith's son – in the back and shout, 'Can't you get that into your thick, good-natured head?'

In a flurry of snow they drew up at the house. On the steps his father stood with the traditional dish of bread and salt.

'Come on,' he growled, 'it's too damned cold to stand about.' He offered the dish to Kasia who broke off a small piece of bread, dipped it in the salt and ate it; he did the same to Henryk. Then he leant forward and kissed his daughter-in-law on both cheeks.

'Welcome to Lipno,' he said gruffly. He patted Henryk on the shoulder, then blowing his nose loudly he turned and stumped off into the house, bellowing for Stepan to bring him something in a glass.

'It doesn't matter what. Today I'll drink anything.'

*   *   *

And he did. Vodka, beer, wine, his favourite mead, everything except tokay. That he refused to touch, even when Kasia herself brought him a glass.

'Try it,' she urged. 'Just try it once. You'll love it.'

But he shook his head stubbornly, sucking the drops of dark brown Polish beer from a moustache which had lost its previous neatness and now hung down over his mouth like that of a Cossack elder.

'He's got himself quite a woman there,' remarked Count Branicki, puffing away at his old pipe, watching Kasia as she moved among the guests, the nobles and the peasants, with flushed and sparkling eyes.

'Yes,' he added, 'he's a lucky fellow, that son of yours.' He drew thoughtfully at his pipe. What did they know of her beyond the fact that she was half a Czartoryski and that she had been a lady-in-waiting to Catherine of Russia? A use might be made of that. He knocked out the dead ash against his heel and began to refill the crusted bowl. Yes, definitely something could be made of that.

'Come on,' Barinski shouted at him. 'Don't look so gloomy. Great God, we're not so old that we can't enjoy ourselves, are we?'

With a great roar of laughter he looked round the big barn which had been cleared for the occasion. At one end a fire blazed and the rich smell of sucking pigs turning slowly above the flames mingled with the thick odours of hot, excited bodies, of spilt wine, of beer, smoke and all the mountains of food piled on the long, trestle tables: smoked trout from the Dniester; pickled cucumbers; ham with buckwheat and huge piles of *kluski*, those small, fat dumplings that soaked up the vodka so well. Long loaves, round loaves, honey cakes, sugared cakes: the spread was gargantuan, the tankards never empty.

Large tallow candles burned in home-made sconces on the rough pine walls; every so often small boys, employed for the purpose, threw buckets of water on the wall nearest the fire under the supervision of a worried looking Globnik.

Henryk sat on a bench with Josef Pulawski and Jan Dombrowski. He was watching Kasia with pride in his eyes and a deep and tender joy in his heart; Pulawski was, for him, in jovial mood but Dombrowski seemed morose and pre-occupied and Henryk noticed his eyes followed Kasia wherever she went. Well, who could blame the lad if he fancied her? Henryk felt tremendously magnanimous towards all the world.

Suddenly his father's powerful voice was heard above the laughter and snatches of song starting up here and there in different parts of the barn.

'Henryk! Henryk! where the hell are you?'

'It sounds as if I'm needed,' Henryk said. But, as he pushed his way through the happy, back-slapping throng, he thought, it should be Adam. Then he saw his brother in a corner, very happy with Marishka, the bold-eyed, well-formed daughter of Pawel, the chief forester. Do him a power of good, he thought as he dodged the well-wishes of a dozen beaming faces. Just what he needed.

'The gipsies, Henryk! Why aren't they playing?'

Count Barinski's face was by now the colour of a winter sun seen through fog.

'What do they think they're here for? To drink all the vodka and seduce all the girls? Get the fiddles going, Henryk, and let's start with a polka!'

Six young men with eyes as black as their greasy hair laughed with a flash of white teeth and took up their scarred flutes and violins. A space was cleared on the earthen floor. Men and girls took their places.

In the talented, dirty hands of the gipsies the violins became alive; they laughed, they sobbed, they set feet skipping and stamping short, quick steps. The full petticoats flew out like flowers in a breeze flattening the candle-flames with the bright swirl of colour: the bows flashed over the wailing, throbbing strings as the dance grew faster and faster until with a final crescendo of music and thumping of feet it ended, to a chorus of disappointed cries for 'More! more!'

Flushed and shining faces, eyes alight with the excitement and, in many cases frank passion as hands and bodies touched; the blood, fired by the intoxication of the wild, gay barbaric dance, ran hotly in bodies ripe for caresses; rosy parted lips yearned for kisses.

Henryk, his arm round her waist, guided Kasia to where his father sat, still clapping, still stamping his boots. Count Branicki rose and offered her his chair.

'May I congratulate you on your dancing,' he said gallantly.

'No, please. I'm too happy to sit down.' Her body was still moving slightly from the rhythm of the polka; her hand pressed Henryk's tightly.

Stepan, with a higher colour than usual and a step even slower and more unsteady, brought them wine.

'Not wine,' said Henryk, panting from the exertions of the

dance. 'Vodka, Stepan, vodka.' The old man gazed at him with little, blurry eyes.

'Yes, Master Henryk.' He mumbled. 'Vodka.' He turned away swaying perceptibly.

'Never mind, Stepan. I'll get it.'

As he fetched a jug from the table Henryk saw that Jan Dombrowski was still sitting on the bench, alone now, for Pulawski had disappeared.

'What's the matter, Jan?' Henryk held out a glass of vodka. 'Come on, drink this down and join us.'

Dombrowski shook his head, then, realizing this was no evening to spoil things for Henryk, he summoned a weak smile.

'I'm sorry. It's my head. It's bursting like a bloody clap of thunder. I think I'll go out for a breath of air.'

But he did not stir as he watched Henryk moving away among the crowd, stopping here and there to exchange laughing greetings. Beyond, he caught sight of Kasia's blue dress. It was not his head. It was her. Since the first time he had sat beside her at dinner she had never been far from his thoughts. She fascinated him; she intrigued him; she attracted him. And now she was Henryk's wife. Tonight they— But that would be nothing new to them. It was not that which worried him; no, like Count Branicki, he asked himself continually, What do we know of her? A friend of the German murderess, could she be trusted? For all her Polish blood where in fact did her sympathies lie?

'She is Henryk's wife,' Pulawski had said, 'and that is good enough for me.'

Finding his thick fur coat from among the pile of cloaks, coats and sheepskin jackets, he pushed his way through the packed barn and out into the night.

The cold cut across his face, freezing the fumes in his bursting head until slowly his maudlin thoughts began to quieten. The snow had stopped and the sky was clear. For a while he walked, the squeak of packed snow clear under his knee-boots and then, gazing up at the vast spread of the night filled with the icy glitter of winter, he grew slowly calmer and went back inside.

They were dancing a *mazurka* and the noise filled every corner of the huge raftered roof of the barn; well primed with vodka the gipsies shook the very smoke with the frenzied skill of their playing.

Henryk and Kasia were with his father, clapping their hands in time, throwing back their heads in utter happiness, turning to each other with their glasses raised and touching.

'To you.'

'And to you, my darling.'

Count Barinski winked at his old friend, the Grand General, who smiled his slow, understanding smile.

'Great God,' shouted Count Barinski at the top of his voice, 'that's not the way we danced the *mazurka* in my young day. What have they got in their veins nowadays? Water? By God, Branicki, they're half dead!'

Henryk was delighted to see Dombrowski in the thick of the dance, his face split in a great laugh of enjoyment.

'They're happy, darling,' Henryk said, his lips searching for her ear through the thick curls of hair.

'They don't know what happiness means.' He felt her mouth brush his cheek. The dance came to an end amid tumultuous applause. The gipsies wiped the sweat from their faces, accepting the drinks thrust at them from every side.

'Now we'll eat,' said Count Barinski. 'Globnik can play his damned fiddle. It sounds like a scalded cat but if it gives him pleasure— Come on, Branicki, we'll make pigs of ourselves.'

While everyone stuffed themselves with everything they could lay hands on, Globnik, who normally contented himself with perhaps three or four glasses of wine, stood up at the end of the table and played a selection of tunes on his fiddle, most of them slightly off-key, to the uproarious delight of the peasants of Lipno who shouted and banged the table, laughing until the tears poured down their cheeks as the strings squealed and shrieked like small animals in pain.

The sucking pigs vanished from the spits to be replaced by others by the cooks; logs were thrown on the fire; water was splashed on the wall by the small boys, and Globnik, drunk as a newt, coaxed weird sounds from his violin no longer caring whether or not the sparks soared to the roof.

One would not have thought it possible for one building to contain so much noise without bursting apart.

The gipsies were playing their own tunes: sad, gay – it did not matter; they held the whole of life in their soaring, lingering notes. Here and there a head fell forward on the table, but no one noticed or cared. Tonight the hours belonged to them all; tonight would go on forever. No more work, no cold outside, just this warm, smoky friendship and the vodka that made life into something worth living. And next door, in the small barn where the hay was piled high, soft and fragrant, was the promise of paradise. Under the table hands wandered, above the table the girls giggled and squirmed on the benches.

Someone banged loudly on the table.

'Silence, please for Count—' No one heard the name. He was an elderly man with a drooping moustache stained brown by years of tobacco.

'Quiet,' shouted Globnik, who felt he ought to do something. 'Silence for Count—' But he could not remember the name either which made everyone laugh even more loudly.

'. . . on this great occasion when we are all gathered here to celebrate—' Gradually the speaker made himself heard, and his audience listened owlishly while he rambled on with reminiscences of his own wedding, was it forty years ago, or was it forty-two? Well, they must excuse a failing memory. And they did, with a kind burst of encouragement.

'What I want to say to these newly-weds is this—' He broke off what he was saying. Rows of faces peered at him through the smoke and steam.

'Forty years ago I had to leave my marriage bed—' Groans of sympathy. Fingers entwined more, bodies pressed more closely.

'Yes,' he cried above the titters and smothered laughter, 'I had to leave it to fight the bloody Swedes.'

'Come on,' shouted Count Barinski. 'Sit down and go to sleep, you stupid old fool! You've never even seen a Swede!'

'Let them come,' said a voice, sounding quite sober in the silence.

'Yes, let them all come.'

'Cossacks!' The barn was silent, the only sound the rising

wind and the small sounds of a gipsy trying out a new tune, slowly, plucking at the strings.

'Tatars,' called out someone else.

'Or Russians!' This time it was Dombrowski. Hands pounded the table: some of the young men were on their feet with glasses held high.

'To Poland!' cried Dombrowski in a ringing voice.

'To Poland!' The shout shook the very roof.

Count Barinski was on his feet, hand raised for silence.

'Friends,' he said, 'we are here tonight to celebrate the marriage of my son to Kasia Radienska, not to start a war. Many of you will remember there was a time when the very appearance of someone with that name on this estate would have meant calling out the hounds—' There was some suppressed laughter as they all watched to see how the new Countess Barinska was taking this.

Kasia sat with a radiant smile, nodding her head as if in agreement. Then she also got to her feet beside her father-in-law.

'And if any Barinski – except one,' she smiled down at Henryk, 'had ventured on to Volochisk we wouldn't have bothered with hounds.' She paused. 'We'd have got out the s-sabres.'

They loved that, rolling against each other in exaggerated mirth.

'But now that is all in the past,' Count Barinski went on, putting his arm round her shoulder. 'It's all over.' A heavy thud announced where someone's head had fallen forward on the table; there was a moment's commotion then the shining faces turned back to their host.

'A pity he could not have lasted to take part in the last toast of the evening,' he said drily.

'To Kasia and Henryk!'

'To Kasia and Henryk!' shouted those who in the cold, sober light of day would never have dreamt of addressing either of them as anything but Your Honour or Your Excellency.

'And now I want to see you all dancing – those of you who can still stand.'

The gipsy violins played faster and faster, the bows oiled

with vodka and mead; the skirts whirled and flared, higher and higher; the atmosphere grew thicker and thicker as the birch logs were thrown on to the fire, hurling red sun-bursts of sparks high through the smoke.

Henryk danced the next *mazurka*, returned to his seat, hot and gasping from the energy of the dance.

'Where's Kasia?' asked Count Barinski.

'She's gone to change.'

'Change? Into what! Nothing wrong with that dress, as far as I could see.'

'She'll be back in a minute and then you'll see.'

His father grunted.

Then he saw her, coming through the door. She removed her cloak and was no longer dressed as a grand lady but was wearing the clothes of the Ukraine, the clothes of her youth: embroidered blouse and wide red skirt, soft red calf-skin boots. Her hair was braided in a single gleaming plait hanging down over one shoulder.

Henryk went to her.

'Well?' she asked.

'You're lovely,' he said. They might have been alone; the music, the stamp of dancing feet, all were forgotten; there was nothing in the world but each other.

'It's fourteen years since I've seen you dressed like that.' He held her outstretched hands, leaning back so as to look at her better.

'I borrowed them from Zonia. A little tight round the hips but—' She shrugged gaily. 'She's only eighteen.' A little tight round the breasts he thought, but that he did not mind.

Count Barinski was delighted.

'That suits you, my dear. By heaven, that suits her, doesn't it Branicki?' His old friend opened one eye. 'Yes,' he agreed, and closed it again.

At this moment, Pawel the forester came up respectfully and, bowing with great courtesy to Kasia, said:

'When you were young I once had occasion to visit Volochisk and saw you dance the *gopak*. Would you dance for us tonight? We will play for you.' He and his son held their *banduras* under their arms.

'No, really, I can't. It's been so long. I've forgotten the steps.'

'Go on,' urged her father-in-law. 'Of course you can do it.'

Kasia glanced at Henryk questioningly.

'Yes, darling,' he said.

It was so long since she had danced the wild dance of the Ukraine. The last time had been to the light of great bonfires reflected from the red rippling surface of the Don.

But that was many years ago.

'Very well,' she cried impulsively. 'Why not?'

'Thank you,' said Pawel gravely. Filling his lungs, he shouted, 'The *gopak*!' Five young men came forward to volunteer.

To the plucking throb of the *banduras* and the shrill wail of the violins Kasia danced. And Henryk watched her with a great pride in his heart. He knew it was a Cossack dance but tonight it did not matter; tonight nothing mattered but the knowledge that after all they had been through, after all these years, she was now at last, unbelievably, his wife.

The leaping, bounding figures threw their distorted shadows across the walls; they span faster, faster, hands beating at the hard earthen floor.

'*Ahi, dou, dou, dou, dou!*' they cried as they danced and the spectators joined in with clapping and stamping until at last Kasia gave up and came, gasping and laughing, to Henryk.

'Bravo! Magnificent! Here, some wine.' Count Barinski's eyes were as proud as those of his son. Kasia leant against Henryk, her head on his shoulder and he felt her hair damp on his cheek, the quick heave of her bosom.

'You were wonderful.'

'In my young days I could have gone on all night. But now—'

'Now you're just a poor old thing who ought to be in a wheel-chair.'

The dance went on. Another girl had taken her place, and another; more young men joined in, trying to show off their skill and strength, but many simply fell over and lay, rolling helplessly in drunken mirth, while the others leapt round or over them.

When she had regained her breath Kasia turned to her father-in-law.

'Thank you for a wonderful evening—'

'Nonsense,' he said. 'Why not? After all, the first wedding we've had here since – since—' He buried his face in his huge tankard, remembering how they had danced in this same old barn when he and Wanda had married; how they had slipped away into the summer night.

'Be off with you. Go on, Henryk, take her away.' He waved his hand towards the door, disturbed by the vividness of his memories.

After the deafening din of the barn the night was amazingly quiet as they walked slowly to the house, the noise fading behind them, the sigh of the wind in the leafless branches becoming louder as they neared the house. A few snowflakes were falling, melting at once to the touch of their hot skins. They did not speak. Now and then Henryk looked at her face, shadowed by the sable fur of her hood.

There was candle-light softly shining through a gap in the curtains of their room.

'The house is waiting to welcome us,' Kasia said.

In the porch he brushed the little white rim of snow from the fur and slowly pushed the cowl back from her face and hair.

'Tonight it will be different,' he whispered. She nodded.

'We'll love each other as we always have, but tonight it will be different. Tonight as I make love to you, I can call you wife.'

She pressed forward against him. Beyond the sheltering roof of the pillared porch the snow was falling more heavily now, obscuring the dark branches of the lime trees clawing at the sky, black and hard in the whiteness.

His fingers found the lacing of the blouse. With her mouth on his she shook her head.

'Wait, my dearest, my heart. Take me to bed – husband.'

And, as the sigh of the wind became a steady roar in the branches and the snow drove against the house in white fury, Henryk and Kasia loved each other with a new tenderness, a new passion they did not know could exist between a man and a woman so that at times, as her cries and moans of love mingled with the rush and swoop of the storm, she knew an exaltation

218

so exquisite that it was almost a kind of fear that she might lose her mind through the sheer ecstasy of her body.

It was nearly dawn before they slept. The wind had gone, the snow fell very gently, very delicately and the ugly winter branches, quite still now, became as rounded and softened as a woman's arms.

'I love you, Henryk,' she murmured drowsily. 'I love you so very much. I don't think you'll ever realize quite how much.'

But he was asleep. Smiling, she closed her eyes, holding his head in the soft crook of her shoulder.

*   *   *

'We cannot defeat them in pitched battles. That surely must be clear to all of us here.' Henryk looked round the faces of the five men seated at the table. It was the Grand General of Poland who answered first; as usual he was stuffing his pipe with the black, evil-smelling stuff he called tobacco.

'And how to you propose we fight them then?'

'By taking to the forests and operating from bases hidden in the foothills of the Carpathians, from the great marshes of the Pripet.'

'That's no way to beat the Russians,' argued Dombrowski. His skull was splitting from the night before; there was a foul dryness in his mouth. 'Skulking in the woods and swamps.'

'I hardly think that's what Henryk has in mind,' said Pulawski.

Henryk listened for a while as they bickered. The day following his wedding night and he was spending it planning for war – and with no more than three hours sleep behind him. What a honeymoon! But his marriage had been an excellent excuse for the Grand General and Pulawski to visit their old friends at Lipno. With an effort he dragged his mind from the wonders of the night.

'We must form an army of light horsemen as Lisowski did last century. Horsemen who can strike, here, there and vanish back into the forests before the heavy Russian cavalry has time to deploy. In fact we have got to fight on the ground of our own choosing.'

'And how many men do you visualize in this army of yours?' asked Branicki.

'I know thirty who will join me tomorrow.'

'Thirty? That is not many with which to take on Catherine's armies,' remarked the Grand General, but his eyes through the pipe smoke were bright and interested.

'Thirty men, well trained—'

'And well led,' said Pulawski.

'Yes,' Henryk agreed, but he was not boasting.

'These men can inflict pin-pricks which will encourage others to join. One success.' He struck his open palm with his fist. 'Just one success. That is all we need and our thirty will become thirty hundred, thirty thousand.'

Once again, seeing the fire in his eyes, hearing the hot enthusiasm of Henryk's words, Pulawski thought, Yes, this could be the man to save Poland.

'And as the pin-pricks become bludgeon blows so more and more men will join the standard, and Poland will have an army again.'

'But will Radziwill join?' asked Count Barinski.

'I think so,' said Branicki. 'As Henryk says, success will bring him down from the north.'

'The time for private armies is over.' Henryk watched Kasia in the garden throwing crumbs to the hungry sparrows gathered round her feet; the sun was shining and the snow-glare beautiful. Watching her his resolution almost weakened. Would they never have a peaceful life together, seeing their children grow up? This woman was his wife. Had he the right to expose her to the dangers which he knew lay ahead? Yet she would be the last person in the world to hold him back. She bent down, holding out a piece of bread to the trusting birds, her lips moving in words he could not hear.

Behind him he heard his brother's voice.

'But we are not at war, are we?'

'No,' said Branicki. 'We are not at war – yet.'

'We will be.' Henryk turned round to the room. 'It will be forced on us and therefore I say we should strike first.'

He spread out a map of the district on the table. The others leant forward to look more closely. Here and there they could see little circles drawn in ink.

'Now, we know there are Russian troops – here.' His finger pointed to the local town of Rabka. 'More are reported on the march from the north-east. Infantry, cavalry, guns, supply trains, ammunition waggons – everything an army needs that is going to war. The road from Lvov to Krakow runs here—' He traced the road along its route just north of the Carpathians. 'As we all do, I know it well and personally would not like to lead a column containing guns and waggons along certain stretches if I knew that enemy forces were likely to be waiting in ambush.' He stabbed a finger at half a dozen spots on the map, all over Poland.

'And that is how we must begin – by ambushes, sudden quick raids, by cutting off stragglers. In fact, gentlemen, by making life so hard for the Russians that they won't be very willing to venture outside the towns.'

'These efforts must be co-ordinated,' put in Adam. 'To achieve any sort of success there must be an overall plan.'

'Agreed,' said Henryk. 'But first, as I said, we need a success. And that I intend to provide. Somewhere between Lvov and Cieszyn. I think probably just to the west of Rabka.' They sat digesting his words for a moment.

'You mentioned the Pripet Marshes,' said Branicki. 'What have you in mind?'

'I suggest as a start four commands: one in the province of Krakow, one in the Ukraine, one on the Bug, east of Warsaw, and another in the area of Vilno. The road from Russia to Warsaw, to the heart of Poland, runs not far to the north of the marshes. To anyone who doesn't know the area it is a trackless waste of water and reeds yet an army could hide there.' Henryk looked straight at Count Branicki.

'You see what I mean, sir? With their two main supply routes into Poland threatened the Russians may perhaps think twice before launching an all-out war. More especially as they may soon be facing trouble from the Turks.'

No one spoke. Henryk watched their faces. Adam looked doubtful, Pulawski impassive, Dombrowski his usual pugnacious self, still unwilling to accept the fact that the days of the

Winged Hussars were over. Count Barinski smiled at his son, nodding his head encouragingly; and the Grand General sat very still, hidden in his cloud of tobacco smoke.

Then he got up and limped slowly to the window where he stood with his back to the room, his head sunk in thought. He too saw Kasia like a brilliant scarlet tulip against the snow, her cloak spread wide by the skirt.

Again the thought entered his head, insidious as some slow poison: what did he know of her? Beyond the fact that she was a very attractive and intelligent young woman and that she was the wife of the man planning to lead Poland to war? But how far was she to be trusted? For that matter how far was anyone to be trusted at a moment like this?

'So you intend to set up a system of bases hidden in the forests, each one entirely independent, in some cases hundreds of miles apart, is that it?' Adam asked.

'But you must have co-ordination,' Adam repeated. 'One bee sting is uncomfortable, a whole swarm is deadly.'

'Adam's right,' said his father. 'That's been Poland's trouble for the last hundred years: acting in bits and pieces.'

'There must be a system of communication set up.'

'They taught you long phrases at the Military Academy,' said Henryk with a smile. He had a quick memory of the 'system of communication' used in *Huntress*: midshipmen posted at each hatchway, passing on the information and orders. If only it could be as simple.

'Between us we will work out something.' He knew it sounded lame but this was going to be the stumbling block; this he had always known.

'What about artillery,' asked Adam. 'We've got no guns, except the ones guarding the Royal Palaces.'

'And if Poniatowski becomes King, he's going to need them all to keep him on the throne,' said Dombrowski bitterly.

'Guns can be captured,' Henryk said. 'I imagine Russian cannon can be fired just as well by Poles.'

Count Branicki listened as they talked, his eyes still on Kasia as she moved slowly and gracefully between the apple trees, shining in their sheaths of ice; he watched her stop and speak to the man clearing the fresh snow from the path, saw him smile at something she was saying, then laugh. She had a way with her, that one, and not only with men.

'If we choose the first—' he hesitated, searching for the right word, 'skirmish – for that's all it can be with only thirty men – with care, and are successful, then there's no reason why we shouldn't have the guns we need.'

'Yes.'

'You realize, don't you,' asked Count Branicki, returning to the table, 'that this "skirmish", as you call it, may lead to a war that will ravage Poland from end to end?'

'Yes,' said Henryk. 'I do. But either we fight, or go under to become a province of Russia.' He was on his feet now, sweeping them with fierce eyes.

'We *must* fight! Don't you see. We must!' His voice trembled slightly with the strength of his emotion.

'We have no choice.' Dombrowski agreed with equal passion. His anger grew as he looked at Branicki who sat without answering, his eyes heavy with worry. Oh, the damnable caution of the old: weighing up this, weighing up that, until in the end it was too late anyway.

'Supposing,' said the Grand General, 'I was to forbid this enterprise?'

'With all due respect, sir, I think you would be wrong,' said Henryk firmly. His father felt a surge of pride for his son.

'You mean you would go ahead – with your thirty men?' A hint of a smile showed on Branicki's old, worn face.

'Yes.' After a silence Pulawski said, 'What kind of men are these?'

'Seven from the Royal Horse Guards. Fifteen gentlemen, all expert horsemen and hunters. Four artisans: a blacksmith, a carpenter, a cobbler and a stone-mason.'

'My God,' exclaimed Pulawski admiringly, 'you've been thorough.'

'I've had time in the last three months to do more than get married.'

They laughed.

Henryk went on. 'If we want a sabre sharpened we won't always be able to go to the local blacksmith.'

'The most important factor in the type of warfare you're proposing is to win the respect and trust of the people,' said Pulawski.

'Since when have the Poles not fought for their country?' Dombrowski demanded.

'In any people, however patriotic, there are traitors,' said Pulawski calmly.

The Grand General tapped the table for silence.

'When can you be ready?'

Henryk's face lit up. 'You mean—?'

'I said, when can you be ready?'

'Early December.'

'I see.' Branicki thought for a moment. 'There are some who must be told of this.'

'Not too many, sir, I beg of you.'

Branicki nodded in agreement.

'Next time I come I shall bring my son, Casimir,' Pulawski said. 'He has much in common with you, Henryk. I think he could lead another of your groups.'

'And you, Josef, what will you do?'

'Well, I shall certainly give up being a lawyer, for it seems to me that shortly there will be more important affairs to attend to.' His thin lips twitched slightly.

'All news from Warsaw – and St Petersburg – will be sent here in the usual way,' said Count Branicki. 'At least we have our system of couriers well arranged.'

Suddenly an embarrassed look came over his face; he fiddled with his pipe, began rummaging in one of his baggy pockets for more tobacco.

'Forgive me,' he said to Henryk. 'But your wife—' He broke off at the expression in Henryk's eyes. 'I mean no offence,' he continued, but—'

'If you mean, is my wife to be trusted,' answered Henryk in a hard voice, 'the answer is, yes – with all our lives.'

'And with the future of Poland?' Count Branicki obviously hated the words he was speaking.

'And with that too, sir, yes,' said Count Barinski. He saw the little muscle twitching in Henryk's unscarred cheek. He knew his son's temper, and so did Dombrowski who kept his

224

thoughts to himself. But they raced to and fro in his mind, mixed up with his feelings for her as a woman.

Henryk voiced them aloud in a tight voice.

'Because she has been in Catherine's service,' he addressed Dombrowski. 'Because she was her friend – *is* her friend – you think she can be told nothing. Is that it?' Only Pulawski met his eye. 'Count Branicki meant no offence,' he said. 'It is simply that, knowing how much is at stake, we must be certain.'

'Well spoken, like a true lawyer.'

Pulawski ignored the angry contempt.

While they waited for Dombrowski's answer Count Barinski wondered to himself what in hell's name they would think, and say, when they discovered that Kasia was returning to Petersburg to take her final leave of the Empress they all thought of as an enemy. What a damnable situation, he thought, as savage little needles of pain shot up his leg from the swollen foot.

'Well?' said Henryk more loudly. 'You've usually got plenty to say for yourself.'

'I've got plenty to say now.' Dombrowski leapt to his feet, scarlet with rage.

'Keep quiet, both of you,' shouted Count Barinski furiously; his leg was aflame and here were these two hot-heads going for each other like a couple of spoilt children. Why the devil had Branicki brought up the subject at all? Bloody old idiot.

'And what am I supposed to do?' Henryk was shouting as well. 'Just ride off for months, years perhaps, without saying a word to her?'

'Yes, Henryk, if that is what they want.'

Faces turned to the door, mouths agape. Kasia stood in the doorway, pale but meeting their eyes very steadily.

'I'm sorry,' she said with a slight smile. 'You were making such a noise I couldn't help hearing some of what you were saying. It was about me, wasn't it?'

'Yes, my dear.' Count Barinski struggled to rise from his chair. Henryk went to his wife and, taking her hand, led her into the room.

'Sit down,' he urged tenderly.

'I've arranged refreshment for you,' she said to break the awkward silence. She called and servants brought in trays of wine and cakes.

Jan Dombrowski got up and offered her his chair. Though, in his mind, anyone who could even consort with Catherine must of necessity be either mad or bad, or both, he was finding himself being increasingly drawn to Kasia, won over by her charm, friendliness and gaiety.

'I think, g-gentlemen, that before anything else is said I should tell you something.' Here she glanced at Henryk as if for confirmation. For an instant he hesitated then, with a slight shrug he nodded.

'As you all know I have spent the last years at the Court of the Empress Catherine. Not only that but she is a friend.' She paused, but no one spoke. 'And now I have to go back.'

'Go back? Go back where?' Naturally that was Jan. She smiled at him.

'To St. Petersburg.'

'St. Petersburg! St.—' Words failed him. Just married and already preparing to go back to – to that – that ... Even his thoughts failed him.

'I know all about this,' said Henryk. 'She has to go. Whatever we may think of Catherine she has shown herself to be a good friend to Kasia.' He stood behind her chair his hand on her shoulder.

'Naturally I'm not exactly attracted to the idea,' he said, 'but she feels she has a duty at least to tell Catherine she must leave her service.' Kasia's hand came up to rest on his. 'I think you all know she's not one to creep away like some miserable little creature in the night.'

The silence was broken by the tapping of Count Branicki's pipe against his heel; a sure sign that the Grand General was disturbed in his mind.

'You really *have* to go back?' he asked kindly.

'Yes, I must.'

'I see.'

'And you think she'll let you return just like that?' Pulawski looked at her curiously. Yes, she was certainly the wife for Henryk.

'I've no doubts at all. Not when she knows I'm married.'

'Will you tell her your husband's name?' Pulawski was beginning to probe like the lawyer he was.

Kasia thought for a moment before answering.

'Yes. Catherine knew Henryk as a boy when she came to stay at my home. If I know her as I think I do, she'll be delighted. She's got no reason to be otherwise.'

'Countess Barinska!' exclaimed Jan. 'Soon the whole of Europe is going to ring with the name Barinski—'

'I think you're doing me a little too much honour, Jan,' murmured Henryk.

'No, it's true. And then what's this Empress going to think of you?' Jan's eyes challenged Kasia for an answer, but it came from Henryk.

'By then Kasia will be safely back in Poland,' he said. 'So it won't really matter, will it?'

His father shifted his bad leg with a small grunt of pain.

'You and Kasia must do as you think best,' he said firmly. 'I think the whole idea's damned crazy but—' he spread out his hands in a gesture of resignation – 'you aren't children any more. But come back,' he added. 'The house will be dead without you.'

Count Branicki roused himself from the refilling of his pipe and looked up at Kasia. 'Please do not be insulted at what I'm about to say.' He saw Henryk stiffen, the dangerous look come into his eyes: the look they were all going to need, that Poland was going to need.

'Would you be so good as to leave us, Countess.'

They all stared at Henryk. But the old man spoke as the Grand General of Poland; Count Barinski nodded at his son.

There was complete silence as Henryk went with his wife to the door; they all stared at the table or munched self-conciously at the tiny sugared cakes. At the door Kasia turned with a little smile on her lips. She gave a small curtsey, half polite, half mocking.

'Gentlemen.'

The door closed behind her.

Dark with anger Henryk demanded, 'So you don't trust her then?'

Count Branicki regarded him calmly. 'Sit down,' he said, 'and listen to what I have to say.' Again it was the Grand General speaking.

'For her own good it would be better if she knew nothing – or, at least, as little as possible.'

'I'd trust her with my right arm,' said Henryk.

'Or any other part of his anatomy,' put in Pulawski drily.

'Except one.' Count Barinski chuckled coarsely, but the laughter was brief.

'I have lived a long time,' said the Grand General, 'and one of the things I've learnt is this: if someone knows nothing then they can tell nothing.'

And Henryk, remembering the blood-splashed dungeons of the Secret Chancellery, knew he was right.

'Perhaps,' said Pulawski casually, sipping his wine, 'perhaps your wife could be of great use to us. After all,' he paused, 'a confidante of the Empress—'

'You mean—' began Henryk.

'Yes.'

An uneasy moment followed, then Count Branicki asked as though talking to himself, 'What was it one of the Borgias said? It is well to beguile those who have shown themselves masters – or, in this case, mistresses of treachery.' He stamped tobacco into his pipe.

'Your wife is a highly intelligent woman, and one with great charm.'

'But she won't spy on her friend, if that's what you mean. I know her. She'll do many things, but not that.'

'Not even for her country?' asked Jan, surprisingly gently.

'No, not even for her country.'

Jan nodded his head, disbelieving and yet understanding.

The Grand General looked at Henryk for fully half a minute before he spoke.

'If we trust Henryk then we trust his wife.'

His old friend, Count Barinski said two words:

'Thank you.'

And Jan Dombrowski thought as he drank his wine, By God, I envy him.

*　　　*　　　*

That night before they went to sleep Henryk said, 'You know they'd like you to act as a spy – at least Branicki and Jan would.'

'A spy?'

'As a friend of Catherine's they know you could discover a lot.'

Kasia lay open-eyed in the darkness.

'Is that what you'd like?' she asked.

'I'd like to find out what was in her mind, yes. What merry little surprise she is planning for Poland. I know you're the one person who could do it but—' He paused. 'Don't worry, darling, I'd never ask you to spy on her. Because you'd never consent.' She heard the smile in his voice.

'But they don't understand that. To them Poland comes first, before anything.'

Again she lay silently seeing many pictures clearly in the darkness.

'Tell me something,' she said. 'If you were faced with the choice of Poland being destroyed or you and I never seeing each other again, which w-would you choose?'

'Is that a fair question?'

'Perhaps not, but supposing it came to that very unfair choice,' she persisted.

'You like to have everything cut and dried, don't you?'

'Over anything to do with us I do.'

'Well,' he said pretending to consider deeply, 'as a true patriot I shouldn't say this but, surprisingly enough, I think on balance I'd choose you.'

'You're laughing at me again.'

'No, my dearest, over this I am not laughing.' Pray God, he thought, we're never faced with such a choice.

Kasia bent over him shrouding his face and shoulders with her hair; very softly she kissed his eyes, then his lips, and lay back, her soft flank against the hardness of his body.

'Thank you, sweetheart, for the most wonderful compliment any woman could have received.'

He rolled on his side and threw an arm across her breasts, pressing his lips to the rounded curve of her shoulder.

'Henryk.'

'Yes?'

'Don't tell me anything, you know, about what you're going to do. Not until I get back.'

He did not answer but his arm tightened protectively round her.

'I am mad to let you go.'

'But you must, you promised. And it'll only be for four m-months then we'll be together for always.' She was crying softly and he kissed the tears from her cheek-bones, whispering words of love and comfort.

Summoning a light-heartedness he did not feel, Henryk said, 'You can always keep your ears open. Some useful information is bound to creep into them.'

But she was still crying helplessly at the thought of the few days left to them and he took her in his arms. And soon her sorrow was drowned in a torrent of passion that arched their bodies and scored his back with the long marks of her nails. They were consumed by the white heat of their mutual love and lust until, emptied and satisfied, they lay exhausted and quivering in each other's arms.

'Thank you,' they whispered. 'My love, my own, thank you.'

And on the wind, the wind from the west, from the Carpathians, there came the faint howl of hunting wolves, running down a panting, quivering stag through the snow.

*   *   *

Major Skurin turned from the map pinned on the wall of the farmhouse. 'What I want to know,' he demanded angrily, 'is what we are supposed to be doing here?' His mouth had grown harder, thinner, during these last few months in the Ukraine; his blue eyes looked out on the snow-covered world even more coldly. There was murder in his soul.

'It's not a war. Not a musket has been fired except to kill an occasional mangy pig. The men are fed up to the teeth. And now this!' He swore obscenely. 'Instead of going home for Christmas what happens? We're ordered to march west.'

'Well, Major, that at least should please you. You've always said you wanted to get into Poland, to where the war will have to be.'

Colonel Glebov sat hunched over the glowing stove, a faint smile on his podgy face. He did not like Skurin, for, unlike the Major, he was not a cold, merciless professional. In fact he had never heard a shot fired in anger. Skurin ignored the remark.

The room was darkened by the snow plastered thickly on the small windows.

'So I am to lead this column as far as some miserable, stinking little Polish town called Rabka and just sit there waiting for further orders, is that it, Colonel?'

'Yes, Major, that is it.'

'But this place is in the foothills of the mountains. What in hell's name are we going to do there? Dragging guns and waggons into the mountains. Christ, they must be crazy!'

'Those are the orders, Major Skurin. And you start within the week.'

'Give me two thousand men,' Skurin rasped, 'and I'll take Krakow for you.' With that he saluted curtly and stamped from the room, shouting for his orderly.

'Oh dear,' murmured Colonel Glebov to himself. 'These keen soldiers!'

*　　*　　*

They left Lipno as a red sun came up through the freezing mist of a day in early December.

'St Nicholas's Day,' Kasia said. 'The day for children.' As if to bear out her words the children of the village ran beside the sledge waving and shouting out to her, 'Goodbye, *Pani*. Come back soon.'

'I will,' she called with bursting heart. 'I promise.' She took Henryk's hand in hers and they did not speak until the village was far behind.

At the house Count Barinski and Adam stood watching until the two sledges were out of sight beyond the trees.

'Your mother would have loved her,' said the old man heavily. He turned and hobbled into the house that had grown suddenly very cold, very quiet, very empty. With that he said no more but went to his room and shut the door.

And Adam, who possessed more imagination than many

thought, tried not to think of what it would be like for them in a few hours' time when they had to part. At least, he thought with sudden wry sadness, if you didn't love then you were spared such moments as these.

*   *   *

The few hours had come to their end.

In the distance beyond the great white plain, where once the Golden Horde had grazed their ponies, rose the snow-capped domes of Kiev. It was there that the escort sent by the Empress of Russia would meet her friend and escort her in safety to St. Petersburg.

And it was on this little hill dotted with small dark trees that Henryk and Kasia were to say goodbye. She leant against him under the heavy fur rugs, her hand tightly in his. Now that the moment had arrived there was so much to say which should have been said but Henryk had been sunk in silent gloom and her few efforts to cheer him had sounded false.

The driver got down from his seat and stamped his feet then he went back to the second sledge – the one that was to take Henryk home. Kasia heard the mutter of their voices. Oh, God, this was awful. Her resolution was weakening. Why should she go back to Catherine? This is my husband I'm leaving. This is the man I love more than life itself and yet, of my own free will, I am leaving him. If he was to take her in his arms and beg her to stay, order her not to go – but he also had given his word, and he said nothing.

'You won't be doing anything – anything dangerous while I'm away?' she asked.

'Not till you're safely home.' He put his arm round her and pulled her very close.

'It'll only be four months,' he said with a smile. 'We've been apart for longer than that, haven't we?'

She nodded, looking away, unable to speak. He tried to summon the courage to get out of the sledge but could not move.

'If I'm away Adam will let me know when you are safely back at Lipno.'

'But you said—'

'Nothing dangerous, darling. I may have to be away in the mountains. A hunting trip.'

She did not feel hurt at the lie. He would tell her everything in his own time.

'Take care – on this hunting trip of yours.' She smiled back at him, her courage greater than his. 'You're very precious to me, Henryk.' Her lips trembled slightly but she still smiled.

'Don't worry. You know me. I'm much too fond of my own skin.'

'You're a fool, Henryk Barinski, but I love you very much.' This time the smile crumpled and her face was buried in his neck; he felt her shoulders shaking.

'Don't,' he whispered. 'Please, sweetheart, don't.' He lifted her head and kissed away the tears. 'Only four months,' he kept saying. 'And think how much you'll have to tell me when you get back.'

Kasia nodded.

'I'm sorry. That was very s-silly of me. It only makes it harder for you.' She brushed away the tears, with the back of her gloves where they froze into tiny spikes of dark fur.

'Kiss me, my darling,' she said quickly. 'Kiss me and then go.'

The strength of his arms was crushing her body as his mouth was bruising her lips.

At last they broke away.

'God bless you, my dearest,' he muttered, hardly daring to trust his voice, 'and keep you safe.' Pushing aside the rugs he jumped from the sledge, beckoning fiercely to the driver who came running.

'There'll be an escort of Russian cavalry waiting at the Dnieper bridge. You will not leave Countess Barinska until you have seen her safely into the charge of the officer in command. Is that clear?'

'Yes, Your Honour.'

'If anything happens to my wife between now and then, don't come back to Lipno. If you do I shall flog you till your backbone's bare.'

The old man who had known Henryk since he was a boy and

was the most faithful servant to the Barinskis knew by his face it was no idle threat.

'I'll take good care of her,' he said quietly.

'Now go!' Henryk shouted, gesturing towards the city.

'*Hah*!' cried the old groom. 'Get on there!'

With a creak of harness and crackle of snow the sledge began to move.

Kasia's face as it was turned towards her husband looked very small and white within the sable hood, her eyes enormous and full of grief.

Henryk raised his hand then let it drop helplessly to his side

'Don't look back,' he called. 'Please don't look back.'

He watched through blurred eyes as the sledge taking her from him grew smaller until it was no more than a speck of soot in the vast white wilderness and the brisk little tinkle of the bells had ceased.

'Come back to me,' he whispered aloud. 'You must come back to me.'

Then he turned and ran to the waiting sledge.

'I'll drive.'

Henryk drove like a man possessed so that the runners sang shrilly in the hard snow, white spray blinded him, and behind him sat the second groom, his hands clenched, eyes closed, thinking, Christ in Heaven, the parting from his wife had driven the Count mad.

And if sudden appalling loneliness can drive someone half crazy then the man was right.

PART SEVEN

THE winter of 1763 was very hard. In the mountains it was even harder. It was night and the pine branches, bent beneath the weight of snow, were ghostly white in the light of a half moon.

Hidden deep in the forest in a hollow clearing among tall straight pine trees that ringed them like sentinels stood half a dozen woodmen's huts. Until Josef the carpenter had got to work, these huts had been rotting and derelict but now they provided warmth and shelter for the twenty-six men who had joined Henryk Barinski to form the nucleus of Poland's new army.

Near but not near enough so that the sound of its rushing water would drown the approach of an enemy, the headwaters of a mountain stream ran down among the ice-glazed rocks to join the larger Skawa a mile below and thence in time to swell the Vistula.

The forest was silent under the icy pall of night; not even the owls planed silently on the still air.

Four men sat in one of the huts. It was well made by Josef, of pine-branches and planks cut from the trees. A stove crackled happily in the middle of the earth and sawdust floor, rich with the scent of pine logs, the smell of drying clothes, powder and cooking. Small oil lamps burnt on the rough table, smoky and flickering but adding to the warmth.

Along the walls were bunks covered in deep pine branches and animal furs.

'All right,' said Henryk. 'That man has complained. Why? Because he has been asked – asked – not told, to stand guard from two till four in the morning.' He looked round the others in the hut.

'Is that going to kill him?'

'No', said Jan Dombrowski uncertainly. 'But—'

'But what?'

'He's sick. He's got pains in his belly.'

Henryk looked at him and Dombrowski's eyes fell away.

'It's getting cold in here,' Henryk said. 'Would you put some more wood on the stove.'

Casimir Pulawski got up. Henryk watched him as he shoved the logs into the stove. Lean, dark, his face alight with intelligence; dressed like a Cossack with a waisted red coat and belt of white fur in which were stuck two silver-mounted pistols. He wore his fur cap at a rakish angle, cocked forward over one sharp, brown eye.

'Those aren't the clothes for war,' said Henryk with a grin to soften the reprimand. 'Not this kind of war. For this you need to wear the colour of the trees and the earth: sometimes of the snow.' He himself, like the other three in the little cabin, was dressed roughly and very soberly in browns and faded greens; white sheepskin coats hung on pegs; muskets, pistols and sabres hung oiled and ready for instant use along the walls among the pelts of wolf, stag and bear. The little smoke-blackened room smelt of war: powder, leather, grease.

All the men were bearded except for Casimir whose face looked very young. Henryk's swarthy skin was even darker now from the winds and the burning frosts of mid-winter, but the tiny lines at the corners of his eyes were paler from constantly screwing up his eyes, looking into the distances across sunlit snow.

He looked very much as he had done during his time at sea.

'So your father is gathering an army in Warsaw,' he said, spearing a piece of venison on his knife.

Casimir laughed.

'Hardly an army. He is, shall we say, sounding out friends.'

As Adam was doing in Krakow, Henryk thought.

'What you mean is, they're all waiting to see whether we are successful or not. Is that it?' Dombrowski spoke with all his truculent forthrightness, but if Pulawski minded the tone he did not show it.

'I think some of them are more deeply committed than that,' he replied pleasantly.

236

'Soon all Poland will be committed.' Father Gurowski spoke for the first time. He was a sad-faced man of about fifty – 'far too old for sleeping in a pile of half-cured skins,' he was always grumbling in his lugubrious way. But then he was always inclined to grumble over almost everything: his corns, the cold, the Church, with which he had become disillusioned many years before. But Henryk knew him to be a reliable, loyal character with a bitter hatred of Russia and anything to do with her. A priest better with the sword than with the prayerbook. 'Another Reverend Debolecki,' Jan used to tease. 'Are you going to lead the light horsemen to Moscow?'

'And then,' said Father Gurowski, 'may God help her.' His deepset eyes reflected dark, unspoken thoughts.

'It's for Poland to help herself,' said the fifth man. A young man in his late twenties with a round, bland face and deceptively soft blue eyes, Jacek Zalinski was the second son of an estate-owner near Lipno. He had joined Henryk not out of any warlike ambitions but mainly to escape the stifling influence of a possessive mother, and that, as Henryk realized, might well turn him into a good soldier.

'Yes,' he agreed. 'And all we can do is to guide her on her way.'

They ate and drank for a while in silence, each one of them occupied with his own thoughts. And the silence, broken only by the sounds of their eating, the sputter of the lamps, the spitting crackle of the logs, could have been the only silence in the whole world.

'Tomorrow I have to leave,' said Casimir. 'I have to get back to Warsaw.'

'Don't wear that coat then.' Dombrowski picked his teeth with a pine splinter. 'Or you'll be seen all the way from here to Kiev.'

'A pity,' said Casimir sadly. 'I rather like the colour.'

'I like the colour of a Cardinal's hat,' said Father Gurowski. 'But somehow I feel I shall never get one.' He did not sound too worried.

'What message have you for my father?' Casimir asked Henryk.

237

Henryk stirred the remnants of the game stew with the long blade of his hunting knife, chasing the bits of meat with intense concentration.

'Tell him this,' he said. 'As soon as the Russians move we will move faster.'

'And the Grand General?'

'The same.'

No one else spoke. They could hear the trees crackling in the frost. Then they heard the bang on the door.

Casimir's hand went to one of the pistols but no one else moved.

The door opened and Sergeant Nym stood there, huge and stolid.

'What is it, Nym?' Henryk asked.

'It's Bludhorn, Your Excellency,' said Sergeant Nym, black in the doorway. 'He says he's sick.'

'What did I tell you?' Dombrowski's expression was smug. 'Too sick to stand sentry?'

'That's what he says.'

'All right,' said Henryk, 'I'll come.'

Sergeant Nym vanished into the silver, shadowy night.

'Hasn't got the guts of a louse.' Dombrowski belched loudly. 'Why the hell did he think he could cope with this sort of life, if he's going to faint like a bloody woman the moment he feels ill?'

There was silence. It was difficult to know how to answer such a wild question.

'Sometimes,' said Father Gurowski, 'a man feels very close to death. Who are we to say he doesn't?'

Henryk put on his white warm coat and went to the door. Casimir followed.

'I'm going to bed,' said Jacek Zalinski. 'God knows what's going to happen tomorrow.'

'Very wise.' Father Gurowski yawned, leaning back from the table.

'If at any moment we're expected to fight for our lives,' Dombrowski agreed, 'then surely we can at least be allowed a good night's sleep.'

Henryk stood outside the hut breathing the frosty air. No

snow fell for it was frozen to the branches. No wind blew for it was frozen silent in the air.

'Sergeant Nym!'

'Your Excellency.' The vast shadow appeared with a scrunch of snow.

'How many times have I told you not to address me as Your Excellency?'

'Often,' said Sergeant Nym imperturbably. He knew his commander and just how far he could go. The only regular cavalry soldier among what, in his own mind, he termed these odds and sods, Sergeant Nym had only recently been employed in the Royal Bodyguard of Augustus the Third of Saxony – and, by some flight of fancy, of Poland too. The young nobles and sons of squires did not mind obeying the orders of a man who before he joined the army had been a mere peasant. For he, except Henryk, was the only other professional among them.

Having no wish to serve under King Poniatowski he had volunteered to follow this Barinski who, they said, was a man who would lead you to glory, or death, or both.

'Do you think Bludhorn's too sick to take his turn of duty?'

'I'm not sure, sir.'

'For God's sake, Nym, yes or no.'

'Yes.'

'Very well then.'

They stood by the door of the hut, their breath steaming in the air.

'Just because we don't wear cuirasses and plumes it doesn't mean we can do without discipline.' Casimir Pulawski listened to the calm answer and, somewhere in his brain, something registered. This was a man that one listened to.

Henryk thought of Captain Primrose, of Jem Pike and the lash. If the British Navy had taught him anything it was that you could not fight successfully without discipline. In fact, he thought suddenly and very unexpectedly, you could not live without discipline.

But discipline came in different forms. There was that of the gallows, the yard-arm, and the rope's end. There was also that imposed by a man who could lead, who could inspire, who, if

239

he had to, could kill. Either they trusted you, or they feared you; sometimes both; they were rarely fond of you.

Two tracks led into the camp. One came from the north, the road leading from Rabka to Cieszyn; the other, climbing steeply into the mountains, would lead them to safety should the camp be discovered and attacked.

But where they joined the road Henryk had insisted on a maze of well-trodden paths which continued, churned up by horses' hooves and boots, well into the trees before becoming the single entrance track. Only by the greatest bad luck would an enemy find his way into the camp. To assist the deception, logs were piled at the edge of the trees; now and then they were cut, and fresh chips lay on the snow; branches were burnt and passers-by saw wood-cutters at work who shouted greetings, leaning on their axes.

'He's a good man, that Bludhorn,' said Nym, breaking into his thoughts. 'If he says he's sick then he's sick right enough.'

'They're all good men. Does he need a doctor?'

'Too much pork,' said Sergeant Nym.

Two days before Zalinski had shot a boar; yesterday evening a young stag drinking at the stream. So far he had not failed to keep them supplied with fresh meat.

'Give him a clean-out with herbs and he'll be all right.' Nym was a great one for herbs, trusting them to cure all ills from gout to colic.

'Do as you like,' said Henryk with a smile. 'But I want him fit to ride – and fight – within two days.'

'Two days!' Casimir whistled between his teeth. 'As soon as that?'

'The Russians are in Rabka. By what I've heard it's a large column, too many men merely to occupy a little place like that. They're on their way to the west, and that must bring them past here.'

'By God, I wish I could stay with you for it,' Casimir spoke wistfully.

'You'll get your chance.'

Sergeant Nym cleared his throat. 'Will there be anything else?'

'No, Sergeant, thank you.' With anyone else he would have

checked that the sentries were posted but he knew the sun was as unlikely to rise as Sergeant Nym to leave sentries unposted.

'Goodnight, Your – sir.'

'Goodnight, Nym.'

The two men stood quietly as Nym went round the other huts. At each door his great bulk was silhouetted against the red glow and the snow crystals glittered like a sprinkling of golden dust.

'If more like him join us,' said Casimir with feeling, 'we can hardly fail.'

Henryk did not answer. Nym had vanished into his own hut. There was silence except for the muted murmur of men's voices; the distant icy tinkle of the stream. Here and there moonlight broke through the roof of white branches; a wolf howled far away to be answered by another high in the mountains above them.

'The Grand General. Prince Radziwill. Oginski. What will they do if you fail?'

'Do?' said Henryk with a shrug. 'Nothing. Publicly they will probably disown me. I don't know.' He felt depressed; the silence of the shrouded trees bore down heavily on his spirit; he was very tired and the bayonet wound of Rossbach ached dully. He longed to mount his little mare, Rasulka, and ride away secretly; ride to Lipno where his wife waited. For Adam had come a few days previously with the news he had hoped and prayed for; Kasia had returned safely from Petersburg.

'How is she?'

'I had the devil's own job preventing her from coming with me.' Adam had chuckled. 'She's got quite a temper, that wife of yours. It only abated when I'd told her you'd expressly forbidden her to leave Lipno.' He paused. 'But she said that if you weren't back within a week then she'd come and find you herself if it meant combing every inch of the High and Low Tatras.' He had become serious.

'If anything happens to you, Henryk, I think she'd die.' Then brusquely, embarrassed at his words, he added, 'Father and I would be quite upset too.'

Adam had left with the parting words, 'Soon I shall join you. Globnik can look after the estate.' He had sounded guilty to be leaving his brother to the forest, the snows and danger of death.

'Are we right to do this?' Henryk now asked wearily. 'Are we thinking enough of the consequences? God. I wish I knew.'

'You're playing for the highest stakes there are,' said Casimir. 'The future of our country.'

'If I fail, what do I lose? Twenty-six men. If I win, I may gain an army.' Henryk was speaking aloud the thoughts and doubts which had been burdening his mind for weeks. Casimir let him talk.

'Whatever the result down there—' Henryk pointed through the blur of the trees – 'Russian soldiers will lie dead. We're not at war, yet Russians will die, and Catherine will want vengeance. This I do know. There will be burning and murder and rape, famine and disease.'

'These things will come anyway,' Casimir interrupted firmly. 'There are sixty thousand Russians poised on the frontier. Sooner or later they'll attack us. At the moment they hope to take Poland by peaceful means. Are we going to stand by and allow that? Surely it's better to go forward and meet what's coming than just to sit and wait?'

'You're like Jan,' said Henryk. 'How old are you?'

'Twenty-one.'

'Twenty-one. I'm thirty-six. I've fought in battles on land and on the sea and I've seen what war can do. Some of it is not very pretty.'

'Slavery is not very pretty either.'

'It's a difficult question, but I think I'm probably on the same side – except that slavery goes on longer than death.'

The wolf howled again, longer on the wind.

'And the peasants?' asked Casimir. 'What if they take them and put them to the torture?'

'I know. I've thought of that. There'll be reprisals.' Henryk sighed. 'Some of our countrymen will hate us; some will try and betray us and then we shall have to kill them. And so the hatreds will grow.'

'But you're right to do this. You must believe that.' Casimir spoke with passionate intensity. 'Within a few months, perhaps weeks even, of the first shot being fired you'll have all Poland behind you. These forests—' he gestured round the silent trees – 'will not be large enough to hold the men who'll come to join you.'

Henryk kicked at the frozen crust with the heel of his boot, bent down and scooped powdery snow into the palm of his hand. He watched as the little white cone very slowly dwindled and melted away into the warmth of his skin.

'I wonder,' he said heavily. 'I very much wonder.' Then, in an attempt to throw off the moment of depression he smiled and clapped the young man on the shoulder.

'It's time you got some sleep. You've a long ride tomorrow.' He smiled again and this time the smile turned to a chuckle.

'As far as Rabka you'll be honoured by a servant. I shall ride with you to the town. Behind you, of course, as befits a groom.'

'But – is it wise?' Casimir touched his own face involuntarily.

'The scar, you mean? I've never been to Rabka and, as far as I know, no one from there has ever visited Lipno. I shall be an old soldier, veteran of Zorndorf, full of vodka and boring tales of forgotten campaigns which I'll inflict on the first Russian soldiers I can find in a drinking mood. In exchange I hope to learn a little of their future movements. And that shouldn't be too difficult. Oil a Russian soldier sufficiently well and he'll soon be telling you everything from the personal habits of his officers to what he particularly wants from the woman he's looking forward to having in the next town.'

'You're a bit crazy sometimes,' said Casimir with an answering laugh. 'But I see why these men follow you.'

Henryk watched him go inside their hut then went to the one where Bludhorn slept.

The five other men playing cards got up from the table as Henryk came in.

'Lucky as usual, I see, Lazienski.' The man grinned sheepishly, glancing down at the pile of little wooden counters by his hand.

'He never loses, that one.' He was a tall, red-haired man with a slight cast in one eye.

Bludhorn lay on his bunk. Every now and then his face tautened from the griping pain of his bowels. There was sweat on his skin and his fists were clenched.

243

'How is it, Bludhorn?' Henryk asked gently.

'Not too good.' He tried a weak smile.

'Will you be fit to ride in a couple of days?'

'Yes. If I have to be tied into the saddle.' He gritted his teeth against the next fierce spasm.

'He's better than he was,' volunteered Lazienski with a wink at his companions. 'Most of the day he's been in and out of that bunk like a jack rabbit. Then he got a damned great spoonful of Nym's herbs pushed into him and at least he hasn't left his bunk for over an hour.'

'The Sergeant and his herbs,' said one of the men, shaking his head. 'They either clear you out or close you up.' Henryk joined in the laughter.

'Who's on sentry?'

'Kolbe and Ducek.'

For a moment Henryk stood looking down at the sick man. 'See that he's kept warm and given plenty to drink.'

He wished them goodnight and went out to see Kolbe.

It was impossible to walk silently; every step crunched against the silence of the night. Though he knew exactly the whereabouts of the sentry-posts – one, seventy yards down the track, the other some forty yards farther on – Henryk was startled by the sudden quiet challenge. In his white coat and sheepskin cap Kolbe could have been a white space between the trees, the musket cradled in his arm a black branch. He emerged from the little shelter made of branches cunningly entwined to break the bitter force of the blizzards that roared through the trees, turning the days to a thick grey murk, the nights to impenetrable, choking darkness.

'Nothing to report?'

'Nothing to report, except that the cold's nipping my toes like a pair of hot pincers.' He stamped his bulky felt boots.

'If that's the worst any of us have to worry about things won't be too bad.'

Kolbe patted his musket. 'It's time she had something better to fire at than deer.'

'She will, Kolbe, she will.'

Farther along the track he found Ducek at the entrance to his little shelter. For a while he talked with the man but it was not easy for Ducek spoke in monosyllables, being a shy and uncommunicative person, and, after a long look down to the thin white ribbon that snaked among the trees to the road, Henryk returned to his hut.

The others were asleep; Father Gurowski snoring as if wanting the monstrous sounds to be heard in Petersburg. Casimir lay curled up like a baby.

Henryk longed for sleep but his mind was too keyed up; the thoughts raced through his head. He watched the glowing red eye of the stove and his imagination was filled with the sight of burning villages, fire licking the blackened sides of the *Richelieu*. He remembered ghastly wounds he thought long forgotten, the screams of men and horses, the howl of grapeshot and little Cornu falling, clutching his throat.

Try as he might he could remember nothing but war. Within the week he, Henryk Barinski, he himself, would trigger off events which could only lead to slaughter, burning, famine. By this decision he would once again release the Four Horsemen to ride the flame-tinged skies.

He asked God for guidance but no revelation came. Now, at last, alone among those who slept peacefully, he knew what it was to be a leader – and not even Captain Primrose had had to face a decision of such terrible magnitude.

But Kasia had agreed and she had suffered and was willing to suffer again. He was overcome by so sharp a longing for her, not only to make love to her but just to have the comfort of her presence beside him, that he had to bury his face in the rough pillow to stifle the audible groan.

It was better to think of tomorrow; of Rabka and of what would follow when the Russians entered the defile this side of the ford. He had to lead these men, and he had to lead them well. And then, when that was over, he could go to Kasia.

When at last he fell asleep it was to a night of fitful slumber, sudden awakenings and strange, phantom-ridden dreams.

*　　*　　*

The two riders passed few people on the way to Rabka. It was a crisp, crackling morning aglitter in the thin winter sunshine, without a breath of wind, and the frost hung in the branches and from the dead grass showing above the snow in shining cobwebs. At the turning to Krakow they met a small procession of peasant carts laden with firewood.

Casimir gazed at them haughtily, raising his whip in a slight gesture of response to their polite greetings.

'Good day, Your Honour.'

'A warning, Your Honour: there are Russians in Rabka.'

'Yes,' cried a young girl excitedly. 'We saw them, and guns too. Great big guns.'

Casimir nodded coldly, as though Russians meant no more to him than so many midges. But Henryk answered and Casimir was astounded to hear his voice; it could have been the meanest serf speaking.

'They must be blind these Russians to let such a pretty girl go past them.' He spoke in a sort of nasal whine.

She flushed and broke into peals of giggles. Whips cracked, men shouted as the long carts rumbled slowly away over the brownish, hard-packed snow. And if any of the woodcutters gave a thought to the magnificent horse ridden by the scarred man in a dirty, matted sheepskin with heavy rags wound round his legs and feet, they assumed it was the servant riding his master's spare mount.

The girl, watching till they were out of sight, thought, admiring Casimir's erect carriage in the saddle, remembering his arrogant good looks, Why couldn't it have been that one, in his splendid coat with a sabre at his belt, to pay the compliment, and not the dirty, miserable-looking thing slouched in the saddle like a sack of rotten potatoes?

As they entered the defile Henryk closed the gap between them to a few paces, ready to drop back to a respectful distance should anyone come in sight.

'It's here we'll ambush them.'

'A perfect place,' said Casimir, looking at the high banks topped here and there by clumps of scrub birch and occasional young pine trees.

'The best shots up there.' Henryk pointed to the trees. 'In front of them charging horsemen; at their back the ford. But it'll all depend on their order of march.'

'And whether they have cavalry,' Casimir said, looking to right and left, taking it all in.

'That's my biggest worry. A squadron of heavy cavalry – even a troop – and our chances are rather too slim for comfort.'

'I wouldn't like to be in their commander's boots if they haven't.' Casimir laughed. 'You'll cut them to pieces.'

'They fight well, these Russians.'

'So do Poles.'

At the end of the defile they came to the ford. Ice reached well out from both banks separated by a narrow flow of black water. The ice splintered sharply beneath the horses' hooves.

The water rose until Henryk felt the intense cold soaking through his foot wrappings and envied Casimir his solid riding boots.

'They won't haul guns through this in a hurry,' observed Henryk. 'Nor waggons either.'

The trees grew close to the water's edge and so thickly that they gave little chance of escape off the road.

'If all goes well they'll have to run all the way back to Rabka.'

The small market town lay about two miles beyond the ford, perched on a slight rise so that the wooden spire of the church showed clearly visible above the treetops. Before they came in sight of the first houses Henryk dismounted, and leading his horse some way up a tiny track and into the hidden shelter of the trees he tethered it. From the sack at the back of the saddle he took an armful of hay and spread it on the snow.

'There you are, get on with that until I come back.' He patted the horse gently on the neck and rejoined Casimir, having cut himself a long, crooked branch. He walked, bent-backed and exaggerating his limp, now and then hawking and spitting into the snow.

'How does it look?' he asked, in his beggar's whine.

'Marvellous. The very picture of a penniless old soldier.' Casimir's laughing glance turned serious.

'Well, this is where we say goodbye.'

'We'll meet again,' said Henryk in his normal voice.

'I know. Perhaps in Moscow. Until then all our thoughts will be with you.' He pointed in the direction of the ford.

'Send us word about – about what happens here. Send it at once, for we must know.' Taking a quick look up and down the road Casimir leant down with outstretched hand.

'May God be with you and your men – and I wish to heaven I could be with you as well.'

Wheeling his horse abruptly he put spurs to its flanks and cantered away, kicking up snow.

'*Au revoir*, Henryk,' he called without looking back, raising the whip to his fur hat in salutation and farewell.

'*Au revoir*,' echoed Henryk softly. 'God knows when we may meet again.'

He set out on his hobbling progress into Rabka. At once he began to see Russian soldiers; the whole place was crawling with them and he saw from the uniforms that they were the men who had been billeted at Lipno under the hard-faced Major Skurin.

* * *

'That's a hell of a scar you've got yourself, friend,' said the Russian corporal, smacking his lips over the last swig at his beer-mug.

'Zorndorf,' Henryk answered. 'A bloody Prussian sabre. One of Seydlitz's swine.' He wondered if Seydlitz and his cavalry had in fact been present at Zorndorf.

'Zorndorf? You were at Zorndorf?' A large private with a square head looked at Henryk with new respect.

'For my sins, yes.'

'I'll buy you a vodka, by Christ,' shouted the man above the din of the smoky little tavern. Every corner was filled with the green and yellow tunics of the Smolensk Regiment whose owners seemed all to be yelling at the pitch of their lungs and emptying a solid torrent of beer down their open throats.

'What brings you to Poland?' asked another man at the table.

'I had a Polish mother,' Henryk said truthfully.

'Ah.' They thought about that for a little while.

'And what brings *you* to Poland?' Henryk asked blandly.

The soldier looked at Henryk for a moment before answering.

'Our much-loved commanding officer, Major Skullhead Skurin, he's what brings us to this God-forsaken place.' He laughed drunkenly.

'There are better places to spend the winter,' agreed Henryk. The soldier made an unsuccessful attempt to light a filthy little pipe, cursing as he burnt his fingers.

'Oh, we're not staying the winter here. Our precious commanding officer waits until we're just beginning to get settled and choosing ourselves the best girls, and believe me, friend, some of these Polish whores are—'

'I had a Polish mother,' Henryk reminded him with just the right amount of indignation.

'Too many Poles,' said the man thickly. 'Shouldn't be any Polish mothers, then no more Poles and we could go home.'

'I wonder where your officer will be taking you next?'

'The Lord knows. Some other stinking little town to the west,' the sergeant said. 'On the march again in two days' time, so wash your feet and oil your boots, and off we go again, boys.'

The square-headed soldier pushed his way back with Henryk's vodka.

'To Zorndorf,' he cried raising his mug.

'To Zorndorf,' cried Henryk, finishing his vodka in one clean swallow.

'The happiest day of my life,' he added for good measure. 'They may have beaten us but, by all the fires of hell, we gave them something to think about. We showed the world that day that we Russians can fight as well as any of 'em – Frenchmen, English, Austrians, Prussians and all the rest.' Warming to his theme he was attracting more and more listeners to the table.

'He's right there.'

'With the Empress to lead us we'll march to Berlin.'

'And Paris too, if we have to.'

'Who were you with?' asked the corporal.

'The Preobrazhensky,' Henryk said after a tiny pause, hoping fervently that the Guards Regiments had fought that day, and not been on duty in Petersburg.

'Another vodka for an ex-Guardsman,' called a voice.

'We missed it. They had us stuck out on the steppes at Orenburg watching for a few miserable Tatars.'

'Did you see Orlov?'

'I fought beside him for two hours.' Henryk tossed down the raw spirit. 'For two hours we stood against the fire of the Prussian guns and threw back their infantry at the point of the bayonet. Oh, I tell you, my friends, the world will never see another such battle as Zorndorf.' He held their rapt attention with an entirely fictitious account of the day, heavily spiced with memories of Rossbach. After all, for the infantryman, most battles were much the same: who can hang on the longest.

Then, at last, when his imagination was running out and he knew he had drunk enough vodka he got unsteadily to his feet and raised a hand for silence.

'And now I must leave you. I have a long road home and a wife who has no great liking for vodka – nor for husbands who drink it.'

There was a roar of laughter at that.

'Shove your head in a horse-trough!'

'What's a bad-tempered wife to the victor of Zorndorf?'

'If we'd cavalry like the ones riding with you lot we'd have sent old Seydlitz flying up his own backside.' Amid the laughter someone shouted, 'We've got no bloody cavalry. We're foot-soldiers like yourself. We walk everywhere.'

'The only horses we ever see carry old Skullhead and any other officers mad enough to serve under him.'

'And a few old nags to haul the baggage waggons.'

'And the guns,' said Henryk, slurring his words on purpose.

'Call those guns! Put a ball into one of them and it'd be just as likely to come out of its arse as its mouth. They were old when the great Peter was on the throne.'

'Well, thank you for your hospitality, gentlemen. Perhaps I'll shee you in Cieszyn.' He winked and leered. 'The girlsh there are—' He drew curves in the air and then lurched for the door.

'See you there in three days' time, friend,' the corporal shouted after him.

Until he was well out of sight of the tavern Henryk hobbled

and weaved his way along the road, now and then bursting into some unsteady singing which drew reproving glances from women in their doorways and laughter from a crowd of children who followed him to the outskirts of the town, chanting derisively: 'Hop-skip, Hop-skip!'

By the time he reached the trees where he had left his horse the sky was overcast and dusk falling early, the wind was rising and there was a look of more snow to come from the east.

Henryk rode through the ford and the defile, planning minutely the exact position to be occupied by his ten musketeers. He hardly needed to touch his horse who could have found his way back to the camp blindfolded. As he dismounted the first small hard snow was rattling in the branches, and the little cracks of reddish light looked very warm and inviting, but first he tethered his horse with the others in the sheltered lines: a rough, three-sided wall of thick pine bark, roofed with branches. He threw a rug over the animal and gave him a generous bunch of hay.

When Henryk entered his hut he was greeted by a chorus of questions. But he shook his head and sat down. Zalinski brought him a bowl of hot melted snow with which he washed the dirt from his hands and face. He threw the flea-ridden old coat into a corner and slowly unwound the sodden rags from his legs, and all in silence.

Jan put a dish of steaming pork stew in front of him and a jug of mead. Henryk nodded his thanks and took a deep draught of the heady, sweet liquid.

'Ah,' he exclaimed. 'That takes away the taste of cheap vodka.' He started on the stew, revelling in the warm food passing down his throat, revelling in the heat of the stove and, mischievously, in the barely contained impatience on the faces of his expectant companions.

It was Jan who spoke first, as he knew it would be. Impetuously he burst out with, 'Well, what happened? What did you see? What did you find out?'

With exquisite slowness Henryk poured himself another glass of mead. Leaning back he looked round the little room, letting his eyes rest on each man in turn. Smoke puffed from the stove as the wind rose to a sudden roar in the trees.

'We have two days in which to prepare,' he said slowly.

His head was beginning to spin. The Russian hospitality, the raw vodka coupled with the cold ride home and the warm mead was having more effect than he cared to admit. Moving carefully and with the extreme concentration of one who is determined to show himself completely sober, Henryk rose to his feet and walked very purposefully towards his bunk.

'Tomorrow, we will go into the plan in minute detail.' He clambered in and fell thankfully into the nest of furs, closing his eyes against the roof of the hut which seemed to be lowering itself at him, now a blur, now so clear he could make out every cobweb, every vein of wood.

'Tomorrow,' he repeated. 'You all know what we have to know. It only remains—' He stopped, trying to remember what the devil it was he was going to say. Zalinski winked at Father Gurowski who shut his eyes and lifted his face as if praying.

Jan who was cook that week banged about at the stove.

'Not so much noise,' said Henryk. 'Please, Jan, have a heart – not so much bloody noise.' Henryk groaned softly. 'Tomorrow we'll look at it on the actual ground – but tomorrow's a long way away – thank God. Oh, and they've got no cavalry. Thought it might interest you.'

With that Henryk turned his face to the wall and almost immediately lost consciousness.

*   *   *

Major Skurin sat in his billet – two rooms in the best house in Rabka – and studied his orders sourly. Like his men he had just got settled. His unwilling hostess was a good-looking woman, a widow in her early forties, and he was beginning to hope that perhaps she was becoming slightly less unwilling. And now this! Pack up and march to some unholy place with an unpronounceable name. He went to the small window; light snow fled past dancing in the wind. He'd had just about his bellyful of marching through snowstorms. But his orders were very definite: he and his detachment were to be in Cieszyn by the evening of Thursday.

Once again he measured out the distance by road: thirty odd miles. An easy seven-hour march for his men, but burdened with these damned guns, which seemed to need greasing every other mile, and the creaking stores carts it was going to be nearer ten hours. Being the experienced soldier he was, Major Skurin hated night marches, especially through thickly wooded country.

For the tenth time he reminded himself they were not at war. But why the hell hadn't they allowed him any cavalry? Thirty miles into a snowstorm and nothing between himself riding at the head of the column and any crazy Pole who took it into his head to loose off a musket at the officer on his big black horse.

And, on top of everything else, he was still lumbered with that young nincompoop, Ensign Potovski.

The door opened and the Polish woman came in carrying a bowl of *bortzch*, and some bread and cheese. Major Skurin rose gallantly to his feet, smiling his bleak smile, and was disappointed to see no answering expression in the blue eyes beneath the beautifully marked black eyebrows.

'Thank you,' he said in Polish. Wordlessly she left the room to return with the mug of beer he drank with every meal. This time he said nothing but the look in his hard eyes was softer, almost pleading. Her handsome mouth curled slightly – was it contempt, or worse, was it pity? She went from the room and left him to his solitary meal.

For the first time in his forty-four years Major Skurin realized how lonely he was. Except for his profession he had nothing, absolutely nothing. At that moment, if he had been the sort of man to indulge in self-pity, tears would have filled his eyes. But instead he forced his mind back to the immediate problems: would the ford be too deep for the guns? Was this snowfall going to increase to a blizzard? Orders or no orders he was not going to march thirty miles into the teeth of a raging blizzard. He half hoped the wind would get up. Then he could stay in the warmth and at least he could look at the proud widow and enjoy the sight of her high firm bosom. If they were at war, he thought, then he could take her as a conqueror's right. Not normally a lustful man, Major Skurin felt his body stirring at the idea of her struggling beneath him.

He began to tremble and sweat and only with a great effort pulled himself together as he heard the tramp of heavy boots and Ensign Potovski came in.

'God, it's cold!' He held his arms above the stove so that the snow melted and drops of water darted sizzling about the glowing top.

Major Skurin did not answer. He was intensely irritated by the inane grin on the young man's weak face. At last he could stand it no longer.

'What in hell's name are you smirking about?'

Ensign Potovski's grin widened.

'Good news, sir.'

'We've been ordered back to Petersburg,' grunted Major Skurin sarcastically. Or you have, he thought sourly; that would be better news than most.

'Ha, ha.' Potovski laughed dutifully. 'No.' He paused. 'We've got some cavalry at last.'

Skurin sat up very straight.

'If this is one of your infantile jokes, Potovski—'

'No sir, really. I've just seen them. The troop sergeant's coming to report to you when he's got his men settled in somewhere. They're dragoons, sir.'

'A troop of dragoons.' Skurin sighed. 'Ah well, better than nothing, I suppose.' He drew towards him his map and the paper.

Slowly, thoughtfully, he began to scratch out what he had written and to substitute new orders.

*　　　*　　　*

By the early morning of Thursday the blizzard had blown itself out. A few flakes floated gently down out of the metallic dawn sky as Major Skurin put on his heavy cloak and picked up his hat. Outside he heard the rattle and jingle of harness as the dragoons trotted forward to take up their position at the head of the column, the sound of the hooves muffled by the thick, powdery snow.

He turned to his hostess.

'Thank you for your hospitality,' he said in his slow stilted Polish. 'Perhaps one day, should we return, I— ' He stumbled lamely to a halt. She stood very still staring straight at him with eyes as cold as the dawn outside, and never said a word.

Cramming on his hat and giving her a short, curt nod he strode from the room, pulling on his thick riding gauntlets and shouting angrily for Ensign Potovski.

Moving quickly the woman shut the door behind him and put up the bar, then she ran to the back door, popped her head out and called softly, 'It's all right, Piotr, he's gone.'

Sergeant Nym stepped out from the shelter of a little out-house and followed her inside.

She faced him then, with a cry of love and welcome; she was in his arms bringing warmth to his taut, frozen face with her kisses. He almost crushed her ribs with his great strength as he felt her heavy breasts tighten against his chest.

'Oh, Piotr darling, how I've missed you.'

'And you, Marishka.' He buried his mouth in her neck and she gasped. Then he held her away from him. There was colour in her face and a velvet glow in her eyes; she tried to get back close to him but he held her away.

'Did he—' he nodded at the sounds beyond the window – 'did he try anything?'

'No.' She laughed gaily, showing strong even teeth. 'No. Major Skurin was most correct. Not that he didn't want to, mind you.' She laughed again, more mischievously.

'If he'd so much as laid a finger on you I'd go out now and kill him.'

'And be cut down by the dragoons. That wouldn't be a very good start to our life together, would it?' But Nym did not seem to hear; he was gazing at her in disbelief.

'*Dragoons*? What dragoons?'

'A troop of them, darling. It's only a troop.'

'Are you sure? Have you seen them?' He had seized her by the shoulders and was shaking her.

'Don't, you're hurting!'

'I'm sorry, Marishka, I didn't mean to, but – oh, my God, cavalry.' He reached the window in one long stride and peered cautiously out. To the left, just visible above the tall mitre hats of the infantry he could make out the blue cloaks of the dragoons. In front of him, level with the window, Major Skurin sat his horse, watching as the four guns and ammunition limbers creaked into their place in the column.

'Come on,' he called. 'Hurry it up there!' In rear of the guns another small detachment of infantry halted and stood blowing on their hands and stamping their feet.

'I've got to get back at once,' said Nym.

Marishka went to the little dresser and took out a handful of small cakes. 'Here, take these.'

He shoved them into his wide pocket beneath the wolfskin jerkin. 'You're a lovely woman, Marishka, and I love you very much.'

She clung to him biting back her tears. 'When will I see you again?'

'As soon as all this nonsense is over. Keep a corner of the bed warm for me.' She smiled, brushing at her eyes with the back of her hand.

'Don't go doing anything stupid, numbskull.'

'I've done it already by promising to marry you.' He kissed her hard on the mouth and went.

After he had gone she watched through the little frosted window, her heart in her mouth in case his departure from the back was noticed. But she need not have worried. There was far too much noise as the Russian column formed up. And, besides, no one out there was thinking of anything but his own discomfort.

Sergeant Nym led his horse quickly and silently along a narrow lane running behind the houses, his hand clamped firmly on its muzzle to prevent it calling to its Russian cousins. Two hundred yards from the village and out of sight of the leading dragoons, he mounted and rode at full gallop, bending low in the saddle. And as he rode he thought of what he had seen – one tiny corner of his mind kept asking, as the trees flew by and the freezing air whipped cruelly at his narrowed eyes, Doesn't she realize what she's getting herself into, for God's sake?

He splashed through the icy waters of the ford, through the

defile – covered every inch of the way by ten muskets: five men under Zalinski on one side, five under Kolbe hidden among the birches opposite. And beside each man lay two other muskets, loaded and primed, and two pistols.

Fifty well-aimed shots by men who had practised for months at targets ranging from a drinking stag to a running wolf would turn the defile into a panic-stricken death-trap.

Two hundred yards beyond the western end of the defile Henryk waited in the deep shadow of the trees, within sight of the road. Beside him Jan Dombrowski sat his horse in the deceptively casual way he had, as if he would never dream of exerting either the animal or himself.

Behind them fourteen men shifted in their saddles, muttered to each other in low voices, checked their holster pistols for the dozenth time or drew their well-oiled sabres half way from the scabbards. Now and then a horse tossed its head with a sharp little jingle or pawed impatiently at the snow.

'What's keeping him?' Henryk asked curtly. 'He should have been back by now.' If the Russians arrived before Nym – well, they'd just have to suit their plans to the occasion.

'Marishka,' said a voice and there was some subdued laughter. They all knew about the widow in Rabka.

Henryk turned in his saddle and looked at them with a half grin. 'Not even the love of a good woman would keep Nym at a time like this.'

They smiled back, teeth white in bearded, weather-beaten faces. They were dressed in the toughest of their animal skins, bulky in jerkins and fur to smother a ball and dull a sabre cut. But their sword arms were free.

'All right, Bludhorn?'

The man nodded. He looked ghastly but his face no longer twisted from the griping pains in his stomach. Out of them all he was the only one who carried a lance. At first Henryk had forbidden it but having seen the way Bludhorn could transfix the swinging bag at full gallop and pick up a small square of leather on the lance-tip in the way of the Cossacks, he had allowed him the distinction of being known as Bludhorn the Lancer.

'There's a horse coming,' said Jan, a thrill of excitement in his voice. They could feel the drum of the hooves through the hard ground rather than hear the sound.

Sergeant Nym reined to a halt in a shower of fine snow.

'They've got cavalry, Your Excellency. Dragoons. A troop.' He tried to get his breath.

'Cavalry!' The word travelled among them, and Henryk could hear the nervousness in their voices.

'There's nothing to worry about,' he said. 'It simply means a slight change of plan, that's all.' He hoped his voice sounded calmer than he felt. His mind began to race.

'How long before they reach the ford, Nym?'

'They were pretty well formed up when I left. Perhaps an hour.'

'I agree. The dragoons won't make them march any quicker; they'll still have to keep down their pace to that of the slowest waggon or else get spread out over about two miles of road and I don't think our friend Skurin will allow that. Presumably the dragoons were in the van?'

'Yes,' said Nym. 'By the look of it about a hundred yards ahead of the first detachment of infantry. Then the guns, then—'

'Draw us a picture, Nym.'

They dismounted and gathered round as the Sergeant drew out the order of march in the snow with the point of his sabre. Henryk stood for a moment with his head on one side, thinking hard.

'Horsemen, infantry, guns, then the waggons. Is that right?'

'As far as I could see, sir.'

'How many men would you say they had, Nym?'

'Counting gunners and waggon-men—' Nym scratched his head. 'I'd say about two hundred or so.'

'Two hundred!' Someone drew in his breath sharply.

'And we've got twenty-six,' said Henryk. 'But we've got something more important than numbers – we've got surprise, complete and utter surprise, and that's worth a hundred men. Now, listen carefully, all of you. This is what we'll do.'

He went through his new plan quickly and clearly, now and then glancing at his battered old campaign watch. 'Do you all understand?' he asked.

They all nodded; no one spoke.

'Basically it's the same as before except we now have these horsemen to deal with, and I think this is the best way in which to do it.'

'Wouldn't it be better if Kolbe's men were to open fire on the dragoons in the defile where they'll be helpless? At that range they'd be bound to get at least ten or twelve and—'

'What, and block the road with dead men and horses so that we can't charge? No, Jan, our main objective is to capture these guns and the best way to do that is for the musketeers to kill the gunners when the guns are crossing the ford and inflict as many casualties as they can on the infantry while they're trapped in the defile; then we can finish them off, tumble them back across the ford.

'So we wait till the dragoons are just below—' He pointed down at the road. 'Then we hit them in the flank, scatter them and wheel right along the road and into the infantry.'

Dombrowski looked as if he was going to say something but shut his mouth at the look on Henryk's face.

'Sergeant Nym.'

'Yessir.'

'Ride along and tell Kolbe and Zalinski to ignore the cavalry and carry out their original orders. Right?'

Nym galloped towards the defile. Henryk looked at his watch again.

'About quarter of an hour, gentlemen. Remount please and draw sabres.'

He drew the executioner's black mask over his face. That had been Jan's idea. 'If Skurin recognizes you he'll remember that Lipno's your home and then – after today – well, God knows what might happen to your home and family.'

'Besides,' Zalinski had added, 'it'll frighten them out of their wits.'

Henryk had seen the sense of the idea. At this stage he could not afford to be recognized. And so the widow Marishka had fashioned a tight-fitting mask of black cotton material.

'By heaven, you're enough to make the Devil turn and run,' Jan laughed.

It was a long quarter of an hour; for Henryk the longest of

his life. There was still time to call off the attack; just sit and watch the Russians go past. What he was about to do was an unprovoked act of war. But it would have to come; it was bound to come. And what right had Russian troops to march across Poland? His men sat very silent behind him and he wondered what they were thinking. The thoughts that any man feels before going into battle for the first time: in some, a trembling excitement, in others, a stoical hoping for luck; in all, the prayer that he would acquit himself well.

Among them Henryk was the only one who knew what war was really about. But at least this would be different; this would not be standing on a wooden deck waiting for the first broadside to tear and mangle; this was not waiting on a road in Saxony for the order to advance at a walking pace into the mouths of the Prussian guns.

This would be the wild exhilaration of the charge with a sabre in his hand and possibly the future of Poland depending on the result of that charge.

Sergeant Nym had returned and sat motionless beside him, his deepset little eyes bright with anticipation.

'They won't fire until they hear the sound of our attack.'

Flurries of snow were whipping round them, coming from the west. That was good; the wind would drive it into the Russian faces.

The quarter of an hour became twenty-five minutes; half an hour. Men began to fidget. Perhaps they weren't coming after all. What did one feel? Disappointment? Relief? A little of both?

'*Sst*!' Sergeant Nym's head was up, his eyes half shut, listening like a hunting animal.

'They're coming!'

He's got the ears of a lynx, Henryk thought. Strain as he could he only heard the wind in the trees, the loud rattle of a bit.

Then he heard it: the distant tap of a single drum. He glanced round and nodded at his men with what he hoped was an encouraging smile. His mouth was very dry; his heart seemed ten times too large for its lodging. For something to do he checked the girth, stirrup leathers, stroked Rasulka's silken mane. Her ears were pricked up; she was looking intently in the direction of the enemy.

He had time for one last short prayer: 'Please, God, don't let her fall,' and then the leading dragoon came into view through the thickening snow.

He was shapeless in his long cloak, head down against the snow, sabre safely sheathed. Behind him his comrades rode in files of three, their hunched shoulders white with snow. They rode slowly by, quite silently like a troop of ghostly horsemen looking to neither right nor left.

The muffled tapping of the drum was louder now. The rear file of dragoons was directly below and the solitary figure of Major Skurin appearing through the drifting white cloud when Henryk shouted his order:

'*Now!*'

Slithering, sliding, picking up speed, the Poles charged from the trees.

'Into them, boys!' roared Nym. They struck the dragoons full in the flank. Henryk had a brief, blurred sight of terrified faces, mouths wide with shock and fear, astonishment as the Russians struggled to get their sabres out. Engulfed for a moment in the sea of dark cloaks the Poles hacked and slashed; a head leapt from the spouting neck and dropped among the milling hooves. Men were yelling obscenities and formless, bestial shouts.

There was the vicious clash of steel as a few of the Russians fought back. Henryk parried a savage cut and lunged hard. With the full weight of Rasulka and his own body behind it the blade drove through till the hilt struck the man's breast-bone. His body toppled sideways across Rasulka's neck and the blood rushed from his open mouth, staining her mane deep crimson.

Henryk grabbed a pistol from the dead man's holster and fired into the broad face of a gigantic dragoon, but snow had dampened the pan and no shot came. He hurled the weapon into the man's panting mouth and heard the ugly crack of splintering teeth.

'Fight them! Fight them, you lousy dragoons!' The cry rose above the sounds of the battle. That must be Skurin. Henryk rose in his stirrups, trying to see beyond the shining helmets. The snow had slackened and he saw the figure of Major Skurin on the same black horse, galloping into the *mêlée*.

From the corner of his eye Henryk caught sight of a bright blade raised to slash down at his neck and, even as death stood poised above him, remembered with awful clarity the sight of the Turkish scimitar which had so shockingly scarred him.

He ducked away with upraised arm and as he did so a pistol went off and he saw the whole of the Russian's jaw vanish in a spray of red and white flesh and bone.

'He's one who won't try that again,' shouted Jan with a wild laugh. The dragoon rode away uttering a continuous bubbling scream. The sound was infectious; his comrades turned their horses and fled behind him, along the road to Cieszyn, carrying a cursing Major Skurin with them. The dragoons had had enough.

'Wheel right!' Henryk shouted above the cries of triumph. He got them into some kind of order. Two hundred yards down the road the leading column of infantry, unable to turn and run, trapped as they were in the defile, resolved under Ensign Potovski to sell their lives dearly. The front rank knelt; behind them the next ranks stood ready, presenting a hedge of bayonets.

Farther back towards the ford where gunners and horses thrashed and struggled in the icy red water some of the infantry were trying to claw their way up the steep, frozen banks to get at the sharpshooters who were making such deadly execution, but one after the other they rolled back, dead or wounded, among their comrades.

'*Charge!*'

Unarmed except for one pistol Henryk set Rasulka at full gallop down the road towards the glinting bayonets, the rest of his men close at her heels, their reddened blades pointing forward to challenge the bright bayonets. Jan was shouting, 'Poland! Poland!' He'd be wiser to keep his breath for what lay ahead, Henryk thought grimly, putting the mare's head at the very centre of the Russian front.

They were very close now and he could see the kneeling

soldier's cheeks laid along the butts. These were disciplined men who were not going to break without a fight. Another hundred yards; he dug his spurs savagely into Rasulka's flanks so that she hurled herself towards the green and yellow wall with ears laid back and her blood-stained mane streaming like red flame. Sixty yards. Forty yards.

The levelled muskets, here and there trembling at the sight of the horsemen coming at them full-tilt, spat a solid flicker of flame. Bending forward, close into Rasulka's neck, Henryk heard the wicked 'swish' of the balls through the crash of the volley, felt a heavy blow on his hip, then again he jabbed Rasulka without mercy and she cleared the kneeling men as though they were a thorn hedge. In her great leap, her razor hooves smashed the skulls of several men standing in the second row and, as she landed, the weight of her flying body scattered men like broken dolls.

A musket exploded close to Henryk's face, the blast singeing his skin, half blinding him. He shot the man in the throat, then reversing the empty pistol in his hand he clubbed right and left.

He saw a young Russian officer on horseback, waving his sword and exhorting his men with high, shrill cries, blood streaming down his face.

The rest of the Poles, ten of them now, crashed into the gap opened by Henryk and his little mare, their blades sweeping up and down, cutting as scythes lop the purple heads of thistles. In the middle of the shambles stood the little figure of the drummer boy beating at his drum, an expression of frozen horror on his childish face.

'Run,' yelled Henryk. 'Run, you little fool! Save yourself!' But the boy did not move except to go on beating out his pathetic defiance. A sabre rose, flashed down. The sound of the drum ceased as the boy sank slowly to his knees as if in prayer to his bloody drum, then pitched forward on his face.

'Oh, Christ!' Henryk found himself repeating. 'Oh, Jesus Christ!'

The Russians in the rear, closest to the ford, were turning now, struggling desperately to get back across the river, but their way was blocked by the dead gun horses, the guns and limbers stuck in the swirling water; and as they struggled, gasping, panting, screaming in their panic, the men under Zalinski and Kolbe shot them down with ruthless efficiency.

Henryk saw that many of them were throwing down their muskets, huddling together in dazed groups or lying, trying to get cover behind or beneath the bodies of their dead and wounded comrades.

He forced Rasulka through the infantry, most of whom gaped at his black executioner's mask, eyes glittering through the narrow slits and the horse's crimson mane as if they were apparitions straight from Hell. Resistance had faded to an occasional musket shot or wild thrust from a bayonet.

Those few brave men were cut down and quite suddenly the awful sounds of men killing each other had ceased. But still the shrill cries of Ensign Potovski continued, as he ordered them to die where they stood. If it had only been the six horsemen they would have killed those impudent Poles without too much difficulty but it was the deadly fire of the marksmen hidden above them they could no longer face.

'Stop firing!' Henryk held up his hand. 'No more firing! Kolbe! Zalinski! Hold your positions. Don't show yourselves. Be ready to shoot again.' To Ensign Potovski he called, 'Give up! Surrender and save your men!'

In answer Potovski swore horribly and rode at Henryk with raised sword. All round them men stood motionless or sat slumped in their saddles uncertain whether or not they were still fighting. Except for Bludhorn who spurred forward, lance couched. Seeing the point coming at him Ensign Potovski's courage failed and he reined to a halt.

The lance, red half way up the shaft, pointed unwaveringly, the tip against his chest. Potovski did not move. Tears of rage and humiliation trickled down his cheeks, making pale furrows in the blood.

'That's better, my young cockerel,' said Bludhorn in Polish. He smiled thinly. 'Move an inch and I'll split you just like that.' One of the Poles laughed hoarsely.

The six horsemen looked round them with the expressions of men who could not believe what they had done; they glanced at each other with grins of savage triumph, teeth bared like animals, and held their sabres loosely, swinging from tired wrists, dripping slowly into the trampled snow.

'Thank you, Bludhorn. I'm very pleased you were able to get out of bed.' Henryk's smile was strained. 'Sergeant Nym'.

'Sir.' Nym looked as unruffled as if he had merely been exercising a troop outside the royal palace in Dresden.

'See to the disarming of the prisoners. Collect as many horses as you can and get those guns harnessed up and dragged under cover. Any man who resists from this moment on will be killed. Is that understood?'

'Completely, sir.'

Rising in his stirrups Henryk addressed the Russians in their own language.

'Throw down your arms in a pile over there.' He indicated a spot at the foot of one bank. 'Then collect your wounded. Bring up the baggage waggons. Cut the dead horses from the guns and drag the guns to this side of the ford.' He saw them glancing uncertainly at their own officer, at each other; a few of them were still holding their muskets as if prepared to use them.

'If I give the order another ten of you at least will die. And so will he.' Henryk gestured at Ensign Potovski. With a savage grin Bludhorn drew back the lance about two feet.

'Tell them,' said Henryk to Potovski.

'Do as he commands,' cried the Russian officer. Sullenly his men threw down their muskets in a growing pile. When every Russian was unarmed Henryk ordered the ten men down from their positions among the birches.

'Well done,' he said quietly. 'Did you lose any men?' Both Kolbe and Zalinski shook their heads.

'Thank God.' He saw their faces as they counted what were left of the horsemen.

'Watch their officer,' he said and rode back down the short distance of the charge. Four of his men lay on their backs dead from that first volley which miraculously had somehow spared him. Jan rode beside him, very silent. He had never seen death before: especially such careless, untidy death. He had never before seen snow stained with the blood of men who were his friends, with whom he had been laughing and joking only a few hours before.

Father Gurowski had sheathed his sabre and got out his bible and was giving what comfort he could to the wounded of both sides.

'Four dead,' said the priest, 'and four wounded. None too badly.' Henryk noticed a dark red thumb-stain on the page of the open bible, and the thin lines of blood snaking between Gurowski's fingers.

'And you?'

'Just a graze on the arm. It's nothing.'

'You know those old derelict huts by the river.' The priest nodded.

'Get the wounded there and find out if the Russians have a surgeon with them.'

Father Gurowski spoke adequate Russian. He made the sign of the cross over a dying Russian and went off down the road calling for the surgeon.

Henryk decided on his next orders.

'Jan.'

'Yes.'

'See that the guns are got out of the water at once and taken under cover of the trees.'

Left to himself Henryk tried to think calmly of what should be done. On no account should the Russians be allowed to return to Rabka. Cieszyn was twenty-five miles away. Searching for his watch he found it a twisted mass of metal and shattered glass. He remembered the blow on his hip. Turning the remains over in his hand he thought with a kind of wonder that if it hadn't been for this little object he would be lying down there like the Russian at his horse's feet; he'd be lying biting back the agony of a shattered hip or a punctured stomach. Henryk put it back in his pocket and glanced at the sky. Clouds were piling up from the west, heavy with the yellowish tinge of snow.

They'd just have to march the twenty-five miles. And when they got there? Would Skurin take reprisals on innocent citizens? Henryk gazed at the Russian dead, very colourful against the snow; somewhere a man was screaming without pause; a horse stood mutely with its broken foreleg dangling; a green tunic dragged itself slowly across the snow. There seemed to be blood everywhere. He remembered how Captain Primrose had stood gazing helplessly at the carnage of his beautiful ship.

Henryk felt like that: utterly exhausted by the reaction, drained of strength, of the will to do any more. But there was much to do and he was the man they would turn to. He heard a wet choking sound as the Russian's life rushed in a torrent from his mouth.

'Oh, Christ,' whispered Henryk, loathing himself for what he had ordered to be done. He watched the man's head fall back into the sodden snow and the light fade from the surprised blue eyes.

'God forgive me,' Henryk cried aloud.

Then he straightened in the saddle. The decision had been taken and now the fight must be fought to the bitter end. And here was Nym riding towards him obviously with the first of many questions on his lips.

'Yes, Nym, what is it?'

If Primrose could do it then surely to God so could he.

*　　　*　　　*

The four of them sat on the rotting branches in one of the huts by the river. Henryk, Father Gurowski, Jan and Ensign Potovski, his head missshapen in a clumsy bandage. He was shivering under the blanket which draped his bowed shoulders.

'Here, drink this.' Henryk held out the mug of vodka. Potovski shook his head.

'Go on, take it.' This time he took a long draught, and they heard his teeth rattle against the tin rim. Colour slowly tinged his grey face.

'You understand what I've said?' asked Henryk sharply. Potovski nodded.

'You will take your men to Cieszyn. Ten of them will be allowed to carry their empty muskets with bayonets fixed.' He paused. Potovski saw a flicker of amusement in the eyes regarding him so steadily from the slits of the mask. 'At this

267

time of year the wolves are hungry and much braver than usual.'

'We wouldn't want you to lose any more men,' put in Father Gurowski. There was a silence in the miserable little room; a few flakes of snow fell through the holes in the roof. From outside came the creak of wheels, shouts in Polish and Russian; whips cracked, horses whinnied and the great booming voice of Sergeant Nym could be heard shouting orders.

'Why have you done this?' Potovski ground out between clenched teeth. 'In God's name, *why?*' He gestured with his hands. 'Twenty-four men dead, eighteen wounded. And we aren't even at war.' He drank more vodka. 'It was murder. Sheer bloody murder!'

'What's he saying?' Jan asked impatiently.

Henryk translated.

'Tell him this,' said Jan, his eyes very bleak. 'Because he and his kind are in Poland – that's why. And we'll go on doing it until the last Russian soldier is off our land. Tell him that, Henryk.'

Potovski listened to Henryk's words then he said in a trembling voice, 'You must be crazy. Six horsemen left, and you talk as if you had an army at your back.' There was a hint of unwilling admiration in his tone.

'Next time I shall have an army at my back,' said Henryk. 'Today it is six. Tomorrow six thousand. The next day the whole of Poland. You can tell your Empress that.' Henryk had a vision of Catherine and how she would look were Ensign Potovski to give her that message, not envying the unfortunate young officer.

'This'll mean war,' said Potovski. 'If you think we're going to sit back and—'

'The prospect shouldn't worry you,' broke in Father Gurowski drily. 'After all, it's your trade, isn't it?'

'War would have come sooner or later,' Henryk said. He got to his feet. 'Now, as I have nothing more to say to you and you have a long way to march, I suggest we see you on your way.'

The snow was falling quite heavily now. The Russians were drawn up in some semblance of military formation, the snow already thick on their shoulders. Their wounded were in one

268

waggon, sheltered as best could be done under a canopy of blankets. Their dead were piled, neat as logs, in the second cart.

In rear of the carts Zalinski and Kolbe and their men sat their horses with drawn sabres resting on their shoulders.

'All ready?'

'All ready, sir.'

Henryk beckoned Zalinski close and spoke in a low voice.

'Stay with them for five miles, then drop back slowly. They'll never notice in this.' The wind was whipping the snow into solid white drifts. 'I want you back as soon as possible. We've got to get the guns to the camp and hidden before we're caught in a full-scale blizzard.'

He rode to a position where he could be seen and heard by the enemy column.

'Listen to me! You have twenty-five miles to march. I have left you food and water in case you have to make camp.' He spoke very clearly, very incisively, and they watched his masked face as if mesmerized. 'I did not enjoy having to do this.' The Russians shuffled uneasily; there was some low angry muttering.

'And one more thing,' he added, raising his voice. 'If so much as a single hair on the head of any Polish citizen, man, woman or child, is touched then we will hunt down those responsible and destroy them without mercy.' His tone was ruthless. 'And take no prisoners. Remember that.'

And Sergeant Nym thought: eighteen men at his back and he speaks to them as the leader of a great army.

Ensign Potovski walked bravely enough to his horse but they had to help him into the saddle.

'Till next time,' he cried defiantly. 'Next time things will be different.'

'If there is a next time then I shall have to kill you,' Henryk answered. He watched as the carts rolled slowly away and the groans of the wounded came to him for a long while after the horsemen had vanished beyond the swirling veils of snow. Poor devils, he thought with real compassion, remembering his own dreadful journey from the field of Rossbach in a springless cart.

'Don't reproach yourself, Henryk,' said Father Gurowski gently. 'It had to be done.'

'I suppose so,' said Henryk dully, tearing the mask from his face. 'I suppose so.'

*　　　*　　　*

Though it snowed without pause for two days it was not till the evening of the second day that the full blizzard struck.

Eighteen men crowded into Henryk's hut, and though the storm raged through the trees, battering at the hut and filling it with smoke from the stove; though outside in the darkness, the cold was so bitter that the wind would flay the skin from a man's face in a matter of seconds, the packed room was so warm that sweat ran down Henryk's skin as he spoke.

'We have done what we set out to do. Our task is – for the moment – finished.'

They had hidden the guns under canopies of canvas piled with pine branches; thickly greased, they would remain there till the spring thaw, four mounds of snow indistinguishable from many others round them.

They had buried their five dead – one more had died beneath the unskilled knife of Father Gurowski as the priest vainly dug for the musket ball lodged deep in a lung, the ball which was killing him anyway, slowly and very painfully.

Gurowski had said a few hurried prayers over the holes hacked from the iron ground – it was too damned cold for the living to stand about. Josef, the carpenter, had fashioned beautifully carved crosses, and hammered them into the graves.

'The Russians will never find this place, not till the snow goes, and even then the chances of them stumbling on it are practically impossible.' Henryk said. 'So what I propose is this—' he looked round the faces turned towards him – 'that we disperse to our homes until the spring.' He held up his hand as he saw Jan's mouth open, an expression of dismay on his face. 'During these next two months we won't be idle. We will be recruiting men. I have plans for more camps of this type in the mountains from here to the Lvov area. There will be other groups forming all over Poland after this small success of ours.

These groups must be co-ordinated. There will be a lot for us all to do. Just to sit here trapped by the snow, out of touch of what is going on in the country is not only a waste of time, it's sheer stupidity.' Though he addressed them all, he kept his eyes fixed on Jan. He knew the hot-headed young man wanted to fight another action as soon as possible, whenever a target presented itself. But no target would. Not within miles of either Rabka or Cieszyn, not while the land was gripped in winter. The Russians would not move until the late spring or early summer.

'Next summer,' he went on, 'we'll have all the opportunities we want. And let's hope it won't be only eighteen of us.' A few men laughed. 'Go home, gentlemen. Resume your lives as idle, rich young noblemen whom no one would suspect of doing anything more dangerous than chase wolves or bears. I will keep in touch with you all.' Smiling, he turned to Sergeant Nym. 'I don't suppose you'll mind spending the next few weeks in Rabka?'

Nym's face reddened at the roar of laughter that shook the room. But he grinned widely.

'Just as Your Excellency says.'

'You'll never see him again,' called a voice. 'Not once he gets to the widow.'

When the mirth had died down Henryk said, 'Fill up the mugs, would you, Jan.' He was relieved to see that Dombrowski had decided to accept his decision without argument.

Jan went round, pouring the vodka from the stone flagon.

'A toast, gentlemen.' Henryk raised his mug. 'To the next time we meet under these circumstances and to those we hope will have joined us.' They drank.

'To our five friends who lie under the ground.' The mugs were raised again.

Then Jan Dombrowski stood up. 'To Poland,' he said quietly.

'To Poland,' they echoed.

'And to the man who leads us in her name,' called out Sergeant Nym. 'To Count Barinski.'

Henryk felt a lump rise in his throat as he thanked them with an inclination of his head.

'And I drink to you, my friends, who fought so well in our first action. Thank you,' he added simply.

Someone began a song and Kolbe joined in with his fiddle. Henryk, tossing down his vodka, joining in the gay chorus, thought with a feel of wondrous joy flooding his whole body. In a day or two, when the wind drops, I shall be going home, to Kasia, my wife.

*　　*　　*

'So you are really determined to go back?'

'I am married, Ma'am. My husband's in Poland. I have to go back.'

It was late at night: the Palace was quiet, the tread of the sentries muffled by the snow. One of Catherine's dogs whickered in his sleep, twitching his whiskers.

'I shall miss you, Kasia.'

The flames cracked in the open fireplace and the damp birch logs hissed and bubbled.

'Perhaps, one day, we will come and visit you.' But Kasia knew that Henryk could never return to Petersburg. Nothing would drag him there but chains.

'No,' said Catherine sadly. 'Though I count you as my friend—' She paused. 'Well, you are a Pole. Your people are stubborn.' Seeing the expression on Kasia's face, she stopped. 'We can never agree over this. It is better we don't discuss it.' For a moment they watched the dancing flames, deep in their own thoughts.

'You are packed and ready for the journey?'

'Yes.'

Again a silence.

'I shall never forget you, Kasia. Nor what you have done for me.'

'I feel the same.'

A log fell apart in a burst of sparks.

'Twelve years is a long time.'

Kasia did not answer. What was there to say?

'So you married your childhood sweetheart.' There was sadness in Catherine's voice, and also a little envy. 'Henryk

Barinski. The boy with the black curly hair and drooping grey eyes. I remember him: he had a most infectious laugh.' But, Kasia thought, you do not remember him as De Bonville, the Frenchman with the terrible scar who came to your bed; who vanished to Siberia.

'How does he feel about Russia – about me?'

'He thinks first and foremost about Poland.'

'I see.'

She sat in silence, as if mesmerized by the leaping tongues of fire.

'That I can understand,' she said quietly. 'And admire.'

She picked up a poker and stirred the fire.

'Whatever the future may hold for us, you and I, you know one thing, my dear. I shall always be your friend. You know that, don't you?'

'Yes, I know that.'

And so did Henryk.

'You paid me a great compliment by coming back. The compliment of complete trust. And I admire Henryk for allowing you to come. Tell him that from me, will you?'

Kasia nodded. She reflected sadly on the irony of the fate that was sending her back from Catherine, her friend, to the arms and the love of a man who was one of Russia's most implacable enemies. Before many months were past Catherine would certainly hear the name of Barinski and her admiring memories of a handsome boy would turn to hatred; her soldiers would be harried, some would be killed. In her imagination Kasia could hear the anger in Catherine's voice, see her eyes turn as bleak as a frozen wind. 'I want that man. I want him dead or alive, but I want him.' And yet, remembering her friendship for his wife, perhaps – no, Kasia knew her too well. Over anything that threatened Russia, or herself, she would be utterly ruthless.

'My God, I do envy you,' sighed Catherine. 'To love, to marry, to live quietly with the man of one's choice, and with children.' Seeing Kasia's expression Catherine burst out laughing.

'How well you know me,' she said. 'Domesticity is not really for me. And yet – sometimes—' Her little smile was wistful.

'Should you have children, and I'm sure you will, try and tell them that Catherine of Russia is not quite the dreadful ogress she's made out to be.'

'I'll tell them that Catherine of Russia is more of a woman than any other I have ever met – and more of a friend.'

'Thank you, my dear.' There were tears in her eyes when she looked up from the fire.

'You are ready for the journey? You have everything? The sleigh, the escort, they are arranged, I think. Now, one last thing.' She got up and went to her little inlaid bureau, unlocked an inner drawer and took out a long flat jewel case.

'Here,' she said, suddenly shy, and thrust the box into Kasia's hand. 'Something to remember me by.' In a bed of crimson velvet lay a superb necklace of emeralds and diamonds flashing and sparkling in the candle-glow: chips of green sunlit ice and huge frozen tear-drops.

'Oh, Ma'am!' Some of her own jewels were very beautiful but this – this was—

'Now, go, Kasia, before I disgrace myself.'

Kasia took up her dark blue travelling cape, edged with Imperial sable, and put it round her shoulders. Her throat was choked and the room was hazy through her tears.

'Perhaps one day,' said Catherine in a muffled voice but trying to speak lightly, 'if you need the money some jeweller in Warsaw or Paris might be generous if you say it once belonged to the Empress of Russia.'

'What c-can I s-say?' She sank down in a deep curtsey.

'No, no, not that, not now!'

Kasia felt Catherine's lashes wet on her own cheeks as they embraced, clinging together for a moment, then Catherine gently pushed her away.

'God grant you happiness with your Henryk,' she whispered in a choking voice. 'For you of all people have earned it.'

'And may God look after you, Figgy.'

As she went from the room Kasia turned in the doorway. Catherine's back was turned, her head leaning on her arm stretched along the mantelpiece.

Kasia did not look back at the Palace as the sleigh drove away through softly falling snow, across the square and along the bank of the frozen river, past the spire of the Admiralty, shrouded by the gentle fall of snowflakes. Behind it trotted the troopers of the escort, their faces tucked deep into the high collars of their cloaks, cursing the thought of the long winter ride when they could have been warmly installed with pipes and beer and women on their knees.

She thrust her feet deeper into the straw that covered the floor, her hands deeper into the big ermine muff. And, as she listened to the hiss of the runners, the tinkle of the bells on the high horse collar, the thin, curling crack of the whip, knowing that every stride the horses took was tearing her farther from Catherine and a life she had lived for fifteen brilliant, exciting years, Kasia had a sudden premonition that the threads of their three lives, already so closely ravelled, would one day cross again. So strong was the feeling that it left her breathless.

But now, through the snow, with the thud of escorts' hooves beside the sleigh, she was going home.

*　　*　　*

He had ridden for two days through the filth of the thaw and was coated from his heavy riding-boots to the shoulders of his patched and faded green coat with the black mud of the Ukraine. He had ridden with hardly a pause, merely taken a short stop now and then to rest Rasulka and snatch a couple of hours' sleep.

But now, as he came in sight of his home, all his exhaustion lifted from him and Rasulka, as if sensing his mood, increased her stride.

Kasia heard the sharp clatter of the hooves on the cobbles of the yard and her heart jumped to the sound of Henryk's voice calling for the grooms to take care of his horse. She flew along the corridor, calling to her father-in-law, 'He's back! Henryk's back!'

Not caring who was in the yard to watch, she ran to his outstretched arms. He held her to him fiercely, with a kind of desperate violence. Then he pushed her away from him.

'You're very lovely today,' he said. 'Don't spoil it by crying, darling.'

'It's not crying, you stupid fool. It's laughing.'

He looked her up and down, realizing how desperately he had missed his wife and wanted her during the frozen nights in the mountains.

She was dressed very simply in the clothes of the Ukraine, of her youth: her hair was not swept up and bejewelled in Court fashion but braided in heavy shining coils; her skirt was blue, beautifully embroidered, her shirt soft and white and the tight little bodice rounded her breasts in so sensual a fashion that he gave a little gasp and his eyes darkened. She met his look with excitement growing in her body; his grip hardened on her arms.

'Soon, my love,' she whispered. 'Very soon.'

He nodded, never taking his eyes from her face. 'Four months is a long time.'

'Your hunting trip has done you good,' she laughed.

He was thin and hard; only the top part of the scar stood out white against the brown skin, the lower half hidden by the thick beard. His eyes were tired but bright. The life in the mountains suited him, she thought. His old green coat was faded to a sort of dingy grey, even more patched and worn; a dark, rusty stain discoloured the frayed cuff of his right sleeve.

'Henryk!' Count Barinski stood in the doorway, leaning on his stick.

Henryk went to his father and embraced him. 'You're looking well, Father.'

'Fine, except for this bloody leg. And you—' he regarded his son with affection – 'you look like some kind of a tramp who's been dragged through a swamp.'

Both men laughed but Kasia just stared, her face shining with love, unable to take in the miracle of Henryk's presence.

Then Stepan appeared, grinning a toothless welcome, and old Katushka who threw up her hands in horror at Henryk's appearance.

'Mother of God, a beard!' she exclaimed shrilly. As though faced by the Devil himself she turned and hobbled back into the house muttering loudly to herself.

'Well, that's a fine way to welcome the returning hero,' said Henryk smiling.

Katushka's quite right, Kasia thought. He won't be allowed to keep it. They went into the house, Henryk with his arm round Kasia's shoulder, while Stepan hurried ahead as fast as his legs would carry him to fetch wine, vodka, mead, beer — everything he could think of, and so excited he might well pour the whole lot into one jug.

'Where's Adam?'

'At Uman,' Count Barinski said tersely, 'Buying more horses. He'll be back within the week. It's all he seems to think about,' he added grumpily.

But those horses were going to play their part in what was coming — perhaps within the next few months.

'You have no baggage,' asked Count Barinski, after many suitable home-coming toasts.

'Only what I stand up in.'

'You must have lived rough on this hunting trip of yours,' his father said.

'Oh, we were quite comfortable.' Henryk twirled the stem of his glass. 'You've heard nothing?'

'What about?' Kasia wanted to be done with this talk, wanted to be alone with her husband, in his arms, but she knew they could not offend the old man by leaving him before he gave them some sign.

'About a successful hunt,' Henryk said.

'No, we have heard nothing,' said his father, glancing at Henryk shrewdly from beneath his great bushy eyebrows. So Rasulka brought me home before the news that would soon have spread the length and breadth of Poland.

'Was it wolves or bears?' Kasia's tone was light, but her eyes were serious.

'Bears.'

There was a short silence.

'So,' said Count Barinski in a low voice. 'It has begun.'

'Yes.'

'God help Poland now.' Count Barinski's voice was sad but resolute.

'*We* will help her,' said Kasia.

Her father-in-law glanced at her with all the admiration he had come to feel for her courage and intelligence.

'You chose well, Henryk,' he said. He stifled a yawn. 'Now I'm tired. I think I'll rest a little. This evening at dinner we'll hear all about your adventures.' As Kasia bent to kiss the top of his head he added, 'You'll have better things to do than sit gossiping with an old man.'

Their looks met and the message in their eyes was the same.

Henryk half drew the curtains in their room so that a thin shaft of pale sunlight fell on her body as she lay waiting for him, turning her skin to golden satin. He stood over her for a long moment, as he removed his coat and let it fall to the floor, then, unbuckling his belt, he knelt beside the bed and very gently, very tenderly, he brushed his lips across her breasts. Her arms came up and pulled his head hard into the hollow of her bosom. Then all gentleness faded and they fought each other with a wild and savage passion. He felt the sharp bite of her little crooked tooth and the strong searching of her long fingers; his kisses travelled from her neck to the soles of her feet as she arched and strained beneath him; her lips were wet and as soft as the April rain which had begun to fall outside so that the room darkened and her eyes stared up at him huge and black.

Then he went into her as she cried out, 'Now, my darling! Now!' and the bed rocked to the violence of their consummation.

He continued to lie on her body which still moved beneath him, gradually becoming still. Her breathing steadied and she asked softly, 'Was that all right, dearest?'

'Was it for you?'

She smiled, stroking the back of his neck. 'You know it was.'

'Except for one thing.' He had forgotten how much he loved her husky little laugh. He waited in silence, wondering if, in some subtle way, he had failed her.

'Your beard tickles.'

He rolled off her and lay with his eyes shut, one arm across her breasts. For a while he slept while she watched him. The rain was heavy now, drumming on the roof and splashing on the gravel below their window.

Before he was fully awake his hand had begun to move,

hardening her nipples, then slowly down to her thighs. This time it was slow, languorous almost; he was not rough, she did not bite, they took each other with utter tenderness. Then they both fell into a deep sleep. The shower passed and a dusty sunbeam played for a while on their wet and shining skins before it moved past the parted curtain and gradually the room grew darker. They slept the sleep of the dead, completely relaxed, until woken by a banging on the door and Katushka's angry old voice.

'How much longer has the dinner to spoil?'

Kasia quickly drew the coverlet over their naked bodies. The housekeeper came in and plonked down two chamber candlesticks.

'Your father's waiting,' she grunted, her eyes averted from the bed. 'But I daresay he'll forgive you both just this once.' She uttered the cackle which passed with her as a laugh and went away.

They dressed quickly, talking and laughing all the time and Kasia wore the blue dress embroidered with gold and silver flowers which she knew was Henryk's favourite.

Before they left the room, he stood back from her, nodding gravely.

'Yes Countess Barinska, you're just as beautiful as I've always thought.'

'Thank you, darling.' Her eyes crinkled. 'But I'm not so sure about you, not with that beard.'

'You won't mind if it tickles you again though – will you, my love?'

'Not tonight, I won't, no. Come, your poor father's waiting.' Kasia took her husband by the hand and led him from the room.

*　　*　　*

Count Barinski leant back in his chair with an expression of admiration on his flushed face. They had dined long and well and he and Kasia had listened with fascination as Henryk described his life in the forests and the attack on the Russian column.

'You did that with only twenty men?'

'Twenty-six.'

'Twenty – twenty-six. What does it matter?' Count Barin-ski's blue eyes sparkled with pride.

'By God, but your grandfather would have been proud of you. What d'you think, my dear?'

'He would indeed,' Kasia answered. But in her heart there was a heavy feeling of dread, a small stab of fear as she thought of the future and what it might bring to them all.

'And what will happen now? What will your friend Cather-ine have to say about this business, eh?' Her father-in-law asked the question with a note of triumph in his voice as if he personally had dispatched at least a dozen Russians to their Maker.

'I don't know,' Kasia said. 'I honestly don't know.'

She remembered Catherine's words very clearly: 'Whatever the future may hold for us, you and I, you know one thing. I shall always be your friend.'

But would she be the friend of the man who defied the might of Russia, who killed her soldiers and thumbed his nose at her ambitions? Kasia looked across the table at Henryk who sat staring into his glass, running his finger idly round the rim, and she wondered, as she often did, what were his true feelings where Catherine was concerned.

At last he spoke.

'She'll do one of two things,' he said. 'She'll either order a full-scale attack on Poland' (And God knows, Kasia thought, from her point of view she has every right to), 'or she will pretend to ignore what was after all only a small skirmish, launched by a handful of irresponsible bandits, and continue with her policy of conquering this country by peaceful means—'

'Through *King* Poniatowski,' interrupted his father bitterly.

'Exactly.'

'They are saying in Warsaw that the Election Diet is to be held next month.' Count Barinski refilled his glass and took an angry drink.

'And how will this Election be held,' he asked grimly. 'I can tell you in four words. Under the Russian guns.' He drank again.

'With Keyserling in command of the proceedings.' His eyes suddenly lost their ferocity and saddened. 'And that is how low Poland has fallen.' In his mind was the tremble of the ground as the squadrons of her famed cavalry led the Poles to victory and conquest.

Outside the rain was falling again, this time in a steady downpour.

'When the thaw is over,' said Henryk, 'then we go back to the mountains.'

'Do any of the others know?' Kasia asked.

'I have sent Jan to tell them,' said Henryk.

They listened to the rain.

'That old fool Globnik,' said Count Barinski. 'I've told him about that leaking gutter a hundred times. What the hell do I pay him for?' He scowled at the curtained windows. The slow rhythm of the clock broke the silence with quiet, calm sanity. Then the moment was shattered.

'Will they fight? Will they *really* fight?' There was anguish in his voice.

'Yes,' said Henryk, calmly and confidently. 'They will.'

'Thank God,' said the old man. 'Thank God for that.'

Kasia raised her glass to her husband.

'And I agree,' she said.

*　　*　　*

They were in bed. A single candle still burnt by the bed. Henryk lay back with his arms beneath his head, stretching his whole body luxuriously.

'It's only when you've slept without sheets for months that you really appreciate the feel of them.' He could just see the tips of her nose and chin beyond the dark curtain of hair.

'Like a woman,' he added with a quick smile.

She turned her face towards him. 'A wife,' she corrected.

'A wife, yes.' He stroked her hair. 'But very much a woman.' His hand felt through the hair for the warm curve of her shoulder.

'No, darling. Not now. We'll sleep first.' She kissed his hand with the corner of her mouth. 'Then you can wake me – in any way you like.' A rat scampered in the wall behind their heads; some piece of furniture creaked and they heard the distant double call of an owl; then the house was silent.

'We've got our lives together now,' she said. 'No more partings. Can you realize that, Henryk? Can you really take in the wonderful, marvellous fact that we have our lives before us?' He saw her eyes shining in the smoky light, and watched her with great love in his heart before answering.

'You know I'll be going back in a month or so?'

'To the forest? Yes, I know.'

But there was no sadness in her voice.

'Why should I mind,' she asked. 'I shall be with you.'

He knew she would say that; he'd always known it.

'War's a filthy business,' he said, 'and no place for a woman.'

'So what exactly d'you propose? That I sit at Lipno sewing or playing the spinet? Oh, no, darling. From now on, where you go I go. And no argument.'

'Supposing I forbid you to come.'

'You can try it,' she said happily. 'That's a husband's privilege. But it's also a wife's privilege not to listen to nonsense.'

His answer surprised her.

'Someone once told me I was born under the star of war. Yet, especially now we're married, I long for a life of peace in which we can see our children grow up. I just want to lie in the grass and listen to the wind in the trees and watch the wild geese flying north in the spring – with you beside me to share the moments. But instead all I will bring you is danger, hardship, stretching into the future as far as I can see for the rest of our lives.'

'I'm used to hardship. Life on the Don was not exactly a minuet.'

'There'll be no grand dresses; all your jewels will have to go to buy food, horses, ammunition. Instead there'll be fear and perhaps death—'

'And does death matter all that much,' she said. 'Provided we're together when it comes?'

He took her hand.

'We'll always be on the move; we'll be chased and harried.'

'I can ride just as well as you. I've used a musket and a pistol – and I can cook.'

'And if you have a child, what then?'

'We'll think of that when the time comes, my sweet silly love.'

He lay staring at her in sort of wonder.

'To say I love you, Kasia, no longer means anything. What I feel for you is something so – so—' He gave up, spreading his hands palm upwards in a gesture of despair, shaking his head.

'I know,' she said. 'I know, my own dearest heart. It's how I feel; there are no words.'

'I'll try in my feeble way,' he said smiling. 'I love you more than life itself, far more. Everything I have in my heart and body are yours for as long as you want and need them.'

She took his face between her hands and kissed him with a tenderness he had never experienced, not even from her.

'And that,' she whispered, 'will be forever.'

And round the house the soft sigh of a sudden little breeze echoed their mood as Kasia put out the candle, and turned with a deep sigh of contentment to her husband.

ESTHER BY NORAH LOFTS

He was King of Persia, Lord of one hundred and twenty-seven provinces, master of an Empire which stretched from India to Ethiopia – and yet his wife treated him with barely concealed contempt ...

And so the unhappy king began his search for a new bride. From every corner of his Empire came girls whose beauty matched their ambition – a princess from Egypt, a shepherd's daughter from Esdraelon, a red-haired Kurdish maid from the north ...

But the most unexpected – and unwilling – applicant for the royal throne lived in the Jewish quarter of his own capital city – and on the appointed day the dark-haired girl called Esther was brought before the King ...

0 552 09304 1   30p

THE MARIGOLD FIELD

BY DIANE PEARSON

The Marigold Field is a story of poor, proud, high-spirited people ... people whose roots were in the farming country of southern England ... in the bawdy and exuberant streets of the East End.

Jonathan Whitman, his cousin Myra, Anne-Louise Pritchard and the enormous Pritchard clan to which she belonged, saw the changing era and incredible events of a passing age – an age of great poverty and great wealth, of the Boer War and social reform, of straw boaters, feather boas, and the Music Hall ...

'Powerful, articulate, teeming with marvellously real people. This is the sort of thing that keeps the novel alive.' – Monica Dickens

0 552 08525 1   30p

BY PHYLLIS HASTINGS, author of
All Earth to Love

SANDALS FOR MY FEET

The world, for Lee Lindridge, consisted of what she could see from the windows of the house in Bartholomew Street – dirty pavements, crumbling houses, shabby people. From her wheelchair she watched them all – the children, the slut at number eighty-eight, the factory workers hurrying up to Blakemores.

And then one day the family moved her wheelchair out on to the pavements so that she could sit in the sun. And that was where Kyre Blakemore – who was rich, and vital, and . . . odd – saw her. A frail, beautiful girl, unlike any woman he had ever known before . . .

0 552 09202 9   35p

STEAMBOAT GOTHIC

BY FRANCES PARKINSON KEYES

Clyde Batchelor was a rugged man, a self-made man. Reared in a St. Louis orphanage, he had made his fortune playing the steamboats of the Mississippi, plying a disreputable and hazardous trade on the great floating palaces that sailed down to New Orleans.

And finally, his fortune secure, he was free to do the things he most wanted – buy one of the great plantations along the river . . . acquire a home to which he could bring a bride . . . And there fate played her most curious trick. For Clyde Batchelor, the tough, lawless, self-driven man fell overwhelmingly in love with Lucy Page – Lucy was frail and beautiful, and came from one of the most aristocratic families of the South . . .

552 09279 7   50p

BLACKSTONE BY RICHARD FALKIRK

Edmund Blackstone is a Bow Street Runner of doubtful parentage and background, the best if far from most conformist in the force who secretly applauds the robbers he hunts. He is also one of the best shots in London, an expert in almost all areas of crime, and a ruthless man with a reputation for courage and persistance.

In this, the first of a series, Sir Richard Birnie, the Bow Street magistrate, has appointed Blackstone to guard the heir to the throne, the young Princess Alexandrina Victoria. Among the Runners this is considered an honour but Blackstone feels it is all a waste of time, even a punishment. Then Blackstone himself is attacked outside his lodgings – and there's something about his assailant that seems oddly familiar . . .

552 09303 2   35p

Further adventures of Phillip Hazard, R.N.

BY VIVIAN STUART

BLACK SEA FRIGATE

As Acting-Commander of H.M. steam-screw frigate *Trojan*, Phillip Hazard is at sea when the great storm strikes the Crimean coast with devastating fury on November 14, 1854. Carrying troop reinforcements for the garrison at Eupatoria, Hazard has strict orders to land them as soon as possible. But as the *Trojan* battles her way through mountainous seas and a hurricane-force wind, distress rockets are sighted from the shore. Should he risk his ship and the much-needed reinforcements to go to the aid of another vessel, or adhere to his orders and plunge on to Eupatoria . . . ?

0 552 09159 6   30p

A SELECTED LIST OF FINE BOOKS FOR YOUR READING PLEASURE